Mountain Angel

Mountain Angel

A Northstar Novel

SUZIE O'CONNELL

SUNSET
Rose
BOOKS

Copyright © 2014 Suzie O'Connell

Second Edition / March 2014

ISBN-13: 978-1-950813-01-8

For Mom, Mark, Maddie, and Holly

One

ANY DAY THAT INVOLVED closing a case or didn't involve opening a new one was a good day. By that rule, today had been a good day, but from the moment he'd opened his eyes with that long-familiar tension coiled tightly in his neck, nothing else about today had been particularly agreeable. It was just one of those days that had no reason to be bad beyond the inexplicable fog of depression. Pat was eager to go home, fix himself something for dinner, sit on his well-worn couch with a book, and wait for the day to be over.

He was just getting ready to head out the door when a request from his boss put his grandiose plans on hold.

"Pat, meet me in my office in a minute."

Pat, his boss had called him, not *O'Neil*. Whatever Bill Granger wanted to discuss, it was personal. Anxiety curled more tightly in his gut. One subject had been flirting with his mind all day, and he had no desire to be dragged down that road right now. On a good day, a trip down that bleak alley was a painful experience, but on a day like today, such a trip would leave him exhausted and incapable of doing more than pulling the covers of his bed over himself with a prayer that sleep would relieve him from the bitter memories and empty stomach.

To pass the time, Pat studied the photographs in Bill's office. In a log frame on the wall behind the desk was a poster-sized photograph of a two-story cabin illuminated by filtered rays of golden sunlight. The structure was nearly an A-frame, but the peak was not as steep as the sides. In other photographs, Pat recognized Bill's incredible, dark-haired wife and his sister and brother-in-law. There was a new picture of a beautiful young woman with strawberry-blonde hair and striking, deep green eyes wearing a DayGlo orange vest and matching stocking hat. There was a rifle slung over her shoulder and a triumphant smile on her face as she knelt beside a magnificent four-point whitetail buck. She gripped the antlers with long, graceful fingers to hold the animal's head up for the camera. Pat knew she was his boss's niece and had seen her face smiling from a multitude of other photos, but he hadn't yet met her.

Pat turned his attention from the pictures to the matching pair of four-tiered, wrought-iron filing shelves. He hadn't seen them before. The craftsmanship was stunning and, along with the collection of rustic picture frames, did a lot to reduce the beige sterility of the room.

Bill's boisterous laughter rumbled through the closed door from the workroom. With his back to the door, Pat smiled as his boss entered noisily.

"Afternoon, Pat," was his greeting.

"Afternoon, Bill," Pat replied as the older man sat down behind his desk.

"Sorry about the delay, but Garrity made another smart remark about my age, so I had to remind him of how thoroughly I trounced him at racquetball over the weekend."

Pat chuckled. Bill was only fifty-three and still had the body he'd had during his enlistment in the navy. His rich brown hair was only starting to gray on the sides and in his short beard, and he looked anything but old.

"He'll learn one of these days," Pat remarked. He inclined his head toward the filing shelves. "Did your niece make those, too?"

"She did. She's had a lot more time to build since she went back to Montana." Bill paused to look at the photograph of his niece. "Her friend June took this picture and the one of my sister's cabin on the wall behind me. So, Pat, you don't have any plans tonight, do you?"

"No more than usual."

"Good. Mary wanted me to invite you over for dinner. She said something about not bothering to come home tonight unless I brought you with me."

Pat chuckled. "I suppose I shouldn't keep you from your wife's good cooking... not that you couldn't stand to miss a meal or two."

"Keep it up, smart ass." Bill opened one of the drawers on the desk and took out a manila envelope. "See you at the house?"

Pat nodded and left.

As he drove to Bill's house, he decided that an evening with Bill and Mary was the perfect medicine for his ailments. So long as *that* subject wasn't broached. However, Mary was always careful to steer Bill clear of it, especially on days like this one. As much as he didn't like talking about that weekend three years ago or the miserable months leading up to it, he knew he'd have been lost if Bill and Mary Granger hadn't been there to pull him back from the proverbial cliff's edge. As it was, he still wasn't too many steps back from it.

"Pat, welcome!" Mary greeted him with a warm hug when he arrived at the Grangers' modest house on the bluff overlooking the Indianola beach. "I'm so glad you came."

So am I, he thought. "Can I help with anything?"

"No. Everything's ready. We'll just wait for Bill to get home. He called a few minutes ago to say he was leaving. Would you like anything to drink? Beer? Wine? Juice?"

"Water would be fine, Mary," he replied.

He followed her through the house to the back deck. The handiwork of Bill's niece was everywhere. More frames of weathered wood, like those on Bill's desk at the sheriff's department, hung on the walls, filled with family photos and more of his sister's cabin in Montana. Walking through the Grangers' home was a stroll through a Rocky Mountain dream. Mary dabbled in interior design as a hobby, and she'd put the rustic furniture and decorations to perfect uses. Her house could have graced the pages of a magazine devoted to Western living.

Pat would love to meet Bill's niece someday. Bill had tried to introduce them in the past, but work, school, distance, or something else had always prevented it. Admiring her work, he got the sense that she was dedicated, driven, and artistic but also giving, loyal, and he suspected a little stubborn. Any woman who chose to make her living in a field that traditionally belonged to men was no soft lady to take what life handed her.

Pat followed Mary outside to the deck. Below him, the tide washed up the broad sand spit, reaching toward the rocks farther up the shore. The old ferry dock stretched far out into the glassy ripples beneath a cloudless sky and to his left, Seattle glinted in the distance, bathed in the rich golden light of the westering sun. It was a rare, perfect March day laden with the promise of the warmer months to come.

"Oh, I wanted to ask," Mary said. "Do you know if Shannon got the birthday present we sent? It was supposed to be there yesterday, but I haven't had a chance to call your mom to ask. I'm sorry it was late, but it took longer than we expected to ship."

"It was waiting for her when she and Mom got home from Seattle. She loved it."

"Did you change your mind and meet them?"

Pat shook his head. "No, but I talked to Mom yesterday. I still can't believe my little sister is seventeen already."

"Neither can I, but I can't believe you'll be twenty-nine in a few more months, either. It doesn't seem like so long ago that your father was more excited about your birth than graduating from college." Mary smiled fondly and patted his hand.

"Are you calling me old, Mary?"

She laughed. "Indeed not. You're just a pup. I'm calling *me* old. Was Shannon disappointed you didn't go?"

"No. I think she understands."

Mary hesitated a moment, then said quietly, "I'm glad Bill convinced you to come work for the sheriff's department. I think you're happier here than you would have been if you'd stayed with the Seattle PD."

"It's certainly a much quieter job. Grandpa Antony says the Kitsap Peninsula fits me better, and he's right." Pat smiled fondly. "He was so proud that I'd seized the opportunity to become a detective and glad that I was happy."

If Mary noticed how his voice hitched on the last word, she didn't say anything. Instead, she pointed out the beach party below them. A group of teenagers had broken away from the bonfire and were now racing across the sand toward the water's approaching edge, followed by a black lab, a border collie mix, and two smaller mutts. Their excited, carefree voices rang wonderfully in the still evening, and Pat's depression slipped away.

Bill arrived a scant twenty minutes later to find his wife and Pat laughing uproariously at the antics of the teenagers and dogs.

"Glad to see your mood's improved, Pat," Bill remarked as he joined them.

"Your wife is a charming woman," Pat said. "I can't help myself."

"She certainly is."

Mary went back inside, leaving them to talk. Dread wormed its way back into the pit of Pat's stomach. There was nothing overly prodding about Bill's demeanor, but Pat suspected his enjoyable evening was about to head in a direction he didn't want to go.

"Before you give me your usual, evasive responses, hear me out."

"Do I have a choice?"

"Absolutely not." Bill took a deep breath and plunged ahead. "You're regressing. Over the last few months, I've watched you slide back down into the pit. I'd be willing to bet a large sum of money that you've had as many bad days as good in the last three months. That worries me, Pat. You've worked too hard to recover from Sara."

And there it was.

"I want you to take a vacation."

"I'm fine, Bill."

"I'd be more convinced by the truth, and we both know that isn't it."

"C'mon, Bill. It's been a long, wet, gray winter. Everyone's been—"

The look Bill gave him—brows lifted, mouth flat—silenced him.

"There's a trend here, Pat. Every time something reminds you of Sara, you have one of these days after. What did you see, hear, or do yesterday that reminded you of her?"

"My mother mentioned her. First time I've talked to my mother in two months, and *she* came up. She always does."

"What do you mean, *mentioned her*?"

"Mom thought I should be warned, but I wish she hadn't told me. Apparently, yesterday when she took Shannon shopping for prom in Seattle, they bumped into Sara at the mall. She asked how I've been."

"That little...." Bill shook his head. "I'm sorry, Pat. I shouldn't be dragging you through this tonight. It just makes me so angry. What you need is a good woman like my niece to show you Sara isn't worth any of the pain she's caused you." He cleared his throat, and Pat sensed he was stalling. "My niece is the other reason I wanted you to come to dinner tonight."

Pat sat back in his chair and gaped. The situation had suddenly gone from depressing to absurd. "Oh, no. They've finally gotten to you, haven't they? Listen, I'm sure she's a very nice girl, but…"

Bill's laughter rang out in the still evening air. He kept laughing until his eyes glittered wetly. "You think that's what I'm trying to do? You really know how to bring a man to tears, Pat." He wiped beneath his eyes, still chuckling. "I'd bet my niece would be a much better match for you than any woman anyone in the department can find, and as much as I'd love to have you legally a part of my family as a nephew, I'm afraid my reason for mentioning her is more serious."

Bill pulled the manila envelope out of his bag and handed it to Pat. On the cover was one of the more unique names he'd seen. He knew it was the name of Bill's niece, but Bill had always pronounced it like the flower alyssum when he wasn't calling her what sounded like "Allie."

Inside the envelope was what appeared to be a criminal file but less official. It included a sheet of personal data with the last known address, phone number—both of which were months out of date—the physical descriptions of the man, and a photo. Pat narrowed his eyes. There was something about the hazel eyes that hooked his attention, a contained fervor shimmering beneath a placid surface. The man had the look of someone who had spent his entire life reaching for something unattainable and had not yet realized the hopelessness of his endeavor. The longish, messy medium-brown hair was further evidence, but beneath the mop, the man could be called good-looking. What a pity. Behind the photo was a copy of a restraining order. There were a few more pages, but Pat shifted his attention for the time being back to Bill.

"What is this?" he asked.

"The biggest favor I'll ever ask of you. Aelissm called me two days ago. I told you that she moved back to Northstar but not why. Adam Winters—" Bill tapped the picture from the file. "—won't leave her alone. We filed a restraining order against him, and he's broken it, but he's off the grid. I can't find him to arrest him."

"So you want me to find him."

"Yes and no. There's more to it. The night Aeli's boyfriend, Brent Ellington died, he tried to rape her. Adam heard her scream, came to her rescue and started to strangle Brent. Aeli ran out. Brent died a few hours later of a burst aneurysm, possibly brought about by being throttled, but there's no way to prove that. A neighbor saw Brent stumbling back to his apartment later that night. She thought he was drunk, and he was. By that time, Adam was long gone, so Brent was still alive after Adam left. The landlord found Brent's body in the morning when he entered the apartment for a routine testing of the smoke alarms. It's a mess."

"Sounds like it."

"Anyhow, a copy of the statements and records of Brent's death are in the back there, along with the statements Aeli gave to get the restraining order and what she dictated to me over the phone the day before yesterday." Bill paused and took a deep breath. "Adam has had a thing for her since they met a couple years ago. At first, she was flattered, and I thought he would have been a better match for her. Until this mess happened, I liked him. I still want to like him because I think he's a good man beneath it all, but something snapped that night. He's become obsessed with her."

"Obsessed how?"

"Calling her, writing her letters, and proclaiming his love for her. A couple times, she arrived home to find him sitting on her couch."

"Sounds like a bit of a creep."

"I hate to say it, but yes. She changed her number a couple times, and when she decided she had no desire to finish her master's degree in Seattle, she moved in with her parents here in Indianola for a few months, but he didn't get the message."

"And now she's in Northstar. How did that come about?"

"Her grandparents called about six months ago and asked if she was interested in taking over operations of their inn. Her grandmother also works at the local post office, and the inn is getting to be too much work. She said yes, and the move has been good for her because she enjoys the work at the inn and the blacksmithing class she teaches one night a week at the college in Devyn, and she's been able to unwind. Until Adam called her two nights ago."

"So, how do I fit in to all this?"

"This is your vacation. I want you to go to Montana, take a couple months to relax and clear your head. And, while you're at it, find anything you can about Adam Winters and protect my niece if the need arises."

Pat considered Bill's request, then laughed. "Good one, Bill. You almost had me, what with the file and the story."

Bill's eyes hardened. "I wish to God this was a joke. There isn't much Aeli can't do, but when she told me Adam had called again, she was in tears. I don't trust anyone else to do this, Pat, and even if I did, I'm not kidding about wanting you to take a break. You need to get away for a while, take a step back, and forget about Sara."

"It's not that simple, Bill."

"I understand that. I also know that working yourself half to death hasn't done you a bit of good. I'm hoping a good, long vacation away from everything that reminds you of her will succeed where distraction has failed."

"I suppose you have it all figured out," Pat said sharply. He winced. He hadn't meant that to come out so harshly.

"You'll stay with Aelissm, of course. She could probably use a little extra help at the Bedspread, and it would give you something to do." Bill held Pat's gaze for a moment. "I love you both. I hate to see either of you struggling."

"How long do you expect me to stay there?"

"As long as necessary, on both counts, even if I have to pay you out of my own pocket."

Pat sat back in his chair, stunned. This was one hell of a favor, and he wasn't sure if he was up to the challenge. He glanced at Bill, saw the silent plea in the older man's gaze, and considered it. He very briefly thought about turning Bill down, but his boss—his *friend*—had done a lot for him over the years.

"Do you need a day to think about it?"

Pat shook his head. "I'll do it. And I'm sure you're right that I should get away for a while. Maybe it *will* help."

Bill scribbled some notes on a piece of paper and stuffed it in the file. "All right, then. It's all here. We've notified the local law enforcement about the restraining order, so if you *do* find Adam, he can be dealt with legally. Aaron Hammond lives in the valley and is a sheriff's deputy, so if you need any help, call him. I've included his contact information in the file as well as all the numbers for the Devyn Police Department and the county sheriff's office. I really hope you won't need any of it. I keep hoping Adam will come to his senses and just leave Aelissm alone."

Mary's return with dinner brought an end to their head-spinning conversation. They talked about other things while they ate, but as Pat listened and talked and laughed with his friends, his thoughts were focused on what he might be facing and how he could best tackle the task. It was… refreshing.

"I really appreciate this, Pat," Bill said as Pat was leaving. "You have no idea what peace of mind I'll have knowing you're there with Aeli."

Pat nodded and tucked the file under his arm. He leaned down to embrace Mary and thank her for dinner. As he drove away, he began to wonder what he'd gotten himself into. When he got home, he picked up his road atlas and glanced at the notes Bill had scribbled as he studied the map of Montana. There it was, a tiny dot in the southwest corner of the state. The nearest town of any size was Devyn to the east with a population that nearly matched its elevation of just over five thousand feet. Beyond that, the closest city was Butte, many miles more to the north. His eyes traveled back to the little dot that would be his home for the next little while.

"Northstar, here I come," he sighed. Then he chuckled as he recalled the picture of Bill's niece with her buck. "Looks like someday is just around the corner. It'll be nice to finally meet you, Aelissm Davis."

* * *

"Uncle Bill, I didn't want you to send me a protector. That's the last thing I need."

"Then you shouldn't have called me."

"You're wasting his time." Aeli glanced at her friend, rolled her eyes, and sighed. "When I called you the other night, I only wanted to let you know Adam had called me again. That's all."

"You're not fooling anyone, Aelissm, except maybe yourself."

"I don't know how Adam got the phone number here, but he can't find me. Hell, Unk, *you* couldn't find this place last summer, and you've been here before."

"You thought Adam wouldn't find you when you moved to your parents' house, too, remember?"

"Yes, but—"

"Humor me, Aelissm."

"I don't need someone to watch over me like I'm a child."

"I know you can take care of yourself, Aeli darling, but Adam is not the same man he used to be." Her uncle sighed, and she pictured him sitting in his recliner at home, massaging his temples. "I chose Pat because I trust him and because I know he can protect you. Knowing he's there will ease my old heart."

"Old? Ha!"

"I'm serious."

"I know you are. All right, fine. It might be nice to have a man around."

Bill laughed. "I know that tone. You're a devil, you know that?"

"Yep. Anything else?"

"Yes, actually. Make sure Pat relaxes while he's there."

"Will he be here on vacation or to protect me, Unk? Because that seems a little contradictory."

"Both. He went through a bad break up a few years ago and hasn't given himself the chance to get past it, so I'm using one stone to kill two birds."

"A bad break up, huh? You're not playing match-maker again, are you?"

"No, but it certainly wouldn't break my heart if the two of you got together."

"Uh-huh."

"Just make sure he gets some rest while he's there, will you?"

"I'll see what I can do. Well, I should probably get off this thing. I don't want to run up June's phone bill."

"All right. Love you, Aeli Girl."

"Love you, too, Unk. G'night."

She set the cordless phone back in its cradle and glanced at her friend, who sat on the couch with her scrawny, twelve-year-old foster son, Luke, curled up beside her. It amazed Aelissm how much their lives had changed in the last year. And yet, here they were, together in

Northstar again. Suddenly, she was very grateful her grand-parents had asked her to start taking over management of the Bedspread Inn because, until she'd returned to Northstar six months ago, she hadn't realized just how much she'd needed to come here. The utter peacefulness of the remote valley was such a welcome relief to the constant pulse of Seattle. Besides, this was *home*.

She flopped on June's matching love seat and exhaled.

"I take it Uncle Bill is sending one of his detectives over?" June asked.

"Yeah. Patrick O'Neil."

"O'Neil? As in…?"

"The son of Uncle Bill and Aunt Mary's friends from college, yes."

"Why do I get the feeling Uncle Bill is meddling again?"

"Because he probably is. You know Unk."

June glanced at Luke and smiled fondly. "Yes, I do. When's your bodyguard supposed to get here?"

"Most likely in the next couple days. I don't need someone to protect me."

"Maybe you do."

June's tendency for being right was sometimes very aggravating, Aeli mused, but it was also nice to be slapped with the truth now and again. She'd thought that coming out here, to Northstar, would end her problems with Adam, and for a pleasant six months, it had. Then, two days ago, he'd called her parents' cabin. She'd held the phone against her ear with a trembling hand, frightened beyond words at the sound of his voice. *Just leave me alone*, she'd finally told him. Then she'd hung up. Running away never solved the problem, she thought, only postponed it.

"It's almost like old times, isn't it?" June asked. "Back in college when we used to sit up in your cabin, reading and snacking on Spaghetti-O's while it snowed."

Aelissm smiled, and some of the tension she hadn't realized was binding her shoulders slipped away. "Those were good times."

"Grandma Davis told me about you singing Christmas carols at the top of your lungs," Luke said.

"While we were out chopping wood," Aeli remarked. She tried not to look surprised that he'd spoken, but the boy was usually so quiet that it was hard not to. "I guess we were making a bit of a racket."

"I like it up here," the boy said.

June pulled her fingers through the boy's blond hair. Aelissm wondered, as she often did, what had possessed June to agree to Uncle Bill's plea that she take him. Luke was a good kid—very quiet, well behaved, and disturbingly tidy—but June wasn't even twenty-five yet. A little voice in the back of Aeli's mind retorted rather coldly, *What possessed you to go out with Brent?* It wasn't a question she was willing to ponder. *Chalk it up to a disastrous lack of judgment*, she told herself, *and leave it at that.*

"I should have known Unk would do something like this," Aelissm muttered. "Poor Deputy O'Neil is in for a shock when he sees where I live. I swear, if he complains about the lack of creature comforts, I'll strip him down to his birthday suit and leave him out in the snow."

"Aeli, it's really not nice to judge people before you've met them," June said. When Aeli opened her mouth to object, her friend held a finger up for silence. "But if he complains, I'll help."

"You've got a deal. Now, I don't know about you, but watching a movie sounds dull. How about we go take a dip in the hot springs?"

"Sounds like a plan to me. Luke, run upstairs and get your swim trunks."

The boy nodded and leapt off the couch. He raced across the living room, skidded around the snack bar and counter that divided the kitchen from the living room, and bounded up the spiral stairs. Aeli shook her head and chuckled. "He's a cute little monkey, I'll give him that."

"Yes, he is. You know, Aeli, I've been thinking."

"That's dangerous."

June frowned at her but continued. "I want to adopt him."

The flood of maternal warmth surprised Aeli, but June's admission didn't. She and Luke had built an incredible bond in just eight months, so unbelievably like that of a mother and her child despite the circumstances. It wasn't just the golden hair and blue eyes. Luke *looked* like her son and had already shown a lot of the same characteristics, right down to June's quirky sense of humor and uncanny intuition.

Aelissm shook off the tingle of envy. What had happened to them, to their promise that neither of them would ever have kids until they were ready or be dependent on a man? Life happened, Aeli thought. Yes, they were still young, and though she often scorned girls her age who already had children, she found it harder and harder to deny that she envied the wives and the mothers. When she'd told

Uncle Bill that it would be nice to have a man around, she hadn't been entirely joking.

"Hey, June, why don't you call Aaron and Henry? They always like hanging out with us."

"Yeah, because they still have the naïve hope that we might yet go out with them."

"It's not naïve. It could happen."

"Please, Aelissm. If I were to go for one of the Hammond boys, it would have been Nick, but I don't date married men."

"And sweet Beth is about to pop," Aeli muttered. "Yeah. Henry's still too much of a partier, and Aaron…. Well, he's just not my type."

"Do you even have a type?"

"Not yet. Get your damned suit, and I'll call them. With Luke around, they won't dare try anything scandalous."

She picked up the phone she'd abandoned moments ago and June's Northstar Directory. With her thumb hovering over the buttons of the cordless handset, she stared at her own name, then at her phone number. Outside of the valley and the directory, only her parents, Uncle Bill, her father's brother in Ohio, and June's mother and stepfather knew the cabin number. Anyone else wishing to contact her were given her grandparents' number. They hadn't mentioned any suspicious phone calls before they'd left for Ohio two weeks ago. What if Adam had somehow gotten hold of the directory? Panic raged like a blizzard through her veins. The only way he could have gotten one was from someone who lived in Northstar. What if he was in the valley right now, looking for her?

Stubbornly, Aelissm straightened her spine and refused to give in to her wild thoughts. This valley was a very close community, and anyone out of place quickly became the subject of the grapevine. If Adam was here, she would have heard about it. Taking a slow, deep breath and letting it out even more slowly, Aelissm reasoned that she was just jittery from his phone call the other night. He'd gotten the number from someone else. That had to be it. After all, he knew all of her friends in Washington, and breaking and entering didn't faze him in the least.

"Aeli, are you all right?" June asked, coming down the stairs. "You're shaking."

"I'm all right now. I just had a scare. I thought maybe Adam had somehow gotten hold of one of these," she replied, holding up the directory. "But I'm sure he must've found it a while ago. Maybe he picked it up from my apartment in Seattle or something."

"Are you sure you're all right?"

She nodded, then dialed Aaron Hammond. He wasn't home, and his twin brother Henry wasn't, either. Then she remembered. It was their mother's birthday today, so they were all probably down at the main house celebrating.

"That's okay. I didn't really want their company, anyhow."

June wrapped her arms around Aelissm. Aeli drew a ragged breath and assured her friend that she would be all right.

"Maybe Uncle Bill sending Mr. O'Neil will help," Luke said, joining them in the living room. "You know, maybe he'll be able to chase Adam away."

Aeli smiled and draped an arm around his narrow shoulders and around June's. "Let's go take a dip, shall we? Just the three of us. You don't mind two such gorgeous ladies as June and me hanging on your arms, do you Luke?"

He grinned. "I'll be the envy of the valley."

June reached over and ruffled his hair affectionately. She glanced at Aeli and asked, "So, what do you think?"

After nineteen years of friendship, she didn't have to ask what June was talking about. Aeli considered what June had said, about adopting Luke, and gazed at the boy. In just the eight short months he'd been here, he'd already come a long way. She glanced at June and nodded. "I think you should."

They climbed in June's pickup and drove up to Aeli's cabin so she could grab her swimsuit. When she opened the door to her cabin—which she rarely ever locked unless she was going to be out of the valley—she saw that there were two messages on her answering machine. She hit the play button. The first was from Bill, letting her know that Pat O'Neil was leaving early in the morning with plans to be in Northstar tomorrow evening. He reminded her to keep detailed notes of Adam's calls. He also recommended that she sign up for caller ID. The moment the second message started playing, Aelissm froze.

"What is your problem, Aelissm? You didn't have to talk to me like that the other night. I didn't mean for any of this to happen, and I didn't want Brent to die, but you don't care about that. You think I'm a monster now, but you're too much of a bitch to remember that he tried to hurt you, that I only hurt him to save you. Why can't you see how much I love you?"

The message ended, and Aeli stared at the machine. With that rough, desperate voice, he barely sounded like the Adam she knew. Shuddering, she picked up the note pad beside the phone and jotted down the time of the message, the date, and exactly what he'd said. Then she erased the messages, grabbed her swimsuit and a towel, and trotted back out to June's truck, locking the door behind her.

"He called again," she told her friend as they drove down the mountain.

"Oh? What did he have to say?"

"More or less the same things he always says."

Twenty minutes later, Aelissm slid into the soothing embrace of hot water in the Ramshorn's larger pool. She and June and Luke were the only people in the pools, and she was grateful for the solitude. With a sigh, she settled on the steps, submerged in blissfully warm water up to her neck. She tilted her head back and stared skyward. Steam rose in drifting clouds beneath the blue-white light of the lamps around the pools, randomly obscuring and revealing the glittering stars. The night was crisp and fresh with all her favorite scents of home—pine, sagebrush, and snow. There were still almost six inches of the latter in places on the boardwalk around the pools, and Aelissm grabbed a handful and held it under water, amused by how it tickled as it quickly melted.

June joined her on the stairs and they watched Luke swim around for a while, silent.

What's happened to me? Aelissm wondered. She'd never run from anything in her life until that night. Yet, here she was, hiding in a remote valley in Montana, terrified that Adam would find her. She could argue that she'd come home to Northstar to help her grandparents, but the truth was that she probably wouldn't have said yes to them if Adam wasn't breathing down her neck. She probably would have muscled her way through the last of her master's classes and continued on with her plan to teach at the college level. *At least I'm* sort of *still on that path*, she thought. *But one class isn't a full-time position, and I still have those classes to finish. When am I going to do that?*

"I'm scared, June, and I don't know what I'm going to do," she admitted. "I'm staring into a blank future."

Her friend looked at her with concern etched in her face. "Then maybe it really is good Bill is sending Pat. Having a big, strong man around might give you peace of mind or, if nothing else, a distraction."

"Maybe."

June smiled and returned her attention to her foster son. The boy was down at the deep end, hanging off the side to catch his breath.

"Let's fling him," Aeli said. "Hey! Luke! C'mere!"

Obediently, Luke swam back to the shallow end. June and Aelissm faced each other with their hands locked together underwater. The boy grinned and put his feet in the cradle, and they launched his small body skyward. He went in head first, then resurfaced, laughing.

Aelissm enjoyed herself, and slowly, the anxiety eased out of her. Everything would be all right. She had her best friend close by, good clean mountain air in her lungs, and two good jobs. Except for Brent's death and Adam's obsession with her, life was pretty good. She helped June launch Luke again and decided things could be a lot worse and would someday get better. Look at Luke. Eight months ago, after his father had been killed, Luke had been sickly, pale, and skittish, and now he was healthy and happy.

"He's still skinny, though," Aelissm murmured.

"Not because he doesn't eat," June remarked, watching the boy swim. "He's tiny now, but I'll bet he's going to be tall." She turned her eyes on her friend. "But that's not what you were thinking."

"No, I was just thinking that I'm glad I came back to Northstar. If I have to face Adam, I'd rather do it here."

Two

PAT FOUND IT DIFFICULT to concentrate on the road as he turned off the Interstate just past Devyn, Montana, and headed west on a two-lane highway. Some people might say that the stretch of road between Coeur d'Alene and Missoula was prettier, but Pat disagreed. The seemingly empty stretches of rolling sagebrush hills on the edges of the expansive valley around Devyn touched something deep in his heart. The mountain ranges that bordered the ranching valley on all sides were breathtaking, untamed, and still white with winter, though the valley was clear and straw-gold beneath them. It was nearly April, but from what Pat had been told, snow was possible—probable, even—into May, and the area had merely been experiencing a bit of a warm spell over the past week.

As he drove higher up the slopes toward Northstar,

he began to see more patches of snow in the shadows of the trees and hills. Pat wished it were warm enough out to roll his window down. The air was so clean. *Just a brief taste*, he thought and rolled his window down a crack. It might be warm by local standards, but the blast of air was frigid. He glanced at the digital thermometer in his rearview mirror. The outside temperature hovered just a few degrees above freezing.

He'd left early this morning, but seven hundred and some miles was a long way to come, and with the loss of an hour when he'd crossed time zones, the sun was now low in the western sky. By the time he reached Northstar, it would probably be sunset. According to Bill's notes, Aelissm would likely be down at the Bedspread Inn until ten or so.

Pat crested the small pass and followed the highway down and around the southern end of the Northstar Mountains. His first view of the Northstar Valley instantly warmed him to the idea of staying here for a while. Still wearing the tattered but glittering cloak of winter, the valley was gorgeous, bordered by the taller granite peaks to his right and the lower, pine-blanketed mountains to his left. The eastern peaks glowed pink in the failing day while the valley below was wrapped cozily in the cool blue shadows of night.

"Stunning," Pat murmured.

He nearly missed the turn-off to Northstar. The sign was directly across from it, not a few yards before, and listed not just the town but also the establishments of Northstar on a set of wooden slats stained dark brown with yellow lettering.

The road was paved for all of about a mile, then turned over to compacted dirt and gravel. He saw several ranch gateways that looked like they came straight out of the movie and a small schoolhouse. He passed the road that led to the Northstar Post Office. Behind the post office was a single wide trailer with an add-on that almost made it a double wide. Part of it appeared to be a greenhouse. Pat knew from Bill's notes that it belonged to Aelissm's grandparents. Another few miles brought him to the intersection of Northstar Road and Elkhorn Road, and he slowed, at last seeing the dark brown building with white trim that was the Bedspread Inn. He turned left and pulled into the inn's horseshoe-shaped driveway, which looped back toward the main road and was lined with several old buckboard wagons and mine cars.

The inn had ten rooms, five on the ground floor, five above, all facing toward the driveway. He parked in front of the inn's restaurant, which was connected at a ninety-degree angle and looked like a squat A-frame with a front wall that was almost entirely windows. The lights were on inside, and smoke curled lazily from the massive stone chimney.

He stepped out into the chilly evening and stretched some of the stiffness out of his body before he ascended the wide stairs to the deck. *The temperature up here must be at least ten degrees cooler than down in Devyn.*

He stopped on the front deck and gazed over his shoulder. His breath sucked through his teeth at the sight. The Northstar Mountains were bathed in a deep ruby light, and above them, a perfectly cloudless sky changed from the bright blue of day to the darker shades of sunset. A faint haze of wood smoke drifted around the scattered houses and cabins of the valley, spicing the air with cozy welcome.

The bell on the door jingled, and he turned around to see a family of four walk out of the restaurant. They all stopped to look at the mountains, as he had, laughing and smiling.

"Better get in there, 'fore you freeze," the man said to Pat in a thick Southern drawl. "I don't know how these people do it. I wonder if it's really winter eight months out of the year up here."

Curious, Pat watched them until they piled into the Ford Explorer with Georgia plates. He chuckled and took one last look at the mountains before he stepped inside. There was a roaring fire in the stone hearth that commanded the center of the room. It was open on three sides and panels of beveled glass kept sparks and embers from leaping out.

"Marge and Roger are supposed to be back tomorrow, right, Aeli?" he heard someone ask.

He stepped around the fireplace and found two older men sitting at the bar. A golden-haired beauty smiled indulgently at them, and Pat instantly recognized her as the woman from the picture on Bill's desk. Without the vibrant orange stocking cap, she was even more beautiful with a graceful oval face framed by tendrils of hair that had pulled loose from her braid. The reddish cast of that shining mane complemented her soft, rosy complexion and made her dark green eyes glow like polished emeralds. *Striking*, he thought. *Certainly enough to make a man look twice.*

"Yeah, tomorrow afternoon. Ready for another Moose Drool?"

"Nah. I'm done. Thank you, dear. Would you have

Roger call me when he gets in? I need him to look at that hoist again."

"Will do, Matt. John's driving, right?"

"Of course," the man named John replied. "C'mon, Matt. I'd better get your sorry arse home to Livia before she has both our hides."

The two ranchers dropped some bills on the bar for Aelissm and headed for the door, nodding to Pat as they left. He glanced at the only remaining patrons, a couple who must belong to the other out-of-state vehicle. Aelissm wiped down the bar, took the empty glass back to the kitchen. When she reappeared, she spotted him and smiled.

"What can I do for you?" she asked.

"I'd like a cup of coffee, if it's not too much trouble."

"So long as you're a paying customer, it's no trouble at all," she replied teasingly. "You must be Patrick O'Neil. You're the only man who's been in here today tall enough to fit the description my uncle gave me. Six-foot-four, huh?"

"Call me Pat."

She stepped around the bar and extended her hand. He shook it. "Aelissm Davis. Aelissm or Aeli is fine."

"Bill brags about you all the time, so it's nice to finally match the praise to the woman."

"He talks about you a lot, too, so yes, it *is* nice to meet you at last. Have a seat wherever you like, and I'll get your coffee. Cream? Sugar?"

"Just cream."

He watched her vanish into the kitchen again, amused. She was much sexier in person, wearing faded blue jeans and a tantalizingly snug green sweater that matched her eyes. When she returned, he thanked her and paid her for the coffee.

"How long until you close?" he asked.

"Bored already?"

"No, just curious. Need a hand with anything?"

"No, I've got it covered. I close at nine, and if we're lucky, we'll be out of here by nine-thirty."

Pat glanced at his watch. It was a little after seven. Then he remembered he hadn't set his watch forward. Eight. Only an hour until she closed. That wasn't so bad.

While Aelissm checked on her other patrons, he sipped his coffee and watched her. Bill's niece sure was easy on the eyes. She had soft curves that invited a man to linger and was, he noted, deceptively toned. Strong but very feminine. Look twice? He'd be lucky if he could keep himself from staring. He shook his head to clear it of any lecherous thoughts. This was his boss's niece, and besides, he didn't need to be thinking along those lines, not with her safety being his number-one priority. And not after Sara.

"This is a gorgeous valley," he remarked to Aelissm when she joined him at the bar. "I think I'm really going to enjoy my time here."

Aelissm raised a golden eyebrow at him. "Won't you miss your Starbucks?"

Pat lifted his mug. "I'll take a cup of this good brew and the company of an intelligent woman over Starbucks any day."

The quick tilt of her head was barely noticeable, and Pat's lips quirked. She'd been expecting a city boy, had she? He wasn't at all sad to have disappointed her. He smiled, and she returned it, then glanced at the television above the door to the kitchen. There was a commercial on, and she tried to seem interested, but Pat could see she wasn't.

"So, is there anything I should know? Has Mr. Winters tried to contact you again?"

She looked at him with narrowed eyes. At first, he thought she was going to ignore his question or lie to him. She opened her mouth, closed it, then said, "Yeah. He called again last night and left a message."

"Did you save it?"

"No, but I wrote it down word for word. I'm sorry, Mr. O'Neil—"

"Pat. And I understand why you erased the message." He took another sip of his coffee. "There's something else bothering you."

She stood up and walked over to the small desk that sat between the side door and the open doorway to the kitchen. Pat watched her pick up something. When she flopped it in front of him, he saw that it was a phone book of sorts, labeled "Northstar Directory." He glanced through the list, saw Aelissm's phone number and address.

"When I heard the message, I was afraid he might have somehow gotten hold of one of these."

"How would he do that?"

"He'd have to be here to get it, but no one has said anything about a tourist asking about the directory or me, so he probably got it from my apartment in Seattle." She glanced at her customers. "I thought you should know," she added and strode off.

Pat studied first the list then Aelissm. She was so composed with her customers that he almost couldn't believe the show of fear and wariness he'd seen just a moment ago. He couldn't help but think that she was handling the whole situation well. She may be hiding, but she was at least trying to live a normal life. Pat decided it was good that she had come to such a place as this. Surely, being such a small community, anything suspicious would quickly become the subject of gossip. She was probably far safer here than she'd been in Seattle. And if Winters decided to visit, Pat would likely have an easier time singling him out. For that reason, he decided that one of his first tasks should be getting to know the locals.

"Who were those two gentlemen at the bar?" Pat asked when Aelissm came back.

"When you came in? The older is Matt Carlyle, and his friend is John Hammond. Why do you ask?"

"I just thought it might be a good idea to get to know your neighbors, especially since I don't know how long I'll be here."

"Ah. In that case, you're in luck. We're hosting a potluck here tomorrow, and almost everyone from the valley will be in attendance. Jumping back to John and Old Matt, the Carlyles own the second largest spread in the valley, the C Diamond, and the Hammonds own the largest, the Lazy H."

Pat smiled. "No rivalry between clans?"

"Nope. They get along marvelously. In fact, Old Matt's eldest granddaughter, Beth, is married to John's eldest son, Nick. They're expecting their first child any day now."

"Really. So, Old Matt's going to be a great-grandpa."

"And John will be a grandpa. First one."

"I take it you know everyone."

"Just about, except a few of the newbie part-timers. There's a couple who just bought one of the cabins up the road and another family that's renting one of the Struthers' houses."

"Struthers?"

"Steven and Caroline own the Circle S. Steven's younger brother, Marvin, and his wife, Mary, own the Ramshorn Hot Springs."

Pat chuckled. "You've only been back here for six months, and already you're reacquainted."

She shrugged. "Northstar doesn't change much."

Pat thought he caught a hint in her tone that added, *for which I'm grateful.* He drank the rest of his coffee and ordered a cheeseburger from her. As he stared out the window at the twilight and ate his meal, he again thought that this assignment—this *vacation*—might just be rather enjoyable. Aelissm was downright beautiful and quite possibly the most intriguing woman he'd met in a long time, and he *did* need a little time away from his memories. He already felt more relaxed than he had in months. Then he reminded himself not to relax too much because he *was* here for another reason. Bill had asked him to keep Aelissm safe from Adam Winters, not to let himself be distracted by her. Although, Bill *had* said…. Pat shook his head. He wasn't ready for anything like that. At the rate he was going, he might never be.

* * *

"Well, here we are," Aelissm said as she walked up the driveway of her grandparents' mobile home. The ragged snow was crusted with ice and crunched beneath her boots. She stamped her feet clean as she ascended the three steps of her grandparents' front porch, then glanced at the large, round thermometer. Twenty-five degrees. She exhaled, and her breath formed a silvery cloud in the glow of the porch light. The cobalt night sky with its array of bright, shimmering stars was clear, but the air was sharply damp and smelled of snow.

She slid the key into the lock and led Pat inside.

"Sorry, but you'll have to sleep on the hideaway in the den tonight," she told him as she turned on the lights. "It's comfy enough. I'll be in the room just on the other side of that wall, and the bathroom is the second door on the left—right across from the den."

"We're not going up to your cabin?"

"No. I need to get up early tomorrow and head into town to do some shopping. Besides, it's supposed to snow tonight."

He raised an eyebrow, but his lips lifted in wonder.

Aelissm admired his easy-going nature and the way he seemed to take things in stride. The lingering irritation over her uncle's interference dissipated for the time being, and she was looking forward to getting to know Pat. She showed him around, led him out through the den, and then pointed out the refrigerator in the back room that was packed full with goodies.

"Help yourself," she told him.

She grabbed a couple extra blankets and pillows from the closet in the hallway and dropped them on the hideaway, which she'd pulled out and *mostly* gotten ready this morning. Then she went back to the den and stoked the fire while Pat ducked into the bathroom. She sat on the floor in front of the wood stove with one leg tucked beneath her and an arm wrapped around the other with the poker held loosely in her hand. She stared into the merrily dancing flames, mesmerized. Right then, her mind was mercifully devoid of all fears and worries.

There was nothing like wood heat, she thought. It warmed thoroughly to the bone and left a snug feeling of safety that no amount of natural gas or propane or electric heat could give. She could feel it on her face, dry and comforting.

"There's nothing quite like wood heat, is there?"

Pat's voice startled her, and she glanced over her shoulder to find him standing in the doorway to the den. He'd taken off his coat and folded it over his arm, and Aeli tilted her head, riveted. His jeans were just tight enough to give her a taste, and the dark blue sweater he wore fit him just as well. The flickering light and shadow outlined his features exquisitely—the broad, strong shoulders, the sculpted chest, and flat stomach, the long, firm legs. There was a light smile on his face, and in the glow of the fire, he was devastatingly handsome with features that were both smooth and masculine. He looked tired, though, she thought. Granted, he'd driven more than seven hundred miles today and had probably risen well before the sun, but she suspected that was only a fraction of the exhaustion she saw in his eyes.

"Have a seat," she offered.

Pat stretched out beside her, his posture relaxed and open. She was acutely aware of how intimate the situation was and how completely unconscious it was. He wasn't trying to make a move on her; he was just sitting in front of a fire with his boss's niece. What surprised her more was how easy and natural it would be to rest her head on his shoulder.

He exuded serenity, and with her emotions still a little too chaotic after Adam's calls, she was drawn to his unassuming demeanor.

Instead of acting on the urge, she pulled her other knee up and draped her arms around her legs. She had met Pat barely more than two hours ago, and she couldn't trust her instincts. Brent had been a gentleman, too, at first, and Adam had been a funny, lovable companion. Aelissm shuddered.

"So," Pat said as if he sensed her uneasiness, "tell me about your friend June. Bill said you two have known each other since you were five."

Aelissm smiled, grateful for the diversion. "Yep. Uncle Bill and June's stepdad introduced us when Dan started dating June's mom."

"That wouldn't happen to be Dan Blue, would it? Your uncle's buddy from the navy?"

"That's the one."

"I've never met him, but Bill speaks very highly of him. He sounds like a good guy."

"He is. Unk wouldn't be friends with someone who isn't."

"No, he wouldn't. Doesn't June live up by your parents' cabin?"

"Just a couple hundred yards over from it. My parents invited her to spend two weeks with us up here one summer, and she fell in love with the place."

"It's always nice to have a good friend around when times get a little rough."

"Don't I know it. It's been fun, the two of us together on the mountain again." She paused and found herself smiling. "I'm really glad I came back."

Pat nodded but didn't say anything else. They sat for a while, enjoying a contented quiet that was only interrupted by the occasional pop from the fire. Aelissm found herself wanting to explain about Brent and Adam but not in the context of what Pat would want to know for his role as her guardian. She felt the need to explain why she'd fallen for Brent in the first place, but why should she have to explain anything? People made mistakes.

"We should probably get some sleep," she said after a moment. "Hope you don't mind being dragged around tomorrow."

"Not at all. Do you mind if I call Bill? I should probably check in."

"Help yourself. Phone's in the living room. G'night."

She tossed another log in the stove, then shut the door and closed the dampers for the night. Pat followed her out, bid her goodnight at her bedroom door, and headed for the living room. Her guest spoke quietly, but the thin walls made it easy for her to hear every word he said. The conversation was short, but Aelissm was curiously pleased by Pat's glowing compliments of Northstar. Even more unaccountable, she enjoyed the smooth timbre of his voice, and she was disappointed when he bid her uncle farewell. The floorboards of the hallway creaked as he walked back to the den, and she thought she heard him whisper good night to her as he passed her door.

As she lay in the bed, curled beneath the thick blankets, she listened to the snaps of the fire, then the squeaks of the hideaway's springs as Pat shifted into a comfortable position. Those sounds, signs of something as simple as a man preparing for sleep, made Aelissm sigh with relief. For the first time since Adam had called three nights ago, she felt safe. Maybe Uncle Bill was right. Maybe sending Pat was a good idea, if only for her peace of mind.

Too bad Pat had been uprooted from his life to give her that. Then again, maybe he needed the break as much as she needed to be herself again. Uncle Bill *had* asked her to make sure Pat relaxed while he was in Northstar. What exactly had happened, Aelissm hadn't a clue, but Pat had been working too hard to get past it, and that was enough to tell her that Northstar was probably the best place he could have come to get away. Aeli knew it from the weariness about him—the kind of exhaustion a good night's sleep couldn't cure. The only things that could help him were peace and quiet, good company, and fresh mountain air, all of which were abundant in Northstar.

Three

AELISSM THRASHED AWAKE, feeling his hands gripping her arms, smashing her breasts, digging into her thighs. Terror dragged icy fingertips over her skin, and she shuddered against the threatening promise that echoed in her head as she struggled to escape the nightmare. Her chest heaved, and cold sweat trickled down her spine. She felt his touch, but she shouldn't be able to. Brent was dead. She hugged herself and rocked, trying to slow her thumping heart. It refused to obey and continued to pound erratically. The image of Brent's apartment writhing in candlelight and shadow was imprinted vividly in her mind's eye. That apartment—part of his attempt to make his own way without his parents' money—had been more comfortable and welcoming to her than the Ellingtons' opulent mansion… until *that* night. That night, it had turned sinister and become as welcoming as a grave.

Just a bad dream, she told herself.

She glanced around the dark room, comforted by the warmth of her blankets and the quiet. Very slowly, the nightmare faded away, and she sank back on the bed with her hand covering her eyes. She was safe in her grandparents' house in Northstar, and her uncle's detective was sleeping out on the hideaway. There was nothing to be worried about, nothing to fear.

Except that Adam had called the cabin twice now.

Sleep was long gone, so she climbed out of bed and went into the den to stoke the fire. There were just a few coals left, but she tossed in a few slender logs and blew on it until flames were once again devouring the wood. After a few minutes, she glanced toward the hideaway where Pat lay on his back, still peacefully asleep with his head turned to the side. His body was outlined beneath the blankets, and Aelissm's pulse quickened. She squatted in front of the fire for a moment longer, spellbound.

Finally, she shut the stove door and opened the dampers, then closed herself in the bathroom and turned on the shower. Stripping out of her well-worn flannel and boxer shorts, she climbed under the steaming water and imagined the remaining chills draining away with it. By the time she stepped out of the shower, she was much revived.

Walking to the front door, she flipped on the porch light, and her lips lifted in amusement. As she'd predicted, there was an inch of fresh snow glittering on the porch. More still fell from the sky, twirling and glinting in the light. She strode down the hallway and stood in the doorway to the den, silently daring Pat to wake and see her still damp from her shower and hidden from his eyes by only a towel. He didn't stir. Shocked by her behavior, she turned abruptly and fled to her room. She dressed in a sinfully soft, cream-colored sweater, jeans, thick socks, and lightweight snow boots, then set about her morning chores and tried to figure out what had gotten in to her.

When her alarm went off, she dashed into her room to shut it off and stepped into the greenhouse to water her grandmother's plants. Moments later, she heard Pat get up, then the bathroom door closed, and the shower turned on.

After she finished watering the plants, she headed back into the house. Just as she stepped through the doorway between the den and the hallway, the bathroom door opened, and she froze mid-step only inches from Pat. Droplets of water glistened on Pat's skin and ran in rivulets down his toned chest. Their eyes met, and for a long, trembling moment, Aelissm couldn't move, could barely breathe. All she could think was, *Wow.*

"I didn't know you were up yet," Pat said. His voice was disconcertingly soft.

"I've been up for an hour or so."

"Ah."

She noticed how Pat's eyes glanced over her and thought she saw a glimmer of appreciation in them.

"Hungry?"

"What?" he asked, startled.

A little distracted, are we? she wondered, pleased. "Can I make you breakfast?"

"That sounds wonderful. Thanks."

Aelissm turned away and grinned. He hadn't caught her in a towel, but the other way around was just as good or better. There was a distinct spring in her step as she walked into the kitchen and pulled out eggs and bacon. Compared to Pat's delectable physique, Brent had been on the skinny side. While she waited for the bacon to fry, she sat down at the kitchen table and skimmed through the most recent issue of the Smithsonian, but it was difficult to focus on what she was reading, so she put it down again and redirected her attention to cooking breakfast. As she finished the eggs and bacon and popped the bread in the toaster, Pat joined her in the kitchen. He wore jeans and a sweater—green this time. His face was clean-shaven, and his dark auburn hair was almost dry.

"I got caught up in front of the fire again," he remarked when he caught her staring.

"That happens." She looked away to hide the blush that tickled her cheeks. "Breakfast is ready."

She pulled two plates and glasses out of the cupboard, then dug two forks out of the silverware drawer, opened the fridge, and grabbed the orange juice bottle. When she turned around, she nearly dropped it all. Pat stood just inches from her, and had he not reached out to take the glasses, they likely would have crashed to the linoleum.

"Sorry about that. I didn't mean to startle you." He smiled. "Can I give you a hand?"

"Sure. Grab the bacon and eggs and the toast, if you would."

"I can't grab all that in one trip."

"I didn't say you had to."

He laughed, and the rich sound brought a smile to her face. If this morning was any indication, Pat's time in

Northstar was going to be even more interesting than she'd suspected last night.

"Bill hasn't told me too much else about you beyond what I needed to know and that you're an accomplished craftswoman," Pat said, "so I have to ask—and I apologize if you take offense—how ever did you come to have such an unusual name?"

"In high school, my mother and her best friend Melissa were playing around with Double Dutch—it's a playground language like Pig Latin, but you switch the first and last letters. Anyhow, they did that with Melissa's name, and Mom fell in love with the result, thinking it was a cool and different way to spell the flower alyssum."

"I'll bet it made school interesting. Your teachers must've had a difficult time pronouncing it, and I imagine the other kids gave you hell, if they were anything like my classmates."

"What did the kids used to call you?"

"Fat Pat."

"But there's nothing fat about you."

He smiled sheepishly. "And I was about as scrawny as they come back then, too."

"I didn't get teased *too* badly, but there *were* a few times I wished I could change my name."

Pat tilted his head and studied her. "It fits you, though; it's unique like you are, and delicate to say but tough, too."

Aeli lowered her gaze to hide the smile that spread across her face at his quiet praise. "What about you? With a name like Patrick O'Neil, I'm guessing at least one side of your family has some pretty strong Irish heritage."

Nodding, he replied, "My great-grandparents on my dad's side came over from Ireland when my grandfather—Patrick, my namesake—was a little boy. They're all pretty gifted musicians, and for a while, my grandparents made a living playing at various theaters."

"Your dad's a music teacher, right?"

"Yes, he is, and he taught me how to play the piano, which I enjoy, but it was Grandpa Patrick who taught me to play the pan flute, which is my favorite instrument."

"You play the pan flute," Aelissm repeated. She regarded her companion with an even greater interest. Her uncle's detective was turning out to be quite an intriguing man. "And yet you decided to be a cop."

"My Grandpa Antony was a detective for the Seattle PD, and for as long as I can remember, I wanted to follow in his footsteps. Don't get me wrong. I love music, but honestly, my little sister got the lion's share of the musical talent. She is truly gifted. Like you."

Again, Aeli shyly dropped her gaze. "I don't know about that."

"I do because I've seen some of the things you've built." He leaned back in his chair, and she again felt like an open book beneath his gaze. "And now you're sharing that gift with college students, though I recall Bill telling me you taught a couple years of high school shop."

"Yeah…" she said slowly. "Two years in a small town near Billings. Unlike June, I'm not cut out to be a high school teacher. I think I inherited too much of my father's antisocial nature along with his talent for building. Teaching only one class at the college level allows me a lot more freedom in what and how I teach, and because I'm not a full-time faculty member, I don't have to interact with my colleagues much." Recalling the frustrating two years that had played a large role in her decision to pursue her Master's degree made her think of her time in Seattle, which she was in no mood to revisit after her nightmare, so she gestured to Pat's plate with her fork. "We'd better eat so we can head into Devyn."

Their conversation trailed off, but the quiet that followed was comfortable. When Pat finished first, he rose from his chair, but before he turned to take his plate to the sink, he stared over Aelissm's shoulder, gaping.

"Is it… snowing?"

She glanced over her shoulder out the window. "Yes, it is."

"Huh. You were right, then. Neat," he remarked, then started on the dishes.

Ignoring her own proclamation, Aelissm took her time finishing her meal and studied Pat covertly, smiling. He definitely wasn't the city boy she'd been expecting. This might be fun.

* * *

While Aelissm drove back to Northstar after their outing in Devyn, Pat watched her and wondered what had drawn her to Seattle. She seemed so at home here in this sparsely populated corner of Montana that the move didn't suit what he knew of her. He'd barely known her for fourteen hours—much of which had been spent in sleep—but he understood intuitively that she couldn't have been happy in the city. Remembering the light smile he'd seen on her face last night in the firelight, he was sure of it because there was an innocence about her that Seattle and even Brent's assault and death had not touched.

He stared out the window at the white hills half-hidden by curtains of falling snow. What had drawn *him* to Seattle? To be fair, he had gone to follow his grandfather into a career with the Seattle Police Department, but the ceaseless buzz of humanity had never appealed to him. His fonder memories came from the town of North Bend, several miles inland from Seattle, where he'd spent most of his life enjoying the quiet shadow of the Cascade Mountains.

"Earth to Pat."

He blinked at Aelissm, startled.

"Where'd you go?"

"Seattle and North Bend."

"Ah. Well, we're back at my grandparents'."

"You haven't told me why we were in such a hurry to get back here."

"I have a date."

"A date?"

"Yup. With a stunning blonde woman, a devilishly cute twelve-year-old boy, and a lot of flour and apples."

"You've lost me."

"We're baking pies with June and her foster son for the potluck tonight."

Pat cocked his head. "You didn't mention that June was fostering a kid. That's a helluva task for someone her age."

"Maybe so, but so far, it's been a great arrangement for them both. She's had him for about eight months now." Aelissm's expression softened affectionately. "I guess she's seriously thinking about adopting him. I'm surprised you didn't know because Unk is the mastermind behind it, and he pulled all the right strings to get Luke here quickly and without fuss."

"Right now, I can't remember him saying anything about it. So, when do I get to meet your grandparents?"

"They won't be back until this afternoon, but you can bet they'll put in an appearance at the potluck. And I think the plan is to go up to Grandma and Grandpa's cabin afterwards, just the six of us. It'll be a regular party on the mountainside."

"Sounds like fun."

Her answering grin was pure mischief.

Pat laughed. Aelissm, it was turning out, had a wicked sense of humor to complement her talent in a typically masculine field. Even Sara, with all her socialite sophistication, didn't possess nearly the multi-faceted layers as Aelissm Davis. *What has Bill gotten me into?* Pat wondered idly. His boss's niece was the most sassy, intelligent woman he'd met in a long time. Unbidden and potent, the wish that they'd met before he'd gotten mixed up with Sara whispered through his mind.

He shoved it away and climbed out of the cab to help Aelissm transfer groceries to his truck as the one they'd driven in to Devyn belonged to her grandparents.

"North Bend, huh?" Aelissm asked.

"I grew up there. I only moved to Seattle to join the force, and to be honest, I didn't ever completely adjust. I'm glad Bill talked me into moving over to the sheriff's department. I'm a detective now like I wanted, and I much prefer the quiet of Kitsap County to the bustle of Seattle."

"I didn't fully acclimate to Seattle, either," she replied. "I went to work on my Master's and to be closer to my family, and then I met Brent… oh, I guess it was almost two years ago. Wow. He's been dead almost a year already."

Pat frowned at the catch in her voice. He wasn't sure if she was scared, sad, or angry, and the expression on her face was just as uninformative as the tone of her voice. "Are you all right?"

"For now, but if Adam comes here…." She inhaled deeply and began again. "I just want him out of my life so I can put this whole damned mess behind me."

"That's why your uncle asked me to come," he reminded her. More gently, he added, "This is your haven, and I won't let him ruin it."

Her lips quirked upward. "Thank you."

With everything now in the back of Pat's truck, they headed up to the cabin. Pat was nervous about the snow-covered roads, but Aelissm made him drive anyhow.

"Winter might hang on for a while yet, and I don't want to have to chauffeur you everywhere, so you'd better learn how to drive in it," she told him.

Following her directions, he turned right on Elkhorn Road, and she pointed out the convenience store called Ma Burns' Country Market. A short while later, she told him to turn right again, and the road curved up and around through a stand of aspen, then snaked through the sagebrush. A hundred or so yards after the road entered the forest of lodgepole pine, he turned left on an unmarked road. Aelissm told him it was Wellman Creek Road, named for the miner who had mined gold and silver at the end of the road near the cabins.

The road was rough in spots, though the snow helped smooth out the ride some, and Aelissm guided him around the worst rock clusters. Most of Pat's attention was on driving, but he couldn't ignore the wild beauty of Aelissm's home. The meager light seeping through the clouds and flurries reflected off the snow, softly illuminating the forest from below. The trees here had stubby branches and hardy, dark green needles. Beneath them, the steep ground was littered with granite boulders ranging from the size of a man's head to twice the size of his truck. The climate was much drier than Washington, and the pitch of the land and the rocky ground didn't allow water to sit and pool, so the wood wasn't dark and rotting but sun-silvered and perfect for those picture frames in Bill's house.

As he drove higher up the winding backwoods road, Aeli began to talk more. She told stories about riding down the hill on dirt bikes to buy candy and soda at Ma Burns', including one trip when the goodies she'd purchased had fallen off the rack on the back of her bike.

"My brother and June thought I'd lost all of it, so we went all the way back down to Ma Burns'." She laughed, and he could feel her fondness for her brother and friend and for the memory. "I forgot to tell them that I hadn't lost the package of cookies, so I didn't know what they were looking for."

"I'll bet they were annoyed."

"Yeah, they reminded me about it for the rest of the trip. 'Have a cookie, Miss Daisy.' I still hear about it from time to time."

Pat chuckled, glad that she had some good memories from her childhood to comfort her when things got rough.

They reached a closed gate, and Pat stopped so Aelissm could open it and close it behind them. Just as they crested the hill and the road leveled out, a driveway split off to the right and doubled back in a sharp switchback. Aelissm informed him that it was the road up to June's cabin. About ten yards past that was a mound of pale yellow mine tailings and the remains of a one-room cabin. The road continued up into a small clear-cut, at the end of which was a single-story, beige cabin sided with metal sheets like were used on most of the roofs he'd seen in Northstar.

"That's my grandparents' cabin," Aelissm said as they passed its driveway.

She directed him around a short bend and told him to continue around to the right instead of following the road to the left. As her cabin came into view, he recalled the picture of the cabin that Bill had above his desk. The cabin hadn't seemed so tall in the photograph.

"Home sweet home," Aeli murmured as he shut his truck down. "And thanks to June, it'll be nice and toasty."

They sat for a moment, staring at the curl of smoke rising from the chimney.

"I could get used to this," Pat remarked. "No one but a few close friends and the animals to bother me."

She laughed and invited him in.

After they grabbed their bags and as many groceries as they could, Aelissm led him through the front door, which was unlocked. For a moment, Pat was alarmed, but amusement slowly filtered through him. The woman had an obsessive former friend trying to find her, and here she was leaving her door unlocked.

The first room was a utility room with a workbench on the right and a tiny bathroom complete with a claw-foot tub behind the door on the left.

"We didn't used to have electricity up here," she informed him. "Or an indoor bathroom, so be glad that you won't have to use the outhouse."

Inside the second door was a living room that spread across two-thirds of the ground floor, and the first things he noticed after the blissful wood heat were the matching, rust-orange, fuzzy couches that must have come straight out of the seventies. The living room itself had been modernized with sand-colored carpet and pale green curtains.

Pat trailed after Aelissm as she crossed the big room. The remaining third of the first floor was the kitchen. The cupboards above and below the snack bar and a steep spiral staircase separated it from the living room. The dining table sat between the kitchen and the living room, and a china hutch stood beside the back door on the right. Beside it was the refrigerator. Against the wall to the left of the door was the sink, and in the far corner were a wood stove and a newer gas range. *Must be propane*, he guessed.

Aelissm told him to drop the groceries on the table and take his bags up to the bedroom he'd be using. He ascended the steep spiral stairs. Immediately at the top was a bedroom a little larger than the kitchen; it contained two queen-sized beds and an antique chest of drawers. He dropped his shoulder and let his duffel bags slide down his arm onto the bed against the far wall, then peeked through the doorway into what appeared to be the master bedroom. It had a single queen-sized bed against the dividing wall and a long dresser on the left wall. Stacked carefully in the rafters were several boxes, and he wondered what they contained.

"Hurry up, Pat! I don't want to be late for my date!" Aelissm called.

He turned out of the room and headed back downstairs. The way the cabin was set up, if Adam *did* find her, he'd have to come through Pat to get to her. The thought reassured him.

"All right, I'm coming," he remarked. Then he noticed the small caliber rifle standing just out of sight from anyone coming up the stairs. Aelissm was a smart woman. And perhaps more scared than she let on.

He trotted downstairs to see that Aelissm had already put the groceries away and gathered her pie plates in a backpack. She informed him that they were hiking the two hundred yards to June's cabin and suggested he change into his snow boots.

Once his feet were snuggly encased in the boots Bill had recommended he bring, Pat followed his hostess out the kitchen door. They took a well-worn trail through the snowy woods, and though it had been cleared of the logs and rocks that made the steep terrain treacherous, it was still slippery, and he was grateful for the warmth and good traction of his snow boots. When he and Aelissm reached level ground at the end of the old logging road, he had to stop. He prided himself on being fit, but his lungs burned from the exertion. The air at seven thousand feet was much thinner than he was accustomed to.

"Come on, old man," Aelissm remarked. She was breathing harder, too, but she wasn't panting. "I thought you were in shape."

"I am. At sea level."

"It's not much farther. Just around the bend."

Pat straightened and trudged after her through the snow, which was still knee-deep up here on the mountainside. He could feel the cold against his legs and wondered if he should have brought his ski pants. He couldn't remember the last time he'd had to push his way through snow this deep. Probably the last time he'd made it up to a ski hill. He scowled. He hadn't been skiing in three years since the weekend before it had all fallen apart with Sara. He snorted. *Fallen apart* was off the mark. *Exploded* was far more accurate.

At last, they reached June's cabin. It was log with a dark green metal roof and appeared to be slightly larger than Aelissm's. Without knocking, Aeli opened the kitchen door and slipped inside after stomping the snow from her boots. Pat followed and was greeted with the mouthwatering scents of apples and cinnamon. The kitchen was similar to Aelissm's, including the wood stove in the right corner, the snack bar dividing the kitchen from the living area, and the spiral stairs. The upper floor, however, spanned only half the cabin's length, leaving the living room with a vaulted ceiling. A south-facing wall with big windows looked out on the surrounding ridges and the Northstar Valley. There was another wood stove in the southwestern corner of the living room.

A very attractive blonde woman stood at the sink washing apples. She was an inch or so taller than Aelissm— Pat guessed she was around five-nine—with a lankier build and kind, dusky blue eyes. She smiled broadly at Aelissm and inclined her head to Pat. A small boy with the same golden-blond hair as the woman rolled out piecrust on the counter that jutted out from the end of the snack bar. Two pies cooled on the table.

"It's about time you got here. I hope you brought

your pie plates, Aeli," the woman said. She wiped her hands on a dishtowel and extended a hand to Pat in greeting. "I'm June Montana."

"Montana? Really?"

She laughed. "I get that a lot."

Pat took the offered hand and shook it. "Pat O'Neil. And yes, we brought Aelissm's pie plates."

"Good." She wrapped an arm around the boy's slender shoulders. "This is Luke McKindel, my foster son."

"Hi," the boy said shyly.

The boy's name jolted Pat. He'd heard it before, and suddenly, he *did* remember Bill talking about the case, which had resulted in the death of the kid's father and the resignation of the sheriff's deputy who'd shot him. Because it wasn't any of his business, Pat ignored his curiosity, smiled to cover his shock, and said, "I'm glad to meet you both. So, we're making pies."

"Yep. Apple, as I'm sure you guessed. I thought we'd make ten pies—not that they'll last long tonight. We've already finished two."

June thrust a bowl of washed apples and a peeler at Aelissm. When Pat asked how he could help, she told him he could mix the ingredients for the filling and help Aeli peel and slice the apples. She turned her attention to making the dough for Luke to roll out.

"How are you liking Northstar so far, Pat?" June asked.

"I love it."

"He thought I was lying last night when I told him it'd snow," Aelissm remarked. "I hope he's here long enough to drag him up to Sawtooth. Then he can have his first snowball fight in May."

"What or where is Sawtooth?" he asked.

"There's a trailhead a couple miles down the hill from here, and the trail goes up to Sawtooth Lake. We hike it every third week or so in the summer. There are other lakes around that we hike to, some with trails, some without, like the Hall and Hopkins Lakes."

"That's a fun hike," Aelissm muttered. "Remember the first time we hiked up there? Grandpa said, 'at the bottom of the third rockslide, there's a trail that'll take you up to the lakes.' Ha!"

Pat glanced at June.

"There's no trail other than game trails that appear and disappear at random," she explained. "We followed the creek up. It's three miles up and three miles down, but it's a harder hike than Sawtooth, and it's higher, too."

"Sounds like fun."

"Fun?" Aelissm remarked. "You barely made it here. You should have heard him huffing and puffing, June."

"Like we used to?"

Pat was enchanted. The friendship between Aelissm and June was borne of a lifetime spent together, and it spiced the air as warmly as the fragrance of fresh apple pie. He didn't realize the passage of time until all ten pies were cooling on the snack bar. When he glanced at his watch, he saw that it was already three o'clock in the afternoon, which meant they'd finished just in time to allow the last pies two hours to cool before the potluck.

"Thanks so much for coming to help, Pat," June said. "You didn't have to."

"I know, but I'm glad I did. It was really nice to meet

the two of you."

Aelissm reached over to ruffle Luke's hair. The boy squirmed away with his face twisted in chagrin.

"We'll see you in a couple of hours," Aeli's friend said.

On the hike back to Aelissm's cabin, Pat again had to pause to catch his breath, but even as his lungs burned with the lack of oxygen, he found the breath to laugh.

"Don't worry," Aelissm remarked. "You'll get used to it. Luke's from Washington, too, and he can bounce all over these woods now like he was raised here."

"Yeah, but I'm pushing twenty-nine. Luke's only twelve." Pat's lips twisted thoughtfully. "He looks more like eight."

"He's tiny," she agreed.

"I doubt he'll stay that way for long. He's real lean and long-limbed like I was at his age."

"That could be from malnourishment. I don't think he had a very good life before he came here." Aelissm's pretty face darkened with a frown as if she wanted to add something, but she remained quiet.

"That may be, but I'll bet he'll be tall. Mark my words."

"How much would you bet?"

Pat's breath caught in his throat. He wouldn't be here long enough to see how the wager turned out—it might be a decade before the kid stopped growing—but Aelissm's challenging grin made his face lift in reply. "A hundred bucks. And I say he'll be at least six-two."

"You're on, Mr. O'Neil."

"No matter where we are?"

"No matter where we are," she affirmed.

Pat could only smile as he shook her hand to seal the deal.

Four

AN HOUR AFTER THEY returned from June's, Aelissm was in the spare bedroom of her cabin helping Pat unpack. When they finished, she headed toward her bedroom to change, but Pat's voice stopped her. She turned around to find him standing beside the stairs. Beside her gun.

"I've been meaning to ask about this, Aelissm," Pat said. His long fingers toyed with the barrel of her rifle. "And don't tell me it's for bears because even this *city boy* knows it wouldn't do more than piss a bear off."

Aelissm eyed the gun and cursed herself for not putting it away. Supposedly, she didn't need it now, anyway. "It's for gophers and badgers," she replied and added in an exaggerated Western drawl, "You know, varmints."

She tried to sound playful and nonchalant, but the lie was sour in the back of her mouth, and her neck warmed uncomfortably. From the stern shadow in Pat's eyes, she knew he didn't believe it any more than she did.

"Look, Pat, if I was really worried about some*one*, I'd reach for a pistol first. It's easier to maneuver than a rifle."

He lifted an eyebrow in inquiry. The intensity of his gaze made her look away, but when he cupped her chin and tilted her face toward him, the sincere concern that gentled his expression snatched her breath away. Never before had she been read so intimately by a man, and it was as enticing as it was startling. For a moment, she couldn't look away, and as he searched her gaze, she stood rooted to the floor, enthralled. It was the disgustingly girlish wobble of her knees that gave her the strength to turn away.

"Aelissm, I need to know."

"You need to know what?" she asked, bracing her hand on the doorjamb. She stared blindly into her bedroom, her senses a little too in tune to the subliminal signs of another being in her home. She could feel Pat's eyes on her back, worried and curious.

"I need to know everything I can about Adam Winters. Up to and including how you feel about the whole situation."

"I would have thought that was obvious." Her betraying voice cracked. She inhaled and let it out in a sigh before turning toward him. Unable to look him in the eyes again just yet, she trained her gaze out the window beyond and said, "I'm sorry. I'm not usually this emotional, but my nerves are a little raw."

"I understand, Aelissm. It's perfectly reasonable, considering what you've been through in the past year. If you were as steady and unmovable as one of those boulders outside, *then* I'd be worried."

"Well, I *have* been called as stubborn as one before," she replied with an amused twist of her lips.

A trail of shivers coursed down her spine when Pat gently touched her shoulder. She met his gaze again, guarded this time.

"I don't expect you to tell me right now, but soon." He paused, then added, "When you can trust me."

I already trust you, she thought. Her heart fluttered. It had taken weeks before she'd been able to trust Brent enough to let him kiss her, but it was all too tempting to cross the distance to Pat in a step, stand on her toes, and drag his mouth down to hers. She didn't, though neither did she move away, and the knowledge that he was single ignited a flash of desire. To smother it, she glanced at the gun. "We should probably head down. I need to be there early to set up," she murmured.

"Of course. It is your inn, after all."

"Well, it's not mine yet."

"But it will be if you stay here."

If you stay here. At the moment, she couldn't imagine going anywhere else. She'd come to Northstar to regroup, and she hadn't considered what she would do if this mess with Adam was resolved.

"I hadn't thought about staying. Or leaving, for that matter," she said. "I've been living in the here and now lately, and I haven't thought much about tomorrow."

When she glanced at him, she saw Pat frowning.

"You talk as if you aren't sure there will be a tomorrow. Do you really think Adam would kill you?"

She shook her head. "I didn't mean it like that. This

thing with Adam has taken most of my concentration, and I haven't had much time for thinking about anything else. I wish I could say that I haven't been running and hiding, but the truth is, I have. The main factor in my decision to come here was getting away from Adam."

"You're not living. You're existing. Surviving."

"Barely."

Aelissm watched his face for some clue as to what it was in his past that allowed him to empathize with her plight, but his expression was impossible to decipher. "Uncle Bill said you had a bad break up and that you've been losing yourself in work ever since."

"It's been three years, but I'm still not ready to talk about it."

His voice wasn't harsh. He was stating a fact, not snapping at her for prying, and Aelissm was all the more curious. What kind of rocks-for-brains woman would turn a man like Pat away? She shivered. What if the compassionate smile and the kind eyes with their shadows of heartache hid something sinister? She'd been wrong about Brent. What if she was wrong about Pat as well?

No, she thought. Uncle Bill had known the O'Neils since before Pat's birth, and he trusted Pat. He hadn't trusted Brent.

"You said you needed to head down early to set up."

She winced at the thread of cold distance in his voice. Then he smiled, and the memories passed from his eyes. With them went her apprehension.

"Probably ought to change into something that isn't covered in flour."

Pat glanced down at his flour-dusted clothing.

"Good idea."

Aeli stepped into her bedroom and closed the door, then stripped down to her undergarments. She pulled on a soft, black V-neck sweater and jeans before studying her reflection in the mirror. The outfit showed off her shape nicely, she noted with feminine pride. After a few moments of indecision, she decided to leave her hair down and brushed it until it shone like a sun-gilded afternoon.

"Are you decent?" she asked Pat.

"As decent as I'll ever be."

She smiled and opened the door between the rooms. *I could watch him for hours,* she thought, taking in every line of his six-foot-four-inch frame, which was clad to comfortable perfection in jeans and a black sweater. Hastily, she averted her gaze and descended the stairs.

Pat followed her out to her truck and climbed in the passenger side. The conversation on the ride down to the Bedspread revolved around Northstar and its inhabitants, but Aelissm's mind frequently sidetracked to her time with Pat. The memory of their encounter at her grandparents' house this morning kick-started her pulse. He was a distractingly sexy man, and his absolute lack of vanity was refreshing after Brent's preening self-absorption. When she snuck another glance at her companion, she caught him watching her with a bemused expression, and her cheeks and neck warmed uncomfortably.

"What?" she asked.

"Just wondering how long it's going to take you to answer my question."

"I'm sorry, but what did you ask?"

"When do I start work? Your uncle said you could

use a little extra help at the inn."

"How about a week from today? That will give you some time to get rested up and enjoy yourself a bit."

"Sounds good to me."

Aelissm parked her truck by the back door of the restaurant, and she and Pat walked inside together. There were already a few people inside, holding dishes, and Aelissm made a mental list of who was there. The Struthers brothers and their wives were accounted for, as were John and Tracie Hammond and Jim, Jessie, and Erica Robinson. Aelissm also spotted the Hammond twins Aaron and Henry at the bar, and craning her neck a little, she saw Nick and Beth sitting beside his brothers. Normally, she hated social gatherings, but Northstar potlucks and get-togethers were exceptions to that rule. The people of this valley were her friends, and she adored their open, honest company. If Pat was as smart as Uncle Bill led her to believe, he'd let them soothe and repair his bruised heart.

Aeli dragged him over and introduced him to the Hammond twins, who regarded her new guardian with unveiled envy. Her lips twitched with amusement. Aaron, at least, was professional, and he offered to sit down to discuss the matter of Adam Winters at Pat's earliest convenience. Before Pat could suggest they do it right then, Aelissm pointedly reminded them that it was supposed to be a fun evening. She wasn't about to let thoughts of Adam intrude, so she introduced Pat to the eldest Hammond brother and his wife. Nick and Beth warmed to him instantly and invited him to come down to the Hammond spread for a ride.

"Horses, I assume?" Pat asked. His tone was playfully self-mocking.

"Or four-wheelers, if you'd rather," Nick replied.

"I haven't been on a horse in years, so that'd be a lot of fun." Pat inclined his head to Beth. "So, boy or girl? Or are you going to be surprised?"

"Boy," Beth replied, beaming. "I swear it's the Hammond curse because they haven't had a girl in four generations."

Aelissm crossed her arms, and her fingers tapped a rapid rhythm of irritation. It wasn't the way Pat fawned over the parents-to-be that disturbed her; it was her entirely more unsettling reaction to it. If he was so kind and attentive to Beth and Nick, she could well imagine how devoted he'd be to the woman who carried his child.

I don't even want kids, she reminded herself. Looking at Pat's tall, lean body and listening to the warmth in his entrancing voice, the vow didn't feel so solid. *Maybe* hovered in the back of her mind like smoke in the valley on a cold, still day. Maybe, with a man like Pat.... No, not a man *like* him. She'd want Pat. With him, she could see herself in the role of wife and mother, though she was damned if she'd ever play the happy-little-housewife for any man. Brent had wanted that of her, and he was all the more a fool if he'd honestly believed he could turn her in to that. She'd majored in industrial arts, for God's sake.

"Beth, can I steal Nick's muscles for a minute or ten?" she asked, forcefully redirecting her thoughts. "Pat could use the help bringing tables up from the basement. He's not used to this altitude, after all."

"Hey!" Pat retorted. "I just got here. Give me a couple of weeks, and I'll keep up with even Luke."

"Go ahead and take him," Beth said with laughter in

her voice. "Better watch yourself, Pat. Aeli's a hellion."

"I think I can manage."

Aeli was about to tell him just what he could manage, but Nick beat her to it.

"Then you probably haven't met the real Aelissm Davis yet."

"Thanks, Nick," she said flatly.

"Take it as a compliment, Aeli, as I meant it. You'd keep a man on his toes, make life a never-ending adventure. Just like Beth does for me."

"Fine. C'mon, then, gents. Let's get this done. I don't think it's wise to make the mob that is Northstar wait too long."

As Pat and Nick hefted the second eight-foot banquet table, Pat inquired why they were bringing them all up when there was a dining room full of much nicer tables just above them.

"Where do you expect people to eat?" Aelissm replied. "On the floor? We may be a little behind the times, Mr. O'Neil, but we're not *that* far behind."

The men laughed, and she trudged up the stairs ahead of them with some folding chairs. She was greeted at the top by her grandparents. Setting the chairs down, she embraced them both.

Her grandmother looked around. "Tell me, where is this Patrick O'Neil your Uncle Bill sent over?"

"Trying to come up the stairs with a table," Aelissm heard Pat say with a grunt.

Aelissm stepped out of the way so her workhorses could get by. They set the table up beside the other against the east wall of the dining room, and Pat ambled over to greet Aelissm's grandparents.

"How are you liking Montana so far?" Marge asked him.

"It's great. I haven't felt this good in… months."

Aelissm noted his hesitation. From what little she knew, he probably hadn't felt this good in three years. Her grandparents, however, moved on without so much as a pause to consider the sudden distance in her guest's eyes. They launched into a lengthy description of all there was to see and do in the Northstar Valley, and by the time her grandfather was finished, he had enlisted Pat to help him work on the shed for his Model-T as soon as it warmed up a bit.

When June and Luke arrived with the pies, Aelissm stationed June beside the dessert table to stand guard over them and sent Luke into the kitchen for her serving knives. A short while later, the people of Northstar streamed through the double glass doors of the inn's dining room, and the tables Nick and Pat had set up were soon laden with food. Relaxed chatter filled the room, and children's shouts and laughter drifted up from the game room in the basement. As she surveyed the scene from the door to the kitchen, Aelissm knew she was where she should have been all along. Home.

"That's a good song!" Aaron Hammond cheered. "Hey, Aelissm! Turn it up!"

With a smile, she did as he asked. Several members of Northstar's younger generations stood to dance while their parents and grandparents watched, shaking their heads in bewildered amusement.

"Can we let them at the pies yet?" June asked, walking

over to join Aeli beside the kitchen door.

"I suppose so. Pat's already in to them. Hey! Pat!" Aeli barked. "He's as bad as they are."

"At least he helped make them." June laughed. "He does seem to fit in well here, doesn't he?"

"Mmm-hmm."

Aelissm watched him, spellbound. He worked his way through the room, greeting people and introducing himself to the residents of Northstar with a quick and engaging smile, and the way he concentrated attentively on each person he addressed had even stubborn Old Matt Carlyle chatting freely.

"He's fascinating to watch, isn't he?" she asked June.

"Apparently so. If you stare any harder, your eyeballs are going to pop out of your head."

Scowling playfully, Aelissm glanced at her friend, whose steady blue gaze held hers, probing deep into Aelissm's innermost thoughts in a way only June had ever been able.

"I don't think I've ever seen you look at a man like that," June said after a moment. "So be careful."

"Why?" Aeli asked, curious. June was an insightful woman and very adept at gauging people, and Aelissm wondered if her friend saw something worrisome about Pat. The thought made her shiver. "He's not Brent."

"No, he's not."

June started to add something else but instead shook her head. Aelissm glanced at Pat to find him making his way back across the room toward her with an inviting grin on his face. When he held out a hand, she cocked her head, realizing that a slower song was now playing on the radio, one that had even the old married couples on their feet and swaying.

"Dance with me?" Pat asked.

Her pulse quickened delightfully as she laid her hand in his. "I wouldn't want you to be the only man here without a partner," she replied. The softness of her voice blunted the teasing edge of her words.

She was acutely aware of the strong hand resting on her waist and the quiet grace of the man who led her so steadily in the slow, rocking dance. God, he was tall, she thought, staring up into eyes that were such a captivating blue-flecked hazel.

Nervously, she looked at June, who watched them from the bar with Luke perched on the stool beside her. There was a matching grin on both their faces that went far deeper than the amusement they took from Aelissm's predicament, and Aeli realized that Luke's place in the valley had just taken the first step to becoming permanent.

"Welcome home, Luke," she murmured.

She glanced up at Pat, who also gazed at June and Luke with a smile of happiness for them on his face, and she again felt that unfamiliar warmth spread through her. June was right. Pat really did fit in well here, and it wasn't just that he could work a crowd. He genuinely cared about the people even though he'd only just met them.

She rested her head against Pat's chest, noting with a smile that the beat of the song perfectly matched the beat of his heart. Why did everything have to feel so incredible? His career and his life were in Washington, and now that she was home in Northstar, she had no desire to return to the state where she'd spent most of her childhood and adolescence. The dull ache of loss coursed through her even as she stood wrapped in Pat's embrace, and she thought she understood what June hadn't said. Her friend was right to warn her to be careful because Pat *was* dangerous, though not in the way Brent had been. He was dangerous because he was already under her skin, and she stood to lose more than she ever had with her late boyfriend if she got too attached.

* * *

"What are all these cars for?" Adam wondered as he drove past the Bedspread Inn. "There can't be more than a hundred people up here."

The looped driveway of the inn was lined with vehicles all the way out to the main road. Most were trucks, and all had local plates, he noted. Something was going on. He pulled off the road into the short driveway of the Northstar Volunteer Fire Department, which was a glorified garage that might house a couple of smaller fire trucks, if such a thing existed in this remote valley. He pulled his recently purchased truck up beside the building, out of sight from the inn. Aelissm wouldn't know the vehicle, but Adam didn't want to chance her getting suspicious. He'd even checked into the hotel in Devyn under a false name and paid cash. The forty-some-mile drive up here was a pain, but seeing Aelissm again after six months was worth it. She'd better be there this time. He didn't want to have wasted another night without seeing her. The last time, someone else had been working, and he'd since learned that she'd had class down in Devyn. He'd probably passed her going one way or the other.

Yanking on his coat, he stepped out into the night.

Damn, it was cold here. He walked the quarter mile to the inn, careful to stay out of sight as he snuck around to the back door of the dining room. It was a potluck, he decided, glancing at the multitude of home-cooked dishes.

What a happy little picture, he thought, sneering. Aelissm was out of her mind if she really enjoyed this life. There was nothing here but snow and a bunch of cows and a room full of country bumpkins. Irritation flared when he spotted June Montana sitting at the bar beside a young boy. Of course she'd be here. He recalled Aeli saying that June had come out here to go to college and stayed, that she'd built a cabin on Aelissm's family's land. He'd met her a couple of times in Washington when she'd returned to visit her family and Aelissm, and after his initial, fleeting attraction to her, he'd come to realize he didn't stand a chance with her. Brent had mentioned feeling the same, but she'd seen right through him. At the thought of his friend, guilt stabbed him, icy and vicious. Adam shrugged it away. Brent shouldn't have hurt Aelissm like that.

His heart leapt when he spotted his beloved Aeli, pounding erratically with a confusion of emotions. She was so incredibly beautiful and moved with such grace that he couldn't breathe. He was so enraptured with his first glimpse of her after six bleak, lonely months that he didn't pay her dance partner any attention until he noticed how she looked at the tall man. There was a wonder and contentment in her expression he'd never seen before, and the chill of unease doused his excitement. She had never looked at Brent like that, nor had she ever danced so closely with him.

Adam shook it off, figuring he was imagining things;

time had a strange way of distorting memories. Still, he studied the man, jolted by a vague sense of familiarity. He'd seen Aelissm's partner somewhere before, but when he tried to recall where, he drew a blank. Rolling his shoulders to dispel the irritation, he committed every detail he could to memory, took one more, lingering look at Aeli, and turned away before someone glanced out the window and caught him.

Again cursing the snow, he trudged back to his truck. He wanted to stay longer, but he restrained himself. Aelissm would be his soon enough, and then he could watch her all he wanted. Until then, he needed to be cautious. She was too easy to spook these days and he didn't want her to run off again. It had taken him far too long to find her this time, and he knew that if he scared her away again, he'd never find her. And that was intolerable. His life would be worthless without her.

Five

A WEEK AFTER THE POTLUCK, Pat could still feel the softness of Aelissm's body tucked against him and see the contentment and wonder on her face as clearly as if she had only just left his arms. As he watched the last customers stroll out of the bedspread's dining room, he wished he could turn up the radio and dance with her again.

Instead, he helped her clear the table and take the dishes into the kitchen. "So, boss, how'd I do?"

"I should give you a hard time and tell you that it's going to take a lot of work to turn you into a half-decent waiter, but I'm actually pretty impressed," she replied. "And I believe that was the bell on the door, so get out there and impress me some more while I get everything back here cleaned and ready for Kelsie and Mason's shift."

Pat strolled back into the dining room and was

immediately greeted by a couple looking for a room for the night. Following the steps Aelissm had shown him earlier, he completed the task to get them checked in.

"We hear there's some hot springs up here somewhere. Can you point us in the right direction?" the woman asked.

"That'd be the Ramshorn," Pat replied. "If you take the main road north another few miles, you can't miss it."

"Thank you."

"You're most welcome. Here are your keys. Room ten is on the second floor at the end of the building. Enjoy your stay."

"Well done again, sir," Aelissm remarked from the kitchen doorway after the guests had left.

"Thank you, ma'am."

The very song they'd danced to came on the radio, and Pat turned it up, unable to resist an excuse to hold her close again. When she strode past him with a rag and a bucket of bleach water to wipe down the last table, he snatched the supplies from her and set them on the bar and rested one hand on her waist. With his other, he took her hand, pressing their palms and fingers lightly together, and was momentarily hypnotized by the subtle heat of her skin. Her hands were callused but delicate and surprisingly soft. Rotating his hand against hers, he slowly curled his fingers around her hand and stepped forward. She moved instinctively with him, trusting him implicitly to lead her. That faith was provocative. So was her unassuming nature. With Sara, he'd always felt inferior, but with Aelissm, he didn't feel the need to check his every move in fear that he'd be judged and found lacking. She took him for who he was and seemed pleased with what she saw, and in the past week with her, he'd found a freedom Sara's shadow had never allowed him.

The same enraptured smile added a new level of beauty to her face, and Pat didn't want this moment to end.

"What's the occasion?" she asked breathlessly.

"I enjoyed dancing with you so much at the potluck that I wanted a repeat."

Her smile turned playful. "If I didn't know better, I might think you were trying to seduce me."

Am I? he wondered. There was no doubt that he was attracted to everything about her, and it was possible that he was so out of touch with dating rituals that he wouldn't recognize it if he *were* flirting, so he said, "That was not my intent, so I apologize."

"Why? I didn't say I was opposed to the idea."

Pat leaned back in surprise. Before he could respond or begin to analyze her statement, the phone rang, and she slipped away to answer it. A sudden and perplexing chill crept over him in her absence, and he could almost feel Sara's breath on his neck and hear her whisper in his ear.

Silly Patrick. What makes you think you'll ever be man enough for a woman like that?

His body convulsed, and he closed his eyes, but she was still in his head. It had been three years since they'd spoken, but she still had her talons in him, piercing his heart and denying him escape. Bill was so right. He wasn't getting better, or hadn't been, but in the seven days since he'd arrived in Northstar, he had taken what he hoped were the first genuine steps toward recovery. Was he not more at peace than he'd been since before he'd met Sara? Had

Aelissm once insinuated that he was weak or incompetent? No, she had not, so he must not be as worthless as Sara had made him believe.

He drew a deep breath and let it out slowly. There were bound to be bad days ahead of him yet, but he hadn't had one in the past week, which was a victory in itself, and even though this felt like the beginnings of one, he hadn't yet sunk below the surface of it. Another triumph. If a week had given him this much composure, how much would a month give him? Or two months?

I'll be all right, he promised himself.

"I swear, Unk, he is already doing much better," Aelissm said, echoing Pat's thoughts. She smiled at him. "I think I'm going to take him up to Baldy Lake soon, even if we have to use the snowshoes. Yeah, that's the one we took you up to last summer. It wasn't too bad, was it?"

Pat leaned on the bar and let her voice soothe his memories away.

"Yep. He's right here. Pat, it's Uncle Bill."

He took the cordless from her. "Hiya, boss."

"Hi, Pat. Sounds like my niece is giving you a workout."

"Oh, not too bad."

Bill cleared his throat. "I hadn't heard from you in a few days, so I thought I'd better call. How's everything going? Any word on Adam?"

"Nothing. I've been getting to know the locals, explained what Winters is like, showed people his picture. No one has seen him."

"That's good. Maybe Aelissm was right. Maybe he can't find her there. It *is* rather remote, after all."

"It is that. I had my doubts when you asked me to do this, but now that I've been here a little while…. It's incredible. The air is so clean, and have you seen the stars?"

"I told you a spell in Northstar might do you some good, didn't I? Listen, Pat, I have some bad news."

"I don't like bad news," Pat replied.

Bill didn't answer for a long while, and dread settled in the pit of Pat's stomach.

"Bill…. Just spill it."

"Sara's been sniffing around, looking for you. I haven't talked to her, but Redford did."

Pat balled his hand into a fist. With his mood already balanced precariously on the knife's edge, the mere mention of her name might be enough to tip him over to the wrong side. "I hope he told the bitch to—"

"He told her she was not welcome in the station unless it involved official business, and if she was looking for you, she could go to hell. Exactly what I would have told her. Look, Pat, I don't want you to worry about Sara. I sent you on vacation for a reason. Keep your mind on having a good time and keeping my niece safe."

Pat glanced at Aelissm and found her watching him quizzically. "Is that all?"

"Yeah, that's it. Get some rest; you've more than earned it, and I know you need it. Tell Aeli I love her."

"Will do. I'll call you as soon as I hear something, if not sooner. Have a good one, Bill."

"Same to you."

Pat pulled the phone away from his ear and pushed the call-end button before he turned to Aelissm. She still wore that same, questioning expression.

"What?" he finally asked.

"Who were you talking about?" Aelissm responded.

Pat shifted his weight. Her eyes were determined, and after the jolt he'd received from Bill's news, he was just as determined not to talk about it. He turned his back to her, but she sidled around him and put her hands on his chest to keep him from walking away. He shuddered. She must have noticed because she backed away, her green eyes soft with concern.

"What did she do to you, Pat?" Her voice was quiet, enticing him to trust her. He wanted to, but he hadn't been able to trust anyone with his secrets since he'd been stupid enough to ask Sara to marry him. Bill knew the details—he'd been the one to press charges—but even he didn't understand how it continued to torment Pat. He tried to summon the courage to allay Aeli's concerns, but he couldn't speak around the lump in his throat.

She persisted. "You don't strike me as the kind of man to call a woman a bitch without a damned good reason. Did she hurt you that badly when she left?"

"She didn't leave. I did."

Aelissm's brows dipped in confusion. "Unk gave me the impression that she's the one who ended it. So, now I *really* don't understand."

Was it fear or hatred or self-loathing that prevented him from explaining? Helplessly, he held Aelissm's concerned gaze, wishing he could just open his mouth and let the memories out. It wasn't healthy to keep them locked inside, but when he tried to speak, nothing came out but an apology for his inability to enlighten her.

"I'm sorry, too," she replied gently. "Because you're

a great guy, and she obviously doesn't deserve any part of you—especially not your misery."

When Aelissm hugged him, he could only cling to her and whisper, "Thank you."

The bell on the door jingled again, and Aelissm's waitress, Kelsie, strolled in with the cook, Mason, right behind her. Aelissm stepped away to transition her evening crew in and her and Pat out, and he wiped down the tables and bar, using the task to distract himself. With his mood spiraling in the wrong direction, he was not looking forward to spending the evening alone while Aeli taught her class forty-five miles away in Devyn.

They left the Bedspread Inn and returned to the cabin so Aelissm could grab a quick dinner. All too soon, Pat stood on the front steps, watching her truck disappear down the driveway. He turned and went inside to seek any form of distraction, but he simply needed company, so he drove over to June's. No one was home, and he remembered that she had a date in Devyn tonight. Sighing, he headed down into the valley. An unexpected smile teased him as he ran through the list of people who had given him an open invitation to visit, and the realization of how many were on it was liberating. Back home in Washington, he had few friends and had become so accustomed to turning to work to distract himself that it was strange and wonderful to turn instead to people.

He stopped by Aaron Hammond's house to see if the sheriff's deputy had heard anything about Adam Winters—he hadn't—before heading to Aelissm's grandparents'.

Marge greeted him with a smile and a hug and welcomed him inside. Roger was watching TV from his recliner, and June's foster son sat at the kitchen table working on homework. Not in the mood for television, Pat joined Luke in the kitchen.

"Hi, Pat," the boy greeted.

"Need any help?"

"Nah, I got it. Thanks, though. Do you want to play Rummy with Grandma and me when I get done?"

"Sure."

Pat sat across from the boy, and Marge took the seat to his left. While they waited for Luke to finish, Aelissm's grandmother quizzed Pat about his first week in Northstar, and after Luke informed him their discussion wouldn't disrupt him, Pat detailed his outings and visits with the locals for her.

"I think I've put more miles on my truck this week than I do in a month back home," Pat remarked. "And you were so right about the scenic byway up into the Crystal Valley. It's gorgeous."

"Just wait until the snow melts and all those meadows and pastures turn green," Marge replied. "I'm sorry I haven't had much time to sit down with you, but I hear you've made quite a good impression on everyone."

Pat brushed her praise aside but couldn't ignore the impact that simple statement had on him. "The people here make it easy."

"Now, today was your first day at the inn, right?" When he nodded, she asked, "How did it go?"

"Great. I enjoyed it a lot more than I would have thought." He found himself smiling again. "Of course, that probably has a lot to do with your granddaughter. She's a remarkable woman and great company, but you already know that."

"I do, and Roger and I are very proud of her." Marge rose to pull a deck of cards off the shelf beside the window. "There's only one thing she's done in her life that I wish she hadn't."

"What's that?"

"She got involved with Brent Ellington. He was never right for her."

"Did you ever meet him?"

"A couple times when we visited our son and his family in Indianola. He struck me as being rather arrogant and selfish, and I don't like the way he looked down on Aelissm. He wasn't obvious about it, of course, and she's always been sure of herself, so it didn't bother her."

"I can see that. What about Adam?"

"I met him just the once, and I liked him. He seemed like such a sweet young man, very humble, funny. I would never have thought him capable of strangling his own best friend."

Almost exactly what Bill said, Pat noted, saving the information for later.

"I wish she hadn't met either of them. If she hadn't, none of those things would have happened to her. I think she's handling it very well, however, and I know it looks like she came here to hide from all that, but she didn't."

"I don't think she's hiding at all," Pat said. "Getting away from Adam and what happened may have been a factor in her decision, but I think this is the choice she would have made in the end regardless of the circumstances. She's happy here."

"She's a lot more relaxed now than when she first

came back to Northstar, too," Luke observed quietly. He gathered his books and notebook and stuffed them into his backpack. "And funnier, too."

"Even though she teases you?" Pat inquired.

He shrugged. "I don't mind because she wouldn't bother if she didn't like me. Anyhow, I'm done with my homework."

Luke was a quiet kid and frequently appeared much younger than his twelve years, but once in a while, he said or did something that spoke of someone much older and wiser, and Pat suspected there was a lot behind his statement. However, the abrupt dismissal of the topic said plainly that he didn't want to talk about it, and as Pat understood that all too well, he let the kid have his privacy. Still, he couldn't stop himself from asking, "I guess that means you're pretty happy about June adopting you."

A broad grin shattered Luke's cautious reserve, and Pat caught his first glimpse of the extraordinary young man Luke would become in June's patient and compassionate care. He thought of the bet he'd made with Aelissm and hoped he'd get to see that transformation, even if only from a distance.

"All right," he said. "Let's play this game, shall we?"

By the time he headed back to the cabin at sunset—not yet ready to trust his navigational skills in the dark—he'd pushed Sara from his mind again and only allowed himself a moment to appreciate the understanding that ignoring her by indulging himself with the company of friends was far more effective than turning to work. Work only covered up the pain; friendship was beginning to erase it.

* * *

"Ms. Davis? Can we leave early tonight?"

Aelissm lifted the welding mask and paused for a moment to admire her handiwork. The wrought-iron poster frame would be exquisite. "No, Mr. Daniels, I don't think we can. You still haven't shown me that you can twist a piece of iron yet, which means you can't move on to making your section of the wrought-iron banister, and you were supposed to have started *that* last week."

"Ah, c'mon, Ms. Davis. I'm trying."

"Try harder. You're talented, Bobby, I know you are, but you're lazy. It wouldn't kill you to come in a couple extra hours a week while Dr. Barth is in here."

"Yeah, but—"

"That's your problem, Bobby. 'But' this and 'but' that. If you spent as much time working as you do making excuses, you'd be ahead rather than behind."

"Sounds like something I might say to some of *my* students."

Aelissm nearly sighed with relief at the sound of June's voice.

"Hi, Ms. Montana," the boy said. "Ms. Davis won't let us go home early."

"I agree with her."

Muttering to himself, the student trudged off toward his friends. Aelissm shook her head in despair. "I'm half tempted to take that lump of metal he's working on and beat him over the head with it. Are your students so obstinate?"

"If not worse," June replied. "Of course, then you have assholes like Jake Sterling who make kids like Bobby Daniels look like angels."

Aelissm turned to her friend with a brow raised. "I

take it your date didn't go well." When June shook her head and scowled, Aelissm added, "I wondered why you were here."

"I need a ride home. There was no way I was getting back into Jake's truck. I knew there was something about him I didn't like."

June kept any further comments to herself as another of Aelissm's students made her way over. In beautiful contrast to Bobby Daniels' hurried work, Amber Jones' wrought iron was fine enough to accent the bedroom set the Industrial Tech club was building to be raffled off at the rodeo team's banquet.

"This is gorgeous, Amber," Aelissm said, beaming. "In answer to the question you asked at the beginning of class, yes, you can leave early."

"Ah, Ms. Davis!" Bobby Daniels moaned. "How come she—"

"Don't 'ah, Ms. Davis' me, Bobby. Put some effort into it, and you could turn out pieces every bit as nice as Amber's."

She watched the student skulk away before turning to find Amber still standing beside her. "I thought you were leaving…?"

"Actually, I'd like to work on a side project. There's this new cook at work—Brandon—and he really likes that I enjoy this kind of stuff." A shy smile lit up the girl's carefully made-up face and glittered in her rich brown eyes. "He wants to see something I've made, but I haven't made anything that I can bring in to work to show him."

"I'm guessing you like him."

"Yeah, but he's not the kind of guy I usually go for."

"Sometimes that's a good thing."

"I think so. He's kinda quiet and shy, but really polite and sweet, you know? I think he's a little down on his luck right now, but he's pretty cute, and he doesn't mind working hard, which makes him really great to work with."

"I'm sure it does," Aelissm replied. "I've heard enough about the Parasite to know it's not too great a place to work. I still say you should come work for me at the Bedspread."

"You know I'd love to, but I can't afford to commute right now."

"Maybe this summer. Anyhow, yes, go make something to impress this Brandon guy while I go ride herd on these cats."

Amber laughed and walked away.

Pat's impromptu repeat of their potluck dance flirted with the edges of Aelissm's mind, and she would rather be anywhere but teaching her class right now. Demonstrating technique for the students who seemed to need a dozen reminders about how to heat and twist metal didn't give her an opportunity to revisit either the dance or her conversation with Pat about his ex, and her curiosity, having been piqued, demanded to be sated. Surely, if he'd been the one to end the relationship, he was glad it was over, and that belief was reinforced by the memory of his expression when he'd called the woman a bitch. She'd seen hatred on his face and something else she couldn't put a finger on. Was it fear or disgust? Either way, none of those emotions matched his easy-going nature.

A crash in one of the welding booths yanked her attention back to her class, and she strode over to find Bobby

Daniels leaning over to pick up a piece of scrap metal that had fallen off the table. His shoulder was just inches from the red-hot stick of iron he was supposed to be twisting, and Aelissm shoved against his chest to save him from a burn.

"Do me a favor and start using this," she said, poking his forehead. She turned around just in time to see another student preparing to weld with his mask on his head instead of covering his face. "Harrison, unless you *want* to go blind, put that mask down."

Sighing, she shoved her questions about Pat from her mind.

True to her word, she kept the students who were behind her deadlines until the very end of class. At ten o'clock, she finally let them go, smirking when several muttered their unhappiness as they stepped out into the unseasonably warm evening. June, who had been sitting unobtrusively in Aeli's office since she'd arrived nearly an hour and a half ago, came to stand beside Aelissm in the shop door. Her expression was no less sour, and Aeli thought it might even be darker.

"It must have been a really bad date," Aeli remarked.

"You have no idea. First, I had a student ask me to help her after school a couple days this week, and he complained about that. Then he asked me when Luke's social worker was going to start looking for a permanent home for him, and when I said I had begun the adoption process, he went off about how I was too young to tie myself down like that, and he called Luke a leech. I didn't stay to hear the rest." June snarled. "I already felt bad enough for going out without Luke, and now I feel even worse because I did it for *that*. Why did I even agree to go out with him?"

"If Jake was that pissed, he needs to get over himself. C'mon, June. You have two jobs and a foster son who needs a lot of attention. If Jake's too insecure to understand that, it's his loss." Aelissm offered her a smile. "Shall we head home?"

June nodded.

By the time they got back to the valley, it would be eleven, and by the time they finally reached the cabins, it would probably be midnight because they had to stop in at Aelissm's grandparents' to pick up Luke, so she quickly checked to make sure all the welders were turned off and locked the shop. The night air was pleasant on her face. Spring was finally gaining some ground against winter, she decided. There wouldn't be too many more snows or frigid days. With a sigh, she admitted that she was ready for the warmer months because it had been a cold, wet winter, starting just after she'd arrived in Northstar back in September.

As Aelissm pulled out of Devyn, the conversation shifted kindly to past adventures—snowball fights up at the lakes in July, digging for quartz crystals at Crystal Park, riding dirt bikes and four wheelers all over the mountain, and lazy afternoons spent at the Ramshorn alternately sunbathing and diving back into the hot waters to escape the horse-flies. They had so many wonderful memories, she and June, and not just from the valley. They'd spent most of their lives together in Western Washington, safely across Puget Sound from Seattle on the quiet Kitsap Peninsula. They'd spent countless summer days as children sprinting through sun-warmed tide pools on the Indianola beach or building forts in the cool shade of the dense forest just out her parents' back door.

She selected a CD her brother had burned for her for a trip they'd all taken to the cabin before she and June started college in Devyn. Turning up the volume, they sang along, just as they had on the long drive from Washington. All those sweet, precious memories swirled around her, swinging vividly from the notes of the music.

She had nearly lost this when she'd moved to Seattle. Looking back, she understood that she hadn't truly been herself for the duration of her relationship with Brent. She had been happy enough, but she's been someone other than Aelissm Davis. The city lifestyle—and Brent's upper class roots—had never suited her, and though she had muddled through well enough, she'd secretly cursed and bemoaned it all.

Adam had been the only friend of Brent's that she'd connected with. She'd been able to talk with him in a way she hadn't with Brent because, born and raised on the high end of society, her ex-boyfriend couldn't fathom the poorer side of middle class that Aelissm had known growing up. Aelissm didn't doubt Adam felt nearly as out of place as she had, but he also wanted what Brent had. She didn't.

"Whatever you're thinking about, stop," June said as she unhooked her seat belt.

"Yes, mother," Aelissm retorted.

Abruptly, she realized she'd pulled up in front of her grandparents' house, though she couldn't recall the last ten miles of the drive. Her grandmother greeted them on the porch, and Luke came out right behind her and ran to June.

"I'm sorry I'm late, sweetie," June told him. She

leaned down and kissed the top of his head. "I'm just sorry."

"It's okay," he murmured, clinging to her as if she would evaporate if he let go. "I did my homework, and Pat came down and played cards with us for a little while."

"He's quite a nice young man," Marge remarked, pausing as if she expected Aelissm to respond. Finally, she said, "Well, come on in. I have your mail. June, I have yours, too."

"Thanks, Grandma," June replied. Luke was still glued to her side.

They followed Marge into the trailer. Roger was snoring lightly in his favorite chair, and Aelissm was grateful. She loved her grandfather dearly, but tonight, all she wanted was to pick up her mail, get up to her cabin, and head straight for bed, something that would be much delayed if he was awake.

"Here we are. June, these are yours. And here you go, Aeli. There's a letter in there with no return address. It's postmarked from Seattle."

The warmth drained from her body, chased away by waves of cold fear. Despite her concentration, her hand shook as she took the thin stack of mail from her grandmother.

"It could be from one of your friends over there," Marge said.

Aelissm shuddered. She forced her eyes from the nondescript envelope to her grandmother's concerned face, then smiled. "It could be."

She saw June's sharp glance from the corner of her eye and winced.

"We'd better get Luke home before he falls asleep,"

June asserted.

"All right. You girls have a good night. And Luke, we'll be looking forward to reading your science report."

"Okay," Luke replied with a yawn. "Good night, Grandma Davis."

"Good night, Grandma," June added and gave Marge a hug. "Thanks for watching Luke for me."

"Always a pleasure. I'm so glad he'll soon be a part of the family. He already is, of course, but it'll be nice when it's official. Aeli, tell Pat hello for us."

"Will do." Aeli embraced her grandmother, ignoring the inflexion in Marge's voice that added, *It'd be nice if he was part of the family, too.* "G'night, Grandma."

She herded June and Luke out to her truck. She felt her grandmother's worried eyes on her the entire way, and when she turned to open the driver's side door, Marge was still standing on the front porch, watching.

"You lied to her," June remarked as soon as they'd climbed into the cab and shut the doors.

"Of course I did," Aeli replied, waving farewell to her grandmother. "I had only one friend in Seattle."

"Adam."

"Yup."

"Which means he now has your phone number and your mailing address."

"Yup."

Aelissm rested her forearm against the window. She couldn't rationalize it at the moment, couldn't figure how he'd found out. The Seattle postmark meant little to her. Adam knew what town she lived in, and as small as it was, Northstar *was* on most maps of Montana. Her hands trembled despite her death-grip on the steering wheel. How long would it be until Adam found her physical address? And why wouldn't he? He was a determined man.

Aelissm was grateful that her cabin was so hard to find. Even if Adam somehow managed to learn its address, he'd still have to find it, and Wellman Creek Road wasn't marked. The knowledge didn't settle her fears as much as it perhaps should have. Knowing Pat would be there helped more until an image flashed in her mind of him spasming on the floor, fighting for life as Adam's hands tightened around his throat. Nausea bubbled in her stomach, and she swallowed hard. Adam had attacked his best friend for her without a second thought. What would he do to the man who stood between him and his prize?

Realizing that her companions had been silent for most of the ride up the mountain, she glanced over at them and saw that Luke had fallen asleep with his head on his foster mother's shoulder while June stared out the window, lost in her own tormenting thoughts. Aelissm pulled up to the gate, and June got out to open it after carefully pushing Luke upright. The boy murmured incoherently as his head rolled back against the seat, then he slipped into sleep once again. What a pair she and June were tonight, Aelissm thought, watching as her friend swung the gate open with fury stiffening her movements.

All it had taken to shatter their brief moments of carefree abandon was a letter from Seattle, which made Aelissm feel all the more trapped and helpless. There had been a time when no problem had ever lasted long, when something as inconsequential as a bad date would have been shrugged off in a handful of heartbeats. That was perhaps one of the worst things about Adam's obsession with her. The hiding and the anxiety was all temporary—it had to be—but what if, when this was all over, she couldn't return to herself?

Aelissm thought of Pat again. She didn't want to spend the rest of her years like that, existing, and she didn't want him to, either.

Uncle Bill, June, Luke, and her grandparents all loved him already and trusted him with her, and without word from Adam, she'd been able to believe he was here solely for a little rest and relaxation. Her uncle *was* most likely playing the meddlesome matchmaker again, but considering what she'd seen so far from her uncle's detective, Aelissm understood and appreciated Uncle Bill's enthusiasm.

June climbed back into the cab after shutting the gate behind the truck. When they reached her cabin, they said nothing more than a dispassionate goodbye. June roused Luke, and Aelissm watched the pair until they reached the front door, then headed back down the driveway. As she came closer and closer to her own home, her dread grew. In just a few short minutes, she would open the letter, read it, and then Pat would read it. And then what? There was never anything beyond the next few minutes anymore.

Aelissm pulled up beside Pat's truck in front of the cabin and shut off the engine. She sat for a moment in the dark with her heart thumping wildly. Instead of going inside, she turned on the dome light and opened the envelope of Adam's letter with her truck key. She willed her fingers to be still and strong, but they disobeyed. Carefully unfolding the letter, she found—as she knew she would—Adam's shaky handwriting and read the passages three times before their words finally sank in.

My dearest Aelissm, he wrote. *I don't understand why you keep ignoring me. You can't run away from what happened forever. We have to deal with it so we can move on. I wish I knew what I could do to make you understand that I did what I did for you, that no one else will ever love you as much as I do. Why do you keep pushing me away and running from me? Why can't you see how much I love you? I will find you again, and somehow, I'll make you understand. See you soon, Aeli.*

His closer nearly made her cry, reminding her of the shy, outcast boy she knew he'd once been. *Love always, Adam Winters.*

Aelissm pinched her eyes closed and pressed her knuckles to her lips, trying in vain to stem the frenzy of confused emotions. What had happened to her lovable friend? Dread infused with grief and regret tightened its grip on her as she recalled the Adam he'd been before Brent's death— always smiling or cracking a joke. That Adam had vanished, replaced by one who rarely smiled and was consumed by a guilt-laden moroseness and an irrational belief that Brent's death had cleared the path to Aelissm's heart. She would have welcomed the old Adam to Northstar with open arms but prayed this new Adam wouldn't be able to find her here.

But he's already two steps closer, she thought as she glanced at her address on the envelope.

Shuddering, she balled up the letter and climbed out of her truck. When she stepped into her house, she was greeted by the soothing heat from her wood stove and a handsome, smiling man.

"How was your class?" Pat asked.

She opened her mouth to answer but couldn't find

her voice. She met his gaze, begging for something she couldn't name, not knowing what she needed from him. The tender concern in his eyes invited her to let go, to stop trying to be strong, and to let him take care of her. Something in her fractured and broke open, and the heartache and fear of the last year pummeled her. A strangled, wordless plea escaped her. Her knees wobbled, and when she tried to take a step forward, they buckled, but he caught her, and she found herself supported in his arms, held firmly to his chest. In distinct contrast to the rampaging quivers of her own body, Pat stood steady.

"Aelissm? What's wrong?"

At the moment, she didn't have the power to answer. The only strength she seemed to have was in her fingers, which gripped Pat's arms so tightly she expected him to complain. He didn't but slid an arm behind her malfunctioning knees and lifted her the rest of the way off the ground—bag and all—so effortlessly that she might have been a small child rather than a fully grown woman. She felt fragile and treasured as he carried her to the love seat, and the combination was deadly to her tattered nerves. Tears threatened, and she swore to keep them contained.

He settled her gently on the love seat and sat beside her, for which she was grateful. She needed something to hang on to, and as far as that went, there was nothing or no one better than Pat at this particular moment. He set her bag and mail on the floor. The letter from Adam was still clutched tightly in her fist; a corner peeked through her fingers. He glanced at it, but didn't ask about it.

"Talk to me, sweetheart. What happened?"

"He knows where I am," she choked out. Tears

seeped from her eyes, but she no longer cared.

"What do you mean?"

"He sent this."

She opened her fingers, cringing at the ache in her knuckles from clenching them so tightly. Without releasing her, Pat uncrumpled the letter and read it.

Aelissm couldn't seem to get hold of herself. Her body shook uncontrollably, and the only two thoughts in her head that were clear enough to grasp contrasted each other so sharply that she couldn't draw a deep breath. Adam knew about Northstar, and he would find it. But Pat was here; he would keep her safe.

"He'll find me again," she murmured. "I can't… I can't deal with him. He's not the same anymore, and he scares me."

"You don't have to be afraid, Aeli. I'm here."

A fresh round of tears sprang to her eyes at those words. Pat couldn't know what it meant to have him watching over her, and that made his assertion all the sweeter.

"It's just a letter, sweetheart, and it's post-marked two weeks ago from Seattle. I'm not saying your worries are unfounded because I don't think they are, but all he has are your phone number and your post office box."

"And Northstar. Pat, he has Northstar now. Don't you see?" She sat up and stared at him, using his face to fight the hysteria that lanced through her veins. That face, so strong and yet so beautiful, helped her keep her shaky grip on her sanity.

"Yes, he has Northstar, too, but Northstar is a difficult place to find."

She shook her head fervently. "Not for him. Oh,

God. What if this never ends?"

Pat grabbed her shoulders and held her gaze. The pressure of his fingers restored some sense of order to her chaotic mind.

"I swear to you, Aeli, it will end."

"Don't say that if you don't mean it."

"I don't make empty promises." He brushed her hair back from her face with such tenderness that she closed her eyes and involuntarily leaned into his touch. "My poor, sweet angel. No one should have to live like this."

"You do," she whispered, her eyes still closed. When she slowly lifted her lids, Pat frowned with memories darkening his eyes.

"That's different."

"Is it? How is working yourself to death to hide from your past any different than me hiding in Northstar?"

At long last, Aelissm found her strength again. How could he pity her situation and not see that his own was so similar? She waited for him to speak, expecting him to deny the truth. For a long time, he remained silent, his brows furrowed in deep thought. When he finally addressed her accusation, his words were to the point but not what she expected.

"You're right."

Her mouth fell open.

"Not what you were expecting me to say, is it?" he asked. "But you're right, Aeli. I *am* hiding."

"And?"

"That stops right now. I'm on vacation, after all."

"Of a sort, I suppose."

He rose to his feet and offered a hand to help her up.

"It's late. We should probably get you settled down and then toddle up to sleep."

She took his hand and smiled. The last remaining shivers from Adam's letter slipped away, and she wallowed in the simplicity of enjoying the company of an attractive, attentive man. Pat, she decided, was exactly what she needed right now. It had been so easy, so nice to fall apart in his arms.

Six

"LONG WAY OR SHORT WAY?" Aelissm asked Pat after closing June's back door behind them.

"Long way this time," he replied.

Without waiting for her, he stepped off June's deck, and she had to stretch her legs to keep up with his long strides.

Pat glanced at her with a mischievous grin. "Now who's huffing and puffing?"

"Oh, hush up."

"I told you it wouldn't take me long to get acclimated."

"I never doubted you, but you know me. I couldn't resist teasing you." Aelissm laughed. "Is this what you do in your spare time when I'm not around to entertain you? Hike around the cabin?"

"Maybe."

He chuckled and playfully hip-bumped her. It was difficult to ignore the instinct to take his hand, and as the days marched by, the strength and persistence of urges like that grew, incited by living with him for the better part of a month in her parents' secluded cabin. The way he lightly touched her arm when he needed to step around her and the feel of his body against hers when they'd danced and when he'd held her the night Adam's letter had arrived excited primal desires and felt so natural. She'd never shared anything like this with Brent, and *this* was only simple friendship. The comment she'd made to June before Pat had left Washington—that it might be nice to have a man around—sprang to mind, and with it came the ache of loneliness. Pat was a delightful companion, and she could easily imagine getting involved with him, but he wasn't ready for a relationship, and really, neither was she.

They continued down June's driveway, turned onto the road, and passed the mine tailings in silence. When the road leveled out just below her grandparents' cabin, Pat paused, and a smile of pure contentment softened his features as he lifted his face to the morning sun and closed his eyes. She wondered if he had any idea how beautiful he was with his hands tucked loosely into the pockets of his jeans. Just the way he stood, so gracefully untroubled, made her heart trip over itself.

"I could get used to this," he murmured. Slowly, he opened his eyes and turned to Aelissm. "You're lucky."

She could think of all kinds of things that he could get used to that would also make her a lucky woman, but she knew by the innocent enjoyment on his face that he wasn't thinking along the same lines.

Too bad, she thought and scolded herself. "How so?"

"You've always had this."

"For a while in there, I lost sight of it," she remarked quietly. She glanced back at June's cabin. "When we were kids, June and I used to talk about living up here, about how our kids would grow up together, like we did, and learn to love all the things we enjoy. When I was dating Brent, that dream slipped away. Yet, here I am, walking up Wellman Creek Road, and if I look just up the hill, there's June's cabin, half-hidden in the trees."

"So your dream came true."

"In a way, but a lot has changed. June has Luke, and as envious as that makes me some days, I can't see myself having kids. Life is just too unstable to bring a child into it."

"But before Brent, you wanted kids?"

"I've never been one of those women whose sole purpose in life is to reproduce—wow, that sounds really condescending. I can't say that I understand that drive, but please don't think that I believe I'm better than them because I don't. I'm just different."

"You're babbling, sweetheart."

She laughed. "So I am. In answer to your question, yes, before Brent and this mess with Adam, I thought I'd have kids someday when I could provide a stable life for them."

Pat watched her with such gentle compassion and empathy that she wondered what things he had once wanted from life. Certainly he hadn't envisioned himself alone at twenty-eight, working himself too hard to escape the memories of a woman. She knew she shouldn't pry, but curiosity got the best of her.

"What about you?"

He shrugged, and for a disappointing moment, she thought he wouldn't answer. Then he said, "I suppose the same things—a career, marriage, kids. Now, I'm like you, just trying to get through without being buried by the disappointments of life."

He started walking again, and Aelissm tried to reclaim the calm she had found again only in the last couple days. In the three weeks since Adam's letter had come, he hadn't given her much chance to recover from the shock of it. He'd called four times—once every four days like clockwork—and left messages that ranged from pleading to nostalgic to angry. He'd always managed to call when no one was home, almost like he knew her schedule and had planned it that way, and the caller ID was next to useless because the number he'd called from was restricted.

It had now been five, almost six days since his last call, and Aelissm was thrilled to finally be settling down again, even if she still jumped every time the phone rang. The constant anxiety had taken a toll on her, and she had been downright surly, snapping at her crew down at the Bedspread and treating Pat, June, Luke, and her grandparents with irritability. She knew she could be sarcastic and abrasive at times, but rarely was she mean. The only times she hadn't been swamped by anxiety she had been too busy admiring and thinking about Pat to worry.

"Can I ask you a question about Adam without upsetting you again?" Pat asked in a voice that sounded more like he was thinking out loud than addressing her.

"I think I'm okay now," she replied.

"What is it about him that scares you? Was it his part in Brent's death?"

"No…." Aelissm frowned. Recalling the strange shine in Adam's eyes that night still made her shiver, but that wasn't it. Honestly, she couldn't pinpoint exactly what frightened her, so instead of replying, she shrugged.

"You're not ready yet. So, tell me," he said as he stripped out of his sweatshirt. "Is spring here always this unpredictable?"

"Yup," Aelissm replied with a quick grin. "So don't be surprised if it snows again tomorrow."

She closed her eyes to concentrate on the air. It was still a little cool but warming quickly, and the crispness that had been in it yesterday was gone, leaving behind the gentle weight of humidity. Well, as much humidity as there ever was so far up in the mountains. Opening her eyes, she glanced around her. Snow still blanketed everything, but it had a crystalline and slushy inconsistency, and tiny canyons were forming in it on the road as the strong spring sun began to melt it.

"You're serious? You really think it might snow tomorrow?"

"The weather's going to change, but in the opposite direction."

Amusement played across his face, and it delighted her to think that he belonged in a place like Northstar with the mountain air in his lungs and peace in his heart. Even as she chided herself yet again when her thoughts detoured into romantic territory, she understood that her curiosity and attraction to him was normal and healthy and a sign that maybe, just maybe she was on the mend.

"Isn't that your phone ringing?" Pat asked as they reached the cabin.

"My phone?"

"Yeah. Hear it?"

Aelissm raced inside, but when she reached to answer the call, her hand hesitated. "For God's sake, this is stupid," she muttered and snatched the cordless. She recognized the number, and breath rushed from her lungs in a sigh of relief. "Hi, Nick. How are Beth and your little monkey?"

Nick chuckled. "You *would* call him that. They're fine. Hey, that's why I'm calling."

"I'm not baby-sitting for you, Nick, so don't even ask." Actually, Aelissm admitted, the thought was rather appealing. Irritated with the unexpected turn of her thoughts, she glanced toward the door as Pat walked inside.

"That's not why I called. Beth threatened to skin me if I didn't stop fussing over her and Will, so I thought, with the weather so nice, it'd be a great day to take Pat on that ride."

"Your dad doesn't need you to help with plowing?"

"No. He's got Aaron and Henry."

"Well, in that case, I'm sure he needs you."

"Ain't that the truth? But he's got Pete Landers and a couple other valley hands helping out today. And Old Matt's down there, too." Nick paused. "You know, Aelissm, it almost sounds like you're trying to weasel your way out of something… or into it. You can't tell me you want private time with Pat because you live on the side of a mountain. Only way you're going to get more privacy is to hike up to one of the lakes. I recommend Sawtooth.

"You *recommend* Sawtooth?"

"That's where Will happened."

"I really didn't need to know that, Nick, but thanks because I hadn't thought about that one. I'll keep it in mind." She was only half-joking, and she blushed, glad Pat couldn't hear Nick's side of the conversation. "Truth be told, I was trying to talk myself off the back of a horse."

"Oh, come on, it'll be fun."

"You forget that I don't like horses much."

"I didn't forget."

"Damn." Aelissm glanced at Pat. "Let me ask him. Pat, Nick wants to know if you're up to sitting on a horse for the afternoon."

"You didn't have to say it like that," Nick remarked.

"Nick Hammond? Sure. Sounds like fun," Pat replied.

"Yeah, we'll do it," she told Nick with a sigh of resignation.

When she turned to Pat after hanging up the phone, he was smiling and shaking his head at her. "What?"

"You can tell the weather's going to change just by the feel of the air, but you didn't hear your phone."

"Oh, shush."

Pat's smile softened, and the amusement in his eyes shifted to a disarming tenderness. "It's good to see you smile again," he said. "You haven't since the letter came."

"I've smiled," she retorted.

"Not really. Not like that."

She wasn't about to tell him what had made her smile *like that*.

Aelissm bowed her head for a moment. He'd noticed her distraction, but how could he not when he'd been sent here by her overprotective uncle to keep watch over her? He'd need to be aware of how Adam's oppression was affecting her, but that wasn't all of it. Pat's concern for her was deeper than his promise to her uncle to keep her safe.

Pat slid his hand under her chin and lifted her face. She met his eyes without fear or hesitation. There was nothing to be afraid of in Pat. But she'd thought that about Brent, too, at first. *No*, she thought, *don't liken him to Brent. He's not like Brent.*

"Don't leave me, Aelissm. Don't lock yourself away again."

"I won't." Her voice wavered, and her eyes burned with tears. She blinked to clear them. Why did he have to be so sensitive and caring? And why, when she needed it, did he have to be so strong? It was too perfect. Why couldn't he just not give a damn? If he didn't care about her, it wouldn't hurt so bad when he left, and it would because she was already too attached.

He brushed his thumb across her cheek. There was something decidedly intimate about the situation. Aelissm's gaze drifted from Pat's keenly beautiful eyes to his lips, and she noticed how close he was standing. The warmth of him penetrated her clothing and skin, igniting her soul. She yearned to lean into him, to find again that comfort she had found in his arms after she'd read Adam's letter.

She didn't know who initiated the kiss, but Aelissm suddenly found her lips pressed to Pat's. She opened her mouth in invitation and surprise. Pat took command, but he was gentle, and affection flooded through Aelissm, washing away all her doubts, leaving only the pure and single-minded pleasure of the moment. She was drawn into him with the length of her body pressed firmly against his as he clasped her face in his hands. All she knew was the tenderness of Pat's kiss and the firmness of his body, and all she wanted at the moment was him. All of him.

Abruptly, Aelissm pulled away. For a brief second, confusion hazed Pat's eyes, but it fled quickly as realization struck.

"I'm sorry," he said. "That shouldn't have happened."

"No," Aelissm replied. *But it did. And I enjoyed it.*

Neither of them moved away.

"We're not...."

"I..." he started. "It won't happen again."

"You're right. Let's not complicate things. Neither of us needs any more pain."

Aelissm turned away and grabbed her helmet from the hooks behind the door and tossed her father's helmet to Pat. "We'd better head down to Nick's. And you'd better be a greenhorn."

"Don't worry; I am. Unless you're talking about the dirt bikes. I've been on a few of those before."

"I was talking about horses." She started out the door, then turned around again to face him. "Oh, and Pat?"

"Hmm?"

"I thought I knew who Adam was. I thought I could trust him."

"What?"

"You asked what it was about him that scared me the most."

Pat tilted his head and studied her, then nodded. Through an unspoken agreement, the kiss and Adam were dropped from their conversation.

Aelissm watched Pat for a moment as he kick-started the dirt bike she and her grandfather had gotten running again yesterday, and the memory of his lips against hers brought another genuine smile to her face. The kiss might have been a mistake, but she was glad it had happened.

* * *

He shouldn't have done it, but even as he chastised himself, Pat couldn't seem to make himself believe it was wrong. At least, not in the sense that his bruised and tattered heart thought it *should* be wrong. He shouldn't have kissed Aelissm for the simple reason that it was dishonorable. When he'd given in to the moment—to clarify, the other side of his brain argued, she'd been just as much a participant—he hadn't thought of what it might do to her. She'd nearly been raped by a man she'd thought loved her, and even if that hadn't happened, she deserved nothing less than a man who could devote every ounce of himself to her, and Pat couldn't. Not after Sara. At this point, he wasn't sure he'd ever completely heal from that disaster. So, he shouldn't have kissed Aelissm.

The thought did nothing to erase the desire to kiss her again.

Sighing, he shifted his attention to the woman at the center of his thoughts. Despite her grumbling, she looked quite at home on the back of the bay gelding with strands of her strawberry-blonde hair pulling loose from her braid. She was adorable, stunning, and confident all rolled into one.

Since that line of thought was only worsening the situation, Pat yanked his gaze away. There was plenty else to see, and he couldn't have asked for a more incredible day. It was a downright balmy afternoon, and they'd spent the last four hours riding across the northern stretch of the Lazy H beneath a brilliant cobalt sky dusted with streamers of gossamer cirrus clouds. Pat couldn't recall ever seeing such a deep, pure blue. The quaking aspen were blooming, the willows down along the creek were opening their peach-fuzz flower buds, and after the wet winter and the past couple weeks of intermittent warm weather, the hay fields were already vibrantly green.

"Do you bale hay, too, or put it all up in stacks?" Pat asked Nick, inclining his head toward the towering stack of golden hay that resembled a giant loaf of bread.

"We actually bale most of it these days," Nick replied, "but since we like to keep the old traditions alive, we still stack a lot of what we don't sell."

"How do you do that?"

"Using that contraption there—it's called a beaverslide. We push loads of hay onto the basket and use a pulley system to hoist it up the slide and into a box made by those panels attached to the sides and a back panel."

"I'll bet that's a lot of work."

"It is, but I love it. Maybe, if you're still here when we cut, you can give it a try."

"You're on."

"I'll bet you can't last an entire day at it," Aelissm remarked playfully.

"Are you sure you want to keep betting me, Aeli? I'm not a stranger to work."

"We'll see how you feel when you get off that horse," she replied. "And if you're sore then, just imagine what you'll feel like after a full day of stacking."

Pat grinned. She certainly was a feisty thing, and after Sara's cool reserve, he appreciated that. There were other things about her he appreciated, too, like her eyes, which were so close in color to the lush hay fields. The beauty of her body was not lost on him, either. From the silken gold mane that tumbled nearly halfway down her back to her firm, perfectly shaped breasts, trim waist, and smooth hips all the way down her long, toned legs, Aelissm Davis was a beautiful woman.

Suddenly uncomfortable, Pat turned his gaze to the countryside below him. From their vantage, they could see down to where Nick's father and brothers were plowing the highest field, which sat at the apex of two ridges below the mountain Aelissm called Alturis.

The sun was still high, but it was beginning to slide westward, and Pat shifted in the saddle. Four-plus hours was a long time to be on a horse for someone who wasn't accustomed to it. Nick must have noticed because he chuckled.

"What d'you say, folks? Shall we call it a day?" he asked.

"I hate to admit it, but yes," Aelissm replied. "It's been fun, Nick. Even being on a horse for so long."

"Did you honestly think I'd lie to you, Aeli?"

"No, but I'm done. Besides, I know it's killing you to be away from your wife and son."

Pat thought he heard a hitch in her voice. Was she jealous?

Nick beamed. "He'll be a week old tomorrow, you know."

"You've only told us twenty times today, as if we didn't already know that," Aeli remarked, rolling her eyes. "C'mon, Nick, this is Northstar. Of course I know how old Will is. And now, I even know where he was conceived. However, I will spare everyone else that bit of Hammond trivia."

Pat wanted to laugh. She *was* envious, though she was trying to hide it. So there *was* a girl beneath that tough exterior that still wanted the more domestic things in life, as he'd expected. She may have said kids didn't seem a part of her future anymore, but she didn't seem opposed to the idea, either.

He wasn't sure how he felt about her indecision—or his own, for that matter—after the kiss that shouldn't have happened. She made him feel things he wasn't sure he wanted to feel again. Most of all, she made him *feel* again. He hadn't realized just how hard and cold and lifeless he'd become over the past three years—five, counting the two he'd wasted with Sara.

Nick started toward his house. The ride back was silent, and Pat tried to stay above the surface of his memories, refusing to be pulled under by them. The day was too incredible to throw away to the darkness of his past. With a sigh, he closed his eyes and allowed himself to take in the sounds and sensations of the valley. The sun beat down at him as if trying to warm away his unpleasant reveries, and it was hard to remain entrenched as the sounds of cattle and horses and birds drifted to his ears on the light breeze.

"I can unsaddle the horses," Nick offered when they arrived back.

"That's all right. We can help," Pat told him.

After the horses were unsaddled and brushed down, Nick released them into the corral behind his home.

"Nick, thank you for the wonderful afternoon," Pat said, extending his hand.

Nick shook it. "You're welcome back anytime, Pat. Aelissm, you too, but you should already know that."

"I do. Thanks, Nick. All right, Pat, we need to scoot. We're supposed to meet June and Luke at the Ramshorn for dinner and swimming when she gets off work, and it's already almost five."

"All right. Tell them hi from us."

"Will do."

Aelissm climbed on her dirt bike and kick-started it. Pat followed her example and waved farewell to Nick. He wasn't feeling the effects of an afternoon of riding just yet, other than his bruised backside and the tenderness where the stirrups had rubbed, but he was sure he would come morning. Maybe the hot springs would help take some of it away, he thought, anxious for that swim.

The wind on his face was pleasant as he sped up the mountain after Aelissm on the dirt bike. There was no better way to enjoy a place like this and still get to your destination quickly than on a motorcycle. It combined the elements of open air and speed, and before he knew it, they'd arrived at the cabin, hurriedly stuffed their swimming gear in back packs, and were racing down the rock-pocked road called Wellman Creek. Aelissm, by far the more experienced rider, beat him to Ma Burns', where they stopped for only a brief moment to say hello to Betty.

What an amazing place, he thought as he and Aelissm rode the rest of the way to the Ramshorn at a more sedate pace. Northstar called to him, promising to embrace him as his home, and he already knew that saying goodbye was going to be very difficult.

June must have heard them coming because she was on the porch of the Ramshorn Lodge when they pulled up. After parking behind her truck across the packed-dirt drive, Pat and Aelissm made their way up the steep steps to the lodge. It was rustic with hand-peeled logs, a red metal roof, and a very welcoming demeanor. Unlike some vacation lodges he'd seen, with their glossy, milled logs and high-end adornments, the Ramshorn was practical and much closer to what he considered to be a proper high-mountain escape. It felt genuine.

"How was your ride down?" June asked when they reached her.

"Good," Aeli replied. "Pat almost caught me on the flat stretch by Betty's. Been busy today?"

"Steady. So, what did you lazy bums do with your afternoon off?"

"We went for a four-hour ride on horseback across the Lazy H with Nick Hammond," Pat supplied. "That's a beautiful spread his family has."

"It is, but how did the two of you manage to get Aeli on a horse?"

"It didn't take much, which surprises me."

"Oh, don't even start," Aeli retorted.

June grinned. "Fine, we won't. Come on in."

Aelissm frowned. "Where's Luke?"

"Inside doing homework."

Pat followed Aelissm and June into the lodge. Trophy heads lined the walls, ranging from whitetail and mule deer to a moose, a couple of pronghorn antelope, elk, and even a grizzly, a black bear, a wolf, and a cougar. The bar stood to the left of the door and, like the tabletops, was constructed from a planed and thickly lacquered log that must have been at least four feet wide. The long side of it was all one piece, he noticed.

Luke glanced up from his schoolwork, smiled at Pat and Aeli, and resumed his task.

"So, what will you be eating?" June asked.

"Cheeseburger," Aeli replied.

"That sounds good," Pat said. "It's all local beef, isn't it? Or was Aelissm lying to me?"

"Of course it is," June replied. "We all serve local beef. Why wouldn't we when we have such tasty cows right down the road?"

While she cooked their dinner, Pat and Aeli sat at the table with Luke. Aelissm teased him, ruffled his hair, and though he squirmed away, he grinned. Pat watched and wondered what hell he'd been through. He was quick enough to smile and laugh, but often, with people he didn't know as well as June and Aelissm, it lacked genuine emotion. He seemed to test every situation to see if it was safe to open up and take a step forward. It was much the same way Pat had spent the past three years of his life, and the comparison strengthened his belief that Luke also had a very good reason behind his caution.

"Luke, sweetheart, dinner's on it's way," June called from the kitchen doorway. "We can finish your homework later tonight."

"All right," the boy replied and stowed his work in his backpack.

June brought their food out and sat down with them to eat. Luke ate with an appetite that was astonishing for his small size, which made Pat all the more sure he'd win his bet with Aelissm. He'd been just like that at Luke's age, and his mother still saw fit to tease him about it from time to time. He felt a pang of guilt. He hadn't talked to her since before he'd left for Northstar, but he'd called and talked to his sister twice.

Aelissm and June's conversation bounced quickly from one topic to the next. It was a tendency of theirs that Pat had become accustomed to, even if he hadn't quite mastered keeping up with their rapid changes in subject. They slipped from discussing Nick's newborn son to the first appearance of the chipmunks up at the cabins to June's classes at the high school to Aeli's class at the college, and a couple times Pat had to ask them to explain how they'd gone from one to the next without losing a beat.

"When you've been friends for as long as we have, you kinda rub off on each other," June explained.

"Yeah, but what scares me is that Luke can launch in any time and know right where you're at and exactly how you got there."

"Well, he's smart. And he's been with me for over half a year now," June replied. "You'll catch on, too, Pat. Just wait. We'll have you thinking you're crazy."

"If crazy is what it takes to live life again, then that's not so bad."

His comment must have caught them by surprise because they fell silent and stared at him. Then understanding dawned on Aelissm, and she nodded.

"I didn't think you were serious. But I'm glad you

are."

June lifted a brow in silent inquiry. "Now, I'm lost."

"Ah, the shoe's on the other foot now, ain't it?" Pat joked.

After that, the mood lightened again, and Pat made a mental note to take caution when he voiced his thoughts. Especially around Aelissm. She was too fragile right now and didn't need him jerking her already frayed emotions around with a careless word.

When they'd finished eating, June cleared their plates, and they headed up the driveway to the pools on the other side of the dirt parking area. By now, the sun was nearly setting, and the sky was a deep blue laced with flares of golden clouds. After strolling down the ramp into the pool house and turning around the corner of the desk, Pat and Luke headed to the left to the men's changing rooms while June and Aeli ducked right into the women's.

As Pat stripped out of his shirt, he heard June and Aelissm giggling.

"Now you're not so upset about Unk sending him, are you," June observed.

"No, I'm actually pretty glad he did," Aeli replied. "And in a few minutes, you'll see one reason why."

"Has a nice body, does he?"

"Not just nice. Gorgeous. Strong shoulders, toned chest and arms, and those legs…. Well, you'll see."

Pat's jaw dropped. "I hope you know I can hear you quite well."

"We know!" they chorused and broke into a new fit of giggles.

While he appreciated the compliments, his face and

neck warmed uncomfortably. He wasn't used to people commenting on his physique, and though he knew he looked good, he certainly wouldn't have used the adjective Aelissm had. What, he wondered, was the point behind her remark when she knew he could hear it? A thought bounded into his mind, twisting his lips in amusement.

"Are you trying to make me blush?" he inquired.

"Of course I am," Aelissm replied. "Is it working?"

"That's for me to know and you to never find out."

"Spoil sport. Would it help if I told you that I really do think you have a spectacular body?"

"Thank you, but I'm still not going to tell you."

"Damn."

Pat glanced at Luke, who grinned. "Are they always like that when they're together?"

"Always," June replied.

"Hey, Luke and I are trying to have a conversation. Quit eavesdropping."

The women laughed again, and Pat listened as their voices trailed off until the sounds of whining hinges and a door slamming announced their departure from the pool house. He shook his head smiling. He might have felt the burn of shy embarrassment, but he *did* appreciate their sense of humor, and it was exactly that brand of friendship that invited him to forget about what was wrong in his life and focus instead on what was worth his time and energy.

"They beat us out," Luke remarked. "You know they're not going to let us live that down, right?"

Pat laughed. He was about to comment when a man sauntered in and immediately caught his attention. His clothing was distinctly incongruent in a place where the standard mode of dress included jeans, T-shirts, and sturdy button-up shirts; his khaki slacks showed crisp fold lines, and the button-up shirt tucked into the waist was a thin and pristine pale blue cotton. His shoes—shiny black loafers—and belt were either brand-new or hadn't seen much wear. More than the clothing, the arrogance in his gait said *outsider*.

"Good evening," the stranger greeted with a practiced enunciation.

"Evening," Pat replied.

"Are you from around here?"

"In a manner of speaking. Why do you ask?"

"I was just wondering if you know either of those two blonde-haired beauties who just walked out of here."

"I do. They're good friends of mine."

"Just good friends?" The man looked Pat up and down.

Pat saw movement in the corner of his vision and noticed that Luke had inched his way toward one of the changing stalls as if to hide. The man glanced at the boy with a sneer, and Pat smiled politely and stepped to block the man's view.

"If you're asking me if they'd be interested in you," he remarked, "I doubt it."

The man smirked. "That's where you'd be wrong." Inclining his head toward Luke, he asked, "Is he your son?"

Pat didn't answer. Anger and adrenaline vibrated through him, and his hands trembled with it as he changed into his swim trunks. The man hadn't said anything threatening, but his haughtiness reminded Pat too much of Sara.

"I'd say he looks a lot like that sexy thing in the blue bikini, but isn't she a bit young to have a kid that age? He must be about nine, right? And she can't be more than twenty-two. I really hope he's her brother because she is way too young and pretty to be shackled to a kid."

"She's not my sister," Luke said quietly. His voice quivered, and Pat saw the shine of tears in his eyes.

"It's none of his business, Luke," Pat said. "Just ignore him."

"Oh, man. She *is* your mother?" The man laughed. "In that case, I'll bet she's a wildcat in bed."

Pat straightened and leveled his gaze on the man. "You might want to stop talking *right* now."

The stranger turned his attention back to Pat. "Why? You said yourself that they're just good friends."

"They are, and they are both way too good for a chauvinist pig like you. Not that you have *any* right to know, but Luke's adopted—or will be soon—and she won't be 'shackled' to him because he is a *great* kid." Pat tossed his towel over his shoulder. "Come on, Luke. Let's get out of here."

Pat rested a hand on Luke's shoulder, and they left the changing room together. Just as they were about to step out the door to the pools, the man grabbed Pat's arm. Pat told Luke to meet his mom in the pool and, clenching his teeth, turned around. It took every grain of self-control he possessed to keep a tight rein on his anger, and only the realization that the fury boiling through him was exactly the same as he'd felt that final weekend with Sara prevented him from losing his grip. *That's not who I am*, he reminded himself. In a carefully controlled voice, he said, "Get your hand off me."

"I just wanted to say… first one to the finish,

asshole."

Pat slammed the man against the wall with his forearm across his throat. The man met his gaze with insolence, and Pat figured his money or position had always saved him from facing any real consequences. Just like Sara. He was the sort who pursued and obtained whatever he wanted without a thought about those he hurt in the process. Snarling, Pat said in a low, deadly tone, "Do not utter even one word to either of those women or that boy."

"Or you'll what?"

Instead of making a threat the man would most likely brush aside, Pat smiled coldly and released him. When confusion darkened the stranger's expression, he knew it was the right move and walked away before the idiot could say anything else to further erode Pat's shaky grasp on his temper.

"Isn't there some rule about not swimming for at least half an hour after eating?" he asked lightly as he joined June, Aelissm, and Luke in the larger pool.

"I don't plan on swimming. I'm going to soak," Aelissm replied, leaning back on the stairs. She rested her elbows on the step behind her to prop herself upright. "And besides, it *has* been a half hour. You two took *forever* to get changed."

"Told you she'd tease us," Luke muttered.

Pat tipped his head back and exhaled slowly.

"Are you all right, Pat?" June asked.

"Yeah. Just had a bit of a run in with a prissy piece of crap thinking he's God's gift to women."

"I'm going to go out on a limb here and say he was dressed in slacks and a blue button-up shirt."

"That's the one."

"We saw him on our way out," Aelissm said. "I thought his tongue was going to hit the floor. I take it you, uh, discouraged any ideas he has for us."

"I did, but watch yourselves around him," Pat said. "He strikes me as the kind who doesn't know how to take no for an answer."

"I can think of another way you can persuade him I'm not available," Aelissm remarked with mischief thick in her voice as she curled her hands around his arm and rested her head on his shoulder. "Of course, poor June's SOL, but she can always say she has a boyfriend."

"If you tell me I should say Jake Sterling is my boyfriend, I will slap you, Aelissm."

"I wouldn't dream of it. I was actually thinking of Aaron. I'm sure he wouldn't mind."

Pat glanced down at Aelissm and had to look away. She was far too sexy in that modest, moss-green bikini and that she seemed oblivious to the fact made her all the more appealing. With the adrenaline not yet fully dissipated, he was far too aware of her. June made just as beautiful a picture in her blue two-piece suit, but there was something about Aelissm that Pat found irresistible. Her body was fuller than her friend's, softer and more inviting.

To distract himself, he watched Luke for a while. The man's comment about June shackling herself to the kid grated as much or more than anything else he'd said. After everything Luke had already been through, the last thing he needed was some random jerk making him feel guilty about what might possibly be the best thing to ever happen to him.

"Luke told me what you said," she said. "Thank you for protecting him like that."

"I should have shut the guy up a lot sooner."

"Maybe you didn't hear me correctly. I didn't chide you for not doing enough; I thanked you for what you did."

He glanced sharply at her, and the way she held his gaze told him that she sensed something of the reason for his hesitation.

"You're an exceptional woman, June."

"Yes, she is," Aelissm remarked.

It was then that Pat realized with a start that she hadn't yet let go of his arm. He should put some distance between them, but just like he hadn't been able to resist kissing her this morning, he couldn't summon the will power to free his arm. Instead, he glanced at Luke again, hesitating to ask about him because he wasn't sure how June would react to the question. His curiosity won out. "I've been debating whether or not I should ask this, but Luke's father was shot by a sheriff's deputy in July, wasn't he, after pulling a gun on the deputy?"

June nodded but said nothing.

"Damn." Pat shook his head. Poor kid. "The deputy, Ben Conner, has been a friend of Bill's for a long time, so I wonder… do you know him?"

"We all went to high school together, in Poulsbo," Aelissm supplied when June didn't answer. "And we've been friends since second grade, when Ben's family moved from Northstar to Poulsbo."

"So you heard that he resigned in October. It's such a pity because he's a good man and *was* a good cop."

June nodded. "Unk told us. I haven't talked to him

since a week or so after the shooting."

"Why?"

She shrugged. "He wouldn't believe me or Uncle Bill when we told him Luke was fine."

"Ah." Pat didn't know what else to say. There didn't seem to be anything, really. He shook his head instead. "What a small world."

"Yeah, and Unk is the center of gravity," Aeli remarked.

He heard the door swing open, then slam shut and turned his gaze. The man from the dressing room had come out and his dark eyes flicked over the three of them, then toward Luke at the deep end of the larger pool. He shook his head and opened his mouth to speak, but before he could, Pat said, "Not one word."

June called Luke over and the boy obeyed without question. She tucked him protectively against her side, and the four of them moved away from the stairs. Rarely did Pat ever feel the urge to use his size to dominate another man, but he made an exception for this one. He was several inches taller and used it to his advantage, looking down on the other man. With a shrug, the man swam to the other end of the pool.

"Do you know who he is, June?" Pat asked quietly.

"No, but we get a lot of people up here who are just stopping on their way through to wherever."

"He reminds me of Brent," Aelissm said, shifting closer to Pat again. "Not in how he looks but how he acts. Arrogant."

"Definitely that," Pat agreed.

The man watched them but maintained his distance.

A half hour later, he left the pool, and Pat breathed a sigh of relief, free at last to enjoy his swim. As he tossed Luke a few times, he tried to forget the momentary flash of aggression the stranger had triggered. In the brilliance of Luke's grin and June's and Aelissm's laughter, it wasn't difficult.

Seven

PAT OPENED HIS EYES and listened for a moment, wondering what had woken him. When he sat up, he groaned at the aches that had accumulated in his muscles after a few hours of sleep. Then he heard whimpers coming from Aelissm's room and pushed himself out of bed. He carefully opened the door between the rooms, and even in the near-blackness, he could see that Aelissm was asleep and that her dreams were not pleasant. He slid onto the bed beside her and called her name.

"Come on, sweetheart, wake up."

"Pat?" she asked.

"It's me," he said. "I'm here."

He gathered her in his arms, and she curled in his lap, clinging to him. She shivered convulsively, so he pulled the blankets around them and let her rest her head on his chest, smoothing a hand over her tangled hair. She seemed so small and fragile pressed against him. How could she be so strong and willful one moment and so weak and terrified the next? He needed to know what had happened with Brent and Adam to make such an independent woman fall apart like this, and he recalled what she'd said about Adam, about what scared her the most. She had thought she'd known who he was.

It seemed like a long time before Aelissm began to relax. When she finally spoke, her voice was so quiet that he almost couldn't hear her.

"I'm sorry, Pat. I don't mean to keep falling to pieces on you. You probably think I'm nuts."

"Not in the least," he assured her. "But you *do* need to stop apologizing for being human."

"Thanks."

"That must have been some nightmare."

He felt her tense up again and stroked his hand down her back.

"It was about Adam… when he…."

Her tears landed hotly on his bare skin but cooled quickly. "Shh. We can talk about it in the morning. Try to sleep."

"No," Aelissm croaked. "I need to tell you."

Pat's chest tightened with the trust she placed in him. He could not imagine her more vulnerable than this as she lay curled against him, still trembling from her dream. She expected him to protect her from her memories and to hold her with no less or deviant intention than to comfort her. Pat wasn't sure he could be all that she needed, not when sleep and his encounter with the man at the Ramshorn had brought his own demons so close to the surface. He felt raw, as if someone had taken sandpaper to his nerves, and his attraction to the slim woman in his arms was iodine in the wounds. Still hazed by sleep, the warm, natural scent of her was a potent temptation, and the feel of her pressed against him threatened to overwhelm him.

Pat blinked his eyes against the darkness and sought any visual distraction. At last, they focused on the glittering, star-spattered indigo outside the window. He tried desperately to train his thoughts on Aelissm's quiet sobs and the night sky… on anything but the flood of desire raging through his veins or the torrent of bitter memories.

"After Brent's death, my life flipped upside down," Aelissm began unsteadily. "All the questions and the people… it was so unreal."

"I can imagine," he murmured.

"I tried to go back to a normal life, I did, but Adam wouldn't leave me alone. He was always asking if I was all right and if I needed him. After I told him I wanted to be by myself for a while to clear my head, he started calling me every day, so I changed my number. I thought that would be enough, that he'd get the hint, but he cornered me outside my apartment building as I was coming home from a night class this past summer. He shoved me against the wall and told me that I was mean to play these games with him, especially after what he'd done for me." She paused to wipe under her eyes and sniff. "I didn't recognize him."

Aelissm's voice was surprisingly steady, and Pat saw again the strength in her. He knew very few people who could have come through such an experience so well, and his respect for her only grew. Resting his cheek on the top of her head, he tightened his arms around her, trying to tell her that she didn't have to face Adam alone anymore. She wrapped her fingers around his forearm and squeezed.

"I moved to my parents' place in Indianola shortly after that and asked Uncle Bill to help me put a restraining order on him," Aelissm continued after a while. "Every time I dream about it, every time he finds me, I wonder if it would have been so bad to be with him. It couldn't be any worse than what I'm going through now. And then I come to my senses and look at who he became the night Brent died, and I know I couldn't do it. I would have killed myself. Or him. Now there's a thought."

The last was said with a thread of humor in her voice, and Pat pictured a self-mocking smirk on her face. "I think he underestimated you."

"It certainly doesn't feel that way."

"I know," he replied. "It's late. We should probably be getting back to sleep."

She was silent for a while, and he wished he knew what thoughts were weaving through her mind.

Finally, she whispered, "Stay with me."

"I shouldn't."

"Please."

He leaned back against the headboard and tugged the blankets tighter around them. "I'll stay."

She snuggled deeper into him and sighed raggedly. Her breathing slowed and deepened, her skin warmed, and her tears slowly dried up. Pat guessed that she must have found the comfort and reassurance that she needed because she was already asleep. He kissed the top of her head, smiling sadly, and took a deep breath.

How can life get so out of control? he wondered. Was there a way to ever regain the balance? He'd been mired in work and self-loathing for so long that he began to doubt.

He knew firsthand how brutal misjudging someone could be. When he'd first met Sara, he'd been fascinated by her. With a mane of shimmering red waves and sharply intelligent honey-colored eyes, she'd been a walking dream. Her laughter had been so rich and vibrant, and the way she could play a room had left him speechless. He'd met her by chance when he'd attended a friend's wedding in the ritzier part of Seattle. Pat had been utterly dumbfounded by Sara's careless wealth. Genuine diamonds and gemstones had glittered at her neck and in her ears and the little combs that pinned her hair back from her flawless, fair-skinned face. Pat recalled looking up to see her standing on the balcony as he stood in the sprawling lawn of the mansion. She'd been sheathed in an exquisitely tailored gown of gold satin. Pat also recalled looking down at his best three-piece suit and feeling as underdressed as if he'd come in ratty jeans and a grease-stained T-shirt.

At first, her superiority had been fun. She'd been the sophisticated older woman, and he'd been the lovesick, inexperienced cop. At twenty-three, he'd fallen into a young man's fantasy. Now, looking back from twenty-eight, the mere thought of her sent a shiver of nausea through him.

His newly married buddy had introduced them. Sara's first glimpse of Pat had been a long one as her experienced gaze raked over him with obvious pleasure. That night had been one of the most amazing in Pat's life and, in hindsight, one of the worst. If only he looked past the stunning exterior wrapped to perfection in smooth gold satin, he might have seen the darkness in her heart and saved himself five years of anguish and torture.

He'd been too awestruck by her and too busy wondering what such a woman could possibly find desirable in him to question the authenticity of her interest. She was, he knew now, a master of manipulation whose every word and action was carefully calculated to produce whatever outcome she coveted. He had been a toy, something to entertain her, and she had played him like a puppet, alienating him from his friends and family with a finesse and cruelty that staggered him. She had made him feel guilty about the friends he kept, and eventually, they had stopped calling to find out when he'd be able to spare a moment for them. It had happened so gradually that he hadn't noticed until the night he'd nervously proposed to her. She had gone out with *her* friends and suggested he do the same, but instead of congratulations, the few friends who had answered his call greeted his news with pity. He had spent the night alone, and for the first time in his life, understood what it was to be truly lonely.

At the time, he'd blamed his misery on his friends' envy, but he was wiser now and knew that Sara had orchestrated every agonizing doubt that had crossed his mind as well as the disastrous interlude when she'd stopped by his apartment for a "breather" in the midst of her night on the town. Under the best of circumstances, her aggressive and domineering sexual preferences had always unnerved him, and he'd known all along that he would never fully sate her appetite, but that night, he'd utterly failed to perform, and he shuddered as he recalled the saccharine way she'd turned the blame on him. Not once had she said outright that he'd disappointed her more thoroughly than ever before, but she'd certainly made him understand it, using his innate tendency to shoulder responsibility to debase and control him.

When the holidays rolled around, he'd made excuses to his family and missed both Thanksgiving and Christmas dinner. He'd broken his father's and sister's hearts. He'd shattered his mother's. Almost a year later, she'd stood in his hospital room after he'd come out of surgery and begged him to forgive her for the mean things she'd said about him and Sara as if she were the one at fault.

Pat pinched his eyes closed and clenched his jaw.

How could I have done that to my family? He wondered, tightening his arms around Aelissm and using her as an anchor. *How did I let her turn me into that?*

He still wasn't sure what was the worst part about it. As a cop, he'd counseled more women—and men—about getting out of abusive relationships than he cared to count, and yet, he'd fallen into the same trap. It was embarrassing, too, for a man his size to be so controlled and degraded by someone as tiny as Sara. She was more than a foot shorter than him and petite. It amazed him, the amount of cold malice and fiery violence he'd found in such a small woman. Then again, dynamite came in small packages, too, and he decided that whoever had said that was a genius.

"I should have known better," Pat whispered. "For God's sake, I've seen it a hundred times, and it's always the same."

He didn't have the excuse of innocence like Aelissm did. It was the ruthless truth, but he'd been swallowed by a fantasy. Sara was, at least on the surface, the kind of woman most men dreamed about. She had a body that belonged to a swimsuit model, a breathtaking self-assuredness, and a quick mind that had been honed by an expensive education—a combination that was deadly to any man's reserve. Even Pat's.

He'd gained *some* perspective of the situation. At the time, he'd been ignorant of the mind games people like Sara played, so perhaps he had been somewhat innocent, but he should have seen the signs. How many times had he told himself that? Yes, he *should* have known, but coulda-shoulda-woulda wasn't going to happen now, and Aelissm was very right. It was time he got back to the business of living. No, business was the wrong word. He'd been working too hard to get past Sara, and it hadn't gotten him anywhere. He needed to learn how to enjoy life again, which was exactly why Bill had asked him to take a vacation.

So, really, had the kiss this morning been so damaging? Aelissm hadn't seemed in the least bothered. As long as that's as far as it went, he wouldn't hurt her, but just because he'd decided to walk away from his past, that didn't mean he could ever let anyone get as close to him as Sara had. He simply didn't have enough left to love again. Although, if he *could* allow himself to love someone new, he could certainly see himself with Aelissm. She was intelligent in a way that Sara never would be, and despite the sarcasm that often rippled off her tongue, she was a caring, compassionate woman.

"Bill would love that," he murmured.

Nick Hammond had it right. A woman like Aelissm would keep him on his toes and make life one grand adventure after another. But he couldn't.

Aelissm sighed in her sleep and shifted into a more

comfortable position. She certainly wasn't inclined to move away, and he didn't want her to. This felt so right, being curled with his boss's niece in a mountainside cabin. Life was so miraculously uncomplicated that his chest tightened. There were no expectations of permanence or perfection, just the pure and simple element of mutual comfort.

Time slipped past in a haze of warmth and sleeping woman. Pat dozed lightly, but he didn't really sleep. No more visions of Sara tormented him, and his half-conscious mind savored these moments of chaste closeness with Aelissm. If only every moment in life could be like this, so peaceful and healing.

Dawn slowly lightened the room with cool blue. Pat narrowed his eyes, studying the clarity of the light. It looked to be another exquisite day. Slowly, the stars began to fade from the softening sky, and Pat found a serenity more complete than he could have dreamed.

"Mmm…" Aelissm purred. "This is nice."

Her words were slurred with sleep, and Pat stroked her fine hair.

"It is," he replied.

"Have you been awake all night?"

"Mostly."

"I'm sorry. I didn't mean to keep you up."

Pat smiled and rested his chin on the top of her head. "There's nothing to be sorry about. I think I needed this as much as you did."

* * *

A contented smile lifted Aelissm's lips. Day was dawning far too quickly, and she closed her eyes to more deeply enjoy the weight of Pat's arms as they encircled her with tender protection. Idly, she wondered if this should feel wrong or naughty. She had just spent a handful of hours with a man in her bed, wrapped around her as comfortably as a lover, so perhaps it *should* feel a little devious. However, as nothing more than emotional reassurance had come of it, she couldn't see where it was wrong. Even the gentleness in Pat's voice as he told her he'd needed this as much as she did hadn't warranted a warning. They both needed to know that they could still find comfort in another who hadn't been privy to all the gory details of their pasts. They needed to know they could still let someone new in. After all, they'd both made rather disastrous decisions in the past.

Don't ruin it, she scolded herself. *Just enjoy the moment. It might never come again.*

"You missed the stars last night," Pat murmured. His voice was an entrancing rumble beneath her ear, and she smiled. "But then, you're used to seeing so many, every night."

Aelissm pictured the night sky over the valley, and her smile deepened. So far away from a city of any real size, there were plenty to see, and though she often took the stars for granted, she could still be awestruck from time to time when she paused to look up at them. It was a stunning sight she'd cherished as a child.

"I'll have to take you camping up to Sawtooth," she said. "There's a meadow at the east end of the lake that is perfect for stargazing."

"Sounds very appealing. So does a blue-sky day, which it appears we'll have."

Grudgingly, she lifted her head just enough to peek out the window. The sky was definitely clear, and her eyes, tired of the snow-choked Montana winter, found the sight alluring. She and Pat didn't have to be down to the Bedspread until four, and she had all kinds of ideas about what she'd like to do with him up here on the mountainside, several of which were spawned by rather questionable impulses.

"Is it me, or does it feel a little cold outside the blankets?" Pat asked.

"The fire's probably out," Aeli replied. "But I don't want to get up to go start another one. Do you?"

"No."

"Hmm. One of us should get a fire going."

"Yep."

"Rock, paper, scissors?"

Pat laughed. Instead of moving her, he readied his hands in front of her, and Aelissm closed her eyes to fully savor having his arms around her. Grinning, she poked her hands out from the blankets.

"Ready?" he asked. "One… two… three!"

Their fists curled into rocks.

"Again?" she asked.

They tied again with scissors. The third time they tied with paper, then with rocks again. Laughing, they agreed to go down together, but when it came to leaving the blankets and each other, Pat seemed no more inclined than she was to step into the chilly air. It was a half hour before he finally flipped the covers back when she offered to make him breakfast.

Shivering, Aelissm leapt from her bed and shrugged into her fleece robe. Glancing over her shoulder, she found Pat still half-buried in the blankets and was rewarded with a nice view of his naked upper body.

"I hope you don't expect breakfast in bed," she re-marked.

"No, just give me a minute."

"Is big old Pat O'Neil afwaid of the cold?" Aeli stuck out her bottom lip.

"Old?"

"Well, you are almost thirty."

"Hey, I'm not even twenty-nine, so quit picking on me."

"Then get out of bed, lazy bones."

"Now I'm lazy, too? I can live with the 'old' remark, but I don't know about this 'lazy' business." He groaned and reached to rub his lower back. "Gimme a minute. I'm a little stiff."

Aelissm's brows rose at his choice of phrase. Her eyes, with a will of their own, dipped toward his nether regions, but his lower half was hidden by the mass of blankets. When she met his gaze again, she saw that he'd noticed her momentary detour.

"Stiff, huh?"

She thought his face pinkened a bit… just a tiny bit. Her face warmed more than she would have liked, too, and she cursed her fair complexion.

"Yeah. This *old* city boy isn't used to sitting on a horse for four hours."

"And I'm sure leaning against a headboard all night didn't help much."

"Oh, that wouldn't have made much of a difference."

Aelissm nodded and turned away. "I'll see you down-stairs."

He came down just moments after her, wrapped in a dark green robe. She glanced down at her own of nearly the same color. For God's sake, even their robes matched. Shaking her head, she stepped out the back door to grab a couple smaller logs and a handful of wood chips to start a fire. Pat took the kindling from her and got a fire going while she started breakfast.

It didn't take long for the kitchen to warm up, and the rest of the cabin was bearable again shortly thereafter. While her father's handiwork may not have been the most aesthetically beautiful, it was far more functional and practical than those massive vacation cabins some people built in Montana. Those huge windows made it much more difficult to hold the heat than the smaller, more economical windows Aelissm's parents had installed. But then, she supposed the people who owned those so-called cabins could afford to heat them. The thought to money that had gone into the design and construction of this cabin reminded Aelissm unpleasantly of where she'd been. The poorer side of middle class she could handle. She'd grown up knowing the value of money, and to this day, she couldn't comprehend the carelessness with which Brent had spent his money. Adam had always been much more cautious, and his thriftiness was the one giveaway to his roots. He knew what it was to count every penny and stretch it as far as possible just like she did.

Brent had never understood that about either of them. Once, he'd even joked that she should be with Adam. She grimaced.

"What're you thinking about?" Pat asked as he stood from adding another log to the fire. He spanned his hands above the wood stove to warm them and watched her quizzically over his shoulder.

"Brent and Adam. You've dealt with all kinds of people, so maybe you can explain something to me."

He shrugged doubtfully. "I can try."

"How could Brent and his family and friends look down on me because I actually have to work for my money?" Her voice quivered with anger. "How can they think they're better than me when they've had everything handed to them?"

"Did Brent look down on you?"

"A little. I think he saw something good enough for him in me, but I always knew I wasn't good enough for his parents or Jeanette—his sister. I mean, how dare I pay my own way through college and take out loans to do it."

Pat stepped over and wrapped his arms around her. She balled her hands into fists against his chest. Until this moment, she hadn't realized she'd been so furious about the way Brent's parents and sister had treated her. Had she been aware of it then? She'd always felt like an outcast among them, but then it hadn't really mattered. Why the hell did it matter now? If a man like Pat could find her appealing enough to kiss, there must be something worthwhile about her. Besides, she'd like to see Brent's prissy sister chop a cord of firewood or turn a hunk of metal into something useful and beautiful. Hell, she'd like to see Brent's snobnosed mother spend two weeks here in Montana in the middle of winter. She'd go nuts.

"Are you all right?" Pat asked after a moment.

"I think I am now. It just… caught me by surprise." Stepping over to flip the pancakes, she said, "I guess I didn't realize how much it bothered me until now."

"Then now's as good a time as any to talk about it." Pat took eggs out of the fridge and cracked them into a bowl to scramble them. "I can tell you from my own experience with certain kinds of people that it's the other way around as often as not."

"Your own experience? Work-related or personal?"

"Some work-related but mostly personal. Sara was the only daughter of an old-money family, and looking back, I see that I was always more of a pet to them, something that amused them. I certainly wasn't ever part of the family."

Aelissm stared at him. That was the first thing he'd ever said about his ex to her.

He smiled, but his eyes were sad. "I know you want to know what happened, Aelissm, but I can't talk about it just yet. I'm getting closer, thanks in large part to you. Can you make do with a promise that I'll tell you someday?"

"I guess I'll have to. It's really none of my business."

"Perhaps not, but I feel I owe you something in return for telling me about things I'm sure you'd rather not."

But I do *want to tell you, Pat. I* need *to tell someone*, she wanted to say. Instead, she asked, "What do you want to know?"

"Everything I can about Adam Winters. You said it scared you that he wasn't who you thought. How so?"

It was a relief to have a point to start on. And it was a valid one, because Pat would need to know Adam's character if Adam found her again. Aelissm suppressed the shiver.

"To answer that, I have to go back a ways." She took

a deep breath. "Adam came from the same kind of background I did, in a way, but his dad left when he was four, and he and his mom struggled a lot."

"Bill told me Adam and Brent were best friends. How did they meet?"

"After Adam's dad left, his mom got a job teaching at the private school Brent went to, so Adam was allowed to attend, tuition waived." Aelissm shook her head. "They didn't start off so well. Brent and his little buddies taunted Adam in gym, but Adam wouldn't fight back because he'd get kicked out of school. Then the gym teacher told him to beat the piss outta Brent if he pantsed him one more time. Brent did, of course, so Adam beat the piss out of him. From then on, they became best friends. Sort of a rite of passage, I guess. Adam had to prove himself to the other boys."

She paused to pour more pancakes. "When I think about that, I remember the Adam I knew before that night. He was always so friendly, and he was as much a social underdog as I was. We only differed in that he *wanted* to be a part of Brent's ring. I didn't. I accepted that, though, because when he and I used to hang out, he was cool. Then Brent tried to prove I was his possession. Adam really did lose it, I think, when Brent hurt me that night. He ceased to be my lovable friend."

"He betrayed you because he changed."

Aelissm tilted her head. In the past year, she hadn't slowed down enough to take a step back and analyze her situation. Pat's words, which sounded more like he was thinking out loud than asking her opinion, were the absolute and painful truth. Why hadn't she ever realized it before?

She smacked her palm against her forehead.

"I'm such an idiot. All this time, I could have been living a normal life," she said sarcastically.

"First off, don't call yourself an idiot. There's nothing farther from the truth."

"Coulda fooled me."

"Okay, there may be a few things less true, but you aren't stupid. I don't think you were wrong about the kind of person Adam was, but he became something you couldn't have anticipated." Pat leaned against the sink and watched her for a few moments before he continued. "I can see why Adam is obsessed with you."

Aelissm lifted a brow in question.

"You're beautiful, intelligent, and strong. You've made your own place in the world, and to hell with what everyone thinks about it. You represent everything he wants to be. And he came from a poor family and grew up in Brent's shadow, so I imagine it killed him that his best friend had everything he didn't. I'm not just talking about money, Aelissm. By social standing, you should have been with Adam, not Brent."

She nodded. That much she'd known from the start. If she believed Pat—and she did, because she knew he was right—she hadn't misjudged Adam, but she *had* been very wrong about Brent. If she had only seen what he was really after, maybe she could have gotten out before everything exploded. Following that logic, she truly regretted her blindness because, despite everything Adam had put her through, she was glad she'd met him. When he'd been her friend, she'd thoroughly enjoyed his company. His easy laugh was infectious, and the never-ending stream of jokes had often made her sides hurt. She missed him, and she wished there was a way to bring that old Adam back, but she didn't know if whatever had fractured in him that night could be repaired.

"You know, June thought Adam was okay, but she never really liked Brent. I'm beginning to think I should have listened to her."

"Hindsight is twenty-twenty, but out of curiosity, why didn't you take her advice?"

"June is good at reading people, don't get me wrong, and she's usually right, but she's missed out on a lot of fun because of it. I had so many good times with Brent and Adam."

Aelissm set the table, and as she and Pat sat down to eat breakfast, she knew that something had changed. It was easier to dissect her relationship with Brent and with Adam and approach it with a calm, rational mind.

"How did you get together with Brent in the first place?"

"We met at grad school, and I was dumb enough to think his pretty-boy exterior was a reflection of what was on the inside. I grew up with very little extra money to blow on ridiculous things like jewelry and flowers, so I was dazzled. I didn't realize that it wasn't something special he was doing just for me, that he spoiled all his girlfriends."

"It's an easy trap to fall into."

"You sound like you know it well."

"Better than I'd like." Pat looked down at his plate. "Don't let me interrupt."

Aelissm hesitated. She wanted to know of this mysterious past Pat hinted at, but she didn't want to stop her own train of thought, fearing that it might derail just when she was making some measurable progress. "You're sneaky, Mr. O'Neil, but I'll play along. Had it not been for the fact that I'm a little stubborn—"

"A little?"

"Oh, hush up. Anyhow, Brent wasn't made of gold, like I'd thought. Just gold-plated with low-grade tin underneath and just like every other asshole who has tried—and failed—to get in my pants."

"You're a virgin?"

"Don't sound so shocked, Pat."

A strange expression twisted Pat's face, one that Aeli couldn't put a name to. She didn't know if he was amused or surprised, pleased or disgusted.

"I'm not shocked. Not really," he said at last. "Honestly, I hadn't thought about it."

"Well, if Brent had had his way, I wouldn't still be."

"Bill told me he tried to rape you."

Putting it into words made her squirm a bit in her seat. Nightmares and the dark memories of that night were unpleasant, certainly, but they were private distractions of her mind. To hear it voiced by another person was something different. It made it more real again. The time between then and now had managed to dull the edges of it, but Pat's innocent comment acted like a whetstone.

"I'm sorry, Aelissm, I didn't mean—"

"It's all right, Pat. It's not your fault. You know, if it hadn't been for Adam…. I still dream about it. All of it. Sometimes, I can still feel Brent's hands on me, and his mouth." She shook herself to dispel the inklings of that memory before it could take hold. "Then I see Adam wrap his hands around Brent's throat and dream about the night he cornered me."

"There's more than what you told me last night, isn't there?"

"He told me that I owe him." Aelissm set her fork down when she realized she was shaking. "Is it true? Do I owe him?"

"It was Adam's choice to do what he did. You don't owe him a damned thing."

Aelissm considered his words for a long time while they ate. She hadn't asked Brent to assault her nor asked Adam to save her.

"You know what? You're right," she announced as she set her plate in the sink. "I didn't do anything wrong, except make a bad decision in my love life, which doesn't justify the way I've been living. I don't owe either of them anything. Not for that. It's time I start acting like it. "

Pat's expression was one of profound pride. She washed her plate, distracted by a memory of the time before her father had installed the hot water heater. Doing the dishes had taken much longer then, having to wait for the water to heat up on the stove and woodstove. She gazed contentedly out the window above the sink and noticed that the snow had melted off enough in the past couple days to reveal glimpses of forest floor. The first shoots of delicate, vibrant alpine grass were already poking through. Spring had officially arrived on the mountain. Movement caught her eye, and she watched a chipmunk scurry down a tree trunk near the outhouse, and she reminded herself to put out some peanuts and sunflower seeds for them later.

When Aelissm had finished her first chore, she

opened the back door and grinned as her gaze landed on a pile of tired snow.

"Would you give me a hand bringing in a couple more logs," she called over her shoulder.

"Sure. Gimme a second to finish eating," Pat replied.

The screen door slammed behind her, but she didn't flinch. The snow was more ice now, hard little crystals that didn't pack well, but it'd do the trick. She dug her fingers into it, curling them around a fistful, oddly soothed by the cold bite of it. In her mind, she likened the snow to the frigid existence she'd been lost in and pictured both melting away in tiny, shimmering streams beneath a blazing mountain sun. Of course, the process would happen much faster if she helped it along.

Finally, as her fingers began to numb, the back door swung open. Aeli hurled her snowball and crowed with laughter as it exploded against Pat's chest. For a moment, he stared at her with his mouth hanging open and his arms and hands loosely outstretched in silent inquiry.

"What was that for?" he sputtered.

Aelissm replied with another snowball.

"All right, little missy, you asked for it!"

With a swiftness her laughter-weakened body couldn't escape, Pat leapt to her side, swept her off her feet, and deposited her unceremoniously atop the snowdrift. Giggling uncontrollably now, Aelissm could only squeal in delighted outrage as he pinned her and dumped an armload of snow on her head. Her sides and face ached, but never had she felt a more pleasurable pain. Something had given way like a logjam in a stream swollen by spring run-off, and joy rushed through her as torrential and cleansing as the rain of a summer thunderstorm. She couldn't seem to stop the laughter or the resulting tears that streamed from her eyes, and she didn't want to. It was so good to laugh like this again.

If Aelissm thought she'd seen Pat smile before, it was nothing compared to the expression he wore now. The most incredible, beautiful grin parted his lips and ignited his eyes with happiness and release, innocence and youth. There was also desire and something else Aelissm was both frightened and hungry to name. There was love in his gaze, but whether it came from romantic or platonic origins, she couldn't say. Right now, it didn't matter.

Breathless from the intoxicating mixture of unbridled happiness and the closeness of such a gentle, incredible man, Aelissm sagged back into the embrace of the snow and beamed at Pat. It felt as though the past year had never happened, and Aelissm was drunk on the sensation. She hadn't been this giddy in a long time.

Aelissm slipped her hands over Pat's cheeks and knitted them behind his head, pulling him toward her. When she kissed him, he responded with dizzying passion and wrapped her tightly in his arms. She released his mouth and rested her forehead against the curve between his neck and shoulder and sighed happily. After a few moments, she let him help her the rest of the way to her feet. She brushed the snow from his robe before she attended to her own, noticing with a flutter of her heart how his pupils dilated. She offered no apology for the kiss, and neither did he. There was no promise of anything beyond the here and now and no facades to maintain. She and Pat were simply being themselves, and nothing could have been more perfect. So, she kissed him again.

Eight

"I HOPE YOU DON'T MIND getting your hands dirty since it's your fault we have to cook tonight," Aelissm remarked playfully as she dropped her shoulder and let her pack slide to the floor beside the inner front door of her cabin. "I wonder if June let you borrow her camera because she knew it'd slow us up. You must have taken enough pictures with that thing to fill two shoeboxes."

Pat shrugged and dropped his pack beside hers. "Better two shoeboxes to help me remember Northstar than none."

Aelissm pointedly ignored his remark and plopped on one of the couches to pull her hiking boots and socks off her tired feet. With a happy sigh at again being barefoot, she wiggled her toes and sank back against the couch. There was little else in the world as relaxing as a hike up to one of the alpine lakes on a day as stunningly clear and perfectly warm as this. Being in the company of good friends only made it better, she mused, recalling the snowball fight of girls against boys that she and June had won. Poor Pat had been half-drenched by the time he and Luke had finally called their surrender.

A smile danced over her face as she closed her eyes and pictured the tiny lake above the Lazy H glittering like a pristine sapphire beneath the grinning sun. Baldy Lake wasn't her favorite, but it was an easy trail and a good start to the hiking season.

After a few moments of rest, Aeli bounced to her feet with an energy that surprised her. She could feel Pat's eyes on her as she sauntered into the kitchen, and she was all too aware of the heat of him when he joined her beside the snack bar. Pretending to ignore him, she turned her attention momentarily to the small stereo on the counter. She'd left a CD in it yesterday, and with a smile of wicked mischief, she selected a sexy, upbeat country song. Cranking the volume, she turned away and opened the refrigerator door. She felt playful but was still shy enough that she didn't act on the wanton impulses flooding her veins.

"So, what are we making for dinner?" Pat asked.

"I thought either spaghetti or tacos. You know, I'm starting to think you're not as acclimated as you want me to believe," Aeli remarked as she rummaged through the fridge. "I mean, we stopped so often for you to take pictures, you couldn't have lost your breath."

"Give an old man a break, Aeli, because I'm rather tempted to prove you wrong."

"Oh, yeah?" With a fleeting thought to caution, she

swiveled around to face him. *Ah, to hell with it.*

Standing on her toes, she dragged his mouth down to hers, giving in to the explosion of desire. Pat stumbled backwards, colliding with the counter. Aelissm curled her fingers around fistfuls of his thick, richly colored hair, claiming him more thoroughly than she would have thought herself capable of. Waves of heat fanned through her, and any thoughts outside of the moment were lost in the hungry contact with this startlingly passionate man. Pat's hands grasped her face, his fingers stroking her cheeks and jaw line with desperate intensity. Aelissm arched against him, pleading for more, and his hands obeyed, stroking down her neck and back to settle firmly on her hips.

Aelissm's deft fingers sought the buttons of his shirt and peeled the soft material back over his shoulders with confidence. She released his mouth to concentrate on his neck, raking her teeth over firm muscle and following gently with her lips, then moved down toward his chest. Pat wrapped powerful hands around her upper arms and pushed her away. Confused, she searched his gaze and stepped back as if she'd been slapped. His eyes were hazed by desire, but anger and fear flared like gasoline on a bonfire beneath the fog. He turned away and tugged his shirt back in place but not before she caught sight of a thick white scar just below his collarbone.

"Pat?" she asked hesitantly.

"Leave me alone, Aelissm. Just give me a minute."

She did as he asked with confusion quickly giving way to fury. She folded her arms tightly across her chest and waited for Pat to speak while her mind darkened with thoughts of rejection and the bitterness of unquenched desire.

"What the hell, Pat?" she asked after several moments passed in tense silence.

"Dammit, Aelissm," Pat snapped. "Neither of us is ready for this."

"Oh, really?" Impulsively, she massaged his inner thigh, pleased to find him aroused. "Your body says differently."

The color drained from his face, and he closed his eyes and swallowed hard. Abruptly, Aelissm snatched her hand back, her eyes wide as Pat slid to the floor. With his knees drawn up and his head resting back against the cupboards, he didn't look at all like the smiling, patient man he'd been only minutes ago. Instead, he looked old and worn out, tormented by memories she couldn't begin to understand. Memories she had somehow provoked.

"Pat, I'm sorry. What did I do?"

"Nothing, Aeli," he replied without opening his eyes. His voice was strained, weary. "It's not your fault, but I need to be alone for a few minutes. Why don't you go over to June's for a bit while I cook dinner?"

She nodded but couldn't find her voice to answer. After stuffing her poor feet back into her socks and boots, she spared Pat another glance before she left. His eyes were still closed, and the muscles in his jaw flexed. She wanted to coax him out of it, but she didn't know what she could do. She'd brought it on, so she couldn't blame him for not wanting her around. She pulled the back door open and stepped through it, then carefully released the screen door so it wouldn't slam. With tears burning in her eyes, she traversed the steep terrain between her cabin and June's, stepping over the rocks and fallen logs out of habit more than conscious thought. What had she done to make Pat break down like that? Why had he pushed her away when his body so obviously wanted to give in to the desire that had been building between them for weeks? Aelissm tried to work the knots out of the tangled mess that was her mind, looking for some clue as to why he would push her away. Was she not good enough for him? He wouldn't be the first man to find her lacking.

Damn it, I'm not going to cry, she thought stubbornly as she wiped beneath her eyes with her thumb.

She was suddenly aware that she was standing on June's back deck and that her knuckles ached sharply from knocking. Her friend stood in the open doorway, smiling.

"I know dinner isn't ready yet," June remarked as she stepped aside to let Aelissm enter. "We just took off our boots."

Aelissm said nothing, just stood there with the back door hanging open.

"Aeli?"

"No, dinner's not ready yet."

"What happened? Adam didn't call again, did he?"

"No. It's not Adam."

"Then what? Did something happen with Pat?"

Aelissm snorted. "You could say that."

"Aelissm… what did you do?"

She finally met June's worried eyes. Her first instinct was to defend herself against her friend's gentle accusation, but a moment's hesitation stopped her. June wasn't accusing her of anything, merely stating the self-assessment that must have been written all over her face. "I don't know what I did. I kissed him, and it was fine at first—great—but then...."

"What happened?"

"He pushed me away."

June's brow furrowed as she embraced Aelissm. "It probably has something to do with his ex. Didn't Bill say it ended badly with her?"

Aelissm nodded, wondering at her own denseness. Why had she automatically assumed she'd done something to make him turn away? Habit. Stupid, self-loathing, and unfounded habit.

"I don't understand what happened. He was enjoying it as much as I was until I started pulling his shirt off."

June stepped back, and her mouth fell open. "Aelissm! You horny little fiend!"

Aeli blushed and looked away, unable to meet her friend's laughing eyes. She sought the reason why Pat had suddenly stopped enjoying the moment, reviewing the whole scene in her mind again and again until she finally knew.

"He has a scar under his collarbone. Everything was fine until I touched it."

"Touched it?" June asked with a lifted brow. "May I ask with what?"

"My teeth."

This time, June's laughter didn't stay contained in her eyes. It came spilling out, and Aelissm was soon laughing with her. Now that she thought back, she was surprised at herself for what she'd done.

"I guess I *am* a horny fiend," she said, still giggling. "But, c'mon, June. He's been living with me for how long now? And you can go straight to a nunnery if you don't think he's damned sexy."

"You amuse me, Aeli."

"Do I now?" Aelissm put her hands on her hips. "How so?"

"Well, you were threatening to throw him out in the snow in his birthday suit if he complained about the lack of creature comforts, and now you want to sleep with him. Oh, Uncle Bill would be thrilled."

"Uncle Bill! Maybe he can tell me where Pat got that scar."

"Aelissm…."

"Can I use your phone, June? If Pat won't tell me what's going on with him, I'll ask Uncle Bill," Aeli said, grabbing the cordless from the kitchen counter. "And don't tell me it's a bad idea to pry. He hasn't told me *anything*, and I've laid it all out for him."

She dialed her uncle's home phone. Bill answered but told his wife, "Corn's fine, love," before asking, "Hello?"

"Hi, Unk."

"Aeli Girl," Bill replied. He sounded happy. "How are you? Everything all right? No more word from Adam since the letter?"

"No. No, everything's fine in that department. But I want to know something about Pat, Unk. How'd he get that scar under his collarbone?"

"He was stabbed. Why do you ask?"

"He, uh, seems a little sensitive in that area."

There was a pause, and Aelissm could just see the grin spreading on her uncle's face as he put two and two together. He wasn't the lead detective in the Kitsap County

Sheriff's Department for nothing, and she swore as her face warmed uncomfortably. This was a bad idea, she realized too late. Bill wouldn't let the matter drop until he heard wedding bells now that she'd given him the smallest clue to the heat between her and Pat. She recalled hearing Pat's name in several conversations with Bill over the past few years, and once or twice, he'd included her in the same sentence, but until Pat had shown up in the Bedspread looking so rugged and handsome, Aelissm hadn't given her uncle's hints much thought.

"Yes, Unk, I kissed him. I know you're wondering, so there you go. Are you happy?"

"We'll see what happens, and I'll let you know. In the meantime, dinner's ready."

That sounded like a cop-out to her, but her uncle bid her goodnight before she could question him further. She hung up and looked at June.

"That was brave, telling Uncle Bill you kissed Pat," June said.

"Tell me about it," Aeli replied. She set the cordless back on the counter, let her hand hover over it for a moment. "Pat was stabbed."

"Ouch. By whom?"

"Uncle Bill didn't say."

June took three bottles of water out of the fridge, handed one to Aelissm and motioned toward the living room. Luke was sprawled on the love seat, reading. He glanced up when they plopped on the couch, said hi, took the water June offered, and returned to his book. Aelissm watched him for a while, wondering who would have stabbed Pat. He seemed like such a likeable guy. Patient.

Compassionate. Affable. Who would feel they had cause to do something so vicious?

Aelissm stood up and paced. "Do you think it might have been his ex?"

"I haven't a clue, but why would you jump to that conclusion?"

"When he was talking to Bill on the phone after he first got here, he called her a bitch. Does that seem right to you, like something he would say about a woman?"

"If she broke his heart."

"But *he* left her."

"Well, then. I don't know what to tell you, Aeli."

Aeli growled in frustration. This time, something in his past had affected her directly, made her doubt herself, so it was time she knew what she was dealing with. "He owes me an explanation."

***

When Aelissm's teeth had touched the scar, remembered pain seared through it, nearly as agonizing as the knife had been in his flesh. The hurt on her face needled through him like icicles, excruciating and pervasive. No matter how hard he tried to out-run it, no matter how hard he worked to close himself off to it, Sara's hatred kept coming back, tormenting him from his memories, and now it was beginning to affect those around him. He had no right to drag Aelissm down with him.

He massaged the scar, trying to work out the lingering ache. It took him a few minutes to find the willpower to push himself off the floor and start dinner. Spaghetti sounded good, he thought, trying to fool himself into being hungry. The hike had tired him, but not enough to explain the deep-seated lethargy that descended on him like a lead jacket. He couldn't let her keep doing this to him, he told himself as he gathered the ingredients and browned the hamburger meat. It had been three years since he'd ended their engagement.

He was just setting the water on to boil when the phone rang, and he absently reached for the cordless as he continued to work. "Hello?"

"Who the hell is this?"

Instantly, Pat's attention was yanked to the call. He vaguely recognized the voice, though he couldn't immediately put a name or face to it. It wasn't anyone from the valley, but the area code suggested the caller was somewhere in Montana, and he thought the prefix might be Devyn. Jogging into the living room, he picked up the pad of paper and pen resting beside the phone's base and jotted down the number on the caller ID, then detailed what had been said so far.

"I asked you who the hell you are."

"Pat O'Neil," he replied at last as realization dawned. On the notepad, he scribbled *Winters*.

"Where's Aelissm?" the man demanded.

"Out. Can I take a message?"

"No, but you can stay away from her."

"I'm afraid I can't and won't do that, Adam."

There was a pause, and Pat strained to hear any background noises. He thought he heard the clatter of dishes, as might be heard in a restaurant, and another man asking when the phone would be free. While Winters was distracted, Pat wrote notes about possible places he might be calling from.

"I'll be done in a minute," Winters replied away from the mouth piece. To Pat, he asked, "How do you know who I am?"

"Call it a hunch. Would you care to leave a message?"

"Yeah, tell Aeli she's mine, and I'm coming for her. And I'll plow right through you to get to her."

"I don't think so, Adam."

"Stay away from her."

The click of disconnection rang in Pat's ear. By the time he'd finished writing, the impatient, broken dial tone was squawking at him. He pushed the end button and set the handset in the cradle before returning to the kitchen. The water was boiling, so he added the noodles, then poured the jar of ready-made spaghetti sauce into the pan with the meat. He crushed a couple cloves of fresh garlic and added a little extra seasoning.

Adam wasn't in Seattle anymore. He was getting closer to Aelissm, and Pat snarled at his own helplessness. He couldn't even tell where the bastard was calling from. He appreciated Aelissm's situation better now and more fully understood her fear and annoyance.

"Son of a bitch," he muttered as the noodles nearly boiled over. He turned the heat on the little gas range down.

Glancing out the kitchen window, he noticed that the light had gone golden as the sun sank westward toward evening. Shifting his gaze deeper into the forest, he spied Aelissm, June, and Luke making their way toward the cabin, stepping and bounding over logs and rocks with enviable energy. All three of them were laughing, and Pat felt his face lift slightly in response. Aelissm was beautiful even frowning, but when that honest smile graced her features, she was exquisite. The light of it danced in her eyes and flowed through the rest of her as she tossed her head back to laugh at something Luke had said. That unbridled joy lent a fluid grace to a body that was already lissome.

The insane urge to slide his hands over those sleek hips again knifed through his tension, and for a moment, he was too distracted by chiding himself to worry about Adam's call or Sara's lasting memories. It would be so easy and so perfect to lose himself in Aelissm. It wasn't just her body that drew him like a dreamer to blessed night but everything about her—the dry wit she frequently unleashed, the talent she had for crafting, and the compassion she often said wasn't even one of her traits. Beside Aelissm's brilliant light, Sara's shadow faded away until he could barely make it out.

The feeling wouldn't last, he knew, but each moment he wasn't plagued by his ex was a blessing and one bestowed upon him more frequently the longer he spent basking in the glow of Aelissm's halo. She caught his gaze through the window. Her lips quirked upward and she made a gesture telling him they needed to talk. His heart sank, then fluttered skyward again when mischief flickered like green fire in her eyes. He laughed.

The trio trooped through the back door still laughing, and Pat asked what was so funny.

"Old times," June replied. "We were talking about our Thursday night card parties back in college. We were playing a game called peanuts—it's sort of like group solitaire—when a friend of ours jumped up on the table in the middle of a particularly frantic game and shouted, 'No one expects a Spanish inquisition!' He scared the crap out of my poor roommate."

Aelissm went over to the stove, where dinner was nearly ready. "I'm impressed, Pat. You actually managed to make spaghetti without burning anything."

Pat rolled his eyes. "I know how to cook, Aeli, even if the sauce is out of a jar. You had a phone call." He hesitated, not wanting to ruin the jovial mood. "Adam Winters."

Aelissm turned on her heel to face him, and her body stiffened. "Adam called?"

Pat nodded. "I took notes."

He watched her walk into the other room with jarring strides. No one said anything while she read what he'd written.

"He's in Devyn," she said at last.

Her voice was icy, but it didn't waver. Pat lifted his brows in surprise. She wasn't afraid. She was angry.

"That son of a bitch is in Devyn!"

June strode into the living room and hugged her friend. Rage vibrated through Aelissm—Pat could see that even from a distance—but fear returned quickly, and her face paled. June murmured something Pat couldn't hear, and Aelissm's blindly staring eyes finally met her friend's.

"I know, June. But dammit, he keeps doing this to me."

"Maybe it'll be over soon," June said hopefully, glancing at Pat.

He nodded, wondering what he should do but understood that he'd do just about anything to keep her safe and free from fear.

Aelissm's blond head bobbed in affirmation. She and June came back to the kitchen and sat down at the table, across from each other. Luke set the table for dinner before taking his seat by the window, and when Aelissm ruffled his hair, he didn't try to duck away, sensing that she needed that gesture of normalcy.

"You're a good kid, Luke," she murmured, "and I'm so glad you're here."

Luke beamed, and Pat exhaled slowly, letting the tension slip away for the time being as he served dinner. They ate quietly, too hungry to talk much. Toward the end of the meal, June asked Pat if he thought he'd gotten any good pictures on the hike.

"I think I took quite a few, actually," he replied. "It's so incredible here. You have no idea."

June smiled indulgently. "Actually, we do."

He laughed at himself. "Of course *you* do. I threw that out more as a generalization. I'd tell the world what they were missing, but I don't want the world to come here and ruin it."

"You hear that, Aeli? He's barely been here a month, and already he's talking like a native! Voice those opinions around any of the rest of the locals, and they might just make you mayor."

"Except that I'm one of those outsiders."

"No, you're not," Aelissm said gently. "Everyone loves you."

He didn't know why, but hearing it made him feel valued and wanted, and the shine of pride in Aelissm's eyes brought him to the gates of heaven. When he'd left Bill's that evening in late March, he wouldn't have believed that coming to Northstar might be the best thing to ever happen to him.

"You're happy here, aren't you?" Aelissm asked with a surprising shyness.

"Believe me this time, at least, when I say you have no idea."

What was happening between them? And could he keep this up until he knew what it was without hurting her? He turned away from her, stood, and started gathering the dishes. June jumped up and took the plates from him.

"Oh, no you don't. You cooked. Luke and I will do dishes," she offered. "Why don't you two pick out a movie, and we'll take it over to my place to watch?"

"I like the sound of that," Pat replied. "Any preferences, Aeli?"

"Nope, you pick it."

They walked into the living room and picked the movie together, deciding on a few episodes of a British sci-fi comedy. Pat excused himself and went upstairs to retrieve his lightweight jacket. Even though each day was warmer than the last, he'd been here long enough to know the nights still frequently brought frost. He was about to head back down when he caught sight of his holstered gun peeking from beneath his pillow. Adam Winters was in Devyn, he thought resentfully. Thus far, his trip to Northstar had been a marvelous vacation, but he was here for another reason, too, and with Adam so close to Aelissm, it might be time to start focusing on that reason. Selfishly, he didn't want to think about it let alone actively find a way to resolve it because that would be the end of his time in Montana.

But you're going to do it because Aeli is the reason you feel this good again, he told himself as he headed back downstairs. *You owe her.*

Minutes later, June and Luke were done washing dishes and ready to head back over to June's cabin. Aelissm grabbed her two spotting lights and her coat before they stepped outside. The four of them made the trek to June's as sunset burned across the sky. Pat paused to admire how the light from the sky colored the land with a warm peach glow and rekindled tranquility in his heart.

Aelissm put the movie on and plopped on the couch beside Pat to wait while June and Luke vanished upstairs to change into their pajamas. June's couch and love seat were perpendicular to each other and gave the open living room a sense of being its own room. There was a lively fire in the wood stove, and Pat was more inclined to watch that or the incredible view out the big front windows than the television on the table below the side window. From the corner of his eye, he noticed something he hadn't before. Across the room on the wall above June's log desk was a poster-sized photograph of a lake—Sawtooth he guessed by the mountain in the background, which distinctly resembled the teeth of a handsaw. The frame's design so closely matched the filing tiers in Bill's office that he knew it was one of Aelissm's creations.

"When did you make that?" he asked Aelissm.

"Over the past few weeks during class."

"It's beautiful. And it fits well in June's cabin."

Aelissm glanced around and remarked, "It's fancier than mine."

"Maybe, but I like your cabin," Pat replied. "It's very cozy."

"Mmm. Thanks. I'll tell my dad you said so." She frowned. "I hate to bring it up right now, Pat, but we need to talk about something. I think I deserve to know some of what happened between you and Sara because I've—"

"Yes, you do, and you have." Pat beckoned her closer, and she scooted over without hesitation. She tucked herself into his side and rested her head on his shoulder. He stroked a hand across her back.

"We'll talk about as much as I can tonight, when we get home. Is that soon enough?"

"It's going to have to be," she replied.

"I'm going to need all the time I can get to work up my courage."

"Courage? I'm not that mean, Pat."

"You're not mean at all, sweetheart, but my demons are."

Nine

"HERE YOU GO, BRANDON."

Adam glanced up at the cute, brown-haired bartender. With a wink, she slid the frosty bottle of Moose Drool across the bar at him, and he caught it deftly. He took a sip and let the liquid swirl through his mouth. Damn, it was good. It looked like he'd be staying in Devyn for a while yet, so at least he had a decent beer to help him pass the time. *And a sexy bartender*, he added, raking his eyes appreciatively over the young woman.

"Thanks, Amber."

"Sure thing, babe."

She moved off to tend another patron, hips swaying sassily. Aelissm may have been the woman he compared every other to, but that didn't mean he couldn't appreciate a fine specimen like Amber. It wasn't only her physical attributes that he found so appealing—though those would make any man pause to admire her. She had an infectious, outgoing personality and a way of smiling at him that made him believe he was something special and desirable. Initially, he'd been determined to ignore her advances and his attraction, but she was in Aelissm's class at the college. He hadn't learned much about Aelissm from her, but he enjoyed hearing Amber talk about her. It made his wait somehow less tedious. Amber seemed to think Aeli was one of the best, most knowledgeable teachers she'd ever had, and Adam knew it wasn't just because Amber and Aelissm were two of only a handful of women in such a masculine profession; he remembered well how talented Aelissm was.

Unbidden, his mind raced back to the phone call he'd made to Aelissm's cabin just a few minutes ago. His fingers tightened in a white-knuckled grip around the bottle. Where had he heard that name? Pat O'Neil. It taunted him, flirting with recollection. Was he a member of Aelissm's family? No, she wasn't related to any O'Neils, even by marriage. Adam scowled when another memory crossed his mind. He'd be willing to bet that the man on the phone was the same he'd seen Aeli dancing with at that potluck a while back—the tall, too-good-looking interloper. He wouldn't be surprised, either, if this Pat O'Neil was also the man that tourist had griped about.

Adam knew he'd gotten lucky when the waitress had asked him to take the order out to the customer, something he usually avoided. The prissily dressed jerk had been in a foul mood, Adam recalled, going off about "Goddamned stuck-up Montanans." The guy had grabbed Adam by the arm and proceeded to say exactly why he thought that, describing Aelissm, June, that waif of a boy, and a big man with indignation.

"I was just trying to find out if either of those women were available—because, *damn*, they were sexy—but he reacted like a rabid dog, pushed me back against the wall, and I thought he was going to punch me. I guess he *was* more than 'good friends' with at least one of them, but he was too much of a dick to come out and say it." The man had leaned back in the booth and knitted his hands together behind his head. "They sure do know how to make them around here."

The guy's tale rang with the undertone of a bruised ego, and it had made Adam sick, not only listening to him describe Aeli as a "hot piece of ass" but to hear that she seemed to have found herself a man—this Pat O'Neil. Patrick, no doubt. Patrick O'Neil…. Where had he heard that name? Frustration gnawed at him, churning in his stomach like a bad meal and pinching his neck and shoulders with agonized tension. He couldn't recall hearing it since he'd been in Montana, so that left Washington. Seattle? Or Kitsap County? And how would the man know who he was talking to?

Call it a hunch.

It was like a spotlight had clicked on in his mind. Detective Patrick O'Neil of the Kitsap County Sheriff's Department. Bill Granger's prodigy. And, if he remembered correctly, Patrick O'Neil was a man with a past.

"Son of a bitch!" Adam snarled.

"What's that, sugar?" Amber asked, sidling over.

He forced a smile and fought to find a convincing lie to cover his outburst. All he came up with was, "I've just remembered something."

"Sounded like a big deal," she remarked.

"It could be. I don't know yet. Hey, do you think Dora would give me a few days off? I'm going to need to go back to Washington for a bit to take care of some unfinished business I forgot about."

"I dunno. Maybe. She'll be in early tomorrow to do some bookkeeping. No harm in asking, right?"

"Right."

"Hey, are you going to invite me over tonight?"

The corner of Adam's mouth quirked upward. "You get off at midnight, right?"

"I certainly hope so," she replied with a playful gleam in her lustrous brown eyes. "But I'm thinking it might take longer than that. Maybe all night."

His smile turned into a broad grin of anticipation. Amber blew him a kiss over her shoulder as she sauntered away again to help another customer. She *was* a delectable thing, shorter than Aelissm and curvier, and she knew how to make him forget everything but her. Amber made him feel witty and attractive. When he was with her, he was the man he'd been before Aelissm, the man who could stand on his own without the thought of *her* to keep him steady.

"Amber, you should know better than to tease the poor boy."

"Oh, hi, JP," Amber called to the new arrival. "And it's only *teasing* if I don't follow through."

Adam swung around on his stool as JP took the empty one beside him. Like Adam, there was nothing particularly memorable about him. He had medium brown hair, brown eyes, a slender but wiry build, and was somewhere from mid-twenties to mid-thirties with a face that was pleasant enough but not so good looking that he would stand out. However, there was something about JP that Adam would never forget, an air of authority coupled with a sense of incongruity. It was that *something* that had first made Adam hesitant to even speak to the man. Oddly enough, though, he'd told JP more about his real reason for being in Montana than he'd told anyone. Anywhere. He'd first met the man that same day that tourist had gone off about Patrick O'Neil. JP had been eating at a table nearby, shaking his head and chuckling.

"Some people are just too pathetic to admit to their shortcomings and blame their failures on everything but their own inabilities," he'd remarked, deeply offending the man. "Go home and take your sob story with you. Come back when you've grown a pair."

Adam had shared a few evenings with JP in conversation over a bottle or ten of beer, and one night about two weeks ago, he'd let it slip that he was here looking for a woman. JP had clapped him on the back and remarked that Adam, at least, wasn't scared to fight for what was his. He knew somewhere in the back of his brain that he should probably be wary of JP, but he couldn't seem to stop talking when they got together in the bar here at the roach motel.

"So, Brandon, any luck finding your girl yet?" JP asked. His voice was quiet so Amber wouldn't overhear.

"Some. I'm still missing one crucial piece of information."

"You don't know where she lives. That puts a bit of a bind on things, don't it? Have you decided how you're going to handle her when you find her?"

"Not really, no."

"Well, whatever you do, you gotta make sure she knows she's yours. No more of this runnin' around bullshit. You've gotta teach her that you're her master, make her pay for all the pain she's caused you."

Adam frowned. That feeling of something being not quite right about his companion danced across his awareness. The way JP slipped from educated eloquence to a relaxed drawl was disconcerting at best, and instinct warned Adam to be cautious. He brushed it aside.

"I know your girl."

"How? I haven't ever told you her name."

"No, but I know her. Reddish-blonde hair, eyes the color of a hayfield in spring. Talented crafter. Aelissm Davis. No one else around here quite like her. Or her friend June. No, they're genuine prizes."

Alarms sounded sluggishly in his mind, muffled by the six beers he'd had. He should walk away right now. There was again that indefinable *something* in the man's voice, a fascination that ran deeper than Adam's predicament. JP's remarks were seated in a personal interest in either Aelissm or June Montana, so it was no wonder Adam had found it so hard to resist chatting with him, but the undercurrent of camaraderie between them made JP all the more risky.

"If I were of a mind for revenge," JP was saying. Adam had the feeling he was talking more to himself. "I'd want to make sure she got the message. Oh, I'd never hurt her physically. No, she's too dear to me for that, and it's not her fault, anyhow. She only did what she thought she had to. For *him*."

Adam frowned in confusion, his buzz fading with

each word his companion uttered. Was he talking about Aelissm or June? Or someone else entirely?

"He deserves to be punished for it." Suddenly, JP's intense brown eyes turned on Adam, seeing him again. "Are you listening to me? You've got to make her understand what she's done to you. You have to make her *pay*."

"And how would I do that?" Adam asked cautiously.

"Use your imagination. You've already tried to tell her directly, I'm sure—letters, phone calls, and the like. Maybe it's time you got a little more… decisive."

Adam doubted he wanted to know anything about JP's idea of "decisive."

"What are you boys whispering about over here?" Amber asked, striding over and mercifully interrupting their disturbing conversation.

"Nothin' important, sweetheart. How 'bout you grab me a Moose Drool? And another for my friend, here."

"Sure thing."

There it was again, Adam thought, intently studying JP's face. The drawl was back, thicker than before. And, with it, the smiling eyes with squint-lines gathered at their corners. The more time Adam spent with him, the more he believed there might be two distinct sides to JP. One was the friendly, harmless ranch hand, and the other was a cold, calculating, and sharply intelligent predator. Still… despite the possible dangers, the man was useful, and if he really did know where Aelissm lived, Adam might be able to finally catch her and claim her.

Amber brought their beers and stayed to chat for a few minutes. Adam was grateful for her presence. As long as she was around, JP couldn't drag him into conversation about things he never should have mentioned to the man in the first place. If it came to it and his patience wore down to nothing, he'd ask for JP's help, but until then, he'd manage on his own like he had since Brent's death.

"Thanks for the beer, JP," Adam said, "but I think I'm going to call it a night. I don't want to be a disappointment."

"I do hate being disappointed," Amber remarked. "See you in a little while?"

He nodded and slid off his bar stool. JP didn't move to stop him, suddenly uninterested in either Adam or Amber. Adam barely swallowed his relief. He left Amber a generous tip and sauntered out the door, resolutely forgetting about JP's oddities and thinking instead of what he'd realized tonight. Dread was swiftly replaced by glee.

Hot damn, things might start looking up again, he thought as he walked through the back gate of the motel complex and down the alley to his rented house.

The place wasn't much—a single room with a separate bathroom off to one side and an old double bed taking up the majority of the floor space in the main room. For two hundred bucks a month, he couldn't complain, and it wasn't like he spent much time in it. Besides, the landlord kept his nose out of Adam's business and didn't ask questions.

When he opened the door, he did a quick scan to make sure everything was exactly how he'd left it. Satisfied, he grabbed his duffel bag and started stuffing his clothes into it. He'd get everything ready tonight so he could take off tomorrow after he'd finished his shift. He had the next two days off, and it shouldn't be too hard to trade a couple shifts with the other cooks to extend his weekend.

He paused in his packing and straightened. Annoyance shimmered through him at the thought of his job. His mother would have been ashamed of him for wasting his talents and his culinary degree cooking at the roach motel, and it certainly wasn't the career he'd envisioned for himself, but he needed Aelissm more than his dream, and to get her, right now he also needed the anonymity the roach motel provided. Few other places were willing to pay under the table or hire someone with as little information as he felt he could safely provide.

As the hopes he'd once had for his life paraded through his mind, he growled. He didn't have much patience left for Aelissm's games. She'd dragged him all the way out here to the back end of Montana—though, admittedly, he shouldn't have been surprised she'd run here, considering how she'd always droned on about this place. He was done playing, he vowed for the hundredth time that week. Now that he knew who Aeli's new fling was, he wasn't going to waste time with scare tactics that wouldn't work anyhow. Pat O'Neil was a sheriff's deputy, probably sent out here by Aelissm's overprotective uncle, so chasing him off wasn't going to be easy, but Adam had an ace up his sleeve.

Sara Montgomery.

What a vicious little bitch she *is*, Adam thought with a shudder.

He knew her through Brent—Sara and Brent's older sister, Jeanette, had been sickeningly close, and he'd gotten to know Sara well because she always seemed to be over at the Ellington's Lake Washington house. *Mansion*, Adam corrected with a snort and wondered what had convinced Sara to lower her standards so far to date a cop. From the first day she'd recognized boys as something other than disgusting, she'd turned her nose up at any would-be suitor worth less than a million in trust funds or toyed with them in the same way that bored house cats toyed with birds. Adam shivered. *Poor bastard.*

He tried to remember what he'd heard in the bar the night he'd been tailing Aeli's uncle about ten months ago. The two of them, O'Neil and Granger, had sat hunched over the booth's table, nursing their beers and ignoring their plate of hot wings. As he recalled, Bill had been trying to convince his underling to take a "well-needed" vacation. They'd talked about Sara for a while, then moved on to something else. Adam had been bored out of his mind and was about to leave when Aelissm's name had dropped into the conversation. Other than a hint about what a nice girl Aeli was, Bill hadn't said anything else about her. So he'd left and given the matter little thought since.

It was strange how something he'd deemed unimportant then had suddenly landed front and center in his brain. At the time, he hadn't bothered contemplating Patrick O'Neil's demeanor when discussing his ex-girlfriend. Now, the little gestures—the grimaces, the flinches, and the darting glances—were branded in his mind's eye. Adam doubted there was anything Patrick O'Neil hated or feared more than Sara Montgomery, and it probably wouldn't take long to scare him back to Washington and back to working himself to death if that socialite bitch came sniffing after him.

"But why would she even care?" Adam wondered.

He'd gotten the impression that Pat had been the one to end it, so maybe he could appeal to Sara's pride. Wringing his hands as he paced, Adam hoped her malicious ego would find vengeance for the insult of being dumped more appealing than seizing the opportunity to take her vengeance on the man who'd killed her best friend's brother. Adam clenched his jaw. As much as it hurt him to admit it, he *had* killed Brent—accidentally, yes, but Brent was dead because of what Adam had done.

Dora had to give him the time off. If she didn't, he'd quit on the spot. He had to get rid of the cop because he couldn't compete with him, and losing Aelissm was not an option. She was his everything, the rope that tied him to the man he wished he could be again, and the only person who knew he'd ever been that man. He needed her to help him find his way back out of this nightmare because he wasn't strong enough to do it on his own.

He jumped when a knock boomed on his door, and his heart hammered against his ribs. It was far too early for it to be Amber. Shaking loose from the lingering nerves, he peered through the peephole to see his boss standing on the other side of the wooden barrier. He opened the door but didn't step back to invite her in.

"Amber told me you wanted some time off," Dora said by way of greeting. "Said you seemed a little edgy."

"Yeah. I have some business I need to take care of in Seattle."

"I see. And how many days do you need to get it taken care of?"

"Four. Maybe five."

Dora lifted her penciled gray eyebrows. "Take five,

then, but if you're not back for your shift after, you can find yourself a new job. I like you, Brandon, but I got a restaurant to run."

"I understand."

The cranky old woman turned and walked away without saying anything more on the subject. Adam took a brief moment to wonder if that heavily painted, wrinkled face ever did anything but scowl. He couldn't see why it would ever have reason to lift in a smile; the motel's owner was an insufferable dick, her husband had left her for a twenty-five-year-old, and her only daughter had recently affirmed that she never wanted to see her mother again. Was Dora a miserable old hag because her life was crappy or was her life crappy because she was a miserable old hag?

Karma, Adam thought. Karma was why he couldn't hurt Patrick O'Neil, no matter how much he might want to. Truth be told, he didn't want to hurt him; he just wanted him out of the way. Grief balled into a lump in his throat. He hadn't wanted to hurt Brent, either, but his best friend had ended up dead. He was tired of pain, but would it ever go away? Yes, if he had Aelissm to remind him that he was still a good person.

He kicked the door closed and regretted it immediately when pain stabbed in his toes. He had to convince Sara to get past whatever dislike she felt for him and help him chase O'Neil off.

Why had he let JP buy him that last beer? And why had he agreed to let Amber come over? He could have been pulling out of town by now, but he couldn't take the chance of one of these Wyatt Earp cops getting a bug up his ass and pulling him over on a whim. So, he'd let Amber's creativity distract him for a couple of hours, sleep off the alcohol, and start out before sunrise.

You'll be mine, soon, Aeli, he thought as he flopped back on his bed to wait for Amber.

When another knock sounded on his door two hours later, he was expecting it and got up to answer it, smiling. Anticipation hummed through him as he pulled open the door and saw Amber standing on the other side.

"Hi," she said shyly and stepped past him into his tiny house. "I brought you something."

She handed him something thin, rectangular, and heavy wrapped rather creatively in a brown paper grocery bag tied with raffia. Adam carefully unwrapped the item, which turned out to be a wrought-iron picture frame. Considering the cold, hard metal, it was surprisingly delicate in design.

"I finally finished something I could show you."

"It's beautiful," he told her. "Even empty. I'll bet your professor was proud."

"She was. I brought my camera. I know you say you hate having your picture taken, but you need something to personalize this place… and I'm hoping a picture of us could be the first thing."

The lonely existence he'd led this past year made her request sound strange. She wanted him to have something to make his bare rental feel a little like home, and she wanted to be a part of that. More willingly than he would have thought possible, he indulged her as she took photograph after photograph of them together. A spark of his old self— a desire to turn the photo-session goofy—flickered.

"Okay, enough," he said at last. "It's getting late, and

I need to get an early start tomorrow."

"Damn. I was hoping I could keep you up for a while tonight."

He shivered as she slid her hands under his T-shirt and peeled it over his head.

"You know," she said huskily, "you have a pretty nice body for someone who claims he doesn't work out anymore."

"It used to be better, but it's been...." His voice snagged in his throat, and he swallowed. "It's been a rough year."

"Is it getting any better yet?" she inquired, leaving a trail of kisses from his mouth to his shoulder.

"It's definitely starting to."

Amber paused in her pursuit long enough to set the picture frame on the dresser, and Adam couldn't help but think that she was every bit as talented as Aelissm. With a growl, he pushed the thought of her from his mind for the time being. Why should he let Aelissm intrude when he had an energetic and willing woman doing everything she could to distract him?

Within minutes, he wasn't thinking about Aeli. He wasn't *thinking* at all. Amber did that to him. Later, when only the soft, sweet fragrance of her remained to remind him of her, he wondered at that. *Nothing* since he'd met Aelissm Davis could make him forget her so completely.

Ten

THE MOMENT PAT HAD been dreading arrived. The credits of the show scrolled up the screen of June's television, and Aeli detached herself from his side to put the disc back in its case. The comfort of having snuggled with her on the couch—there was no point in trying to convince himself they *hadn't* been snuggling—for the better part of two hours distracted him pleasantly for a moment, and he was too amused to question the strengthening bond between them.

A bond that meant he now owed her an explanation about Sara.

Why was it so hard for him to find the courage to tell her about that time in hell? Was he afraid of his own memories or worried that voicing them would bring Sara shrieking back into his life? Or was he simply embarrassed that he'd fallen into Sara's trap? Whatever the reason, he was a coward for not telling Aelissm. She'd been brave enough to bare all about Brent and Adam, and she seemed to be the better for it, so why couldn't he own up to the fact that he'd made a horrible mistake and get on with his life?

"You're at the Ramshorn tomorrow, right?" Aelissm was asking June.

"Yep. All day."

"Mmm. I guess Pat and I are on our own, then."

"I'm sure you'll find something to do," June said as she stood to walk them to the back door.

Luke said a quick goodnight before trotting up the stairs to bed, and Pat shook his head. Oh, to be so young and full of life and energy, to be able to look at life for its promise despite its nightmares. To have hope.

"If we see you, we see you. If not, well, there's always another day. It's not like we don't know where you live," Aelissm said. She planted her hands on Pat's back and pushed him out the door. "Time to go home, Mr. O'Neil."

June's laughter followed them as they started the trek back to Aeli's cabin. Pat recalled his first journey over that stretch of land. It had been daylight then but no less treacherous because of the snow that had blanketed the ground. Now, tender shoots of alpine grass and ankle-high mountain huckleberries blanketed the steep terrain, vividly green in the unnatural beam of his flashlight.

"So, first thing's first," Aelissm said, eerily illuminated in the dark night. "That scar under your collarbone."

Panic clawed at him. They hadn't even reached the welcoming warmth and light of her cabin yet, and in the dark there were too many shadows for his memories to attack from. He took a deep, calming breath and noted that it did nothing to slow his racing pulse, but when he glanced skyward, the flood of stars invited him to let go. There were so many of them, winking and pulsating with cool, brilliant light. Maybe it was better this way. When Aelissm took his hand and gave it a reassuring squeeze, he knew it was.

"Sara stabbed me when I told her I was done with her," Pat said slowly. "With a paring knife from my own kitchen."

If he had thought saying that one thing aloud would help the rest flow out of him, he was sorely disappointed. There was no easing of the tension, no relief at all. If anything, saying it only made beginning more difficult. The old pain flared, hot then frigid, and he shivered. Aelissm must have felt it, because she gripped his hand more tightly. He used the contact with her to focus his thoughts.

"I don't think Sara had ever been left before, but I'd finally realized what she was, and I got out before it was too late."

"What do you mean, 'too late'?"

They'd finally reached her cabin, but instead of going inside, Aelissm sat down on her back porch and clicked her spotlight off. Pat followed her example and plunged them into star-bathed darkness. For a moment, he simply took in the sights, scents and sounds of the embracing mountain night. A cool breeze sighed encouragement, bringing with it a waft of pure, pine-scented air. The promise of home was everywhere around him, offering him security and freedom from his bitter past. Someday, if he stayed here, he really would be free, the wind told him. Open up and let go.

"If I had stayed with her much longer," he began

again, "she would have destroyed me. As it is, I'm not sure I'll ever fully recover from her."

Aelissm curled around him, and the simple offer of support brought fiery tears of shame to his eyes. After so stupidly wasting so much time on a heartless, beautiful snake, he didn't deserve Aelissm, but he selfishly indulged himself with her warmth and friendship and ignored the surge of self-loathing. Part of him argued that after all he'd been through, it was time he had something good, and Aelissm Davis was better than good. She was an honest-to-God guardian angel. He could pour his heart out to her and she would listen without judging, offering words and gestures of comfort that were heartfelt and selfless.

"That last weekend was the worst. I suppose after all the verbal and physical torture she put me through, I should have guessed how she would react."

"She was abusive?" Aelissm asked, surprise shadowing her voice.

Surprise, he noted. Not disbelief.

"I thought there must be something about her to make someone like you call her a bitch. You don't strike me as the kind of man who freely passes out insults."

"I'm not," Pat agreed. "But she deserves the term. I suppose part of me is embarrassed that I let her push me around like that."

"Literally or figuratively?"

"Both."

Aelissm sat up. "Let me guess. She's pint-sized, too. Five-foot-two and eighty pounds fully dressed."

Somehow, Pat found the breath to chuckle. "Five-one and eighty-five pounds. How'd you guess?"

"Little woman syndrome," Aelissm explained. "She has an arrogance problem and is always degrading others because, secretly, she knows she's pathetic."

To hear her describe Sara so succinctly in that sarcastic, analytical tone made Pat chuckle a little harder. At last, some of the bitterness and tension began to slip away. Aeli was the best medicine for him right now; no one else could have made him laugh when Sara was on his mind.

"That sounds about right. The perfect wrapping hid the broken ornament inside, and I'm not proud of it, but I was so blinded by awe that I can't pinpoint when those playful shoves and slaps turned mean. She liked to play rough, and it always made me nervous, but I went along with it. I used to think it was lust that kept me going back for more after she asked me out on that first date, but it was more youthful ignorance and gratitude that someone like her would think I was good enough for her. She damaged me pretty thoroughly, made me believe things about myself that aren't true, and made me believe I wasn't worthy of her." Pat let out a ragged sigh.

"Did you and she ever talk about getting married?"

"We were engaged because I was stupid enough to propose a year after we started dating. I was stunned when she said yes, but she pushed off setting a date, and I began to see that I would never live up to her expectations."

"I can't imagine any expectations you couldn't meet, Pat, except being a billionaire, and if that's all she wants, she's an idiot."

"She is most definitely *not* an idiot, Aeli. She graduated with top honors from Stanford and is the most chillingly intelligent person I've met."

"She's a sadist with an incredible talent for understanding how to manipulate you, and she's doing it right now. Listen to you defending her as if she's worthy of it. Do you still love her?"

He shook his head vehemently, then took a deep breath, and chose his words carefully. "I'm wiser now, and I understand that I didn't love her, so it's not like I'll never stop. I couldn't love her because there is nothing about her that's lovable."

"Now I'm absolutely sure of it."

"Sure of what?"

"That if you couldn't meet her expectations, she set the wrong ones."

It was unsettling, to have someone like Aelissm tell him that there was nothing he couldn't do, and it went a long way toward rebuilding his confidence.

"What made you finally leave?"

"I was on a case, talking with a witness at my favorite diner on a Friday night. She was a sweet woman, about my age, almost as beautiful as you. One of Sara's friends saw me with the woman and called Sara. She stewed outside for an hour before she came in."

Pat swallowed hard. So much for getting easier. The memory was all he could see; every detail was portrayed like a drive-in movie in perfect, painful clarity. The harsh glow of the diner's fluorescent lights heightened the scowl of jealous hatred snapping in Sara's gold-brown eyes. He could still see the nervous, darting gaze of the witness and was reminded of a caged animal looking to escape. Three years removed, the gunshot clacks of Sara's stiletto heels on the checkered linoleum still made him flinch. Several diners had turned to watch the goings-on, and even now, Pat's neck and cheeks flushed and nausea boiled in his stomach.

He described the scene for Aelissm, told her how Sara had confronted both him and the witness, looking down on them the entire time.

"Who the hell is she?"

"A friend of a friend."

"You're cheating on me?"

"Can we take this outside please? Michelle, we'll have to finish this another time."

"Over my dead body. I'd better not catch you near my man again, tramp."

"The poor witness was so horrified that she ran out of the diner. I was lucky she was willing to talk with me again a few weeks later when I came back to work. To make a long story short, Sara accused me of cheating on her. I got the impression that she'd been having her friends follow me when I wasn't with her, trying to catch me at something I wasn't supposed to be doing. That I couldn't tell her who the woman was because of the case only made matters worse."

"What a psycho," Aeli muttered.

"That night outside the diner, Sara was incapable of listening to what I was saying, like she *wanted* to believe I was cheating on her. I shouldn't have been surprised. She never took me for who I am, so why would she believe that I'd never cheat on anyone? Even if she did, accusing me of being unfaithful was just another square on the board, something that moved her ahead in a game she and her friends played. It was a game to them, and I just didn't understand the rules."

"I've never heard of anything so cold."

His emotions were so close to the surface, a raging torrent of disgust, trepidation, and worthlessness that eroded his fragile self-confidence. He didn't know if he would ever comprehend how one human could so utterly degrade someone they were supposed to love. Aelissm tightened her arms around him, and he felt so brittle that he thought he might shatter in her embrace.

"I guess the way she'd treated my witness got through to me, because I yelled right back at her. I mostly held my temper in check, but I did call her a lying whore and a heartless bitch. She was shocked."

"Did she ever cheat on you?"

"Twice that I know of. The second affair ended right before I left, but I'm not sure it played much of a role in my decision. It was the look on that witness's face—she was scared of Sara. She was a victim of assault, but she still found room to pity me. The man who attacked her was a stranger. I set myself up to get hurt, and to see that accusation in her eyes…. It was an uncomfortable thing for me to face."

"I can imagine it was. Does it bother you that Sara was unfaithful?"

"Then? A little. Probably not as much as it should have. Now I see that it probably bothered me *more* than it should have. It was never a sense of possession that I felt. Sara never belonged to me; I always knew that, even from our first date. What really bothered me—and still does—is that she thought so little of me. But she was pretty good at making me feel worthless. Especially in bed. It got to the point that I couldn't perform at all."

"Has there been anyone since her?"

"No."

Aelissm said nothing else, only rested her head on his shoulder. He kissed the top of her head, pausing to inhale the gentle fragrance of her shampoo and the smell of this wild land that clung to her. It was only honest to say that he'd never once had a moment like this with Sara. If he'd had something similar with anyone before her, he could no longer recall. There was nothing before her, and nothing since.

Until he'd walked into the Bedspread Inn and seen Aelissm indulgently flirting with two old ranchers. The memory made him smile, and resting his cheek on the top of Aeli's head, he closed his eyes, allowing the touch of her body against his to protect him.

"That night at the diner was the beginning of the end for me. By Sunday afternoon, I was free of her. A little worse for wear, but free."

"A little worse for wear? Pat, she stabbed you!"

He absently reached for the scar, forced his hand away. "On her third attempt, yes, she did. I've got a few other marks from that weekend, but that's the worst. Some days, I know I was within my right to defend myself, but I was afraid to hurt her."

"Even though she hurt you. How bad was it, Pat?"

"Getting stabbed hurts like hell, but that wasn't the worst." He clenched his jaw, and it took almost a full minute to gather the courage to say, "I hit her when she stabbed me, and even though I know I had every right to do it, I hate myself for it. I hate that she made me do it because I'm not like that, Aelissm. I'm not."

"I know, honey." She put her hand on his chest, over his racing heart.

"I hate what she made me." He took another deep breath, trying to rein in his wild thoughts. "Bill made me take three weeks off to heal after I got out of the hospital. He wanted me to take four, but work was what kept me sane. Maybe 'sane' isn't the best word, but I couldn't stay in my house staring at the walls any longer. During those three weeks, I threw out nearly everything I owned. There's not much in my house now, only the old couch Bill gave me from his basement, some new mattresses, a TV stand, a little table by the door, and the kitchen table and chairs. I have a dresser, too, the pictures of my family, and a few books. That's it. I could fit everything I own in the back of my truck. I had to remove everything that reminded me of her. I almost moved out, but Bill convinced me otherwise. Staying there is the only thing I've done to make a stand against her since that weekend. God, we made a mess. Most of my dishes were broken, and I spent most of my time off repairing the holes in the walls. Why did I let her turn me into that? I look back, and I don't recognize myself as I was that weekend."

He paused for a moment. "I haven't told my parents or Grandpa Antony the whole story. I don't want them to know what I became that weekend."

"You don't talk about your family much," Aeli murmured, "but when you talked about them when you first got here, I had the feeling you were close to them."

"I was, before I met Sara. Most of that last year I was with Sara, I didn't talk to them. I really let them down, and in the hospital that day, my mother told me how badly I'd hurt her. She won't say it, but I think she's still terrified that she could have lost her son without the chance to make things right between us." His throat constricted, and he had to stop for a moment. "There's still a lot of bitterness there, more on my end than theirs, I think. They've forgiven me for what happened, but I haven't yet forgiven myself."

Silence fell between them, and Pat didn't know what else to say. There didn't seem to be any more explanations to help him re-brick the walls that had crumbled as he'd laid his tragic story out for her. He'd never cried about it because he'd never seen the point, but now he did. The only emotions he'd felt then and since were fear and hatred. Now he felt sorrow for what he'd let Sara do to him. No, Aeli would argue, not what he'd *let* her do, what *she'd* done. The tears spilled down his face like liquid fire.

Through it all, Aelissm was there with her arms wrapped around him, supporting him with her understanding silence. Gradually, he cried his frustration out and exhausted himself, but it was a good weariness. He'd be too tired now to think. This wasn't the end of his torment, but right now, he was too drained to ponder what tomorrow would bring. Slowly, familiar numbness crept over him.

After what seemed like hours, Aelissm took his hand and stood. "Come inside, honey," she beckoned softly.

Lacking the ambition to do anything but obey, he let her help him to his feet. When they went inside, she stepped away from him only long enough to stoke the fire. She left the door open and warm firelight illuminated the kitchen, chasing the shadows from his heart. When Aelissm turned to face him, he saw the worry and compassion plainly on her soft, beautiful face.

"Sleep with me tonight, Pat."

"Aeli—"

She put a finger to his lips to silence his objection. "I said sleep, Pat. You shouldn't be alone."

"I don't think—"

"Let me hold you tonight." She slid against his body and tucked his arms around her. "To keep the nightmares at bay."

He knew he should refuse, but it was what he needed. The kiss she pressed to his lips was feather-light and encouraging. It lacked the fiery passion from earlier that afternoon but offered what he needed more: comfort. He tightened his arms around her and drew her deeper against him. His eyes slid closed as her mouth asked for just a little more, and he was stunned to find he could give it. As her hands slid up his sides to his ribs, allowing her to deepen the kiss, thrilled by the unexpected flare of desire. She was as gentle as Sara had been rough and claimed him more completely, but the emotions she evoked with her tender caresses were something he'd never felt before.

Adoration. Trust. Love.

"Come to bed with me, Pat."

She closed the door of the wood stove and lit the hurricane lantern sitting on the counter. It would have been easier to flip the light switch, but Pat was glad for the flame; he didn't think he could handle the harsh glare of electric light right now. He followed her up the stairs and took off his boots and socks. He started to go through the motions of changing for bed when he realized Aelissm hadn't closed her door to undress. Her back was to him, painted with golden light and deep shadow, and he stared, mesmerized by those silky lines of shoulder, back, hip, arm, and leg and by the cascade of shining gold hair and sinfully soft skin.

It was all he could do to avert his eyes when she stripped off her delicate, black satin and lace undergarments. His brain had ceased to function. He couldn't think to find his flannel pajama pants and wondered if that had been her intention. He certainly wasn't thinking about Sara—other than to realize that gym-toned bitch had nothing on Aelissm Davis—because there was no room in his mind; it was full of Aeli's gorgeous body caressed by lantern light.

"Having a little trouble in there, Pat?"

He raised his eyes from the floor to find her buttoning her flannel. Even in that loose shirt and boxer shorts, she was sexy.

"Here, let me help."

Again, she was so gentle that he could do nothing but give in to her. She carefully unbuttoned his shirt and peeled it down over his shoulders. It was an incredible thing to be the center of her attention, to be touched so delicately and with the same curiosity she might have shown an exquisite carving. After she'd pulled his plain white undershirt over his head and tossed it away, she hesitated. Her fingers danced across his bare skin, exploring the physical scars Sara had left and taking in the lines of him. He didn't flinch or pull away, not even when she stood on her toes to kiss his lips again. Not even when she kissed his neck and his chest.

"Shirt or no shirt?" she murmured. "I'd prefer bare skin."

He didn't answer. Couldn't.

She was tender when she unbuckled his belt and

pulled his jeans down. He obediently sat down on his bed, and she freed his legs from his pants, tossing them on top of the pile with the rest of his clothes. She dragged his pajama pants out of the dresser and handed them to him, then turned away so he could finish changing.

"Good enough?" she asked, her voice barely louder than a purr. When he said nothing, she turned to find him clad in his sleepwear. After pausing a moment longer to look him over and smile, she took his hand and led him into her bedroom. She directed him to the bed without any force, sensing, no doubt, that even a playful shove might break the peace she'd woven around him.

She cupped her hand over the chimney of the lantern and blew, plunging the room into darkness. Moments later, she slid into bed beside him. He fell easily into a healing sleep wrapped in her soothing embrace, and his last conscious thought was a silent prayer of thanks for this pure-hearted angel.

Eleven

AELISSM COULDN'T IMAGINE what Pat would feel like come morning. What had happened between her and Brent seemed like a playful disagreement compared to what Pat had endured. Brent had died that night, but somehow even that now seemed detached as though it had happened to someone else and she hadn't been struggling to free herself just hours before he had succumbed to death. Pat had been stabbed. He couldn't escape that memory like she could hers. She hadn't actually seen Brent die, and she hadn't been the one to find his body. The dark wanderings of her mind could be dismissed—though not easily—as being unproven scenarios. The thought of Pat having to relive that moment when the knife had pierced him, unable to hide behind the excuse of "well, maybe it didn't happen that way" made her shudder.

He seemed to be sleeping peacefully enough, she was

glad to note. His breathing was deep and steady, and he hadn't shifted in some while. Unconsciously, she curled a little closer around him, hoping that airing out his bad memories would help him like it had helped her. She knew, without a doubt, that talking about Brent and Adam with Pat had helped her take a step back and look at the whole situation from a new perspective. She'd barely been afraid last night when Pat told her Adam had called, even when she'd seen that he'd called from Devyn. She had reached the point, at last, that she could be angry about what Adam was doing to her. That was a good sign, wasn't it?

Pat would need some distraction tomorrow, she decided, and since it was apparent sleep had no plan to relieve her busy mind any time soon, she occupied herself by making plans for the day ahead. She wondered if Nick would be up for another day on horseback, then dismissed the idea at once. Pat probably wouldn't be up to company just yet, and she selfishly wanted him all to herself. He'd just cut his heart open for her, and she wasn't quite ready to give up the excuse to be close to him.

She was drawn to his vulnerability, and it was better than she'd fantasized to be lying beside this warm, wounded man with her arm around his waist and her knees tucked in behind his. That she wanted to do a lot more with him than *sleep* was a fact she could easily recognize in the dark with only her desire for conscious company.

"What am I going to do with myself when you leave, Pat?" she whispered with a sigh. She kissed his bare shoulder and shivered with a strong flood of possessiveness. "If only you could stay…."

Aelissm pushed the thought away, deciding that she'd

enjoy him—as much of him as he'd allow—while she could. If she was heading for a broken heart, she might as well have a little fun along the way. Live for the moment, right?

She could make him a nice breakfast to start the day off, and after that, they could sit out on the back porch for a while and talk some more. She could show him some of the roads and trails around the mountain, spend the afternoon riding the dirt bikes. Then, she'd finish the day off with a cozy dinner—stew, maybe, or a roast—light some candles and spend the rest of the evening curled up on the couch together or have June and Luke over to play cards. They still hadn't had a card night yet. If Pat was up to it, that might be a good idea. Relaxing morning, a good ride to work out any lingering aggression, and a night full of laughter struck her as the perfect combination to soothe Pat's tattered heart.

Appeal to his subconscious, a sly voice in the back of her mind purred. *Show him how nice staying could be.*

She snorted. Two months ago, worry about Adam finding her had been the forerunning thought in her mind, and now she was incapable of thinking about anything or anyone but Patrick O'Neil. A feline smile curved her lips. There were far worse things to be drowned by. She laid her cheek against his shoulder and closed her eyes. The touch of his skin, hot against hers, evoked carnal urges like she'd never felt.

The only thought that kept her from waking Pat and begging him to make love to her was concern for his state of mind. She'd just asked him to lacerate his emotions for her, and he'd done it willingly, so the least she could do was let him sleep in peace. He needed that sleep and the warmth and comfort of friendship she'd offered. That's why she'd offered it. Or, that was *mostly* why.

"If only sleep would be kind enough to take *me* away," she muttered, pointedly ignoring the little voice in her head that snickered about just wanting to be close to him. *Come on, is that really such a crime?* she asked herself. *Any woman who can call herself a woman would want to be close to him. He's got the sex appeal, no doubt about that. Plus, he's caring and patient. He's good with kids as far as I can tell, and who doesn't love a fixer-upper?*

Normally, she stayed away from fixer-uppers. In her experience, they tended to be more work than they worth, but Pat had everything else going for him in her book, and it wasn't just the qualities her heart had listed out for her that really appealed to her. The most dangerous attribute he had was one he had little control over; she was falling in love with him—honest-to-God, heart-pounding, snuggle-on-the-couch, grow-old-together love.

If she was willing to be perfectly honest with herself—and why the hell not, better late than never—she'd never loved Brent. She'd never been *that* attracted, and she certainly hadn't wanted his lifestyle. Deep down, she'd always wanted the life she'd grown up in—the boisterous family dinners, sitting down to a raucous game of cards or Trivial Pursuit after dessert, and finishing up the night gathered around the television to watch re-runs of their favorite BBC comedies. When she'd realized that teaching high school wasn't what she wanted, she'd decided to pursue her Master's and see where it led her. Why she'd chosen Seattle—to be closer to her family while she figured out what she wanted to do when she grew up—now seemed irresponsible because the fast-track life of the city conflicted with everything she was. Her relaxed Montana drawl had vanished, her quiet breakfast of cereal with the latest copy of the Smithsonian had been replaced by a hurried cup of coffee and a piece of toast, and those laughter-filled family evenings had faded into her past. Some nights, she hadn't come home to her apartment at all, spending them instead in the university's shop facilities.

Brent had come into her life like a parachute, slowing her plunge. He'd worked on her for weeks. Freaked by what was happening to her, she'd finally agreed to have dinner with him. He'd gotten her to slow down and take a step back. Looking back from her newly discovered vantage, she could see that she'd been in love with the change of pace not him.

When Brent died, the strings snapped. Whether or not the back-up chute would open and set her softly on the ground had been a toss up. Now, with Pat's help, her life was slowing to a comfortable pace, and all she had to do now was keep her feet when she landed.

Aelissm inhaled deeply, and her lungs were filled with the beautiful scent of the man in her arms. Her mind became hazy, leaving only her senses aware, and the worlds of thought and dreams blurred. She slipped pleasantly between fantasy and reality, from making love to Pat beneath a smiling moon to finding him tucked snuggly against her. When morning first lightened the star-studded sky, Aelissm briefly woke up lucid enough to wonder if she'd slept at all, then drifted off again, comforted by the inability to recall another nearly sleepless night she'd enjoyed as much or that had felt so perfectly and tantalizingly right.

The treetops were ablaze with golden sunlight by the time she awoke for the day. She stretched languidly, feeling quite like a lazy cat. Pat showed signs of stirring, so she propped herself up on her elbow, gazed down at him for a moment, then slid out of bed.

"Morning already?" he asked groggily.

"Already," she affirmed. "How are you?"

"Feeling like a train wreck, but I've been a lot worse. I'll get over it." He opened those kind hazel eyes and smiled at her. "Thank you."

"For dragging you through hell?"

"You didn't drag me anywhere I haven't been before, Aeli. Thank you for… a lot of things. For getting me to talk about it, for being there while I did. For being you."

"You've been supporting me since you've been here," she said. "The *very* least I can do in return is the same. Breakfast should be ready in twenty minutes or so."

She leaned down and kissed his cheek, then left without another word. The first thing she did after starting a fire in the stove to take the chill out of the cabin was brew coffee. Once that was done, she took out eggs and bread, thinking French toast would be nice. Before long, breakfast was well on its way.

Pat came downstairs, his hunter-green robe only loosely closed, and Aelissm poured him a cup of coffee. She added a little cream, just how she knew he liked it, and refused to let her gaze linger too long on the tempting bare skin peeking from the neck of the robe. He leaned against the counter, drinking his coffee as if this was an everyday ritual they'd had for years not weeks.

"So," Pat said. "What are we doing today?"

Aelissm looked up from the stove and took a moment to study him. He looked tired. That soul-deep exhaustion she'd seen in his eyes that first night by the wood stove in her grandparents' den had returned. Its reappearance made her realize just how relaxed Pat had become these past few weeks and drove home the truth of how much his ongoing battle with his memories hurt him. Aelissm couldn't locate a descriptive harsh enough for Sara. No man deserved to suffer like that, least of all one as sweet-tempered and generous as Pat. It made her furious, and right there in her kitchen, brandishing a spatula like a sword, Aeli vowed she would kill or horribly maim that vindictive, destructive whore if she ever dared to bother Pat again.

"I thought we'd hang out," she heard herself say. "Take it easy today."

Pat took another sip of his coffee and stared out the window. All those jokes about his age they tossed back and forth weren't so funny right now. Pat was only twenty-eight, but at the moment, he looked at least forty. Aelissm's heart sank as she reached the conclusion that staying with her all night hadn't helped him at all, no matter what he'd told her. How could she help him if she didn't know what he needed? Her friendship obviously hadn't been enough.

Stop being so selfish, she scolded herself as disappointment seeped into her blood. Aelissm squared her shoulders, defying self-centered emotions. "Think you might be up to riding the trails? I thought we could take the dirt bikes out on some of the old logging roads around here."

"Sounds like fun," he replied dispassionately.

"Only if you're up for it," she repeated a little more firmly.

"Is that a challenge, Ms. Davis?'

"It is. So, big boy, are you game or not?"

Just like that, he was twenty-eight again.

"You bet your cute ass."

Satisfied, Aelissm turned back to their breakfast. She expertly flipped the French toast with one hand and dunked another piece of bread in the egg with the other. As she cooked, she thought about her parents. Her mother was one of the best cooks she knew, specializing more in old-fashioned, home-cooked meals than worldly cuisine. Her father had worked in construction most of his life, but he had a talent for crafting that put Aelissm's to shame. From them, she'd received her greatest skills, and it pleased her to no end that she'd put it all to good use. She taught in her father's field, and her mother's culinary talents had made her work in the kitchen of the Bedspread a pleasure instead of a disaster. And, thanks again to the many hours she'd spent closeted in her mother's kitchen—occasionally joined by June—she was able to make Pat a tasty breakfast on a day when he needed to be spoiled.

"Have I told you yet that you have the most beautiful smile when you're smug?"

Pat's compliment caught her completely by surprise, and her streamlined food preparation came to a sloppy splat on the linoleum. She glared down at the offending piece of would-be French toast.

"Dammit," she muttered. With an exasperated sigh, she bent down and picked up the egg-coated bread and tossed it in the garbage can. "Don't even think about laughing, Pat, or the rest of your breakfast will join it."

By the look on his face, she could tell he wasn't

fighting to contain a chuckle, but he was watching her with a kind of melancholy amusement. He was teetering on the knife-edge between moving forward and falling back, and Aeli searched for something that would give him a little nudge in the right direction.

C'mon, Pat, honey. Don't go back down there. It's daylight. The sun is up and shining bright. Don't let the shadows take you.

She put a hand on her hip and offered him what she hoped was a playfully seductive smile. "So, how was I last night?"

Pat's brows knitted together momentarily before he caught on. "Fantastic. I'm not worthy."

Not exactly the reaction she'd been hoping for, so she reached a little farther. "I guess we'll have to work on making you worthy. Next time we sleep together, I expect to be reduced to a puddle of mush not left lying awake listening to you snore."

"I wasn't snoring, was I?"

"Nope, but I thought I'd toss that in to make you blush." She frowned. "Hmm. Didn't work. Guess I'll just have to try harder. Tell me, Pat, when do I get to see you naked? I mean, I've seen—"

"Aeli!" he protested. His eyes were laughing even if the rest of him wasn't.

"And… I win," she retorted. "Face feeling a little warm?"

"Blessedly so," he replied. "What would I do without you right now, Aelissm?"

"Since I'm right here, you don't need to think about that." She kissed him on the cheek and grinned. "I'm trying to make myself indispensible. Is it working?"

"More than I can accurately express in words."

She wanted to ask him if it was enough to make him consider staying after this business with Adam was over but couldn't bring herself to give voice to her desire. Before she could call herself a coward, something smacked her straight upside the brain. *When this business with Adam is over. Not if.* For the first time, she could see her situation as temporary. It wouldn't go on and on as she'd feared. There would be a chance to rebuild her life *after*. And her main concern with her life was quickly shifting from keeping Adam out to bringing Pat in. Permanently, on both counts.

"Aelissm?" Pat asked, his voice thick with concern. "You look like you're about to cry."

She gave a bark of laughter. "Maybe I am. I can see daylight again."

How he knew exactly what she was thinking about, she couldn't guess, but he wrapped his arms around her and whispered in her ear, "I told you I'd bring an end to your night."

"I wish I could bring one to yours."

"You are, sweetheart. I can see the first signs of dawn." She felt him take a deep breath, hold it, then let it out slowly. "I honestly didn't think I'd ever come *this* far, and I owe it all to you and your interfering uncle. That sneaky bugger was right."

"I feel like there must be something more I can do."

Pat held her back and narrowed his eyes thoughtfully. "There isn't, Aeli. I'm not going to be entirely myself today, so don't take it personal. The fact that I can be myself at all after going back like I did last night is a sizeable miracle." He stroked her face, then glanced at the stove. "Breakfast is burning."

With a curse, Aelissm yanked the frying pan off the flame. So much for her culinary genius.

* * *

The view from the pullout was incredible. Pat shut the dirt bike down and rested it on the kickstand. There was a small granite boulder beyond the edge of the picnic area, and he climbed up on it. Below him, the Northstar Valley fell away to the south, and its hayfields, pastures, and sagebrush hills resembled a patchwork quilt interrupted frequently by the Northstar Creek and its willow-choked tributaries. Directly in front of him, Comet Mountain rose high above it all. He could see the brilliant emerald patches that were the meadows just above the cabins on the mountain's southwest-facing flank, guarded by a ridge that curled around that haven. Something joyous and persistent stirred in the darkness of his heart. All of this, from the line of mountains proudly watching over the peaceful valley to the aspen groves that shivered in the foothills to the sapphire sky littered with fluffy white clouds, was his now. Northstar belonged to him. And he belonged to Northstar. This was where he was meant to be.

Aelissm joined him on the rock, and he tucked his arm around her before he realized what he'd done. Even as the feeling of at last being truly home intensified, Pat chastised himself for what he was doing to Aelissm. Guilt descended on him as he recalled their conversation that morning. She felt like she wasn't doing enough to help him, but his burden wasn't hers to bear. He should have just given her the bare minimum of details to put her mind at ease, but he'd unloaded everything on her, so grateful to have her there beside him that he hadn't given a thought to how it would affect her.

Why? he asked himself again. He'd always been able to keep his emotions on a short leash every other time he'd shared his memories—at least until he had regained solitude. His family didn't fully understand how deeply Sara's abuse affected him, and he was careful to keep it that way. Only Bill had ever gotten him to open up about it, but Pat hadn't told him about Sara's infidelity or that he still hated himself for striking her, nor had he mentioned how he'd felt so humiliated for the witness, Michelle. Bill knew more than enough to understand when Pat slid down the muddy slope into despair, but no one had ever seen the inside of his mind when he fell. Now Aelissm had.

Panic shot through him. He had to leave before he pulled her down with him, but he couldn't go back to Washington until Adam was no longer a threat to her. He'd told Bill he'd protect her, and he wouldn't back out of that promise, not even to protect her from his misery.

As swiftly as the panic had come, it receded, chased away by the thought of what Aelissm would say if she could read his mind right now.

Stop being an idiot. I can take care of myself.

Maybe he shouldn't be so concerned for her because she was a lot tougher than even she knew. But Pat also knew himself well enough to see that he'd never get over the guilt of breaking her heart. And he would. There was no way to avoid it now. If her sassy taunts this morning were any indication, she was already attached to him, so leaving now would hurt her. On the other hand, staying would only give them time to get closer, and she would be devastated to learn that he couldn't love her as fully as she deserved. A woman like Aelissm shouldn't have to settle for half a man.

If Pat had been in his normal, rational mindset, he might have laughed at himself, but only a small portion of his mind realized how ridiculous he was being about this whole mess. That part of him actually understood that it was a mess and not the end of his world as the rest of his brain was convinced. That tiny fragment of sanity also knew that he was more himself today than he'd been on similar days in the past. He *was* finally healing from Sara, even if he wasn't capable of realizing it at the moment.

"So, how are you feeling now?" Aelissm asked suddenly.

"A little better. Still not myself, but I'm getting there."

"Not good enough. I know just the roads to get that pummeled out of you."

"Oh?"

"Yep. Comet Ridge to the Sheep Field. You'll be too busy concentrating on not crashing to worry about your problems." She grinned up at him. "I was afraid we might need those roads today, which is why we're here. The turn off is just a bit farther up the hill. C'mon, old man, let's ride!"

The start of what Aelissm called Comet Ridge Road seemed tame enough. Two hundred yards later as he was navigating down a steep trail strewn with rocks and dangerously rutted by spring run-off, Pat decided a reassessment of the road was in order. He was so focused on the treacherous path as it wound through dense forest that he had time for only one thought: Aelissm was right. They'd spent the morning and early afternoon exploring the backcountry on comparatively unexciting roads that had been mostly smooth, packed dirt with the occasional rock cluster. *This* road gave him a far greater appreciation of how rugged and untamed this land was, and the unforgiving jolts he received coaxed out his own wildness, beckoning to him and encouraging him to let go of civilization and be a part of his surroundings. Thrill pumped through his veins.

When he did let go and stopped thinking about every little rock and sand bar, he found he was steadier, and the bike bucked less. He passed Aelissm on a rare smooth stretch just as the road leveled out a bit and heard her crow of laughter over the engines. At the next opportunity, she retook the lead and bounced on ahead with a confidence that sent a shock of pride through him. If he thought he belonged here, he had no doubt the mountains were in her very blood.

"That's more like it!" she called as she stopped to let him catch up.

He pulled up beside her and saw they were out of the woods. Below them, the road dropped steeply once again into a small, grassy bowl between hills covered in fragrant sagebrush and crowned by tall stands of quaking aspen. At the bottom of the slope, the road forked, one heading straight up to the hill on the south side of the little valley and the other turning left to run through the bottom of the bowl. There were a few sheep and cattle scattered around the area.

"Sheep Field?" Pat asked.

"How'd you guess?"

"I don't know. The sheep, maybe?"

Aelissm gave him a knowing wink. "The trail on the ridge over there comes out on Wellman Creek Road just up from the Sawtooth trailhead, so it's a longer ride. The sagebrush roots make it a little aggravating, and your ass will probably fall asleep, which is none too pleasant a feeling. The field road is a little rougher, though not as bad as Comet Ridge, and comes out less than a mile from the gate to the cabins. It's your call, Pat."

He debated it for a few moments, and though he would have liked to take a longer road back, he decided that a numb butt was probably a greater annoyance than the extra riding time was worth at this point. Besides, the rate things were going, he was likely to be here for a while yet, so he'd have time to take the other road when his mood had improved a bit more.

"Field road."

Aeli's shoulders dropped in relief. "Thank God. I hate the ridge road."

"Then, why'd you suggest it?"

"Everyone loves options."

The Sheep Field road was better than Comet Ridge, but once it started ascending back up the mountain, it was still rough. As they passed through aspen, he wondered what this field would look like when the leaves turned yellow. Gorgeous, no doubt. He'd have to come back just to see the autumn here.

Though Aelissm had said this was the shorter road, it was still at least three miles long, winding through the valley and up along the northern ridge. At the line of lodgepole pine that signaled the eastern edge of the grazing area, a creek cut right through the road. There was no bridge, and the banks were about three feet high. He considered himself lucky to have made it this far, but he hadn't yet needed to attempt something that belonged in an obstacle course.

"You didn't mention that," Pat told Aeli when they stopped at the stream's edge.

"Didn't mention what? Oh, that? That's nothing."

"Does 'nothing' have a proper name?"

"Wellman Creek. It's the same one that runs by Grandma and Grandpa's cabin."

"Starts from that spring by the Old Miner's Cabin?"

"That's the one. Farther down it joins with Dingley, Clark, and Sawtooth Creeks."

"Ah. So, how do we get to the other side?"

"Don't pop the clutch or hit the throttle too hard coming out of it. You'll already be nearly vertical, and it would really suck to get tossed in the creek."

"I suppose it would."

"Really, Pat, it's not as bad as it looks. I remember one of the summers when June came up here with us. My little brother was showing off, trying to show us girls how to do it and… the bike made it, but he didn't."

"I'll bet he was embarrassed."

"Humiliated. We wouldn't let him go back to the cabin to change since we were heading *down* into the Sheep Field, so he had to air-dry."

Without another word, Aelissm tapped her bike into first gear and went over the edge into the creek. She opened up the throttle a little to get up the other side, and then she was there, making the whole thing look as easy as if she'd traversed it a thousand times. Then again, she probably had.

Pat took a deep breath and started cautiously

forward. Going down was easy enough, so he relaxed a moment, then it was time to go up. He did as Aelissm had and gave it a little gas. The bike leapt forward and zipped up the bank. For a frightening handful of heartbeats, he balanced on the rear wheel, still racing forward, then set down. He turned the bike around in the circular clearing and grinned at Aelissm, his heart pounding with the flood of adrenaline. It wasn't exactly jumping out of a plane or scaling a sheer rock face, but he'd never done something like that before.

"That was great!" he exclaimed. "Can I do it again?"

"Go for it."

So he did. After five roundtrips across the stream, Aelissm finally put an end to his frolicking.

"Dinner time, Mr. O'Neil. I don't know about you, but I'm hungry."

"I am, too, now that I think about it. Guess I was having too much fun to worry about food."

"Better having too much fun than lost in too much misery, eh?"

"That's for damned sure. Any other plans for the evening after we eat?"

"I thought we could invite June and Luke over, maybe Grandma and Grandpa, too, and play cards until the wee hours of the morning."

"That'll be great. You know, we still haven't had one of these card parties you've told me so much about."

"I know. Sorry. I guess we'd better have one tonight. With the summer tourist season starting shortly, we're not going to have too many free nights, and I don't want you to go home disappointed."

I am home.

The thought was unbidden and intense. It took him a moment to force it down. He couldn't stay, no matter how much he wanted or needed to. He couldn't hurt Aelissm more than he was already going to. She looked at him expectantly, waiting for his response, and it pained him to see the hope written plainly on her beautiful, caring face. All he could find to say was, "I do hate being disappointed."

If he'd thought breakfast was good, the beef stew she'd left simmering in the Crockpot all afternoon was heaven. As he savored each bite, he began to wonder just how serious Aelissm was about trying to make herself indispensible. If that truly was her intent, she was doing a damned fine job of it. Pat could cook well enough for himself, but even his best was garbage compared to this. Good, clean air, beauty all around him, fabulous food to eat, and an exquisite woman there to ask him how his day had been and actually mean it…. The reasons to stay here in Northstar were piling up and eroding his vow to leave before the damage to Aelissm was irreversible.

He felt like a foolish boy in high school, but he wondered if maybe he shouldn't talk to June. She had one of the most objective minds of anyone he knew, and since she was watching everything unfold from the outside, she had a far better view. Besides, she was Aelissm's best friend, and he had no doubts about Aeli sharing her innermost secrets with June. If nothing else, June might be able to tell him how he could let Aelissm down gently.

Before he and Aeli had finished eating, June and Luke arrived, barely announcing their presence with a knock before pushing through the back door. Both were beaming.

"Good news?" Pat asked.

"Great news," June replied. "It's official. Luke is legally my son."

Her joy was a palpable thing, and Pat found himself locked in a group hug. When he stepped back, he was astounded by the unbridled emotion on Luke's young face. Pure, unshielded happiness. He'd never seen the boy so unguarded, and the wild urges that had plagued him all day fell silent. Luke was home, and Pat felt privileged to be involved in such a precious moment.

"You've always been a part of our goofy little family, Luke," Aeli said. "I'm so glad it's officially official now."

"Thanks, Aeli," Luke replied, his smile even brighter.

Aelissm spared Pat a long glance that told him in no uncertain terms that she wanted him to be a part of their haphazard family, too, that she already considered him to be. Damn Bill for doing this to them because Pat wanted it to be true.

"June," he murmured to Aelissm's friend. "Can I talk to you when you have a moment?"

She frowned and her blue eyes darted questioningly at Aelissm. "Sure. Aeli, I'm stealing Pat for a few minutes."

"Just be gentle with him. He had a rough night. C'mon, Luke, you can help me get this mess cleared up for cards."

June lifted her brows at Aeli, glanced at Pat, then motioned toward the door she and Luke had just entered through. She closed it quietly behind them.

"What's on your mind, Pat?"

"I love Aelissm," he blurted.

"Well, that's pretty obvious. So, what's the problem?"

"I don't want to hurt her."

"Before I ask how you could or would hurt Aeli, let me first ask what she meant when she said you'd had a rough night. I get the feeling something happened that has to do with this."

"It does. I told her about Sara," Pat explained. "I told her *everything* about Sara. I've never told anyone everything before, not even Bill. And this morning, Aeli told me she doesn't think she's doing enough to help me, which is so incredibly untrue…. I can't find the words."

"And…?"

"Sara really hurt me. I honestly believe she killed me a little."

"Abuse seems to make people believe that."

"How did you…?"

"I'm observant, Pat. I learned young, when my parents divorced, how to read people and situations. It was a useful tool then to help me stay afloat in the battle between them, and I've built on it since. As to you… I put two and two and three together and came up with seven. I've listened to what Aeli and Uncle Bill have told me about you, and I know that look in your eyes. It's the same I see in Luke's from time to time."

"You think he was abused?"

"I have my suspicions but no proof, and he doesn't talk about it. Don't change the subject." June's gaze softened with the deep-seated compassion he'd come to associate with her. "Believing something doesn't always make it true. I think Sara tried to destroy as much of you as she could, but the simple fact that *you* left proves she failed."

"I got out, but that doesn't mean she didn't carve out

a chunk of me."

"Quite literally, I'm guessing, but wounds heal in time, and eventually, scars fade. I'm not saying you'll ever forget because I doubt you will. I'm not even saying you should forgive her. I'm not in a position to rightly believe abuse *can* be forgiven. What I'm telling you is to take that horrible time in your life and learn from it. Appreciate what you have and what you *could* have. Everything that we do and that happens to us makes us who we are. You can let all the bad things drag you down, or you can make them work for you and come out stronger for them. That choice is yours."

"It's not as simple as that."

"I never said it was easy. I'm just painting you a picture." She smiled. "Enough about you for now. Let me tell you something about Aeli. She's always been more open and trusting than I am, but she also keeps everyone but her family and her closest friends at a safe distance. She's never laid herself so completely open with a man like she has with you. She's never been given a reason to before. Think about that when you decide what to do."

"I don't know what to do. Or what I *want* to do. I know I love her enough to want the best for her. She deserves the best, and I don't think I am."

"What's best for Aelissm is what makes her happy and what gives her the support and courage to plant her feet and stop running. From what I can see, that's *exactly* you."

"Me?" Pat asked, startled.

"Yes, you. I'm not telling you what to do, Pat. You asked my opinion, and I gave it. All I ask is that you take what I've told you into consideration before you decide you're so bad for Aeli." She folded her arms and smiled. "Now, this is where our conversation ends because you already have enough to think about. Besides, it's card night, and I heard Grandma and Grandpa pull up a few minutes ago."

Oddly, June's blunt opinions and thorough insight had given him clarity, not more to think about. What he felt for Aelissm was totally new and wonderful, and if June was to be believed, Aeli was on the same mountainside. Why shouldn't they find out where this went? This might be, as some said, the real thing. Even so, caution was necessary. Plowing on ahead with high expectations would only lead to a pair of broken hearts if this was all just an empty promise.

"Thank you, June," he said as they turned back toward the door.

"You're most welcome."

"You know, I'm so used to seeing you here, in Northstar, that I'd almost forgotten you teach high school. Without seeing you in a classroom, I know that you're a great teacher if only because you see people. It makes complete sense, too, why Bill thought you would be a good match for Luke."

"Thank you, Pat," she said quietly—almost shyly. "That means a lot to me. He's come a long way in a short time, but he still has a long way to go."

"And he'll get there because of you." Pat hesitated before opening the door. "Whatever happens… I want you to be part of my family."

"Of course we're part of your family. And, one way or another, you're part of ours. There's no escape, Pat.

You're stuck with us."

"Promise?"

"Promise. Now, we'd better get back inside before they send out a search party."

When they walked inside to find Aelissm's grandparents already inside, it was with an honest smile that Pat greeted them.

"Luke tells us we have reason to celebrate," Marge said.

Indeed we do, Pat thought. He'd revealed his darkest memories and survived. He was almost himself again and in less than a day. In three years, he hadn't made as much improvement as he had in the past two months, and as everyone present congratulated June and Luke, he threw his own, private celebration.

When the phone rang, Pat picked it up, being the closest to it. He glanced habitually at the screen to check the number, but the area code didn't immediately register even though he recognized it.

Seattle, he thought and strode into the living room to retrieve the notepad before answering the call. "Hello?" he asked as he wrote the number down.

"I thought I told you to stay away from Aelissm, Detective O'Neil."

"And I believe I told you I couldn't do that, Adam," Pat replied quietly. He wasn't entirely surprised Adam had figured out who he was; Bill and Aelissm had both called him resourceful. He glanced over his shoulder to see Aelissm still engaged with her grandparents, June, and Luke. When she glanced at him with a questioning look and lifted her hand to her ear like a phone, he pointed to himself and mouthed, *It's for me.*

"In that case," Adam said, "I'll have to employ something a little more convincing to make you leave."

"That's not going to happen."

"You don't believe me? You should. I have ways of digging up the kind of dirt you can't wash off."

Pat snorted. Adam could look until hell froze over, but his record was perfectly clean. "There's nothing to find, so good luck with that."

"Suit yourself."

The click of disconnection echoed in Pat's ear, so he pulled the cordless away and hit the end button, then transcribed the conversation and hid the notepad under a book to be dealt with later. He felt remarkably good but didn't trust the feeling to last if he allowed anything other than the prospect of a boisterous evening with Aelissm and her family to infiltrate his mind, so he pushed everything else out. He and Aelissm could deal with Adam's baseless threat in the morning.

"Who was that?" Aeli asked when he took a seat beside her at the table.

"Nothing we need to worry about tonight," he replied. "You've done a fine job bringing me this far, so how about we finish the task?"

Impulsively, he kissed her firmly on the mouth in front of everyone. No one present was surprised except Aelissm, and the most incredible, open smile graced her face, proving June right and firming Pat's decision to indulge his curiosity because he obviously wasn't the only one who felt this marvelous, dizzying attraction. After the heartbreaks they'd suffered, didn't they deserve something good?

Twelve

"YES, THANK YOU VERY MUCH. That's exactly what I needed. Uh-huh, you, too. Bye." Pat pushed the end button on the cordless and scribbled something in his notebook. Aelissm took the opportunity to admire him, delighted by the easy manner he'd had in speaking with the person on the other end of the phone line. She was more than a little aroused by the lines of his body as he leaned against the snack bar and by the fluid dance of forearm muscle as he wrote down whatever it was he found prudent. His head was cocked slightly to the side, and a frown of concentration occasionally pinched his brows together.

Mama wants to play, Aeli thought, then blushed.

He liked to wear clothes that fit but left something to the imagination, she'd noticed. His jeans and the plain white T-shirt tucked into them were loose enough to be comfortable but tight enough to tantalize her with a glimpse of the toned body underneath. So, subconsciously at least, Pat knew he was attractive, though she doubted even his baser brain knew just how sexy he was. If he wasn't so distractingly handsome, she might have been irritated and impatient that he was keeping her waiting, but watching him was so much more fun than worrying about what he might or might not have found out from his numerous phone calls this morning.

It was a while before Pat looked up at Aelissm. His hazel eyes glittered as he waved the notepad. "Got it."

Aelissm jumped up from her seat on the couch and snatched the notepad from Pat's hand. She scanned down the page, ignoring his notations and froze when she saw it—the address of the phone Adam had called from three days ago. Vicious glee swamped her for a moment. They knew where Adam was. This whole twisted game was about to come to an end. Then, when her mind slowed enough to focus, her heart sank. There was no way this would lead them right to him. It wasn't over yet.

"The Parasite Motel?" she asked. "That's where he was?"

"I wrote Paradise."

"I know." She looked up at him and found him smiling. "What's so great about this, Pat?"

"Where's the motel located?"

"Montana Street. It's the main drag through the north side of town. The motel's almost right across from the northern access to the interstate."

"Convenient."

"A little too convenient, thank you," Aeli replied

unhappily. "Unless you're going to tell me that number is from a phone in a room at the Parasite."

"No, it's not. But it does belong to the pay phone in the motel's restaurant. In the lounge, actually. It's possible he just stopped in to eat and use the phone, but he might be staying at the motel or somewhere nearby." Pat frowned thoughtfully. "We don't know how long he's been in Devyn, or in Montana, for that matter, but we know he's here now. If he's been here for a while, he's probably found some way to get money. Is there anyone back in Seattle who might send him funds?"

Aelissm shook her head. "No. He only ever had his mother, but she died a year or so before I met him. He's pretty resourceful, though—paid his own way through college. I wouldn't put it past him to find a place to work under a fake name."

"A fake name?"

"Yeah. It's still possible in Devyn. Certain places are just glad to get help, so they don't dig too deep, and some of them pay under the table—like the Parasite."

"Is he brazen enough to call from his place of work?" Pat asked quietly, thinking out loud again. "Maybe so. Guess we'll have to ask around, see what we can find out." The last he said more loudly, addressing her.

Anticipation quivered in Aelissm's gut. Freedom seemed so close at hand. She wanted to grab her keys, sprint out to her truck, and race to Devyn. The only thing stopping her was the lack of knowledge. A sketchy theory and the location of the phone Adam had called from were all they had to go on, but it shouldn't be too hard to get some more information. Enough people in Devyn knew her, and most of the population knew of her grandparents, so they wouldn't be too suspicious if she dug around a little. This had to end. It had been a year since she'd slept without worry of being found.

"Aeli. Stop pacing."

She didn't realize she was until he said it. She stopped and found him watching her quizzically. "What?" she asked.

"Relax."

"Relax?" she spat. "Excuse me, but I think I have every right to be a little anxious right now, Pat. Adam is here… or near enough that I can feel him breathing down my neck. That son of a—"

Her proclamation was abruptly cut off when Pat's mouth latched on to hers. He clasped her face with both hands, preventing her from objecting, even if she were able. She was pulled into him, and the wondrous feel of his long, lean body pressed to the length of her own stole away her worries. She had no choice but to give in and melt against him. She moaned low in her throat, pleading for more, as her eyes rolled back behind closed lids. They'd shared gentle kisses and passionate ones, but this was different. This was both and more.

"Are you a puddle of mush yet?" Pat asked against her lips. His voice was a deeply sensual purr.

"Call me goo," she murmured. "What was that for?"

"To get you to shut up," he replied in the same, seductive tone.

"Kiss me like that again, and I may be silent forever."

"I don't want that, but I *will* kiss you again."

The notebook slid from Aelissm's hand and hit the floor in a flutter of paper as he claimed her mouth again. All else but Pat passed out of her mind, leaving only a flood of sensations and emotions swirling wonderfully through her saturated brain. She curled her arms around his neck and buried her hands in his thick hair. If the world crashed down around them, she wouldn't care as long as he was there with her, kissing her like there was nothing more precious or more desirable in the world. It was devastating, and at the same time, it fulfilled her.

He let her go slowly. It took a long time to recover her wits, and by the time she finally realized why she'd been so fired up, Pat was coming back downstairs. He'd gone up to his room and pulled on a dark green button-up shirt, though he had yet to button it, and carried his boots. Aelissm continued to watch him as he walked through the kitchen and into the living room. He stooped to pick up the notepad she'd dropped, then straightened. When he caught her unabashedly appraising him, he smiled uncertainly.

"Do you have any idea whatsoever how sexy you are?" she asked smugly. "And I do believe I just made you blush again, Mr. O'Neil."

"So it would seem. Are you going to finish getting dressed or stand there drooling all day?"

"Drooling over you all day sounds downright lovely, but I suppose there are more pressing things to be done."

Aelissm marveled at the change in Pat. Three days ago, he'd been pale, withdrawn, and unsettlingly insecure. She frowned. He'd gained a rather shocking and sudden self-confidence since he'd talked to June the other night. She tried to figure out what they might have talked about to have such an effect on him. The thought that it had been something scandalous didn't even cross her mind, but she *was* worried what juicy secrets June might have spilled to Pat. No, she thought, June wouldn't betray her confidence like that. Unable to come up with anything of value, Aelissm tried for something a little more direct.

"You seem much happier," she remarked. "What did June say to you the other night?"

Pat smiled. "She gave me some really good advice. Do you know she believes Luke was abused?"

"Yes, I do. Don't change the subject."

This time, he chuckled. "You can tell that the two of you have been good friends for a long time. That's what she told me when I got off track. Word for word."

"Uh-huh." Aelissm lifted her brows and started to say something else but decided against it. She'd get it out of him eventually. With a shrug, she headed upstairs to get ready to leave.

Alone in her bedroom without Pat to distract her, Aeli fell prey to doubt. What if they couldn't find anything about Adam? What if they asked around and described him until they passed out from lack of oxygen and came up without a single clue that might help them? Adam Winters had a talent for disappearing into a crowd; he'd used it to sneak up on her more than once.

Aelissm braced her hands on her dresser and stared at her reflection. The face in the mirror was pale with green eyes rounded with worry and glittering with half-formed tears. She pinched them closed, willing herself not to cry.

"I just want it to be done," she murmured.

"I know."

She watched in the mirror as Pat slid behind her and wrapped his arms around her. He met her eyes in the glass, his expression concerned.

"I wish I could tell you we'll find him today and that he'll be out of your life forever by tomorrow, but I can't, and I don't want to give you false hope by making promises I'm not sure I can keep."

"It's not your place to make promises to me, anyhow," she muttered. "No matter how much I might wish it was."

"And what if *I* want it to be my place?"

"Then we'll see what happens," she replied, ignoring the rush of thrill. "I'm almost ready. I'll meet you downstairs in a minute."

Pat lowered his head and kissed her neck before turning to leave, unbothered by her dismissal. As she brushed her hair and knitted it into a single braid, she tried not to think about what he'd just said or the tremors of comfortable intimacy his gesture had tickled from her. She focused her attention on the morning sunlight filtering through the trees outside her window, on the clumsily stacked boxes in the rafters above her bed. Oh, the memories stuffed in those boxes….

"What was I thinking, going to Seattle?" she wondered aloud. "I belong here. I always have."

She and June, way back when in high school, had spent uncounted hours complaining how much they both despised Western Washington and longed for the pine-blanketed granite peaks of this valley. Somewhere in those boxes was a notebook stuffed with notes she and June had passed back and forth in school, and memory of the words written on those pages brought a smile to her face. Pat might get a kick out of their literary antics.

"Aeli! You coming or what?" he called from down-stairs.

"Yeah, yeah. Hold your horses."

"I'd rather hold you, if I have a choice."

Aelissm grinned. "You might! If you're lucky!"

The sound of his laughter drifted up to her. She could get used to that. If he'd let her.

* * *

Pat drove to Devyn and kept their conversation centered on how to go about their task. Aelissm did her best to quell her irritability. It wasn't that Pat was being so single-minded that bothered her but *why* he wouldn't let them stray. They were going to be walking a tight rope as fine as fishing line today. The slightest fluctuation in balance would have them falling back into the net of helpless waiting. The old familiar tension was back, knotted in her shoulders and throbbing inside her skull. Fear lurked in there somewhere, ready to lunge at her and drag her back under. She'd never much liked yo-yos as a child, and she absolutely despised feeling like one now.

"I think it's probably wise not to mention Adam's name. If you're right—and I believe you are—about him having a job in Devyn, I want to know what name he's been using."

"So how do we ask about him?"

"Describe him like we've only seen him once or twice."

"He's not what you call a memorable person. Medium everything."

"Quit being so pessimistic."

"Can't help it," she retorted. "It's in my nature."

"Well, turn it off for a little while, will you?"

She stared out the window. The hills and valleys were in the full green of late spring, not as vibrant as the emerald of Washington but frosted with the silver-gold of last year's dead grasses. Normally, she would have appreciated the sight, but evidence of Adam's presence in Devyn had cast a foul shadow over her eyes, and she couldn't find the same joy in admiring her home that should have come as easily as breathing. Then again… at the moment, breathing wasn't so easy, either.

"Dammit," she muttered. Returning her attention to Pat, she said, "Okay, I'm sorry. I'm a little out of myself right now."

"Understandably so," Pat replied.

"So, what do you want me to say?"

"I haven't figured that out yet. I thought maybe you could help me with it."

"You're the cop."

Aelissm wanted to slap herself for baiting him like that. He was only trying to help her, but she couldn't seem to stop herself.

"Technically, I'm the cop on an extended leave of absence," he replied. There was a note of exasperation—or was it aggravation—in his voice that caught her off guard. Apparently, his patience was a little short at the moment as well. Which made her feel absurdly better. "An important point we'd both be smart to remember. I have no power to *do* anything, Aelissm."

"Ain't that just the cherry on top?" she snarled. "What did Bill expect you to do, then?"

"Protect you."

"If Adam came to me," she finished.

"I can't bring him in, but I can find him, and then the local police can arrest him for violating the restraining order."

Aelissm snorted, doubtful.

"If that's what you want," Pat added.

She didn't respond. Right now, that wasn't a question she could answer.

They crested Badger Pass and swung around the curve in the road. At the crest of the small hill just beyond, they were awarded with a sweeping view of the broad valley around Devyn. Cloud shadows raced across the land, sliding like playful wraiths over the mountains, hills, and river plain. Rain would fall sometime that afternoon, a penetrating spring shower that would leave the world pristine and refreshed.

Somewhere down there, somewhere in the cluster of buildings and houses that was Devyn, Adam was hiding.

"Just about everyone in town knows my grandparents, and they know I've been taking over operations of the Bedspread," Aelissm said. "We can probably use that as cover."

"We could," Pat replied. "What were you thinking?"

"I don't know. Maybe we're looking for him because he walked out without paying for a meal."

"We'd waste the time and resources to track him down because he didn't pay for a meal? It's not strong enough."

"What if he left something behind? We wouldn't have to tell people *what* he forgot, would we?"

"No. That just might work." Pat drummed his

thumbs on the steering wheel. "We just have to be very, *very* careful. We don't want to run into him, and we don't want anyone we speak to alerting him. We don't know enough to chance him getting suspicious."

"So you said. We don't know *anything*," Aeli muttered.

"I'm trying to make this as easy on you as I can, Aeli. I don't want you to expect too much from our excursion today. I'll be happy just to know how long he's been in Devyn and if he has a job or a residence here. We can find the specifics later."

"Then I guess I'll have to be happy with whatever we find out. I won't get my hopes up, Pat. I promise."

"That's my girl," Pat replied. "So, we decided to start our search at the Paradise—"

"Parasite."

"—because we overheard Winters telling someone he was staying there. Work for you?"

"It'll have to."

"Maybe we'll get lucky."

"That'll be the day."

When Pat growled, Aelissm knew she was frustrating him. She didn't know what she'd expected would happen with Pat here to protect her, but this wasn't it. None of what was happening came within the sphere of what she'd once imagined. There was so much uncertainty in her life right at the moment, and she was all but powerless to make any of it swing the way she wanted. Even if they found Adam and had him arrested, there was no guarantee that would deter him for long. He'd probably pick right up where he'd left off once he got out of jail unless she found a way to resolve whatever issue he thought remained between them. Of course, *nothing* would be resolved if they couldn't catch him. Then there was her relationship with Pat. If she could call it that. She could write a book chronicling the mixed signals he was giving her.

Better not to think about that right now. Like finding the specifics on Adam, it can be dealt with later. When I know more.

Aelissm sighed.

She spent the rest of the drive into Devyn silently musing that the most recent mess she'd landed herself in wasn't any tidier than the one she was still trying to clean up. In fact, it was worse because her heart was firmly entrenched in the muck this time.

By the time Pat turned onto the interstate, Aeli had decided not to worry about any of it. Things would work themselves out however they were going to no matter how she interfered. With a twist of her lips, she wondered how long her resolution would hold up.

Instead of continuing to the second Devyn exit, Pat pulled off the Interstate at the south end of town, and Aeli was grateful for the few extra minutes to build up her courage. As they passed the college, she took it as a good sign that her contract had been renewed for the next year. The administration had asked—and convinced—her to teach two classes in the fall. Her temporary return was fast becoming a permanent move. And that wasn't so bad, now was it?

Two miles and several minutes later, Aelissm's heart had lodged itself firmly in her throat and was fluttering erratically. So much for building up her courage. Pat pulled into a spot near the door of the Paradise Motel's restaurant.

"Cross your fingers and hope all goes well," he said.

"What do we do first?"

"Ask who was working behind the bar three nights ago."

Three nights ago? That long ago already? *Wait*, Aeli thought. *Wait just one minute.* Her palm smacked against her forehead. "I know who was working. Amber, one of my students."

"Well, that could make this easier," Pat replied. "Or more difficult, if she knows him."

Wonderful. Aelissm sneered. Why couldn't something make this easier for a change? She bit her tongue to contain her irritation. She wanted nothing more right now than to march into the restaurant and demand answers, but she was still frightened enough by the possibly disastrous consequences of such rash impulses to wait for Pat's lead.

At last, after frowning at the door of the restaurant for several minutes, Pat got out of the truck. Aeli followed him and hovered at his side as they walked inside.

"Hi, Ms. Davis," said the young woman behind the hostess' desk.

Abruptly, all nervousness left Aelissm as she recognized Amber's bubbly blonde roommate. She returned the girl's smile. "Hi, Jamie. Is Amber working today?"

"Yeah, she's in the dining room. Are you two here to eat?"

Aeli's eyebrow shot up, and her lips quirked. "Am I ever here to eat?"

"Only when your grandparents drag you in kicking and screaming. C'mon, Ms. Davis, the food's not *that* bad."

"You keep telling yourself that, and when you decide you want some *good* food, come out to the Bedspread, and

I'll treat you to one of my mother's recipes."

The girl held her hands up in defeat. "Okay, you're right. The food here sucks. Except when Brandon's on the grill. He's pretty good."

"Uh-huh," Aeli replied, unconvinced. "Bye, Jamie."

"See ya, Ms. Davis."

Pat followed as Aeli turned the corner into the non-smoking side of the restaurant. Amber never worked the smoking side, she recalled, but there was no sign of the girl. There weren't any diners, either. The room was completely empty, the tables all neatly set and awaiting customers.

"Is the food really that bad?" Pat asked.

"It's not great, but it's edible. And it's cheap. Most of the locals eat elsewhere, and since it's midweek and off-peak hours, there probably aren't too many guests at the motel looking for a meal."

"I'll be right out!" came Amber's voice from the kitchen.

"I still say you should come work for me!" Aeli called back. "I'd pay you better."

Amber's beaming face appeared in the scarred Plexiglas window of the swinging kitchen doors, framed by perfect, glossy curls that bounced around her shoulders as she pushed into the dining room.

"Hey, Ms. Davis! What are you doing here? And who's your friend?" she greeted, smiling widely. Her rich brown eyes quickly took in Pat's tall form, lingering just long enough to send jealousy pulsing through Aelissm.

"My friend is Pat O'Neil. Pat, this disgustingly charming young woman is Amber Jones. She's one of my students. Put your eyes back in your head, girl. He's much too old for you. Besides, I thought you were seeing some guy."

Pat and Amber both laughed, though the former clearly wasn't interested in the other, Aelissm was pleased to note. His hazel eyes seemed far more engrossed with Aeli herself.

"Yeah, I'm still seeing Brandon. He's out of town right now, though. So, what can I do for you? I know you're not here to eat."

"No, we're not." Aelissm wanted to take a deep breath to calm her racing heart, but such a sign of fear would be a dead giveaway to her lie. So she lightly steered the conversation in the direction she and Pat had agreed upon. "We're actually here looking for a gentleman. Medium height, about five-ten or so, medium build. Brown hair about chin length and sort of shaggy, hazel eyes."

"That sounds like Brandon."

Thoughts and recollections collided in her mind, rendering her incapable of speech. *Brandon?* was all she could even think.

"Why, are you looking for him?" she heard Amber asked.

"It might not be him, but a gentleman of that description was at the Bedspread a little while back and left something, a piece of paper that looked official," Pat answered as if it was the most inconsequential thing in the world. Only the fingers pressed into Aelissm's neck revealed the intensity of his thoughts. "There was a business card from the motel here with it. Since we were in town, we thought we'd try to track him down. He hasn't been back to get it, so I guess it's nothing important."

"That's possible. He goes out that way a lot. Says he likes the drive. Should I mention it to him?"

"Nah. Like I said, it's probably not that important. Well, we'd better let you get back to work. It was nice meeting you, Amber."

"It was nice meeting you, too, Mr. O'Neil."

"C'mon, Aeli. We've got a lot to accomplish today."

"Bye, Ms. Davis. See you in class."

Pat's fingers pressed deeper into her flesh, and Aeli managed a believably sincere departing remark before he steered her outside. How she managed to wait until they were safely back in the truck and pulling out of the motel parking lot before losing it was a miracle. The implications were too much to handle, and they screamed through her brain, but she wasn't the first one to curse.

"Dammit!" Pat barked. A moment later, he added, "Shit! If she mentions this to him, we're back to ground zero."

"Brandon!" Aeli finally spat. "He's been here as long as you have, Pat. Maybe longer!"

"Living here, working here, and watching you the whole time."

"Oh, my God. Amber. Pat, you have to take me back. I have to warn her. Turn around!"

"No. We can't tell her anything, Aelissm. We may have already lost our only opportunity to—"

"She doesn't know what she's gotten herself into."

"Right now, there's not much you can do about it. Besides, it's her choice, Aeli. She's an adult and more than capable of making her own decisions."

"Don't you get it, Pat? He's sleeping with her!"

"So I gathered, but until this is all over—"

"Then I guess it's time to call the locals in, isn't it? Have them arrest him."

"We don't know where Adam lives or even what kind of vehicle he drives."

"We know where he works."

"But we don't know his schedule, and legally, Adam is the only one who can tell us that. Tell me, Aelissm, is this a restaurant the local police frequent?"

"No, they hardly ever eat here."

"Wouldn't it seem strange, then, if they suddenly started frequenting the place? I imagine Adam is a little wary of the police in general right now, so if they start acting out of character, he'll notice it right off. We can't risk that yet because we don't know enough."

"Then turn around and demand to know everything."

"To what purpose?" Pat snapped. "The only thing going back and demanding information would accomplish is alerting Adam. I can't do a damned thing, Aelissm! All I can do is keep Aaron Hammond and the local police posted on what I know, which is, as of right now, pretty much *nothing*."

"Then find something. That's what you're here for, isn't it? To *protect* me. To find out what Adam's been up to, where he's been. Fine job you're doing. You didn't even know he's been in Devyn for at least two months!"

"That's not fair, Aeli."

"Yeah, well, neither is life."

Thirteen

AELISSM WAS RIGHT. He should have known Adam was in Devyn—should have felt it. But he'd been so wrapped up in the freedom and joy of this place that he hadn't focused on his main reason for being here. Bill had wanted him to relax and to heal, but first and foremost, Bill had asked him to protect Aelissm. And, so far, he *had* been neglecting that duty.

No longer.

For two weeks now, he'd been snooping around Devyn and had learned not only that Adam had taken a job at the Paradise Motel's restaurant under the name Brandon Grimes—a rather fitting surname, Pat thought—but also what vehicle Adam was driving. The inconspicuous white Ford pickup was at that moment parked beside a tiny cottage down the alleyway behind the motel. Pat watched in the rearview mirror as the man himself strolled down the alley toward his rented house, hands stuffed in his pockets and eyes cast downward.

Judging by his attire, Pat guessed Adam hadn't been at the motel to work today. The sweatshirt Winters wore was frayed around the cuffs and more gray now than black. Except the crisp black pants and clean white T-shirts that were his work uniform, most of Adam's clothes were well worn and ragged. Pat doubted he had much more than a week's worth of clothing. Less to pack that way and less to hinder him in his pursuit.

As Adam passed by the Bronco, Pat glanced away. So far, he'd seen nothing to make him believe that Amber had mentioned his and Aelissm's visit to the motel, but that didn't mean she hadn't. It might simply mean that Adam was still secure in his anonymity. Either way, Pat didn't want Adam to see him. For that same reason, he'd been driving Marge and Roger's older Bronco. Since it was usually parked up at their cabin, there was little chance Adam would recognize it, unlike Aeli's or June's trucks or the Davis' newer, white Bronco. The Washington plates on his own truck would have been as clear a warning signal to Adam as the daily noon siren that split the quiet of Devyn.

Pat watched Winters enter the little house, made a couple of notes beside the address in his notebook, and turned the key in the ignition. He waited a few more minutes to make sure Adam wasn't going to pop back out of the house and drove off.

Adam's habits were fairly easy to follow and boring. He spent most of his time at the motel, either working or eating and drinking, and other than Amber and a couple of their coworkers, had no acquaintances that Pat had yet seen. Amber was his only visitor, and she'd stopped by only once during the past week. Adam had been to the house she and Jamie shared with another girl once as well, but his behavior—glancing around nervously while he waited outside for Amber's all-clear—led Pat to believe that Adam Winters wasn't *that* comfortable with his act. He still feared discovery enough to take the precaution of limiting his exposure to as few people as possible. Hence the job as a cook, where he was safely hidden in the kitchen of the Paradise Motel's restaurant.

Aelissm was dead-on in her assessment of Adam's ability to disappear into a crowd. Few people Pat had talked to remembered seeing the man, which had been frustrating until he'd been lucky enough a week ago to be driving down the road behind the motel and glimpsed Adam and Amber climbing into the white pickup. From that point, it had been easy to keep tabs on him. Pat now knew where he slept, what he liked to eat, what beer he liked, that he had no phone, and that he appeared to do nothing in his house but sleep and stare at the walls. He didn't waste money on entertainment and never watched the tiny television that had undoubtedly been provided with the house. The little mail he received was all addressed to Brandon Grimes. The utilities were evidently included in his rent because Pat had not seen any bills in the little mailbox, and all his neighbors had received their electric bills in that time.

Of all that he'd learned about Adam over the past two weeks, Pat was most aggravated and disgusted to find out that Winters ventured out to Northstar at least twice a week—a tidbit he'd realized after discovering what vehicle the man was using. He'd seen that white truck in Northstar twice in the last week and about that often in the past as well. Adam undoubtedly knew Aelissm's work schedule, where her grandparents lived, and possibly, that she lived somewhere up Elkhorn Road. Pat was fairly certain Adam hadn't yet found out where exactly the cabin was because, bless small-town gossip, any strange person or vehicle seen on any of the side roads quickly became a topic of discussion at the coffee table in the back of Betty Burns' convenience store. Pat had taken to starting his day joining what the women of the valley fondly referred to as the Coffee Club. Its members were the ranching patriarchs of the valley and several of the older ranch hands who'd been working in the valley for longer than Pat had been alive. They kept him well informed of valley doings and were also—at his request—on the lookout for the white truck and a man fitting Adam's description. If he so much as turned off Northstar Road, Pat would know it.

So far, no one had seen him. Pat was relieved to know that Aelissm was still safe at home. During the busier hours of operation at the Bedspread Inn, she was safe enough, too; Pat was sure Adam wasn't brazen enough to confront her with so many of her neighbors around, and Pat made sure he was with her at open and close even on the days he didn't work.

Before he knew it, he was turning off the highway onto Northstar Road, and his eyes took in the graceful sweep of the valley with a sense of comfortable familiarity. Washington's tall Douglas Firs, cedars, and dense underbrush were going to look strange after this place, and he was going to miss the wide sky, the pungent sagebrush, and crystalline air.

Knowing as much as he did now about Adam Winters, the time to say goodbye couldn't be too far off. He didn't know yet what he and Bill and Aaron Hammond would do with the information, but it wasn't their decision. It was Aelissm's, but she had not been in a rational frame of mind since learning how long Adam had been in Devyn, and he'd hesitated to share his findings with her because he wanted her to carefully consider the best way to get Adam out of her life and keep him out. The more Pat saw and thought on the matter, the more strongly he believed that Adam needed something from Aelissm to be able to move past Brent's death and the events that had followed. What that something might be, Pat didn't know. However, he *did* know that, until Aelissm made her choice, he would continue his vigil and enjoy his remaining time in Northstar.

He turned right on the road to Aeli's grandparents'. Parking the Bronco beside the post office, he entered through the back door to say hi to Marge. Aelissm's grandmother looked up from her work at the desk and smiled.

"Good afternoon, Pat," Marge said. "How'd everything go?"

"Somewhat boring but otherwise fine."

"You remembered to pick up the hot dogs, right?"

Pat nodded. "Everything's set?"

"I just need to finish up here, turn the Crockpot on for Roger, and then I'll be ready."

"Thanks, Marge. I appreciate it," he said. He leaned down and kissed her cheek. "I saw Roger out working on his shed. I'll go help him while I wait."

"Call June and make sure she's got everything

packed. With Aeli's mood, you're not going to want any delays," she called as he left.

He highly doubted he needed to call June because she'd had almost everything packed this morning before he'd left for Devyn, but he would anyhow to let her know he *had* remembered the hot dogs.

"Afternoon, Pat," Roger greeted from the door of his shed.

"Afternoon, Roger. I'll be out to help as soon as I call June."

"Sure thing. I could use an extra pair of hands."

A quick phone call and five minutes later, Pat was holding a plank up while Roger nailed it in place. It was warm out and Pat was glad to be in the shade rather than perched on the roof. Still, the work was pleasant, and Roger told great stories. At the moment, it was one he'd heard from Aeli and June about the hike up to the Hall and Hopkins Lakes.

"There used to be a trail up there," Roger said. "I guess no one bothered to maintain it after the rock slides, but I didn't know that, and let me tell you, they won't let me forget."

"Oh, don't let them fool you," Pat laughed. "They enjoy that story. June won't let Aeli forget the cookie story either, and I assure you, they both tell that one with equal pride in their adventures."

Roger chuckled. "They're good girls. Been friends most of their lives. I'm glad June's here for Aeli."

"Me, too. Not many people are lucky enough to have a friendship like that. No secrets, no shame, and absolute trust and loyalty and love."

Roger grunted in agreement.

"All right, Roger, let the poor boy go," Marge said as she walked up the driveway.

"He's free to leave whenever he wants. He volunteered."

"I know he did. Both of you, come inside and get cleaned up, and I'll fix you some lunch."

They nailed one last plank up before obeying. Once they'd washed up, Marge promptly put Pat back to work. Chuckling, he gladly reached into the upper cupboard and took down a couple dishes for her.

"Thank you," she said. "Now, go sit. Oh, what do you want on your sandwich? Lettuce, mustard, mayo?"

"All of the above."

Pat joined Roger in the living room, but rather than sit down, he perused the bulletin board completely covered with photos in the hallway. There were pictures of kids, grandkids, pets, cousins, parents, siblings, and landscapes from around Montana and beyond. The only pattern Pat could discern was age. The older photos were mostly on the top, the newer ones toward the bottom. There was one he particularly liked of Aelissm, June, and Luke, taken not long ago at a little celebration Marge and Roger had given Luke in honor of his official entry into the family. Aelissm was ruffling the boy's hair, Luke was trying to duck away, and June was holding her fingers like rabbit ears behind Aelissm's head. All three were obviously laughing, and the pure affection in the shot included those viewing it. There was one up that he hadn't seen yet of him and Roger sitting on the roof of the shed, their legs hanging over the edge. It was a great shot, worthy of a Western-style or cowboy magazine, and he admitted with an uncharacteristic vanity that he looked damn good in it—happy and at peace.

The phone rang, distracting him.

"Hello?" Roger asked. "Hi, June. Yes, he's still here. Well, Marge is fixing us lunch, and then they'll go surprise Aeli. Okay, I'll tell him. Uh-huh. Bye."

"Let me guess," Pat said before Roger could relay the message. "What's taking me so long, everything's ready, and daylight's burning."

Roger laughed. "Almost to the word."

They hurried through lunch and Roger offered to do the dishes so Pat and Marge could head up to the Bedspread. After pulling the Bronco into the cluttered driveway and carefully maneuvering his own truck out, Pat followed Marge as she drove her maroon car. Roger was going to take the Bronco back up to their cabin at some point today, and Pat smilingly shook his head at the shuffling of vehicles. Besides the older Bronco and the car, Marge and Roger also had the newer white Bronco, a truck they used for firewood, a nineteen-seventy-something Oldsmobile, the Model-T, and another, classic Bronco Aelissm's uncle drove when he came out from Ohio.

"And let's not forget the old tractor and the grader parked up at their cabin," Pat added aloud. "And the snowmobiles, dirt bikes, and four-wheelers."

Aeli had remarked once that all those vehicles—not one of which was less than five years old—were Roger's way of coping with retirement. Between the occasional odd mechanical job he still did and all the vehicles he had to tinker on, Aelissm's grandfather always had something to do.

"And if he has someone to talk to while he's at it, he's as happy as a dog with a bone," she'd said.

She hadn't said much to him over the last two weeks beyond what was necessary, which was the reason for his surprise and why Marge was going to be working at the Bedspread tonight for the first time since Aelissm's second month back in Northstar. Pat was going to get Aelissm to warm up again if it took him another two weeks to do it. He sincerely hoped it wouldn't take that long because, as much as he loved Aelissm's sass, she had been downright cold and nasty, and he missed that spark of love and desire that had been steadily building between them. Without it, he felt as if he'd been plunged back into the bitter heart of winter.

"What are you going to do when it's time to go back to Washington?" Pat asked himself. It was hard to think of Kitsap County as home anymore.

His unpleasant musings kept him occupied all the way to the inn. A warm welcome was too much to expect, so he didn't look for one. As he followed Marge into the dining room, Aelissm eyed them suspiciously.

"What are you doing here, Grandma?"

"We thought it was time you started acting like yourself again and stopped being so surly," Marge replied. "So, we're going to do something about it."

Pat winced when Aelissm planted her feet stubbornly, crossed her arms, and turned accusing green eyes on him.

"Who's 'we'?"

"All of us. Your grandfather and I, your workers, June, Pat, and even Luke. He said you snapped at him yesterday."

Guilt flickered momentarily across her face. No matter how angry she might be, her respect of her grandmother and her fondness for June's adopted son could still sway her. Pat could let those emotions do his work for him but steadfastly refused to rely on anyone else to solve his problems. He'd caused this moodiness of Aeli's, and he would fix it.

"We thought it would be nice if you, June, Luke, and I took a camping trip up to Sawtooth Lake," he said. "Right now. Everything's ready, and your grandmother has volunteered to close the Bedspread tonight so you can go."

"No. Even if I was inclined to let her work for me, I have a million other things to do. My summer class at the college starts in two weeks, and I have finals next week—"

Pat closed the distance in one long stride and kissed her. She placed her hands on his chest and pushed. Hard. His eyes narrowed, matching the fury of Aelissm's gaze. Hate and resentment flared, laced with the acidic rejection, and it was difficult to swallow that vicious meal. No matter how bad-tempered and vengeful Aelissm may be feeling, she could never be Sara. That he was remotely reminded of his ex was one more reason why he needed to get Aelissm to relax again.

"There are a few things I could say right now," Pat said, willing his voice to be level. "But I won't because I really don't mean them. So, I will tell you right now, Aelissm, that we've all had it with your attitude. I don't care if it's warranted. It ends now. You're going to come home with me, Marge is going to cover the rest of your shift, and we *are* going to hike up to Sawtooth and spend the night. And you're going to enjoy it, one way or another."

"No."

"Yes."

"Make me."

"All right." Before she could escape, Pat dipped down, wrapped an arm around her thighs, and tossed her over his shoulder.

"Pat! Put me down!"

"Nope." He turned around. "Got it covered, Marge?"

"I've got it covered."

"Grandma!" Aelissm pleaded. "Tell him to put me down."

"Sorry, honey, but I agree with him."

Aelissm growled and struggled to free herself for a moment, then gave up when her attempts gained her a tighter grip. Pat waved his free hand at Marge and headed outside. Aeli braced her forearms on his back and settled in for the ride. He knew if he loosened his hold on her for even a second she would try to thrash herself free. Given the proximity of her knees to his belly, he wasn't about to give her the opportunity.

"Good luck with her!" Marge called.

"I sincerely hope I won't need it," he replied under his breath.

"Oh, you'll need it," Aelissm sneered.

"So might you. I'm not going to give in."

"Great way to get me to warm up to your scheme, Pat."

"I'd sugar-coat if for you, but you'd only throw it back in my face, so I'm not going to waste my energy."

Pat opened the driver-side door of his truck and

dumped her inside. He was mildly surprised that she didn't scoot across the seat and make a go of escaping out the other side. It seemed that staying angry was using more energy than Aelissm wanted to expend. Or it could be she was only waiting to unleash her aggression when there'd be no witnesses. He shrugged.

"You're too proud to ask what I've been doing in Devyn," Pat said, driving down Elkhorn Road. "So, I'll tell you. I've been tracking Winters."

She waited a few moments before impatience and curiosity won out. "And?"

"He's been working at the Paradise Motel, in the kitchen, and he's been there a couple months, but that part you already know from Amber. Everyone he works with greets him like he's part of the crew, but he does like to stay out of sight whenever he can. I also know that he drives a very plain white Ford pickup."

"Marvelous. Only about one of every five people here own one," Aeli muttered. "License plate number?"

"I have it. I'll give it to you when we get to the cabin."

"What about where he lives? Is he staying with Amber?"

Pat shrugged noncommittally. He wasn't about to share *that* information with her because she'd likely do something to get herself in trouble. Adam's license plate number was probably too much for her to know just yet, but he wanted her aware and able to spot the truck for her safety. And he wanted to reassure her that he *was* doing his job.

"Well, I suppose that's something," Aeli muttered after a moment.

"Something's better than nothing."

Grudgingly, she replied, "Yeah, I guess it is."

Pat wanted to smile but didn't dare, feeling she would take exception. He'd prepped her for a return to civility, and a pleasant evening beside a quiet lake after a long hike should have her back to her beautiful, laughing self. He couldn't wait. Neither could he deny that he wanted to kiss her and be kissed in return. Her rejection at the Bedspread hurt more than he would have thought.

Aelissm seemed content with the information he'd given her, and the ride up to the cabin was silent. They had the windows down, and even though it was only just a bit past noon, the air was thick with summer warmth. He'd been here long enough to know, however, that the silky touch of air on the bare skin of his forearm was no promise of a balmy night up by the lake.

"How cold do you think it'll be tonight?" he asked when Aelissm climbed back in after opening the gate.

"I don't know. A few degrees above freezing. We might wake up to a little frost. And the ice might not be completely off the lake yet."

"You and June have subzero sleeping bags, though, right?"

"Of course."

There was a note of anticipation in her voice that made Pat smile.

Less than thirty minutes later, Pat was glad he'd taken so many hiking trips into the Cascades with his parents and Sara. Aelissm was efficient and had her pack ready in an astonishingly short time. Though he'd already settled his own pack, it took him nearly as long to double-check all the gear. He took both packs out to his truck while Aelissm did a final inspection of the cabin. When he came back, she was leaning against the snack bar with her ankles crossed, wistfully admiring his pan flute. She held it gently in her hands as if it were made of delicate spun glass instead of wood. He must have forgotten to put it away that morning before he'd left for Devyn.

"Where'd you get this?" she asked. "And when?"

"My Grandpa O'Neil made it for me when I was a little boy."

"You should bring it to the lake."

"I was thinking about it, but I don't know." He inhaled slowly. "I haven't played it since he passed away."

"I'm sorry."

He shrugged and took it from her. "Not your fault. He wasn't that old, but he went peacefully. I guess by the time I was able to deal with it, I was starting to really get into my work. And then I met Sara."

"She never heard it, then."

It was a statement, not a question. He shook his head and took the flute from her. Running his thumb over the smooth wood, he vaguely felt his face shift into a frown of longing. "No, I never played it for her."

"Good. She didn't deserve it. Or you."

"Truce?" he asked.

He was rewarded with the first real smile from her in two weeks. "Truce."

"Let's get going, then, before June decides we're not worth the wait."

She brushed past him and headed for the door.

"Aelissm?"

When she turned slowly to face him, the familiar concern for him furrowed her brows.

"What is it?"

His throat constricted around the request. Was it too soon to ask? But he needed her. He needed to hold her and be held.

"Kiss me?" he asked, his voice barely a pleading whisper.

For a moment, he thought she was going to turn back around, angry, and storm out the door. It was truly amazing how a handful of seconds could stretch into eternity with only the deep thudding of his heart to count the time by. Then, she took a step toward him, and another, until she was standing barely a hand span away. Curling her hands around his neck, she stood on her toes and pressed her lips gently to his. He wrapped his arms around her and tucked her firmly against him.

"Now, that's what I call a truce," she murmured against his lips. "Does this mean we get to find out if make-up sex is really all it's said to be?"

Pat's head fell back, and he laughed long and hard. "God, Aelissm, I've missed you."

"I know. I've missed me, too." She grabbed a handful of his shirt, playfully yanked him to her, and kissed him again. "For good measure. So, how 'bout that hike?"

Fourteen

DEFINITELY WORTH IT, Aelissm thought as she turned her gaze from the recently erected tents to the glassy surface of Sawtooth Lake. They had set up camp at the edge of the meadow on the east end of the lake, across from where the official trail ended. The ground beneath the trees was worn smooth by the boots of hikers who had chosen this same spot to camp for years, but the lush meadow was as unspoiled as it had been since its formation. Aelissm traced the meandering path of the stream through the thick green grass and smiled. This was, by far, the most popular spot on the lake, but rarely were there multiple parties camped here. As late in the afternoon as it was, Aeli doubted her own little party of four would be disturbed tonight. That suited her just fine. She didn't mind having June and Luke around, but when the campfire died down and the moon came out, she wanted the lake to herself. More to the point, she wanted Pat to herself.

Kissing him this afternoon had re-ignited something that she truly had missed in the past two weeks. After the weeks of sensing the growing heat, she wanted to touch the fire. If Pat thought she wasn't ready or he wasn't, well, she'd have to convince him otherwise. It was time they both got over their fear and reluctance of being with someone else. She was done playing around, done being satisfied with a kiss here and there and the occasional chaste caress.

"Aeli! You gonna help with dinner or what?" June called.

"Yeah, yeah, I'm coming."

When she arrived at the tents, she scowled at her friend. "You know, June, you have a talent for interrupting my daydreams."

"Oh? And what were you daydreaming about?" June asked. Glancing in Pat's direction, she winked and added, "Or should I say whom?"

"Hush up and hand me the lighter."

Aelissm gathered some pine needles and dead grass and made a nest in the ring of rocks in the center of their campsite. How long ago had her father brought her up for their first overnight father-daughter trip? The same summer she'd first met June. June hadn't come that time, of course, but she remembered how cool it had been to have her dad and the lake all to herself. They'd used this same ring then and several times since. In high school, June had started coming up to the cabin with them, and once, the two of them had camped up here all by themselves.

"And we were too scared to go to sleep," she

murmured.

"What's that, Aeli?"

"I was thinking about that time you and I spent the night alone up here."

Her friend laughed. "And we thought we were such tough, independent tomboys. Taught us something, didn't it?"

"Yeah, having a man around to protect us is kinda nice."

They paused to watch the boys prowling through the meadow along the inlet stream. The warmth that churned through her as Pat indulged Luke in some one-on-one boy time had become familiar, and even over the past two weeks, she'd felt it. She could put a name to it but wouldn't right now. Not yet. Tonight, there was a different kind of heat she wanted to feel.

"Do you want me to start the fire?" June asked. "I don't know about you, but I'm hungry, and I know Luke and Pat are, too."

Aeli returned her attention to the fire pit and strategically piled twigs over and around the nest of tinder. She took the hatchet off Pat's pack and used it to splinter some of the larger sticks into kindling. After lighting the fire, she waited a few moments, blowing on it occasionally. When she was sure she had a strong blaze going, she scouted around for some larger pieces and soon had a small bonfire.

"Dinner ready yet?" Pat asked as he and Luke returned.

"Not unless you want it cold," Aelissm replied. "Fire's just about there, though. Git yer pokers ready."

"We've got them," Luke announced proudly,

presenting four slender willow branches.

"Feeling better?" Pat asked Aelissm as he skewered a hot dog on the end of her stick.

"Much, but if you get cocky about it, Mr. O'Neil, I reserve the right to change my mind," she replied. "On second thought—"

"Aelissm! Don't you dare say it," June warned.

"What?" she said. Feigning innocence, she offered June a scandalized gasp. "You dirty-minded little wench!"

"I didn't think it first," June replied tartly. "Pull your head out of the gutter because I'd really like to float by."

Luke looked at Pat questioningly, but the man wasn't paying attention. He'd turned an amusing shade of pink, however. Aelissm silently scratched a tally mark in her mind for a win. She doubted either one of them had missed the conversation. Luke was old enough that his imagination could come up with all kinds of things to fit to the commentary and Pat…. Pat was apparently quite aware of her meaning, and if the light furrow of his brows and half-lifted mouth were any indication, he wasn't as certain regarding what he should do about it. A giggle escaped her.

"She's evil," Pat remarked to June. "But I think that's what makes her so cute."

As they roasted their hot dogs and entertained themselves with jokes, old stories, and tales of recent adventures, Aelissm decided she was feeling deliciously mischievous. She forgot about Adam and the Bedspread and the upcoming finals for her class at the college. Her brain was marvelously devoid of all thoughts other than seducing Pat. Well, almost all other thoughts. There was still enough room left in her mind to enjoy a stunning evening with her closest friends. Embraced as she was by the arms of the mountains above her and the symphony of her home, how could she not be in a good mood?

Pat presented her with an array of condiment packets June had pilfered from the Ramshorn, and she chuckled as she took a ketchup and a mustard. Since packing condiment bottles was cumbersome, she'd been prepared to choke down a dry hot dog. Instead, she was now enjoying the perfect camp-out meal. By the time she'd finished her first hot dog, both Pat and Luke had already scarfed their second.

"How come we never thought of this before?" she asked.

"Well, let's see. Until I started working at the Ramshorn, we didn't have a ready supply of portable condiment packets to borrow."

"Borrow? How do you borrow these?"

"Okay, fine. Mary said I could have them if I promised to bring you back in a better mood."

"Ha ha, very funny, June."

"It's true," Pat told her.

"You've been a pain in the ass lately, Aelissm."

"Thanks a lot, June."

"You're welcome. Here, have another hot dog."

"Can I have one, too?" Luke asked.

When the adults all turned their gazes on him, he shrugged. "What? I'm hungry."

June handed him the package, laughing.

"I really hope you're not a sore loser, Aeli," Pat said.

"Excuse me?"

"Don't tell me you've forgotten our bet already."

Aelissm frowned, trying to remember. Then it hit her.

She studied Luke as the boy fixed up his bun with one hand and held his third hot dog over the fire with the other. He'd grown a little since his arrival in Northstar, but not enough to suggest he'd be as tall as Pat proposed. Still… he had an appetite, and so far, she hadn't seen much of where he might be storing it all. She was reminded of a cat crouched to spring and realized there was a good chance Pat would win their bet that Luke would reach six-foot-two.

"Well, *if* I lose, it'll be a hundred bucks well spent," she replied.

Pat narrowed his eyes, glanced from Luke to June and back to Aelissm, and said, "We might have to give it to June to help keep clothes on him."

"Huh?" Luke asked around a mouthful of hot dog.

"What bet is this?" June inquired.

"We'll let you know when we have a winner. Patience is a virtue, my dear friend."

"Now, that's a fine sentiment, but coming from you…."

"Hush. It's my lie; let me tell it my way."

Her retort was met with a round of laughter, and she admitted it was wonderful to be free to be herself again. Yes, she'd been angry that Adam had been in Devyn so long without them knowing it and terrified to know that he was so close, but she could have risen above it and been a bearable human being. Pat had taken the brunt of her emotions, and to his credit, he'd sailed through it with admirable patience. It had been easier to blame him for not doing his job than to admit responsibility. Adam was a problem she should have taken care of long before her overprotective, beloved uncle had felt the need to send Pat here to protect her.

On that line of thought, however, the logical part of her mind rightly argued that Pat's presence in Northstar had been good for them both. How good had yet to be proven, but that was something Aelissm was determined to discover.

"Pat, take a walk with me," she said.

"I'm still eating," he replied, indicating his half-eaten third hot dog.

"Bring it with you. June, we'll be back shortly."

"Hey, you're both adults, and I'm not here to babysit you."

Aelissm bounced to her feet and offered Pat a hand up. He hesitated, eyeing her warily. When she wiggled her fingers, he took her hand and stood. She led him out into the meadow, wandering toward the lakeshore. They reached the log across the mouth of the inlet creek before she paused. Pat said nothing as she walked across it, pointing her toes out with each step. Halfway across the log, she swiveled and faced him with her hands on her hips. He was watching her with the slightest of admiring smiles on his handsome face, the kind that glowed warmly in his eyes but barely touched his lips.

"I'm sorry," she blurted. There, it was out.

"Wow, Aeli, I really didn't expect an apology so soon."

"Don't be a smart ass," she retorted, hurt by the defensiveness in his tone and the wariness in his eyes. Those beautiful blue-flecked hazel eyes…. Distance was the last thing she wanted to see in them. It gave her the courage to say what she really wanted to. "I wanted to tell you that I'm sorry for the way I've been acting. I really am. It wasn't very fair of me."

"No, it wasn't." Pat sighed. "But I deserve at least some of your animosity."

"No, you don't. I've been a bitch. I can admit that. I frequently do, even when I'm far less deserving of the title." She drew a deep breath and met his eyes. "So here it is. I'm glad you're here, Pat. And thank you for everything you've done for me. I'm glad Uncle Bill asked you to come."

He didn't seem to have a reply, so she stepped down off the log, strode to him, and kissed him hard on the lips. It was a gesture of friendship and gratitude, but when she angled her body against him, she promised more. When she took a step back from him, she found his eyes closed and his brows pinched in a frown. Slowly, he opened his eyes and turned his unfocused gaze out across the lake.

"I hope this doesn't sound callous, but I wonder if we'll ever reach a point when we can just be us without the need to apologize or express our gratitude."

Aelissm considered his words. They'd both been through a lot and brought each other through the beginning stages of recovery. For Pat, his past was just that. Aeli's was still happening. She wasn't through with Adam just yet. When she was, what then? Pat would go back to Washington, and she would stay here, teaching at the university in Devyn and running the Bedspread Inn. Would they have time to reach that point?

"I think we'll always be grateful for what we've helped each other find," she said slowly. "And anyone who can go through life without feeling the occasional need to apologize is a selfish pig. But for us? Why can't that time be right now? Stealing a page from June's mammoth book of philosophy, I think the constant need to express gratitude belongs in a shallow relationship. Between acquaintances. And I think we moved beyond acquaintance a while ago."

What was left unspoken made her pulse quicken. When she lifted searching fingers to Pat's chest, she felt the pace of his heart increase to match hers. Tentatively, she flattened her palm, thrilled, relieved, and afraid all at once. Was she ready to take that irrevocable step? The answer was a firm yes, but that didn't mean she wasn't worried about the consequences for both of them. Contrary to her earlier, private proclamation, she could not honestly go ahead with a to-hell-with-it attitude. Whatever pleasure they found, there would also be matching heartbreak. This wouldn't last, no matter how badly she might want it to. The question was, would that pain be worth knowing what it was to give herself to Pat body and heart?

Yes.

Better to have loved and lost than never to have loved at all, eh? she thought.

"Whatever happens, Aeli, you *are* right," Pat said. "We're more than acquaintances now."

"And you work under my uncle. How hard can it be to stay in touch?"

"Not very, but it's not over yet, Aelissm. I'm still here."

Not, *I'm not leaving yet.* He'd said, *I'm still here.*

Her lips twisted as her sense of humor bubbled free, and she wiggled her eyebrows suggestively at him. "If Adam staying around will keep you here with me, then by all means, I'll give him a down-payment for a house in Devyn."

"You know what, Aeli? June's got you pegged."

"She has most people pegged, but do tell how she has me defined."

"You have no shame."

She laughed until her face and sides ached. "No, I don't."

"That's one of the things I love about you," he said. He slipped an arm around her waist and before she knew it, he swept her off her feet and started back toward camp. She giggled the entire way back.

June had cleaned up their simple dinner and broken out the s'mores fixings. She regarded them with one brow lifted, then smiled and shook her head. Luke watched them with unguarded amusement from his perch in a low nook of a nearby tree. Aelissm, still helpless and weak from mirth, glanced from June over to Luke and up to Pat and soaked up the simple love of her motley family. They may be an odd bunch, and one of them might be gone before long, but for now, they were all hers, and she loved them dearly.

"Why do you put up with me?" she asked.

"Because we love you," June replied. "And because you have a pretty high entertainment value."

"Ah, now I feel all mushy inside. Pat, put me down. Luke, get over here and help me make some marshmallow torches."

"I think we over did it, Pat," June remarked as she tore open the marshmallow bag. "She's gone from one extreme of the Aeli Spectrum to the other."

"Would you prefer the demon spawn from hell?" Aelissm asked.

"No!" three voices replied.

"Then take what you get and quit complaining."

"Yes, ma'am," June replied.

As evening passed into sunset and sunset into star-spattered night, they intermittently darted around the meadow in a spirited game of tag and sat around telling bad jokes around the campfire. Around ten, they tidied up the camp, made sure the food was tied high up away from their tents in case a bear decided to investigate, and headed out to the meadow again to star-gaze. Pat grabbed his pan flute and his and Aelissm's sleeping bags, and everyone else brought their pillows. Careful to keep their fire within eyesight and running distance, they stretched out on a huge, flat boulder on the other side of the meadow.

The night was cooling rapidly, so Pat unzipped his bag, and the four of them snuggled close for warmth. It was about as perfect a night as Aeli could hope for.

"It's absolutely gorgeous," Pat said. He tucked his arm around Aelissm's shoulders.

"I'll never get tired of it," June agreed.

For a long time, they sat in contented silence, speaking only to point out a shooting star. After a while, Luke started yawning, and he and June bid Pat and Aeli good night. Aelissm watched with a rising excitement as they made the trek back to camp. Soon, she would have the night, the lake, and Pat to herself, and she doubted she would be content merely snuggling with him on the boulder, no matter how nice it was to be wrapped so warmly in his arms.

When Pat took a deep breath, Aelissm levered her upper body away from him to look up at his face. She watched, mesmerized, as he lifted his pan flute to his lips and began to play. The notes drifted hauntingly across the bowl of the mountains, and Aeli shivered. It was a beautiful song he played, slow and romantic. She leaned back against him and let the solid warmth of him soothe her as his music touched her heart.

"You don't have to seduce me, Pat," she murmured to herself. "Say the word, and I'm yours."

The playing continued for a little while longer before he lowered the flute again and asked in a whisper, "Are you sure?"

"Yes," she replied. "Make love to me."

"Aelissm…."

"Listen to me, Pat. This is right. When you leave, I don't want to watch you go, wondering and regretting that we never did more than kiss. I'd rather have one night with you to remember than cold emptiness."

There was no hesitation in the hand that stroked her neck, only tenderness and a thrilling urgency. When he lowered his mouth to follow his fingers, she shuddered in pleasure.

"You're not going to argue your way out of this?" she asked, more than a little surprised. "You're not going to say we aren't ready or that we'll get hurt?"

"We probably *aren't* ready, and we probably *will* get hurt, Aelissm. And I'm sure I'll feel guilty as hell in the morning, but you said no more apologies, right? We wanted to see where this would take us, and, God help me, I need you."

She was stunned at his admission, which made her want him more. She took his free hand and dragged it down between her breasts, then sought his mouth with hers. As they joined lips, hungrily devouring each other, Aelissm's desire for him bloomed gloriously through her. She playfully massaged the inside of his thigh, and he groaned low in his throat. Their hands sought every inch of each other's bodies they could reach sitting as they were, until Aeli boldly straddled his lap. The truth of his need for her pressed firmly against her, and her own desire flared in response. His hands burrowed under her shirt, stroking up her back and down again. The feel of his strong hands on her skin was ecstasy. He stoked the fire of her passion with expertise, tantalizing her senses as he raked his teeth over her neck and shoulder. She writhed against him, pleading for more.

When Pat slid his hands down her sides and gripped her hips, she moaned, rocking instinctively against him. Gently, he lifted her and laid her on the cushioning sleeping bag. She barely felt the hard stone beneath it; she was too lost in his touches to notice anything else. Sitting beside her, he slowly, torturously unbuttoned her flannel and peeled it back from her shoulders. Eagerly, she sat up and stripped the rest off. In her haste, her feather pillow snagged on the boulder and ripped open. A cloud of feathers wafted around them, and she giggled.

"Slow down," he murmured huskily. "I want this to be right."

"How could it be wrong?" she asked dazedly.

"I don't want to rush you. I can't make it painless, sweetheart, but I can arouse you until the pleasure overcomes it."

"How many virgins have you had to know so much about taking one?" she asked.

"Just one," he replied. "The night I lost mine."

All thoughts of his previous conquests flew out the window when he pulled her halter top over her head and slid searching fingers beneath her black lace bra. He lay down beside her, propped on his elbow. The newly risen moon glittered in his hair, turning dark auburn to blue-black tipped in platinum. Vainly, she knew the moonlight had bathed her in delicate softness and given her skin the appearance of fragile perfection.

"You're beautiful, Aelissm Davis," he replied.

The heat of girlish coyness warmed her face. To cover it, she pulled his mouth back down to hers. Anticipation surged through her, coiled unsettlingly with hesitation. She may have conquered the kissing part, but everything else was new to her, and she didn't have any clue what she was doing.

"What's the matter, Aeli?" Pat asked, pulling back to regard her with worried eyes.

"I'm a little… nervous, I guess. I have no idea what I should do."

He smiled adoringly at her. "You're doing just fine, sweetheart. Don't think, just feel."

"Take your shirt off," she commanded. "If you get to admire my half-nakedness, I get to admire yours."

Chuckling softly, Pat did as he was told and sat up. As he slid out of the flannel he'd borrowed from her father's dresser and pulled his T-shirt over his head, muscle danced beneath skin silvered by moonlight. She traced the lines of him with her eyes before she realized he'd given her permission to explore with her hands and lips, too. As her fingers trailed over his skin, she felt a strange emotion settle over her even as passion escalated. She wanted to give him the same pleasure he gave her. She wanted to give him every-thing she had and was and wanted nothing more than proof of his happiness in return. Was that love? It certainly wasn't lust. Even in her limited experience with the latter, she knew lust was selfish.

She wouldn't complicate things by blurting it out and didn't want to ruin things by going all mushy in the thrall of desire. But she *did* love him. And if this was as far as things were going to go between them, she could live with that. As long as he was happy. She felt fortunate to have as much of him as she had.

"Aeli… are you *sure* you want to do this?"

"I'm sure, but I'm thinking too much, Pat. Make my brain shut up."

What started out as tender, curious caresses soon turned into fevered strokes and demands. Somehow, they managed to keep the sleeping bags tucked around them, though occasionally, a blast of chilly night air coaxed goose bumps from their flesh.

Aelissm's bra was discarded, and her jeans and black panties followed quickly. With hungry intent, she unbuckled Pat's belt. She wanted there to be nothing between them but heat. He traced circles around her nipples alternately with his fingers and tongue, and she arched up, digging her fingers into his back. She ached for him, and he groaned as she brazenly pushed his jeans down over his hips and pressed herself against him.

"Oh, good lord," he whispered. His hand delved be-tween her legs, stroking her to overload. "I need you, Ae-lissm."

"Then take me," she hissed. "Please…."

Pat braced himself on top of her, but instead of taking her, he trailed kisses from the hollow of her throat to her navel and slid his fingers inside her. She moaned, falling into rhythm with his hand. It felt incredible, but she wanted more of him, and a pleading whimper escaped her. He entered her then, gently, and pain seared through her. She stiffened and bit her lip to keep the cry locked in her throat.

"I'm sorry," he murmured in her ear.

He kept their pace slow and shallow, allowing her to adjust. The pain faded away, leaving only joy and pleasure, and he pushed deeper and faster until he filled her completely, and she gasped. When she thought she couldn't take anymore, he slowed again, giving her a new range of sensations. Time sped out of existence as he thrust into her, taking her nearly to the peak and bringing her back down again. Each time she neared oblivion, the ecstasy grew, and finally, he took her there. The orgasm broke over her thunderously, and bliss and dizziness crashed through her. She clenched around him, pulsing in perfect time with him. As it subsided, her body quivered with raw gratification.

Pat pulled away from her and rolled on to his back, his ribs heaving from the exertion. As sensibility returned, Aelissm propped herself up and gazed down at him, grinning smugly. His eyes were closed, and on his lips was the most beautiful, sated smile. She curled against his side with her arm around his waist, her head on his shoulder, and her legs entwined with his. When he wrapped his arm around her, she knew there was no more perfect a place to be.

I love you, Patrick O'Neil, she said to herself. *And I may get my heart broken when you leave, but I'll never regret this night.*

It was only after they made love again that she

realized they were both decorated in soft, downy feathers. They were going to have some explaining to do in the morning.

Fifteen

AELISSM PROPPED HERSELF on her elbow and watched Pat sleep, bathed in the obscene yellow glow of the tent. The sun had only just risen high enough to crest the mountain and pierce the forest. Peeking out the mesh window, she discovered their temporary home was in one of very few shafts of sharp morning light. Returning her attention to her lover, she traced the lines of him with her eyes, recalling with exquisite detail every touch, every whispered plea, and every quiver of desire from last night. Lying there, gazing down at Pat, she was soothed by the steady rise and fall of his chest and the way contentment and sleep had eradicated the strain that frequently aged his face. Without those lines, he looked younger than twenty-eight, and she hoped the peace he'd found recently would last.

She heard the zipper on June's tent slide and pulled

herself carefully out of the nest of sleeping bags she and Pat had created last night when they'd finally returned to their tent. She crawled to the door and slithered outside to greet the young day with a satisfied smile.

"You two must've had some night," June remarked.

Silently cursing the blush that heated her cheeks, Aelissm met her friend's intent gaze head on. "You might say that."

"There's a trail of feathers from the boulder to your tent. I think poor Luke may have been scarred for life when he went out to water a tree."

Aelissm blanched. This was one of those rare instances when she couldn't read June's scowl. She wasn't sure if her friend was joking or truly angry with her. Sheepishly, she asked why June thought Luke had been traumatized.

"All I know is that he went out, minding his own business, heard music—you never told me Pat plays a flute—and looked up in time to see the two of you making out like a pair of horny teenagers."

"Oh."

"Yes, 'oh.' What were you thinking, Aelissm?"

"To be honest, I wasn't doing much thinking."

"Judging by the state of your pillow, I'd say that's rather obvious. Sometimes I wonder if you listen to me at all."

"What's that supposed to mean?" Aeli demanded as June started gathering wood for a breakfast fire.

June straightened, put her hands on her hips, and gave Aelissm one of her must-I-repeat-myself-again sighs.

"The deeper you go, the more it's going to hurt when he leaves," she said, her voice soft with concern.

"In that case… it's going to hurt like hell because he went deep. And it was incredible, June. Please don't ask me to regret it."

"I'm not, and I never would." June shook her head and laughed. "I can always count on your honesty, even if I don't want or need to know. No wonder Luke was startled. I hope he didn't see that."

"I doubt it. We were in the sleeping bags."

"So you *do* have a shred of decency in you."

By her exaggerated tone, Aelissm knew June was done playing the concerned best friend. She was surprised to find herself disappointed. She *wanted* to talk to June about what had happened between her and Pat last night—not the juicy details but the emotional ones. June, of all people, would be able to tell her if she was either completely insane or if her seemingly irrational desire to have at least one night with Pat was right. She snorted. Wantonly abandoning all common sense and making love to a man she knew was going to leave was most definitely not being responsible, so she already knew June's advice wouldn't lean in *that* direction.

"I wanted to have a memory of him to comfort me when I have to watch him drive away."

June narrowed her eyes and studied Aelissm for a long time before replying. When she finally spoke, the words were the last Aeli expected to hear. "You don't have to watch him drive away."

"How? I don't know when I won't have to worry about Adam anymore, but someday in the not-too-distant future, Adam will be out of my life for good, and Pat will go back to Washington. To his job and his life."

"How much do you love him?"

"I don't recall saying that I did."

"It's written all over you face, Aeli. It has been for weeks."

Damn you, June, she thought without heat. Her friend knew her too well. So well that she had apparently known what Aelissm was feeling long before Aelissm was aware of it herself. Or, at least, before she was willing to put a name to this strange, painful, wonderful, and completely uncontrollable fluttering of her heart.

"Whether you're willing to admit it yet or not, you *do* love him, Aelissm. The question is, how much?"

"You want to know if I love him enough to follow him back to Washington."

June nodded.

"If he wanted me to? I don't know yet, June. I honestly don't." She took a long, deep breath and let it out slowly. "Washington has a lot of bad memories for me."

"I know it does."

"And Northstar is home. Look at us. Our dream of raising our kids together here is within reach."

"Yes, it is."

She saw the point June was trying to make. If she didn't love Pat enough to face her lingering fears and go to Washington for him, it was best if things didn't go any farther than they had already. It wasn't fair to either of them if she couldn't make that kind of commitment, especially if Pat loved her. She couldn't hurt him like that, not after what he'd been through with his ex. Her mother had told her once that when she couldn't imagine her life without a man, she'd found the right one. Well, she could still see her life without Pat in it, but the image was becoming more and more hazy. It was a snap to picture them together... at the altar, celebrating the birth of their first child, spoiling their grandchildren rotten.

"The look on your face right now would usually make you sick," June remarked. "You're dangerously close to impersonating those moon-eyed, love-sick teenage girls we teach."

"Really?"

"Yeah. I'm a little disturbed."

Aelissm offered her friend a playful scowl. "I get it, June."

"Good."

With that, June returned to gathering wood, ignoring Aelissm completely. She'd given Aeli plenty to consider, and she *would* consider it, right along with what she could do to get Adam out of her life. For the time being, however, all that could wait.

She snuck back into her tent and woke Pat with a kiss and a playful caress.

"I know June's up, so don't start anything you might be too embarrassed to finished," he murmured sleepily. His eyes were still closed, but there was a faint smugness about his features.

"Mmm. And what about me has ever given you the idea I'd be so easily embarrassed?"

He opened one eye and looked at her. "The fact that you're blushing right now."

"Okay, fine, be that way. Get your sexy ass out of the sack."

She flipped the sleeping bag back and was awarded

with a beautiful view of a gorgeously built, entirely naked man.

Cursing, Pat grabbed his boxers and yanked them on. "That's mean, Aeli, and cold. What's the temperature out?"

"Oh, probably around thirty-five."

"You're a cruel woman, Aelissm Davis. Gimme that back." He reached for the sleeping bag.

"Nope. It's time to get up. June's starting the breakfast fire, so if you want something to eat, get dressed." She cocked her head, devouring the sight of him with her eyes. "Then again, I'm really liking the scenery, Mr. O'Neil."

"Uh-huh. Be gone with you, fiend."

Aelissm retreated from the tent obediently but unwillingly. Luke was sitting on a log by the roaring fire June had started, rubbing the sleep from his eyes. When he caught Aeli's gaze, his face turned ashen, then red. She apologized for what he'd seen last night, and he smiled timidly in response. The sudden distance he'd put between them shocked her and left her feeling odd, like something she was trying to hold on to was slipping through her fingers. There was so much to consider before she made her decision about Pat, and she had the distinct impression she would miss something.

It would have been a simple choice if her lust had been slaked, but curiously, having known Pat so intimately last night, she was all the more attracted. She wanted to watch him move, to take in the fluid movements of his body and revel in the pleasure of it.

She laughed at herself. Maybe she did love him enough to go back to Washington, but the thought of living so close to the city again and falling prey to the persistent, consuming rush of it made her skin crawl. Since coming back to Northstar, she'd found herself again. The woman she'd become in Seattle, who had given in to the lifestyle and a man she hadn't loved was gone. She was Aelissm again and beyond grateful to be nothing more or less. If she went back to Washington to be with Pat, how long would it be before the woman he'd fallen in love with—*if he loves you*, a vicious voice whispered in the back of her mind—became lost again? Kitsap County wasn't Seattle, but it was too close for her liking. Every time she stood on the Indianola dock or the beach, she'd see the city across the water. Would Pat still love her if she reverted to that impatient bitch, or would he be reminded of Sara and turn away from her in horror?

That was the gist of it. They had no hope of continuing what they'd begun. She couldn't ask him to give up his career any more than she could leave Northstar, so it was probably best that they find a way to resolve his reason for being here in the first place and put a stop to this disaster-in-the-making before the damage became too great.

The shy smiles he gave her all through breakfast and the occasional, fleeting times he took her hand on the hike down the trail from the lake firmed her resolve. Whether or not he loved her was still unknown, but he felt enough for her that, for his sake, she needed to end this. The shadows Sara had put in his eyes had been gone for a while now, and she wouldn't be able to live with herself if she put new ones in their place.

It was when they reached his truck, and she saw his notebook sitting on the dash that she understood what she was going to do. When she had the chance, she'd snoop through it. She wasn't dumb enough to believe he didn't have Adam's address if he had a vehicle description and a license plate number. Even if he didn't, she could use what he'd found so far to do some research of her own. It had been over a year now since her life had been thrown into chaos, and it was time she took control. If she was going to get her heart broken, it was going to be on her terms and her timeline. Not *too* long ago, she'd vowed to June that she was done running, and she hadn't run since. She'd dug her heels in with every ounce of the stubbornness that used to drive her mother to distraction. Now, she was going to play the game *her* way.

Adam, she thought, *it's time you and I come to a little understanding.*

Six hours later, she was standing in front of a tiny rented house behind the Paradise Motel in Devyn, holding a note and a pushpin. Without a moment's hesitation, she tacked the carefully worded letter to the door and took a deep breath. Remarkably, her hand was steady and her legs were firm beneath her. She wasn't doing this because she was tired of Adam's obsession with her or even because she wanted her life back. She was doing it because she'd made a decision about Pat.

"If we're going to make it, my love, it won't be because Adam is keeping you here."

* * *

Much of Pat's day was spent in a haze of daydreams. How he managed to take orders at the Bedspread and serve guests without error was nothing short of a miracle because, when he stepped outside for a break, he was shocked to find it was nearly dusk, and he couldn't remember most of the day. He knew Nick Hammond and his wife and infant son had stopped in for lunch, and Nick's father and Old Matt Carlyle had been in for their nightly beers a short while ago, but there was little else he could recall since he'd kissed Aelissm goodbye and watched her drive off.

He could clearly remember her kissing him awake this morning, however, and he could certainly recall last night without any difficulty. He remembered the feel of her soft skin beneath his hand as if he were touching her now, and the memory of her arching against him and pleading for more was still a raging wildfire in his veins.

"And if you don't stop this train of thought, you'll be sorry," he muttered, cursing the returning ache in his loins.

Besides, he seriously doubted Aelissm would be too understanding of any dereliction of his duties at her inn even if it was thoughts of her that continually distracted him. However, he knew the job well enough that he could get through a day on autopilot. Today was proof of that, he mused, because he certainly hadn't been thinking about the orders he'd taken or the food he'd cooked, and somehow, everything had met or exceeded his patrons' expectations. Aelissm would be pleased about that.

As he took a deep breath, he wondered how her class was going. It was the last of this course, but she wouldn't have much of a break as her summer class would start in just two weeks. A smile touched his face as he thought of her settling in Northstar permanently. She belonged here, and he couldn't see her anywhere else or imagine Northstar without her. It wasn't only that her neighbors adored her or how much she genuinely enjoyed teaching her class and running the inn. It was the private smiles that occasionally brightened her beautiful face for no apparent reason when she was puttering around the cabin or traipsing over to June's or leaning on the porch railing of the Bedspread's dining room like he was now.

A silver truck with the Royal R brand emblazoned on the door in golden yellow pulled into the inn's driveway, and he instantly recognized Jim Robinson behind the wheel and his wife Jessie sitting in the passenger seat. He waved as they pulled up.

"Evening, Pat," Jim said.

"Jim, Jessie. How are you this lovely evening?"

"Good," Jessie replied. "And you?"

"Good."

"Aelissm making you work tonight?"

"Yup," he replied. "She has finals tonight."

"Ah, that's right. I remember her saying something about it."

"You seem to be in a very good mood," Jessie observed. "So I take it that means Aeli is over being crabby."

"I'd say so," Pat replied, wondering if his face was as red as it felt. "It wasn't easy on her, learning Winters has been in Devyn so long."

"I imagine not. The poor dear." Jessie smiled. "But she has you to keep her company."

Pat nodded. "For a while there, I don't think she wanted me for company."

"Nonsense. You were there, so you were just the easiest target."

Pat shifted his weight from one foot to the other, more than a little uncomfortable with the conversation. Jessie must have sensed it because she quickly moved on, asking what the dinner special was. Relieved, Pat led them inside to a table and got back to work.

A little while later, when the owners of the Royal R were well into their meal, Pat leaned against the bar and studied the room. Beneath the dark-stained beams with the brands of the local ranches burned into the wood and painted in teal, the residents of the Northstar Valley enjoyed their meals and each other's company. He'd long ago given up bothering to seat anyone from the valley because they rarely stayed at their own table. Only visitors to the valley remained where he sat them. Aelissm understood her neighbors without thought. More times than he could now recall, he'd watched her glide through them with natural grace and charm, stopping to chat with them all. It was simply who they were. Who she was. And he loved that about her.

A young woman, a daughter of one of the valley's smaller ranching clans, got up to chase her toddler across the dining room. The child squealed gleefully, and the adults in the room laughed indulgently. It was so easy to picture Aelissm chasing her own errant child through the maze of tables, both aided and hindered by her neighbors. The image brought with it a strong yearning that caught him entirely off-guard and a realization that made his heart skitter.

We didn't use anything *last night.*

It was a testament to how caught up in the moment he'd been and how out of practice he was that he hadn't even hesitated to consider protection. What if Aelissm got pregnant?

"Oh, God," he whispered.

"Pat? Are you all right?" Jessie Robinson asked.

"I'm fine," he managed to say. "I just thought of something. I'll be back in a few minutes."

He headed toward the kitchen door, grabbing the cordless phone as he went. With trembling fingers, he dialed June's number. As the phone rang and rang, he prayed she was home. There hadn't been any school for the high school today, but she'd worked at the Ramshorn until six. She might not have made it all the way back up to her cabin yet.

"C'mon, June, please be home. Please, please be—"

"Hello?"

"June! Thank God you're home!"

"Pat? What's wrong?"

All at once, he realized he didn't have a clue what he wanted to ask her or how to ask it. She knew what had happened last night. Even if it hadn't been written all over his and Aelissm's faces and spelled out in a trail of downy feathers, she was smart enough to figure it out with far more subtle clues. His heart raced, pounding painfully against his ribs. He took a deep breath to calm himself, but it didn't help.

"Pat? Is everything all right?"

"I don't know yet." He tried to swallow the lump in his throat. "We didn't use any protection last night," he finally blurted. Once it was out, he found it much easier to breathe.

For a moment, June didn't answer. Pat waited for her to speak, his pulse beating erratically. He tried to slow his thoughts and organize them into a rational pattern, but all those mind-numbing sex ed classes from high school popped into his head. *It only takes once.* Did the possibility of fatherhood frighten him or thrill him?

"If you're worried about Aelissm getting pregnant, don't," June said. "She's been on the pill since before

Brent's death."

Relief washed through him, laden with disappointment.

"How is it that I can be relieved and heart-broken at the same time?" he asked before he could stop himself.

He could just see June's eyebrows rise in surprise, then knit together in deep thought.

"I love her," he said. "But you already know that, don't you?"

"Pretty much."

"She makes me feel things I thought I never would again and things I never imagined I *could* feel." He inhaled slowly and let it out.

"Then you're at a crossroads, Pat. I stand by what I told you weeks ago, that you're good for Aelissm. You make her happy, and I think she makes you happy, but you both have to decide if that's enough. If you decide you want to fight for this, one or both of you is going to have to make an incredible sacrifice."

"All my life, I wanted to be a detective," he murmured. "I never dreamed I would have to choose between that dream and another, or that a woman might be more important to me."

"Is she more important?" June asked. "Don't answer that. Just think about it. And, in the meantime, try to be more careful."

He smiled. "I don't care what Aeli says about you. You're an incredible woman, June. Whatever man finally captures your heart will be one lucky guy."

"Why, thank you, Pat."

"I mean it, June."

"I know you do. Now, get back to work. You put Aeli in a really good mood. Please don't put her back in a bad one."

"I'll try not to."

June laughed. They said goodbye and hung up. Pat stood outside for a little while longer, letting the peaceful evening soothe him. The sun slid behind the peak of the ski hill, plunging the valley into shadow while the eastern peaks still glowed brightly above. The sky was littered with popcorn clouds that turned from gold to orange as he watched.

The sacrifice would be his, he knew, because he couldn't ask Aelissm to leave Northstar. But could he give up his life-long dream? He'd been away from his job long enough that he'd felt rusty the last two weeks tracking Adam Winters. The instincts were still as sharp as ever, but he'd had to stop and think about steps he usually took without paying any conscious attention to them. When had waiting tables, cooking, and washing dishes become more familiar to him than compiling clues and searching for suspects?

Looking around him at the valley and the mountains, then in the window at the people he'd come to know, respect, and cherish, he weighed his choices. His career was in Washington, and Bill and Mary Granger and his family, but there were bad memories there, too. And, as long as he was so near Seattle, Sara would always be there, taunting him and showing up when he least expected it. Here, there were good friends and the invitation of home. He'd likely end up running the inn alongside Aelissm if he stayed. Not exactly how he'd once imagined his life. He watched the woman playing with her child again, noted how everyone joined in the game of hide and seek, and again pictured

Aelissm chasing after a child, laughing and smiling. If this is what he would be trading his dream for, he knew it would be a trade well made.

In the end, the question was, which road would he regret not taking?

Sixteen

"SEVEN O'CLOCK," ADAM MUTTERED, glancing at the clock on the wall beside the kitchen door of the restaurant. "Thank God."

He hastily untied his apron, yanked it off, and hung it beside the others next to the time clock.

"Where do you think you're going, Brandon?"

Adam turned to find Dora pushing through the double doors from the dining room and frowned at the nasty scowl on her face. The owner was in town, and she'd been walking on the proverbial eggshells all day, which had put everyone in a foul mood. Adam had been forced to wait tables for a while earlier that afternoon while one of the waitresses took care of a personal matter. As a rule, he avoided getting volunteered to cover wait shifts, even for a few minutes. Too many people in town knew Aelissm or her grandparents. He couldn't take the chance that she'd start asking people if they'd seen him and finding out that he'd been working at the roach motel's restaurant for so long, but Dora had shot down every excuse he could come up with, and he'd had the displeasure of serving the motel's arrogant owner. Between him and the rest of the irritatingly picky customers they'd had today, Adam was about ready to quit on the spot.

"I'm going home, Dora. My shift's over."

"We've got a rush out there. You're not going any-where."

"You've got Doug and Mitch. They've got it covered."

"Bullshit. Mitch gets more complaints than anyone I've ever employed. He's lucky I ain't fired him."

"See you tomorrow, Dora," Adam said and reached for his time card.

"Punch that ticket and it'll be the last time."

"You won't fire me because you don't have anyone else," he said tiredly. "Either you let me go now or I quit."

Her penciled brows came together in the deepest scowl that he'd yet seen on her haggard face.

"Good night, Dora."

He punched his card and slid it back in its slot. As the door shut behind him, he thought he heard Dora call him an arrogant prick and laughed coldly. Maybe he was, but he'd had more than enough today. He was walking across the parking lot toward the back gate when Amber called out to him. Almost immediately at the sound of her voice, his mood improved, and he waited for her to catch up. The effect she had on him was both unsettling and enticing.

"Dora looked really pissed. What'd you say to her?" she asked.

"I told her I was going home, and if she had a problem with it, I'd quit."

Amber threw her head back and laughed. "I love that about you, Brandon. You don't take her shit. Serves the old hag right."

Adam winced when she used his fake name. The desire to hear her utter his real name had grown into a fever, but how could he tell her without risking his secret? If she knew why he was here, he'd lose her for sure, and she had come to mean so much to him. He wanted to be free and honest with her.

"What?" Amber said, frowning. "What's that look for?"

"What look?"

"The one on your face. Like someone told you your best friend is dying."

"My best friend's already dead," he said. His voice was barely above a whisper.

"Oh, Brandon, I'm so sorry."

Her beautiful eyes rounded with concern and he wanted to dispel her worry. He wanted to tell her he was okay, but he was already lying to her about too much.

"You've never told me that before. How'd he die?"

"Burst aneurysm." No need to tell her that he was probably responsible for it.

She threaded her arms around his neck and hugged him tightly. When she laid her head on his shoulder, he allowed himself to feel the remorse and grief he'd denied. It had been over a year now since he'd nearly strangled the only best friend he'd ever had, and the impact suddenly hit him hard. He shuddered and wrapped his arms around Amber, incredibly glad she was there. Not once in the past year had he slowed down enough to grieve. He didn't want to now, either, but he needed a moment to collect himself, hoping there would come a day when he would be free to mourn his friend and properly reflect on everything that had happened in the last year.

Amber pulled away and held him at arm's length. "What's wrong, babe?"

He shook his head. "Nothing more than usual. It was just a bad day on top of it."

"I hate it when the owner's in town. It's never a good day when he's here." She sighed, then kissed his cheek. "I've gotta head over to class. I'm already late, and if Ms. Davis is in a bad mood, she might not let me take the final."

Annoyance flared at the mention of Aelissm, and he had to force it from his voice when he replied, "I don't think she'd do that to you. I'm sure she knows how Dora is."

"Everyone in town knows how Dora is," Amber remarked. "This won't be the first time I've been late for class because of her. Maybe I should take Ms. Davis up on her job offer. I could work out there for the summer. She said Mrs. Struthers told her I could stay in the apartment above the pool house at the Ramshorn. Oh, man, wouldn't that be fun?"

"Sounds like a great summer."

"You could come, too."

"We'll see. You'd better go."

This time she kissed him on the lips, then deepened it. He had to push her away so she wouldn't be any later. He watched her walk away, smiling when she winked at him over her shoulder. It was strange that he'd been irritated by the mention of Aelissm. He usually enjoyed listening to Amber talk about her, but just now, it felt like an invasion of his private moment with Amber. The revelation was confusing because the need to find Aelissm still pulsed through him.

He turned and started for his house again. What did he want from Aelissm? Once, he'd wanted *her*, but now he had Amber, whom he adored and who returned his affection ten-fold. If it wasn't desire that pulled him toward Aelissm, what was it that kept him alert for any sign or news of her? Did he want her forgiveness for Brent's death or her gratitude for stopping Brent from raping her? And how much longer could he keep playing this game with her? He was tired of hiding. More than that, he was tired of lying to Amber.

When he reached his house, he paused at the sight of a white paper pinned to the door. It was folded in half, and his name—his real name—was printed on it in clear, familiar hand-writing. Trepidation lanced through him, white hot and frigid. His hand shook badly as he took the note down and opened it.

Hello, Adam, it began. *You'll have to tell me how you like being hunted. From my own experience, it's not a pleasant situation. I don't know what you want from me, but you won't get it. We've both suffered from Brent's death, but I'm moving on with my life now, and I'm giving you the opportunity to end this quietly. I want you to leave on your own without making a big deal out of this. If you leave now, I'll have the restraining order rescinded. This whole mess can be over if you just leave me alone.*

There was no flourish to end it, only her signature. Not that he needed it to know the note was from Aelissm. He quickly entered the house and locked the door behind him. How the hell had she found him? The answer was so glaringly obvious that he cursed himself for not being more careful. Her uncle's nosy detective had figured it out. Bill Granger wouldn't have hired Patrick O'Neil as a detective unless he was good at his job because Aelissm's uncle didn't tolerate laziness or ineptitude in his subordinates. If he thought about it, he was surprised he hadn't received a note from him a long time ago. But O'Neil hadn't written the letter. Aelissm had.

"Son of a bitch," he muttered.

He'd have to move and find a new job, just when he'd started to get comfortable. Amber wouldn't understand, and he couldn't see a way to explain it without revealing too much. He could quit and blame it on Dora, but moving? How could he lie that away?

As he thought about it, anger began to bubble. He couldn't just leave and move on. It wasn't that simple. He wracked his brain for the reason why he was still so hung up on Aelissm, but his thoughts stubbornly refused to coalesce into a coherent explanation. After almost an hour, he glanced at the picture frame Amber had made him. Somehow, she'd gotten him to smile for at least one of the dozens of pictures she'd taken that night. That right there was something special.

Crumpling the letter into a ball and hurling it across the room, he stormed out of the house. The door slammed satisfyingly behind him. With his hands stuffed in his pockets, he strode back to the Paradise Motel's restaurant. He perched on a stool in the lounge's bar and ordered a Moose Drool from the bartender, who was so new they hadn't yet met. She was an older woman who reminded him a little too much of Dora, and he'd already heard tales circulating that she was about as pleasant to work with as the manager.

"I thought you said you were going home."

The snide voice jolted Adam out of his unpleasant thoughts, and he swiveled on his stool to see Dora standing behind him. "I did. I'm back. And I'm staying off the clock, so don't even ask." He peered into the dining room. "Besides, it's slowed down."

Dora *humpfed* and stalked away.

"Ain't too many people that can talk that way to that old bitch and walk away with their ears intact."

Adam glanced to his left and nodded a greeting to JP. "I guess I have more job security than most here."

"So it would seem. Tell me, what's got your panties in a bunch tonight?"

Without a word or any of Amber's sassy chatter, the bartender brought his beer, briefly interrupting. When she moved off, Adam informed JP, "The owner's in town. He's got everyone stirred up."

"As usual. I've met him once or twice. Didn't find much of anything useful about the man. But that ain't all that's got you fired up."

Adam shook his head. He really didn't like it that JP could read him so well. There was no lying to the man, and he was one of those people it was hard to say no to. Adam could have told him that he didn't feel like talking about it—which he didn't—but JP would buy him a couple of beers or a couple of shots and get it out of him eventually. He should have just gone to the store and bought himself a case of beer to drink in private misery. It wasn't very often that he set out to get drunk, but tonight called for it. He drained the first beer in one long swallow and flagged down the bartender for another. He hoped JP would get bored and move on to some other topic.

"There's only one thing that makes you drink like that," JP said.

He was, evidently, without luck tonight.

"Your girl. And I'd say she's got you more bothered tonight than usual."

"You might say that."

"What happened?"

Adam frowned at his companion. "You know, JP, it really isn't any of your business."

JP slapped his knee and guffawed. "Oh, sonny boy, she's really got you going tonight."

"She left a note tacked to my damned door. So, yeah, she does, and I'm beginning to question if she's worth it."

"Of course she is."

Adam shook his head, wishing he could loosen the knots his thoughts had twisted themselves into the night he'd heard Aelissm scream. He pressed the heels of his hands to his eyes and tried to block out the memory of that night but couldn't. He'd run into Brent's apartment to find his friend pinning Aeli to the floor of his living room and yanking her clothes off with a disgusting, feral sneer contorting his normally pretty face. He felt again the fracturing of his mind—a brutal snap as if Brent had taken his consciousness and broken it like a twig over his knee—and nearly let out the same savage yell he had that night as he'd rushed Brent.

Queasiness boiled as he recalled the feel of Brent's throat in his hands, saw again the way his friend's eyes had bulged, and heard the sheer terror in Aelissm's screams as she'd escaped out the door he'd left wide open.

What the fuck is wrong with you?! he'd bellowed. *Why did you hurt her?*

When Brent's expression suddenly changed from fearful to agonized, Adam had let go, shocked out of his rage by that unexpected shift. He realized now that that moment was when the aneurysm had burst, but he hadn't understood it then and had fled the apartment unaware that his friend would die within hours.

I killed my best friend, Adam thought, hanging his head.

For the first time since that night, the thought that followed the habitual accusation was not of Aelissm but of Amber.

How can Amber love me? I'm a monster. To JP, he responded, "Maybe she is, but she's not mine anymore."

"Have you listened to a damned thing I've told you? You have to make her understand that she belongs to you."

"But she *doesn't* belong to me. She never did, and I might lose Amber because I couldn't see that."

"You've taken your eye off the prize," JP remarked disdainfully. "You're infatuated with Amber, and I can see why, but once the infatuation wears off, you're going to regret settling for her."

"I am *not* settling for her," Adam snapped. "I don't know yet if I love her, but I do know that what I feel for her is a lot stronger than anything I felt for Aelissm."

"That's fear talking. You're afraid you can't compete

with that detective she has staying with her, so you're settling for what you think you can attain."

Adam dropped his head into his hand and snarled. "I don't really care that Aeli wants to move on with her uncle's detective. Ah, shit. Sara."

"Who's Sara?"

"The detective's ex-fiancée. She is one crazy bitch."

"Crazy can be interesting," JP mused.

"Not that kind of crazy. She stabbed him with a paring knife because he told her he was leaving."

JP's brows lifted. "Hellcat. Why are you suddenly so worried about her?"

"Karma. You remember that trip I took back to Washington?"

JP took a long drink of his beer. "I suppose you thought you could involve her, get her to chase the detective off, and then you'd have your girl all to yourself. Is that it?"

"That was the basic idea, yeah."

JP shook his head, which irritated Adam anew. From what he'd heard about JP's interest in June Montana and his lack of progress with her, the man had little right to tell him what to do.

"What made you think you could control a woman who's already stabbed one man in a rage? A hellcat like that'll just ruin things for you because she has her own agenda."

"I get that now, but what else was I supposed to do? There was no other way I was going to get O'Neil to leave."

"You need to grow a pair and take care of things yourself."

"Excuse me?"

"You can't let this woman take care of your problem for you. Every time you involve someone else and give them that kind of role, it only complicates matters. It makes for too many variables."

"What are you now, some kind of math genius?"

"Nope. Just someone who's taking his time to lay out the pieces just right." JP requested another round for himself and Adam. "That way, when the time comes for me to move, there won't be any variables. Still, the damage is done, so you just need to use what you have and try to make her work for you."

"Do you have a goddamned cotton ball in your ear? I may still need Aelissm in a way I can't explain, but I don't want her anymore."

He thought of Amber, and as he wondered again how he was going to explain everything to her, the realization of why he still needed Aelissm slammed through his brain. He needed her forgiveness. He needed her to tell him he wasn't a monster, that he deserved whatever he'd found with Amber, and maybe, if he could convince her to forgive everything he'd put her through, he could find a way to convince her to help him explain this God-awful mess to Amber. Salvation and redemption—that's what he needed from her. Not love. As he'd begun to suspect weeks ago, Aelissm was the only person who knew that the man he'd been since Brent's death was *not* the man he was. No one else could help him prove that.

He only hoped she had once treasured their friendship enough to give him another chance. Of course, if she was in love with Pat O'Neil, he doubted she'd ever forgive him for involving Sara Montgomery. Adam thought he might puke. Someday, karma was going to come back around and bite Sara in the ass, and he didn't want to be anywhere near her when it did, but simply bringing her into this game might be enough to bring some of it down on himself because he was now just as responsible for whatever trauma befell Pat O'Neil if she caught up to him again.

"I need to get this resolved before she gets here."

"How are you going to do that? Aelissm has the upper hand. She knows where you live, probably where you work, what vehicle you've been driving, and I'd bet she even knows you're banging that cute little bartender. You, on the other hand, still haven't figured out where she lives."

JP was right about that. After hours upon hours of driving the roads of that valley, Adam still didn't have a clue which one she lived on. Most of the secondary roads weren't marked. From the directory, he knew her address; he just didn't know how to get there. There was no map of the Northstar Valley. Apparently, everyone in Northstar knew all the roads and didn't need signs or maps to know where they were going. When he'd followed Aelissm out here, he hadn't thought it would be so hard to find her. No wonder she'd chosen to hide here.

"So what? I'll find her."

"Uh-huh."

He scowled. JP's smug, know-it-all attitude was really getting to him tonight.

"What? You have a better idea?"

"Nope. But, then again, I know where she lives. More importantly, I know how to get there."

Adam stood up. He wasn't about to take aid from JP. God only knew what he'd end up having to do in return for the information. He'd find Aelissm on his own if he had to spend every waking hour prowling every back road out there. He still had a little time until Sara arrived, and Amber was going to be out of town for a couple of weeks after her finals were over. He almost wished he could go with her instead of staying here, like she'd begged, but her absence would give him the opportunity to poke around without her learning what he was up to.

"Going somewhere, Brandon?" JP asked.

"Yeah. I'm going to see if I can convince Sara to stay in Seattle or at least buy myself a little more time."

"Just remember, when you can't find Aelissm on your own…."

JP let the sentence hang, and Adam walked away without another word. Had the man not *just* told him it was stupid to involve other people? Too many variables. He'd wait until there was no other option but accepting JP's help. He'd already made the mistake of seeking Sara's help without first knowing for sure he couldn't get Pat O'Neil out of the picture on his own, and he wasn't going to make the same mistake with a man he was certain was at least half as crazy.

Steeling his nerves, he paid for his drinks and left the bar. He'd need to use the pay phone outside the restaurant because he didn't want to chance his co-workers overhearing his conversation and mentioning it to Amber. When he reached the phone, he was irritated to find it already in use. Impatiently, he waited for the woman to finish her call. As she babbled on to whoever was on the other line about all the fun things she and her husband had done that day, Adam crossed his arms tightly across his chest as his mood continued to darken.

"C'mon, lady. Other people need to use the phone," he said after he'd been waiting for nearly ten minutes.

She glanced over her shoulder at him, sneered, and made a comment to her friend about rude assholes. And went right on talking.

With a growl, Adam walked down the street to the gas station. The pay phone there was mercifully open. He quickly dialed the requisite numbers for his pre-paid card, then dialed the phone number, silently praying she'd pick up even as he dreaded talking to her.

"I thought I told you not to call me, Adam," she said.

All at once, he realized he had no idea how he could convince her to stay in Seattle. She followed her ex-fiancé around, tormenting him by inquiring after him at his work-place or "bumping into" his family or friends. He hadn't needed to ask around to learn her habits regarding Patrick O'Neil. She'd told him herself with a chilling amusement. She was motivated entirely by vengeance, and the fact that she might still love him hadn't crossed his mind. Sara Mont-gomery wasn't capable of love. She wasn't just cold-hearted. That would mean she actually had a heart.

"There's no need for you to come all the way out here," he sputtered. "I was wrong about your ex and Ae-lissm, and he headed back to Washington yesterday."

"Don't try to fool me, Adam. You're not smart enough. I know Pat is still there because *you* are."

"He had to return to work."

"Bullshit. Bill Granger won't let him come back until you're well away from his precious niece."

Adam knew with a sickening lurch of his stomach

that he had seriously underestimated Sara's intelligence and motivation for revenge. "Why can't you just leave him alone? Isn't this whole vendetta a waste of your time?"

"You want to talk about time, Adam? Fine. I spent six months in prison because of him. That is a lot of wasted time."

"Six months for assaulting a cop is nothing. You should have done years. They could've pinned you with attempted murder."

"Six months, six *decades*—it doesn't matter. I owe him for that marvelous little vacation and for the restraining order that nearly got me arrested again."

The fact that O'Neil had put a restraining order on her was funny, but he'd laugh later, when this was all over.

"I hope he loves her. He *is* the sort that would fall for some little backwoods twit. It'll be marvelous to rip them apart." She laughed and the sound sent chills along his spine. "Don't do anything stupid until I get there, Adam. I'll see you in two weeks."

She ended the call abruptly, and Adam retreated to his house. Two weeks. That's all the time he had to find Aelissm and come up with a way to fix this unbelievably sloppy mess.

Seventeen

TWO WEEKS HAD SHOWN PAT that his promise to not get more deeply involved with Aelissm was impossible to keep. They'd made love at least once nearly every night, sometimes more. They never meant to, always saying that this time would be the last. Kissing her or touching her was the sweetest bliss he'd ever known and making love to her…. Heaven itself would have a hard time comparing. Her body was incredible, her willingness was breathtaking, and the pleasure she took from their joinings was the most potent aphrodisiac.

He'd never been unable to resist a woman before, and it wasn't the sex, though there was no denying it was incredible. He loved her spirit and her wit. He found himself wanting to be with her because of who she was. Like today, he'd decided to tag along for the first day of her new class at the college. He'd sat in the back of the room while she went over her syllabus, detailing what she expected of her students, and was amazed. She was good at this. The students listened intently, asked questions, and seemed genuinely interested. It was probably a testament to both her talent and her femininity that there were nearly as many young women in the class as there were men. Many of the girls had already made comments alluding to their joining the class because they'd heard about Aeli's recently concluded blacksmithing course.

Now he was standing with her outside the woodshop, watching and waiting as she bid her students goodbye until the next class.

"So," she said, turning to him after the last student had left. "What do you think?"

"Wow."

"Oh, c'mon, Pat, it's just the first day."

"Not the class, Aeli. You. You're really good at this whole teaching thing, you know that?"

"College is definitely a better fit than high school was."

She smiled and leaned into him. Her kiss was chaste, but desire flared as if she'd initiated a much hotter caress. His eyelids slid closed, and he groaned low in his throat. When he opened his eyes, he found her angled away from him, watching him with a smug smile that was oddly gentle and warm. She was stunning when she looked at him like that, with her eyes full of joy and love. It was gone too quickly for his liking.

"C'mon, Mr. O'Neil, we need to get headed up to the valley."

"Mmm. Anything you say, sweetheart," he replied.

He followed her out to her truck like a faithful puppy, and when he realized it, he was amused at his predicament. He knew that a life spent with her would be a never-ending adventure, but part of him refused to give up his dream of being a detective. The battle was beginning to wear on him, and he could see no easy resolution.

"I'm glad they scheduled my class in the morning," Aelissm said as she drove away from the college. "That way I can still get some work done at the Bedspread, too."

"You're never going back to Washington, are you."

"This is home. I have a great start with the college, and I really enjoy my work at the Bedspread. Besides, it was always my dream to settle down here." She paused. "I just lost sight of that when I went to Seattle."

"I can understand that," Pat said. "All of it."

"You know, this may sound really insane, but I should thank Adam. If it weren't for his refusal to leave me alone, I might not have had reason enough to leave Seattle, and I might never have come back here."

By that single comment, Pat knew that Aelissm's fear of Adam Winters was officially in her past. There were still loose ends to be tied up, but unless Winters did something nasty, Aelissm was done being afraid of him. She was thinking about her future again, not living from one day to the next. The conversation also reinforced his belief that he couldn't ask her to leave this place. It was too much a part of her, and taking her away from it, even if she was willing, would destroy what he loved the most about her.

"What are you thinking about, Pat? And don't tell me 'nothing' because I can see the wheels turning."

"I don't think Adam is much of a problem for you anymore."

She shrugged. "Not like he was, no, but I still have my moments, and I probably will until I know he's gone and out of my life. I've come to a lot of realizations recently, especially about the time I spent in Seattle. I know we said we were through apologizing and thanking each other, but I don't think I could have come this far without you."

He smiled. "Nor I."

The rest of the ride up to the valley was spent in contented silence or light conversation about mundane things like the operations of the Bedspread, Aeli's new students, and Luke's official name change from McKindel to Montana, which had only happened a few days ago when he'd received his new social security card.

Simple conversation like that had been missing from his life for most of the past three years. He'd missed the familial gossip, and though June and Luke weren't his blood relations, he'd come to love them like a second family. It reminded him, too, that he needed to start getting back to that same closeness with his own family.

He stared out the window as they drove up the mountain, amazed by the love that filled him, not just this new love for Aelissm but for everything. He was living again. Like Aelissm, he could start to focus on his future now. No more working himself to death, no more hiding in his bed staring at the ceiling as he waited for morning to come, and no more bad days.

When they reached the cabin, Aelissm walked inside and stopped. She turned to face him, frowning thoughtfully.

"I've been thinking, Pat," she began. "Since you're so

rarely in your own bed anymore, why don't we just make the move official? Sleep with me from now on."

He knew he should say no. Things between them were already too complicated, and yet, he couldn't seem to make his mouth form that simple word. The thought of sleeping in her bed with her tucked snuggly in his arms and waking up beside her was appealing. Since he couldn't answer one way or the other, he did the only thing that came to his mind. He took her in his arms and kissed her. She melted into him, readily giving in.

He would have happily taken her there on the living room floor, but somehow they made it upstairs. Her power over him was awesome, and by the time he laid her gently on her bed, he quivered with raw need. With urgency pulsing through him and desire flooding his veins, he stripped off his T-shirt and hungrily sought Aelissm's neck. She squirmed beneath him, kicking out of her jeans in the same, consuming passion. With their clothes discarded, Pat wasted no time in stroking her to aching need. He fought to control his own raging desire to give her time, but by the feel of her, she didn't need it.

"Quit wasting time, Pat," she said hoarsely.

Obediently, he took her. He kept the pace slow for only a few moments. There was little gentleness in Aelissm's silent demands, only wild, animal hunger, and she urged him with her body. His thoughts scrambled until they were pushed into oblivion by his need. With her tight around him and pleading for everything he had, he had no hope of controlling himself. They raced toward the peak and soared over it, crying out simultaneously in mutual ecstacy.

Still buried inside her, he arched up and gazed down

at her. She reached up and touched his face with all the tenderness their joining had lacked. Her gorgeous green eyes were soft with it, and the smile on her lips was the most beautiful thing in the world.

"You're trembling, my darling," she murmured.

She drew him down to her, cradling his head on her breasts. Lovingly, she stroked his face and ran her fingers back through his hair. He closed his eyes and took a deep, shuddering breath.

"Aelissm…" he croaked.

"Shh, my darling."

"I can't stay away from you," he whispered. "No matter how hard I try. Not even for our own good."

"I know, honey. I can't either. I know this is dangerous, and I know it's going to hurt like hell down the road, but I can't stop." She laid her cheek on his head. "What if this is love, Pat? Not what we thought we had before. I mean *real* love."

He couldn't find his voice to answer. If it *was* real love, they'd fight for it. He thought it might be the real thing, but part of him still struggled against it, the part of him that wanted to be a detective above all else. Only time would tell which side would win. The rate things were going with Aelissm, however, his job was going to lose.

"Pat?"

"Hmm?"

"We should probably, uh, get organized here. We've got to be down at the Bedspread in a little over an hour."

"Remind me why you scheduled us to work tonight?"

"Because everyone who didn't have a class in town is helping the Hammonds with the first cut of hay."

"Ah. That's right. I forgot."

She kissed his forehead. "C'mon, Mr. O'Neil. Don't make me lie and say you're squishing me."

"Am I?"

"A little, but I like it."

Reluctantly, he got up. He paused to admire Aelissm's naked body, noting that her skin was still lightly damp. With a groan, he averted his attention, grabbed his towel and robe and made a beeline for the shower downstairs. Aelissm joined him, and it was only by his steadfast refusal to further delay them that all they did was shower.

When she playfully stroked her hand from his neck to his navel, he grabbed her hand and laughed. "Now, now, Ms. Davis, none of that. We're already cutting it close, so don't start anything we don't have time to finish."

She stuck her lip out in a fair imitation of a pouting child. "Fine."

He kissed her again, though, and she was satisfied with that. She got out of the shower, leaving him standing beneath the steaming fall of water. Leaving Sara had been painful in a very different way, and looking back, it had been a simple decision to get out and save himself while there was still something left to be saved. Survival was always an easy choice. Choosing between one kind of fulfillment and another was a whole different can of worms. Pop the top and pros and cons shot out everywhere. No matter which way he went, there would be pain.

Usually, he'd consult Bill on a matter like this, but he wasn't sure what would bias Bill's advice more—keeping Pat as a detective or gaining him as a nephew.

"Dammit," he muttered. "What have I gotten myself

into this time?"

He turned off the shower and got out. After he'd wrapped a towel around his waist, he walked through the door into the living room of Aelissm's cabin. It struck him then, that it wasn't actually her cabin. It belonged to her parents. Somehow, he couldn't seem to convince himself about that. Maybe it was that he'd only ever known it as her cabin. Thoughtfully, he looked around, taking in the bright orange shag couches, the antique tables, and the various objects Aeli and her family had collected over the years. Could he live here? Happily. It was effortless to picture himself waking up in the master bedroom every morning, checking on his kids as he passed through the smaller room on his way downstairs where he would find Aeli at the kitchen table reading National Geographic or the Smithsonian. And just as effortlessly, with that scenario in his mind, he could imagine himself calling Bill to tell him he wouldn't be coming back to work.

I can't make this kind of decision here. I can't think straight around Aelissm. What if this is all just an amazing dream that ends when Winters is gone and there's no reason why I have *to stay here?* Pat watched Aelissm descend the steep spiral stairs. *Only one way to find out. I have to get Winters out of her life.*

* * *

Aelissm paused in the kitchen to admire Pat's bare chest, wishing there was time to take him back upstairs. The frown of deep thought concerned her, and she wondered what he was thinking about. When he caught her watching, however, the frown evaporated. She could stand there all day gazing at him, but they had to be to work in half an hour, and it would take them almost that long to get down the mountain.

"As much as I love looking at your beautiful body," she said, pausing to let her words sink in, "I'm serious when I say we're going to be late if you don't get moving."

He smiled and started toward her. "I know. I'll be ready in five minutes."

"Good, because that's all you have."

She turned around, faced the mirror to the right of the sink, and braided her hair. Pat walked by and headed upstairs, and she stopped to listen. How could something like the waft of air stirred by his passing or the creak of the stairs evoke such strong yearning? The cabin was going to feel very lonely when he was gone, and Aelissm dreaded similar moments when she would be standing beside the sink and there would be no footfalls above her.

Stop thinking like this, she told herself. *If you aren't willing to go to Washington to be with him, you have no right to ask him to stay here with you.*

Angry with that line of thought and the fact that she hadn't managed to convince herself she could return to Washington, she hurriedly finished braiding her hair and headed outside. Since the first night they'd made love, she'd pondered that question over and over again, and every time she thought about going back, she felt sick. She loved Pat, she knew she did, but she hated that place and all its bad memories. What did that make her? Selfish. She plopped her helmet on her head and yanked the chinstrap tight, cringing as the material slid hotly across her skin.

True to his word, Pat was outside, fully dressed and ready to go, in five minutes. His dark auburn hair was still wet, but it probably wouldn't stay that way long in the warm afternoon, even with the helmet on. He climbed on his dirt bike and looked at her expectantly. She realized she was merely straddling her bike and had not yet kick-started it.

"A little distracted, are we, my dear?" he asked.

"A bit, yes."

Pat wasn't the only thing distracting her. She'd become steadily more confused as to why Adam hadn't responded to her note. Surely he should have done something in retribution by now, but there had been no letters and no phone calls. She hoped he'd decided to up and leave, but doubt threaded itself through her. He wasn't done with her yet, and she wondered at the wisdom of giving in to impulse and seeking him out.

Her ponderings about Adam took her all the way to the Bedspread Inn, where she got the answer she was looking for. Before she'd even walked in the door, the woman who'd been serving all day came outside to greet her.

"Aeli, there was a man in here earlier today. He left an envelope for you."

"A man? What'd he look like?" Before the waitress could answer, Aelissm held up a hand. "No, let me guess. Medium everything."

"Yeah, I guess that's about it. Do you know who he was?"

"We know," Pat said. "May I have it?"

"Sure thing, Pat. I left it by the phone."

Pat strode forward, and Aelissm had to stretch her legs to keep up. He'd gone into protector mode. She recognized it easily now. His back was straight, his shoulders squared, and all the warmth had left his eyes. Before Aeli could reach for the letter, Pat snagged it. Instantly, she regretted not telling him what she'd done. He should know, and undoubtedly, he would as soon as he read Adam's letter. Aelissm decided to break that bit of news first.

"Come back outside with me, Pat," she beckoned.

He obeyed, his brows creased with curiosity. She didn't look behind to see if he followed when she started for the front deck. She didn't need to. She could feel him behind her, warm and comforting, ready to defend her or hold her if she needed him to. His strength was as precious to her as the panorama of the Northstar Mountains that stretched around her as she stepped outside. She took a few moments to admire those mountains and to collect her courage.

"I needed to do it on my own. I needed to know I could."

He looked up from the letter and frowned at her. "What are you talking about, Aeli?"

"Two weeks ago, the day of my last blacksmithing class, I made a visit to Adam's house. I left a note on his door asking him to leave me alone."

"You did *what*?"

She winced at the anger in his voice. It had been extremely foolish, she knew that, but it was done now, and she couldn't go back and undo it. Her reasons for daring to write the short note were still the same and still drove her to defend herself against Pat's rightful fury. That didn't mean it was easy to face him. He'd been angry the day they'd found out Adam was working at the Paradise Motel, but not really with her. Right now, his fury was directed straight at her.

"Do you realize how stupid that was, Aelissm? If he

follows his past patterns, I wouldn't be surprised if he packed up that night. All that work finding him and learning his ways is for nothing now! We have to start all over!"

Fear quaked through her, but it wasn't the same she'd become so familiar with over the past year. She was afraid her act of defiance would push Pat away. The disgust on his face was like a knife to the heart. She swore she wasn't going to cry, but tears burned her eyes anyhow.

"I'm sorry, I didn't think—"

"That's quite clear."

"Pat, please listen to me! I had to do it."

He narrowed his eyes, and she wanted to retreat from the icy glare, but she forced herself to endure it. She'd written that letter to Adam because, with him still here, there was no way to know if this fire between her and Pat was strong enough to bear the sacrifice one or both of them would have to make.

"Do explain what you mean."

Aelissm swallowed the lump in her throat and stared out at the mountains, trying to get the sight of his angry face out of her mind. She felt like a coward for avoiding him. With a deep, ragged breath, she met his gaze again. Her eyes continued to burn with unshed tears, and when she spoke, her voice quivered.

"I'm tired of being the mouse, waiting for him to pounce. But I don't want him gone for the same reasons anymore. I'm not afraid of him, not like I was."

"What other reasons could you have for wanting him gone?"

Contempt and disbelief. That stung. But she refused to give in. He meant too much to her to lose him over something so stupid.

"My reason is standing in front of me."

He blinked in confusion. "What?"

"I love you, Pat."

That certainly took him by surprise. His mouth fell open, and he stared at her with an expression containing so many emotions that she couldn't decipher it.

"I want him gone because I need to know if what we've found can last. I love you, and I want to fight for us, but I can't if he's here because I can't know if you're staying with me because my uncle asked you to protect me or because you feel the same, and—"

His mouth clamped over hers, effectively silencing her flood of explanations. He gripped her arms and pulled her into his body. The tears came then, sliding down her face in trails of hot shame and relief and joy. She tasted the salt of them in the kiss and let go. When his arms came around her, she collapsed against him. He held her head to his chest and murmured wordlessly to her.

"I'm sorry…. I'm sorry," was all she could say.

"Oh, sweetheart," he whispered. "I shouldn't have said what I did. You don't deserve it, and I didn't mean it."

"I know."

"I just saw everything we've won against him crumbling away."

He kissed her again, tenderly, apologizing. Then he held her, and she was content to stay in his arms as long as he would allow.

"What are we going to do with ourselves, Aeli?" he asked.

"I have no idea."

"Can I ask why you thought letting Winters know you knew where he lived would get him out of your life?"

"I thought I could push him into doing something stupid."

"Ah. Well, you know him better than I do. Maybe you're right."

Aelissm pulled out of his embrace and took the letter from him. "One way to find out," she said and tore into it.

That was a nasty trick, Aelissm, but it won't work. I can't leave yet because we need to talk about what happened that night. I'm going to take a leap of faith and stay where I am, hoping that you'll be a better friend to me than I've been to you. Please don't send the cops after me. I just want to talk. I don't know when or where, but it needs to be soon. In the meantime, tell your detective that he should leave before it's too late because he won't like what's coming. He doesn't need to be here anymore, anyhow. I'll never hurt you again.

Rather than the chills she expected Adam's note to evoke, Aelissm felt… confusion. She could almost hear a thread of calm rationality behind his words, and the very phrasing and content read differently than the pleading pledges of his love for her and the vague threats that had populated his earlier notes and calls.

"Looks like you were right," Pat remarked. "He's digging in. All is not lost."

If he was bothered by Adam's mention of him, he didn't show it. In fact, he regarded the letter with amazing aplomb. She wished she could feel so indifferent, but the two sentences concerning him were the only thing about the note that stirred fear in her—and stir it they did. Those lines were too reminiscent of Adam's possessive declarations for her to dismiss them so easily. What was coming that Pat wouldn't like?

What have you done now, Adam? Glancing up at Pat, she asked, "This doesn't concern you?"

"Not really."

"Why the hell not?"

"His apology to you takes most of the immediacy out of the threat," Pat said. Frowning, he added, "I'm not sure it *is* a threat. It reads more like a warning."

"How is that any better?"

"The motivation behind it has changed. He's not telling me to stay away from you. He's just telling me to… get away."

Something had connected in his mind; Aelissm saw it in the dip of his brows and the way he pressed his lips into a flat, contemplative line.

"What are you thinking?" she asked.

"Nothing."

"Bull. Something pinged inside that head of yours. I saw it, Pat."

"Something…. There's something here that I'm not seeing, but I can sense it." He refolded the letter, tucked it carefully back in its envelope, and slipped it into the pocket of his T-shirt before turning a bemused smile on Aelissm. "Since when did you become so adept at reading my mind?"

"Some time since our night at Sawtooth Lake. Speaking of which, remind me to thank Nick for that wonderful idea."

"That day he took us horseback riding…. *That's* the idea you told him you'd keep in mind?"

Aelissm grinned sheepishly. "You *would* remember that."

"Well, you *were* wearing a rather memorable and devilish smile."

"I'm sure I was."

Pat's smile turned to one of adoration as he lowered his head to kiss her. "So, Aeli, since you want to play this game with Adam by your rules, what's our next move?"

She sighed, unready to return to the far less pleasant matter of Adam Winters. "I guess it's time I talked to him."

"Are you sure you're ready for that?"

"No," she replied, "but if that's what it takes to get him out of my life, that's what I need to do."

"When and where?"

"Some place where he won't be able to pull anything. We haven't had a potluck in a while because everyone's been too busy with haying, but give it another week, and people will have time."

"He may be getting desperate, but I doubt he's to the point that he'll talk to you with that kind of audience."

"Then we give the invitation to Amber. She'll beg him to come, and if he cares about her enough…."

"He'll come because he won't want to explain why he doesn't want to." Pat paused for a moment. "And if he shows up, what do you want to do? He's broken the restraining order, so Aaron can arrest him. We could have the Devyn police do that anytime you wanted now, I suppose, but is that what you want?"

Aelissm took a deep breath. It didn't take as long as she would've thought to formulate her answer. "No. I just want to be left alone to live my life and forget what happened in Seattle." She took his hands and entwined her fingers with his. "Truth be told, I want my funny friend Adam back. He's a good man at heart, and I don't want him to suffer anymore, either. Unless he does something…. I just want to talk to him and see if I can convince him to let it go."

"It's a plan," Pat remarked.

"If Amber is serious about working for me this summer, she won't take no for an answer from him."

"Whatever happened to your concern for her wellbeing? As I recall, you didn't talk to me for two weeks because I wouldn't let you go back and warn her."

Aelissm shrugged. "Like you said, she's a big girl. Besides, she seems pretty happy. I got a little tired of hearing about how great 'Brandon' was by the end of class."

"All right, Aeli. We'll drive back in to town tomorrow and give her an invitation. Right now, however, we should probably get to work so poor Janice can go home."

* * *

"What's this?" Amber asked, holding the envelope Aelissm had just given her.

"It's an invitation. I want you to come to the potluck in two weeks at the Bedspread. If you're going to work for me this summer, you'd better be there to meet the locals."

"Sure. Of course, Ms. Davis."

"Call me Aelissm. We're not in class anymore."

"Yeah, of course."

Aelissm smiled warmly. The girl was positively beaming. She genuinely liked Amber and hoped her former student hadn't bitten off too much to chew when she'd gotten involved with Adam.

"You still dating that Brandon guy?"

She blushed. "Yeah," she replied. "I think we're

getting pretty serious."

"Why don't you bring him along? I'd like to meet him. If he's as good a cook as I've heard, I could probably use him."

"Really?"

"Yeah."

"Okay. I'll see if I can get him to go. He's pretty antisocial."

I'm sure he is, Aelissm thought. "Well, see what you can do to convince him."

"Absolutely. I'll be there for sure."

"Good."

Aelissm left the restaurant and joined Pat in the cab of his truck. She leaned over and kissed him. "I think that went well."

Eighteen

ADAM HAD NEARLY FULFILLED his oath to explore every back road in the Northstar Valley. He'd driven more miles and filled his tank more times than he cared to recall and was still no closer to knowing where Aelissm lived. He'd seen pictures of her cabin and some of the terrain around it, but every road he'd been on looked the same.

Then Amber had returned from her parent's house in Bozeman two days ago and put a stop to his frantic searching. Seeing her was akin to breathing again. The tension left him, and he was able to push the note Aelissm had left on his door and Sara's impending arrival from his mind for a little while.

It was probably a good thing Amber was coming over soon. His thoughts had taken a detour again into doubt, and he preferred to focus instead on the woman who'd managed to turn what had begun as a bleak hunt for something he might never attain into the best thing he could recall ever happening to him. Although he doubted he'd ever want to settle here in Devyn, he could do it if Amber asked him to. Now, Bozeman or Missoula or Great Falls or Billings, those places he wouldn't mind. He'd been through Missoula a few times since coming here, but the rest he knew only through what he heard. He just knew they were all more than ten times the size of Devyn, and he could start over more easily someplace where he wouldn't be constantly reminded of Aelissm and Brent and everything else that had happened since his friend's death.

He jumped off his bed at the knock on his door. Yanking the door open, he nearly threw his arms around Amber's neck. Only his unwillingness to alert her to his thoughts kept his embrace more modest.

"I missed you," she whispered shyly. "I know I've seen you at work, but it's not the same."

"I missed you, too, Amber."

She purred against his lips, then deepened the kiss. Yearning came with it, though, disrupting what should have been a mindless descent into sensation. He was so sick of lying to her, and the secrets he kept had begun to gnaw more viciously at him in her absence, but if she knew why he'd come to Devyn, she'd be gone in a heartbeat without giving him even a moment to explain what had changed. *As if I can completely understand it myself,* he thought. *Which is worse, being eaten alive by a lie or losing the woman I love because of it?*

Amber sank down off her toes and studied him with a frown. "What's wrong?"

"I have a problem. I came to Devyn to resolve it, but

it doesn't seem so important anymore," he heard himself say. He turned his gaze directly on Amber, took her face in his hands, and kissed her tenderly. "*You* make it seem like it doesn't matter anymore. But it's still with me, and I can't get past the need to deal with it even though it feels like I shouldn't need to now."

"Then you need to deal with it," she said as if it were so simple.

"I wish it was that easy," he murmured.

He didn't let her respond. Moving her to his bed, he laid her down and kissed her until there was no room left in her mind for anything but the moment and wished his own thoughts could be so quickly dispensed. Why couldn't he just leave well enough alone, take Amber to Bozeman or wherever, and forget what Aelissm had meant to him? Because the past wouldn't leave him alone. It would haunt him and destroy the happiness he'd found with Amber. Until he had closure, he would always see Brent's enraged face and Aelissm's terror-widened eyes.

"More bad memories?" Amber asked, looking up at him.

He nodded.

"Well, quit thinking about them and think about me instead." She playfully wriggled her hips. "C'mon, sweet thing. Show me how much you love me."

"I *do* love you," he replied and sat back to strip off his new blue T-shirt.

"Ooo, someone's been busy," Amber said. She giggled as she reached a hand up to explore the harder lines of his torso.

He *had* been busy with that, too. In the last year, he'd

let himself go, and though he was still fairly lean, muscle had become soft with disuse. Amber had re-awakened his sense of self-pride, and he wanted to get back into the shape he'd been in before everything had gone wrong. For her, not for Aelissm.

With a growl of intent, he sought Amber's mouth and the oblivion he would find in kissing her. At last, he managed to subdue his ponderings as their desire spiraled out of control. It was always like this with her. She was so wild and passionate that he had no hope of keeping his head. As they writhed in that exotic dance, Adam knew he wanted to keep her. For the rest of their lives. But that would come later. After. If she still wanted him when he told her the truth. He would, he vowed, just as soon as he figured out how to do it without losing her. Hope flared that talking with Aelissm might show him the way.

Sometime later, when they were sitting together on his bed watching the static-ridden local news on the little television that had come with his house, his fog of contentment was shattered. Amber bounced off the bed, remembering the envelope she'd brought. She tossed it at him.

"What's this?" he asked, looking at her as he opened it.

"An invitation to a potluck at the Bedspread Inn out in Northstar. Ms. Davis—Aelissm—wants me to come so I can start getting to know the locals. She said you should come, too. Wouldn't that be great? We could live up in Northstar together for the summer, work together...."

Fear leeched through him, cold and nauseating. She knew about Amber. That dread grew as Amber told him about Aelissm's visit—with her detective in tow—to the restaurant quite a while ago now, looking for him.

"Was it anything important?" she asked when she finished her tale.

"If I haven't missed it by now, I doubt it," he replied, drawing a deep breath to settle his skittering pulse.

She walked her fingertips up his naked torso before flattening her hand against his chest. "Brandon?"

"Hmm?" he asked, hoping he sounded sufficiently distracted by what was on the television.

"You'll come to the potluck with me, won't you?"

"I don't know."

"Please come."

"Can I think about it for a day or two?"

"Well, it's the day after tomorrow."

Shit. "Just let me think about it, okay?"

"All right. I should probably head home. It's getting late."

"Please stay," Adam whispered.

"What?" She sat up and stared at him with surprise widening her lustrous brown eyes. "Did you just…?"

"Stay the night. Please," he said more loudly.

A smile spread over her face. "This is the first time you've asked me to spend the night."

"I regret not asking sooner."

"Interesting," she purred, wrapping herself sensuously around him. "You bet I'll stay."

Adam folded his arms around her and sighed raggedly, praying this wouldn't be his only opportunity to hold her all night. Somehow, his two-week window had dwindled away. He had to talk to Aelissm and settle this thing between them once and for all so they could both move on, but to do that, he had to find her and get her alone someplace where she couldn't trap him and simply wait for the cops to arrive. That place sure as hell wasn't her inn during a potluck when she'd be surrounded by her friends and neighbors, one of whom was a sheriff's deputy. Two were, actually, if he counted O'Neil.

He needed to find her cabin, but he had no hope of doing it on his own, and anyhow, he was out of time. Sara was due to arrive in two days—the day of the potluck. If he couldn't warn Pat O'Neil in time—since he hadn't taken the hint and left on his own—any hope Adam had of begging Aelissm's forgiveness was gone.

Two days, Adam thought as he tightened his arms around Amber. *Two days to find a miracle. I wonder what JP will charge for the one he says he can deliver?*

* * *

Adam sat behind the wheel of his truck and stared at the gate blocking him from continuing up the narrow dirt road. It had taken him an hour and three wrong turns to reach it despite JP's directions. And it was locked.

He was certain this was the gate JP had mentioned— its stripes of neon paint were exactly as the man had described—which meant that Aelissm's cabin, her grandparents', her uncles', and June's were all beyond it. He was so close! He could park the truck somewhere below and continue on foot, but he didn't know how much farther up the road to go, and even though JP had given him directions all the way to Aelissm's cabin, Adam didn't trust himself to find the right one. And it would *not* be good if he knocked on the wrong door.

Honestly, he was kidding himself. With the detective

still here, what chance did he have of getting near enough to Aelissm to talk to her? About as much of a chance as he'd had of finding her cabin without JP's assistance. Technically, he *still* hadn't found it, though he doubted JP would consider that grounds to nullify their agreement. For his assistance, JP had asked only that Adam promise to keep his nose out of whatever the man was plotting and not mention a word of their conversations to June Montana or Aelissm or anyone who might pass such information on to either of them. Adam was disturbed enough by the request that he was tempted to break his word to JP.

"The last thing I need to do is get involved in JP's mess. I mean, here I am, sitting in front of a locked gate in the middle of the Montana wilderness," he muttered. "I've been stalking a woman for a year like some deranged psychopath. Yeah, that's a god-damned big enough disaster."

The admission made him shudder. The fact that it was the truth was even more difficult to swallow. *Stalker.* The very word was unnerving. If he had thought he could find denial of what he believed in Aelissm's words—*if* she uttered them—he wouldn't. He hadn't always been a monster, but this past year, he'd turned into one, and maybe he didn't deserve her forgiveness, but he hoped the woman who had once captivated him would free him from what he'd become.

Drumming his thumbs on the steering wheel, he debated his next move. He had tried and failed yet again to meet up with Aelissm on his terms. The thought that the invitation to the potluck was a trap resounded in his head, but if he wanted to clean up this mess, he'd have to take a chance. Maybe, with the surety that she was in the company of people he was certain would do just about anything to protect her, she'd feel safe enough to let him talk.

Reaching into the glove box of the truck, he grabbed the notepad and pen he kept in it and rummaged around for something with which he could affix a note to the gate. He found a roll of black electrical tape in a Ziploc baggie he used to hold various fuses and other quick-fix supplies for his truck. With a trembling hand, he scribbled a note accepting her invitation to the potluck, tucked it in the baggie, and sealed it.

Once he'd secured it to the brightly painted gate, he backed cautiously down the hill to the fork where he could turn around. Tomorrow, one way or another, he would face Aelissm and attempt to put this whole ordeal behind them.

* * *

"What's that?" Aelissm asked, pointing to the gate.

Pat narrowed his eyes at what appeared to be a piece of paper weather-proofed in a plastic baggie, and secured to the gate with black tape. Electrical, he guessed.

"Don't know," he replied and stepped out of Aelissm's truck. First, he unlocked the gate and swung it open. While he waited for Aelissm to drive through, he unwound the tape and peeled the baggie free. As he swung the gate closed and locked it again, he paused to study the tire tracks in the dust. A light rain shower had come through a couple hours ago, puckering the dirt and hiding all traces of traffic from before it. June, he knew, had left for work at the Ramshorn before the rain had come, so the fact that there were two sets of tracks—the one he and Aeli had made just now and another—told Pat that someone had been up here within the last two hours. He knew the other set of tracks couldn't be Marge and Roger because they stopped at the gate, and no one else ever wasted the time to drive up here without calling ahead to make sure someone was home. Glancing at the plastic-shielded paper in his hand, Pat knew who the other set of tracks belonged to. Adam Winters.

"You're brave enough to come up here but not brave enough to go the rest of the way on foot." He chuckled mirthlessly. "So you *still* don't know exactly where she lives."

He pulled the paper out of the baggie as he walked up to the truck and opened it. Sure enough, he recognized Adam's scrawl.

Hello, Aelissm, he wrote. *I've tried to find you so we can deal with this thing quietly. I told you I couldn't leave without resolving what happened, and I can't, so I will come with Amber to your potluck. If you care anything about her or me, you won't make a big deal out of this. I just want to fix things. Tell Pat that he should have left by now. I told him I have ways of digging up dirt he can't wash off. He can still leave; there are still a few hours left. If you care anything for him, Aelissm, convince him to get out of Northstar before the potluck.*

Pat folded the note again and climbed into Aelissm's truck.

"What is it?" she inquired.

"A note from Adam. He's accepted your invitation to the potluck."

The color bled from her face despite what she'd said about not being afraid of Adam anymore. "Maybe this wasn't such a good idea." She glanced at him, and her fear slipped away as a frown pinched her brows. Flatly, she asked, "What's so amusing?"

"Your plan is working, sweetheart," he replied.

"You've driven him to desperation, and he's tried—somewhat unsuccessfully—to find your cabin."

"You're being awfully smug about this whole thing, Pat."

"He's taken your bait, so why are you complaining?"

"Because I still feel like this is completely out of my control."

He leaned across the seat and kissed her cheek. "That's what I'm here for, sweetheart. Whatever happens, I won't let him hurt you."

"What else did he say?"

"He says he just wants to fix things so you can both move on."

They'd reached the cabin, so he pulled her across the seat to him and tucked his arms around her while she read the short note. After she finished, she set it on the dashboard and relaxed into him with the back of her head resting on his chest. Protecting her had become his place when Bill had first asked him to come here. Soothing her worries was a duty he'd taken upon himself.

"This will all be over soon, my love."

"Mmm. My love. I like that."

"I do, too." He picked up the letter and glanced over it again. "I'd say he doesn't seem as determined as he was when I first got here. His letters have changed. Do you think he really loves Amber?"

Aeli nodded. "I know she loves him, and she's not dumb enough to fall for someone who didn't return her feelings."

"I wonder if she isn't affecting his motivation. Or destroying it. I'm not sure I can explain it, but I just get the feeling his heart's not in this anymore. He hasn't vowed his undying love for you in a long time."

"No, he hasn't. And I can't begin to say how big a relief that is, now that you've pointed it out. Let's worry about that later, though, all right? We need to get our dinner fixings inside before they go bad."

Aeli opened the cabin while Pat grabbed the few groceries they'd picked up from Ma Burns' on their way up the mountain, pondering what dirt Adam thought he'd uncovered as he followed his lover inside. There shouldn't be anything. He'd never gotten so much as a speeding ticket, had kept his nose out of anything that remotely resembled a scandal, and had otherwise been a model citizen his entire life. His stomach growled, and he laughed. He'd probably think better once he was fed.

"So, are you and June baking pies for the potluck again?" he asked as he helped Aelissm put the groceries away.

"I thought we might. Why, do you have a problem with getting flour all over yourself?"

"Not at all. I quite enjoyed the last time."

She looked over her shoulder at him and smiled. He watched her get their dinner started, as amazed as always at her efficiency. If something as mundane as cooking a meal aroused such an incredible surge of affection for her, he wondered if he'd ever tire of living with her. He occasionally snatched ingredients as she cooked and she'd swat at his hand every time, giggling. How could something so everyday be so blissful? The graceful movements of her body as she glided around the kitchen absolutely captivated him.

"We should give Unk a call to let him know what's

going on since we actually have something to tell him about Adam," Aeli remarked as she tossed the sliced potatoes she was frying. The aroma emanating from the onions and butter she'd added to flavor the potatoes made Pat's mouth water.

"Probably," he replied, realizing he hadn't told his boss anything of what had happened over the past couple days.

All at once, his mind opened up, and he was able to focus. If Adam *had* managed to find something to use against him, it would have been something in Seattle. It was possible he'd made a mistake as a rookie cop, though he had once been offered a mind-blowing sum of money to look the other way instead of turning the Ecstasy-selling, shoplifting little sister of one of Sara's good friends in. He had staunchly upheld the law. There were other similar cases, and every time, he'd stayed true to his oath. *So, what does Adam think he's found?* Pat wondered again.

Bill might be able to shed some light on the matter, so he took the cordless out to the back porch, scattering a large gathering of chipmunks. While he waited for Bill to answer the phone, he reached inside the door, took a handful of peanuts Aeli kept in a jar beside it, and plopped on the steps to feed the woodland rodents. One of the larger variety had just perched on his knee to take a peanut when Bill answered.

"Hiya, Bill," Pat said, startling the chipmunk. The creature bounded a few feet away and turned to chitter angrily at him.

"Hi, Pat. I wasn't expecting to hear back from you so soon." There was a pause. "What is that noise?"

"I made one of Aeli's chippies angry."

"Sounds like he's cussing you pretty good. Anyhow, how are you? Still enjoying Montana?"

"I'm loving it. I haven't had one of my bad days in a couple of months at least."

"That's great news, Pat. It really is. I told you Northstar would be good for you."

"You have, repeatedly, but I don't remember you saying anything about your niece being the most effective part."

Bill didn't answer right away, but Pat soon heard the sound of his boss's rich laughter. "I believe *you* were the one who accused me of concocting this mess with Winters to get you hooked up with my niece."

"So I did. You were right about her, though. She's incredible. I honestly don't think I could have come as far as I have without her support."

"Do you love her?"

There was no point in denying it because Bill would call him out on the lie—he wasn't the lead detective for nothing—so Pat replied honestly, "I do, but it's all really confused right now."

His boss chuckled again. "Seems I should have placed a bet, after all. I would have won."

Pat laughed, too. "You have about as much shame as she does. Which I can tell you isn't much."

"I should let you get back to her. Mary's finished dinner and you know how I hate to miss her cooking."

"About as much as I'm going to miss Aeli's. I think I'm starting to lose my boyish figure."

Bill's laughter boomed so loud Pat had to pull the

phone away from his ear. "I highly doubt that. My niece may be as good a cook as my sister, but I'm sure she's been dragging you all over the countryside. She won't *let* you get fat, even if you had it in your genetics."

"Ah, shucks, Bill, you're making me blush."

"About damned time you had something to blush about. Now, I'm hanging up, Pat. Take care of yourself and Aeli and keep me posted."

"Wait. I actually had a reason for calling you. I wanted to ask if you have noticed anything unusual over there?"

"What do you mean?"

He explained about Aelissm's impulsive decision to leave that first note on Adam's door and detailed everything that had happened since, including his impressions of Winters' deteriorating drive.

"Hmm. I think you're right, Pat, but that's why you're such a good detective. As far as anything out of place here, no, I haven't noticed anything. I'll look into it and let you know if I find anything. I wonder what kind of surprise he's talking about. If we had a category, that would help narrow things down a bit."

All through their conversation, fear had begun to infiltrate his thoughts. His instincts, his training, and his intelligence had put enough pieces together to form the beginning of a picture. Having concluded that the surprise Winters had mentioned was coming from Seattle, Pat had landed on the only thing Aeli's stalker could possibly use against him. The realization wasn't comforting.

"I have one more favor, Bill. Can you check in on Sara and find out what she's been up to lately?"

"Do you mind if I ask why?"

"If you're thinking I still give a rat's ass about her, you don't need to worry. I have a hunch."

"Oh, goody," Bill said sarcastically. "This is one of the rare times I hate your hunches because they're usually right. Tell me what you're thinking, what you need to know, and I'll do my best to find it."

"See if you can find out if Sara and Adam might know each other."

"You think she might be his surprise?"

"It's not too great a leap to imagine it. They ran in the same circles. Hang on a minute, would you, Bill?"

"Sure."

Pat stood up and poked his head inside. "Hey, Aeli, what did you say Brent's sister's name was?"

"Jeanette. Why do you ask?"

Dammit, Pat thought. Foreboding darkened his thoughts. "Just curious."

She lifted a golden brow but said nothing as she turned back to her task.

Pat stepped back outside and returned his attention to Bill. "There's something I didn't put together until now. Sara's best friend is Jeanette LaRue, but LaRue is her married name. I don't know what her maiden name was, but Aelissm mentioned weeks ago that Brent Ellington had an older sister named Jeanette. Maybe it's just a coincidence, but I doubt it."

"So do I. If Winters has involved Sara, this could get ugly, Pat."

"I know."

"Keep yourselves safe, and I'll talk to you soon."

When he hung up, Pat shook his head to dispel his dread. If he was right—and he prayed that he was wrong—things were about to get rather interesting. The last person he wanted coming to Northstar was Sara Montgomery. He wasn't even sure yet she would be, but already he felt the effects of her nearness taking hold of him like talons of ice, digging into the meat of his shoulders and neck, and he reached back to massage it away. He wasn't going to let her do this to him. She was out of his life, and he was going to keep it that way.

Standing, he glanced in the kitchen window and let the sight of Aelissm soothe him. If he took anything from his conversation with her uncle, it was Bill's support of him staying with Aelissm. He should have guessed Bill would pick adding Pat to his family over keeping him as an employee. Bill was very family orientated. Maybe Pat should be, too. It seemed to make his boss happy. What was so great about the best job in the world if, at the end of the day, there was no one and nothing to go home to?

With a sigh, Pat stood and went back inside to find dinner ready and waiting for him. Aelissm started to sit down, but he beckoned her to him. With thoughts of Sara flirting with his mind, he needed her. She obeyed, and he wrapped his arms around her shoulders and held her, comforted by her nearness.

"I know I haven't said it yet, but I do love you, Aelissm Davis."

Nineteen

AELI WENT OUT TO HER TRUCK to fetch the pie plates and spotted Luke hiking up the hill from her grandparents' cabin. She paused to wait for him and marked the changes in him. The wariness had been shed, replaced by a startling confidence that made him seem much closer to his twelve years. It was as if he finally felt safe and was now free to be himself, and she wondered who he was beneath the quietude.

"So, Luke Montana, how come you get out of baking pies?" Aelissm asked.

"Who says I do?" he asked in reply, grinning.

He's gonna be a heart-breaker, she thought. *It's scary how much he looks like June when he does that.* "Well, we've already started, and you're just getting back from Grandma and Grandpa's cabin."

"Mom sent me down for some more cinnamon," Luke said, holding up the little spice jar. "She didn't think we had enough."

The title caught Aelissm by surprise. Luke had always called June by her name, even since the adoption. Maybe the name change had made it real to him. The same yearning that enveloped her whenever she watched Pat with Luke or Nick Hammond's young son reared back and sank sharp fangs into her. She wanted to hear a young voice call for her, wanting Mommy. She wanted to snuggle on the couch on a snowy winter evening and read a book together with her family. Being in love with Pat made her want so much.

"Why are you looking at me like that?" Luke asked warily.

"You called June 'Mom'."

"She said I could when I asked," he replied shyly.

Aelissm affectionately stroked his shimmering gold hair. "You've found home, haven't you?"

He nodded.

"I am so happy for you, Luke. So, if June is Mom now, does that mean I'm your sarcastic Aunt Aeli?"

"But you're not sisters."

"So? She didn't give birth to you, but that doesn't make you any less her son, does it? We're as close to sisters as we can be without having the same parents."

"You really mean that? You want to be my aunt?"

"I do," Aelissm replied. She wrapped her arm around his shoulders. "You're not the only one benefiting from this situation. June really loves you, and so do I."

He looked up at her and beamed. "Thanks, Aunt Aeli."

She tossed her head back and laughed. "I like it!"

"Me, too. I've never had an aunt."

It was the first time she'd heard him talk about his family. Curiosity nibbled at her, but she didn't want to disrupt his happiness with sad memories. Someday, she'd find out more about him, but for now, it was enough to have him in her family. She'd meant it when she'd said she wanted to be his aunt. And she'd really like it if Pat wanted to be his uncle, but again, she said nothing. She didn't want to traumatize Luke again by making him remember *that*.

"We were about to send out the search party," Pat remarked as she and Luke walked in. "How long does it take to fetch pie plates?"

"Luke and I were having a little heart-to-heart talk," Aeli replied haughtily. "Nephew to aunt. So you just hold your horses."

Pie baking was every bit as fun as that first time when Pat hadn't been in the valley a full twenty-four hours yet, but what had then been polite cordiality had turned into the genuine, familiar love of family, though June didn't find it too funny when Aeli tried to engage Pat and Luke in a flour fight.

"If you destroy my kitchen, I will make you lick it up!"

They'd all come a long way since that first afternoon they'd spent baking pies together and Aelissm could scarcely believe it. That day had really been the beginning of something wonderful, and she dreaded the day when Pat left and took part of their happy group away with him. The mountainside wouldn't be the same without him, and she found herself hoping for a miracle. Luke was a permanent part of her home now, and she wanted Pat to be, too, but she couldn't ask him to give up his dream. As it was, the battle between his calling and the new happiness he'd found was beginning to tear him apart; she could see it in his eyes from time to time, a weariness far too similar to what she'd noticed those first few weeks, and she hated to see the peace they'd won begin to crumble.

It wasn't pleasant, thinking about what she and Pat would have to face all too soon, but it kept her from thinking of other things. Like the potluck in just a few hours. The knowledge that she was going to face Adam for the first time since the night he'd cornered her in Seattle was nerve-wracking if she let herself dwell on it. There was no point in working herself up about it because whatever was going to happen would happen regardless of whether she was calm or in a frenzy. Therefore, she was going to ignore it until she had no choice and enjoy a few peaceful hours.

She found it a little more difficult not to worry about what Adam had planned for Pat. Uncle Bill hadn't called back yet, which meant he hadn't found anything. She was beginning to wonder if Adam was bluffing, but he had a talent for finding what should be damned difficult to locate. She *really* wished Unk would call, if only to tell her everything was as quiet as it ever was in Washington.

The phone rang, and Aeli blinked at it in surprise. June, whose hands were covered in sticky apple pie filling, asked her to answer it.

"Montana cabin," Aelissm greeted, earning herself a roll of June's eyes.

"Very funny, Aeli Girl. I can just see June rolling her eyes at that one."

"She is."

"I called your cabin first before I realized you girls would be baking pies for the potluck. Pat there with you?"

"Of course. We weren't about to let him get away with not helping. At this very moment, he's sprinkled with a rather generous dusting of flour."

"Do I want to know how that happened?"

"Luke and I tried to start a flour fight. June wouldn't let us, but I got Pat before she could stop me."

Her uncle chuckled. "Sounds like everyone is having a wonderful afternoon, but how are you really doing?"

"I'm okay. I'm stubbornly refusing to think about this evening."

"You? Stubborn? Say it isn't so."

"Ha ha, Unk. Did you find anything interesting?"

"I did, actually. Do me a favor, will you? Tell Pat that he was right, as usual."

"Hey, Pat. Unk says to tell you that you're right."

She expected him to smile or laugh, but instead, he closed his eyes and tilted his head back. Worry instantly descended on her when the muscles in his jaw twitched.

"Pat? What's he talking about?"

"Adam knows Sara. Ask him how."

"Pat was right on the money, Aeli. Brent's sister is Sara's best friend. They all went to the same private school, and Adam met Sara through Brent and Jeanette." Bill paused. "A friend of mine with the Seattle PD has been keeping tabs on Sara since she got out of jail. He says she hasn't been doing anything out of the ordinary."

"Well, that's good news, isn't it?" Aelissm asked.

"It was, but she disappeared two days ago."

Fury ignited, burning away her fear. "If she shows her face in my inn or gets anywhere near Pat, I'll put a bullet between her eyes. And I've got plenty of places to bury that bitch's body where no one will *ever* find her. You know I do."

"Yes, I do, Aelissm, but don't go off half-cocked."

"Oh, I won't. I'll be fully cocked when I go off, Unk."

"Aelissm, listen to me. You can't think like that."

Aeli took a deep breath. "I know. If things get out of hand, I'll call the cops so they can *legally* deal with her."

"Thank you. Pat's going to need your strength if she shows up, Aeli. Just as I'm sure you'll need his tonight. I'm glad you have each other."

"Is there anything else we should know?"

"That's everything. I'm scared for you both."

"We'll be fine. Besides, *if* she shows her face in Northstar, I might not have to shoot her. My neighbors are very protective of their own, including Pat."

"Aelissm…."

"I know, Unk. I promise I won't do anything stupid."

"Glad to hear it. Now, I have to get back to work, though I don't have any idea how I'm supposed to concentrate while I'm worried sick about the two of you. I wish I had time to fly out there."

"What good would it do, Unk?"

Her uncle sighed. "None."

"Well, Unk, we've got pies to bake, so I should probably let you go."

"Of course. You'd better call me tonight, or I'll send in the National Guard."

"I know you will. Love you, Unk."

"Love you, too, Aeli Girl. Give my love to Pat and June and Luke, too."

She promised she would and hung up. With a wordless bellow, she turned to Pat to find him leaning against June's sink with his eyes still closed. June and Luke glanced between them, silently asking what they could do to help. Aelissm repeated what Bill had told her about Sara and Adam. Pat opened his eyes at last, and she half-expected to see the same shadows she had the night he'd told her about Sara, but he was remarkably composed. Unnervingly so.

"It is what it is," he said in response to her unasked question. "I guess I'll know soon enough if I'm really past that nightmare."

"*If* she comes. It seems like a bit of a stretch that Adam would be able to convince her to help him."

"I imagine he only had to mention my name."

"June, Luke, will you excuse us for a few?" Aeli asked.

"Sure," June replied. "Take your time."

"Pat, come outside with me."

He followed her out onto June's back deck and stared blindly toward their cabin. Even if she closed her eyes, Aelissm would still feel the undercurrent of panic radiating from him despite the outward appearance of numbness.

"Does she hate you enough to put everything in her life on hold just to chase you all the way to Montana?"

"She stabbed me, Aelissm, so I'd say it's not as big a stretch as you think."

He didn't fight her when she took him by his shoulders and turned him to face her. She studied his expressionless face for a moment, concerned by the dullness in his eyes.

"Pat, are you all right?"

"I don't know."

"I could kill Adam for doing this."

That brought a glimmer of a smile to his face, but it didn't reach his eyes. She could see him starting to shrink away and collapse in on himself, and it killed her. She took his face in her hands and forced him to meet her gaze. All at once, the shadows of remembered pain and terror returned, and he looked down at her, pleading for salvation.

"Oh, sweetheart," Aeli murmured. "Don't let her do this to you."

He drew a deep, shuddering breath. "It's been easy to get over her so far away and with you to show me how good life can be, but I never expected I'd have to deal with her here. Once I get over the shock, I'll be all right. Besides, like you said, I may be completely wrong. Even with all evidence to the contrary."

"The sheriff's department is just a phone call away, and if she comes to the potluck, Aaron Hammond will be there, so he can keep a lid on things."

"I hope you're right, but in my experience, Sara doesn't play by the same rules as everyone else."

Aelissm scowled playfully at him. "Would you quit being such a pessimist? That's my job."

This time the smile lit his entire face, and he leaned down to kiss her.

"That's much better. Are you going to be okay now?"

"As long as I have you, I'll be just fine."

* * *

By the time five o'clock rolled around, Aelissm was

losing the fight with her anxiety. She, Pat, June, Luke, and the three Hammond brothers had just finished setting up the tables. They were running a little late, and there were already a lot of people gathered, patiently holding their dishes and waiting for a place to set them down. Aelissm tried to keep a smile plastered to her face, but inside, she trembled with dread. Any time now, Amber would show up with Adam on her heels and, possibly, Sara Montgomery following two steps behind. If anyone noticed how badly her hands shook, no one said anything.

Pat wasn't faring much better. The unreserved, carefree attitude that was usually in place whenever he was around their valley neighbors was absent, but again, if anyone noticed anything amiss, they kept their observations to themselves. Old Matt Carlyle and his wife Livia arrived, and the first thing they did was tell Pat how nice it was to see him. Not two minutes later, John Hammond and his wife Tracie expressed the same sentiments. Aeli momentarily pushed her own concerns aside; the forced enthusiasm on his face broke her heart.

Slowly, the room filled with her friends and family. They were all oblivious to what might soon transpire. Aelissm located Aaron and pulled him aside.

"What's up?" he asked, distracted.

Aelissm traced his gaze to Jim and Jessie Robinson's daughter, Erica. She lifted an eyebrow. "You ask her out, yet?"

"What?"

"Erica. Have you asked her out yet?"

"Nah."

"Since it looks like you've finally figured out you like

her, you should," Aelissm advised, noting the dopey smile. "But first, Pat and I need to talk to you. Adam Winters should be here soon. I invited him to the potluck."

Aaron finally turned his attention to her. "That's brave. Are you still sure you don't want me to arrest him?"

"I am," Aelissm replied. "Although… if he's brought Sara along with him, I might change my mind."

"Sara?"

"My ex. I'm not positive she's coming, but if so…." Pat unbuttoned the top two buttons of the flannel he wore and showed Aaron the scar Sara had given him. "She's not a pleasant person to deal with."

Aaron let out a low whistle. "When'd she do that?"

"When I told her I was leaving."

"Psycho."

"Anyhow, I hope we won't need you, but I wanted to give you a head's up just in case."

"I appreciate it. Either of you need *anything*, just holler," Aaron replied, glancing from Pat to Aelissm.

"We will."

Aelissm only nodded and went about serving drinks from the bar. Remarkably, she felt much better about the situation.

Five-fifteen came and went, and there was no sign of Adam, Amber, or Sara. Aelissm began to relax a little and started to enjoy the potluck. It was impossible to hold on to her fear surrounded by so many people she adored. The strain was gone from Pat's body, too, so she turned up the music. The people who had finished eating got up to dance, and Aeli was surprised when Pat took her hand and led her into the center of it. Memories of that first potluck frolicked playfully through her head as they danced. So many wonderful things had happened to her since then, and she gazed lovingly up at the man who'd stolen her heart. Warmth shone brightly in his eyes again and melted away her lingering worries.

"Hello again, Aelissm."

Her heart skittered sickeningly in her chest at the sound of his voice, and she nearly collapsed against Pat. Only Pat's quick reaction kept her on her feet. But it wasn't fear that snapped through her. It was anger. With a scowl of disdain on her face, she pivoted around to face the man who'd shadowed her every move for the last year. Facing him sent a surge of old emotions through her, making it difficult to stay the course she'd chosen. It would be so easy to signal Aaron and have Adam arrested....

Instead, as the music abruptly ended, she said, "You're late."

He winced.

"Where is she, Adam?"

"Who, Amber?"

"No. Sara."

She was stunned again when the color left his face, leaving him sickly pale beneath his tan. "Don't pretend innocence, Adam."

"I—"

"Who's Adam?"

They looked up to see Amber walking through the double glass doors, glancing from Aelissm to Adam in confusion. Aelissm felt her face shift into a feral smirk as Adam's expression shifted into a look of utter horror, but miraculously, she also felt a pang of sympathy for him. It was clear that he was in love with the girl, and his dirty laundry was about to be revealed to her before a room full of people who'd been prepped to hate him.

"Seems that you have some explaining to do, *Brandon*," she said. "Perhaps you'd like to tell Amber why you're here."

He pleaded silently with his eyes that she not do this. The part of her that remembered the terror he'd put her through took sadistic pleasure in his pain. The rest of her, which had healed from that trauma, screamed at her to be fair. She wasn't a vindictive tyrant, after all, and she didn't need to start being one now. She studied Adam for a moment before she spoke.

Amazingly, that brief pause allowed her to see that Pat was right. Something *had* changed. His hair, though still longer than he used to wear it, was clean and trimmed, and honestly, it suited him well. He was clean-shaven again, and he had traded in his shabby, threadbare clothing for crisp new T-shirt and jeans that flattered his body. He'd put some weight back on—healthy weight, muscle—and he no longer looked so gaunt. Gone were the shadows under his eyes and the hollows in his cheeks. Most notably, the madness was gone from his eyes, leaving them clear and bright like she remembered despite his obvious nervousness. This Adam she recognized with a happy leap of her heart, and she almost smiled at seeing him again. Almost.

"You two know each other?" Amber asked. Her voice quivered with the battle of emotions clearly inscribed on her face. She was smart. She sensed something out of place, but she was hoping one or both of them would explain it and alleviate her worry.

"We met through a mutual acquaintance back in Seattle a few years ago," Aelissm told her, never taking her eyes off Adam. "He and my boyfriend were best friends. Isn't that right, Adam?"

"Please, Aeli…."

"Why do you keep calling him Adam?"

"Because that's his name. Adam Winters."

"Please, Aelissm. I didn't come here to fight. I need to talk to you about what happened."

Aelissm scowled, then smoothed her expression. She *could* spell out his nasty deeds right then and there in front of everyone, but her conscience wouldn't let her. His demeanor was not that of the man she'd run from, but that of the man she'd known before Brent's death. Her friend.

"Can I please talk to you alone?"

"No," Pat answered immediately.

He still rested a hand protectively on Aelissm's waist, but he was otherwise non-threatening, and Aelissm knew it was intentional; his gaze was trained keenly on Adam. She turned and put a hand gently on her lover's chest. He glanced down at her, and she met his eyes, asking him to trust her. Turning her attention back to Adam, she said, "Not entirely alone. Whatever you have to say, you'll have to say it in front of Pat."

"I'm not going to do anything but talk, Aeli."

"Forgive me if I don't entirely trust you."

"Brandon… what are you talking about? What is *she* talking about? Ms. Davis?"

Aelissm genuinely regretted Amber's innocent involvement in this mess. The girl was a sweetheart, and she didn't deserve to be dragged through the mud with them.

"Amber, I need to talk to her first. Then, I promise I'll come clean about everything."

"Is this about that problem, the one you came to Devyn to fix?"

Adam nodded. When he talked to Amber, his attention was focused entirely on her. Aelissm was suddenly glad she'd decided not to spill the beans in so public a place. If getting Adam out of her life depended on his happiness and *that* depended on Amber, it probably wasn't a good idea for the girl to find out the truth about him so harshly.

"Yes," Adam said. "Aelissm is that problem."

"What the hell?" Amber gasped, jerking back.

"He doesn't mean it quite like he said," Aeli remarked. "Let us talk first, and then we'll explain everything."

The relief on Adam's face reminded her strongly of the man she'd once counted as a friend and made it easier to quell her darker emotions. She could see the same lovable Adam who'd been her only understanding companion in Brent's high society world. He wouldn't hurt her anymore. Whatever had broken the night Brent died had mended, and the release she felt was incredible.

"Let's step outside, shall we?" Aelissm said, motioning for Adam to join her. She took Pat's hand and looked up at him. She spoke softly so only he could hear. "I think everything is going to be okay. He's the Adam I remember again."

"Amazing what love will do to a man," Pat said, his voice all gentle compassion. "It's powerful enough to heal even the wounds we thought would never stop bleeding."

She stood on her toes and kissed him. "Turn the

music back on, June. I want everyone else to go back to having fun. We'll be fine. And, Amber, get to mingling. June can introduce you around."

There was a murmur of support from her neighbors, and she and Pat ducked outside to join Adam on the front deck. Over the past hour, the bright summer sun had been crowded out of the sky by a building thunderhead. Now the valley was softened by the strange glow of reflected light, and the air was heavy with impending rain that would wash the world clean. How fitting. She inhaled deeply and prepared herself to take a stroll down memory lane. The warmth of Pat's arms around her gave her the strength to do it with a clear mind.

"You never looked at Brent like you look at him," Adam observed, inclining his head at Pat. He extended his hand. "I know we already know who each other are, but I want to start this right. I'm Adam Winters."

Pat took his hand and shook it. "Pat O'Neil."

"I also want to thank you, Aeli, for keeping a cool head. I know I don't deserve it, but I really love Amber. I don't want to lose her, and if she finds out what I've done without a suitable explanation, I will."

"You'll have to tell her someday," Pat remarked. "That kind of secret will destroy you."

"I know. I'm hoping Aeli will help there, even though I have no right to ask."

"Let's see how this goes before I agree to that. Your girlfriend is waiting for a conclusion," Aelissm said, "so let's start from the night Brent died."

Adam walked to the railing and braced his hands on it, staring out at the mountains for a few moments before beginning. "I saw him hurting you, and something broke; I actually felt it snap. I couldn't believe—still can't—he could do anything like that." He turned back to Aelissm and added defensively, "He was still alive and conscious when I left him."

His clarity of thought was further evidence that he was himself again. There would be no more hissed threats, no more incongruent requests, and no more maniacal claims of possession. Aelissm took a deep breath and let it out slowly as the last vestiges of apprehension left her. She motioned for him to continue, not trusting her voice.

"The next afternoon, I went by to apologize and to demand an explanation about why he'd done it, but there were cops crawling all over his apartment. That's when I found out he was dead, and all I could think was, *I killed my best friend.* I don't remember anything about the next couple of days, and I still don't remember that night I cornered you, but I know I did because that's when you put the restraining order on me." He paused to consider his next words. "I almost didn't come because of it. I was afraid you were just trying to trick me into breaking it again and that you'd have me arrested as soon as I got out of my car."

"The thought crossed my mind, so I'm a little surprised you're here."

"Then I hope you understand how important it is for me to talk to you. I never intended to hurt you, Aelissm. But I haven't exactly been in full control of my mind since Brent died. I used to think I wanted your gratitude for protecting you from him that night, but that's not right. I need to hear you tell me I'm not a killer, that I'm not a bad man because you're the only one who can. No one else knows that I wasn't always a monster. *That's* why I couldn't let you go. If I had only been able to ask…. But I just couldn't get there."

"What changed?"

"Amber. She showed me that there was still enough good left in me to love."

"How do you know this isn't the same obsessive compulsion you felt for me?"

"Because it feels so different. She makes me feel free and weightless. You…. I always loved you, or thought I did, and you were always so kind to me. I think you were more my best friend than Brent, and after he died, you were the only thing I had to hang on to, the only thing that kept me from completely losing my mind. It wasn't anything like what I feel for Amber. It was chaotic and tense and terrifying, like I was chained to you. Love shouldn't be like that."

"No, it shouldn't," Pat said quietly. "Love should be what you say you have with Amber—freedom and light, not desperation and darkness."

Aelissm glanced up at Pat and smiled before speaking to Adam. "There was a long stretch in there when I didn't hear from you at all. I did a little healing of my own during that time. And I began to move forward."

"I'm glad, Aeli. I really am. You deserve it, and I am so sorry for everything I've done, for what I became. I really lost my mind after Brent…." He paused, and tears welled in his eyes. "Oh, God, Brent. I know what the autopsy said, but I killed him, Aeli."

He collapsed into one of the wicker chairs, dropped his head into his hands, and sobbed.

"Adam. Listen to me. And please believe that I'm not saying it because you want to hear it. I mean what I say."

She knelt in front of him and pulled his hands away from his face. "You are *not* a bad man. What happened was a tragic accident."

"I nearly strangled him. What if I hadn't stopped?"

"But you *did*. You didn't murder him, Adam. And I *am* grateful that you came to my rescue. Because you did, I can still find joy in a man's touch. Pat's grateful, too, aren't you, lover?"

Adam looked up, and his face resembled a Picasso painting. There was regret, relief, embarrassment, and amusement all fighting for control of him. The sight was comical, but Aelissm refused to laugh. He was at too delicate a place to understand it. So was she, for that matter. The idea that her nightmare was finally coming to an end was too new for comprehension.

"I appreciate it, Aeli, and someday I may forgive myself for everything I've done. I think I can start that process now." When a car pulled in the driveway, Adam jumped.

"It's just one of my regulars from Devyn," Aelissm said. She waved a hand in greeting. The man glanced at them and continued inside with little more than a nod.

"I thought it might be Sara." Adam shivered. "I guess that makes one more idiotic mistake I need to apologize for. I never should have told her Pat was here."

Pad shuddered visibly at the confirmation of his suspicion and asked, "Why did you?"

"I wasn't thinking straight yet. This is none of her business, but I thought I needed you out of the way, and I didn't know how else to make that happen. I see now that I didn't have a snowball's chance in hell of getting rid of you." Adam's smile was self-mocking. "I wonder how long it's going to be before I stop making these stupid decisions. I tried to tell her not to come. I even tried to convince her that you had gone back to Washington, but she came anyway, and when I refused to tell her how to find you, she threatened to tell Amber everything I've done, so I told her about the potluck because I knew Aeli's other cop friend would be here."

"So, we can expect her any time?"

"I lied and told her the potluck didn't start until six, hoping she'd believe me, that it might give me enough time to warn you."

Aeli pulled Pat's arms more tightly around her. She was too focused on his state of mind to pay much attention to the sound of another car coming up the driveway. Both Adam and Pat, however, watched the vehicle intently.

"I'm so sorry," Adam added. His voice cracked.

"What's done is done," Pat replied with a shrug.

He stiffened, then released Aelissm and walked to the top of the stairs, and it was then that she noticed the other car that had pulled up—a car with Washington plates. The driver turned out to be a perfectly groomed, expensively dressed redhead with a petite, lithe body and the air of someone who knew her precise effect on everyone around her. Aeli didn't have to think hard to figure out who the woman was, but when Pat spoke, she was chilled to the bone by the frost his voice.

"Hello again, Sara."

The woman's head jerked up as if she hadn't expected him to be *right* there. "Hello, Patrick."

Aelissm thought she now knew what June meant about hating someone on sight. It wasn't just what Pat had told her about the woman. There was something about her that Aelissm didn't like. It might have been how she looked down her nose at them, even from the bottom of the stairs, or it might have been the luxury car. Maybe it was the way she walked, conscious of her every step and throwing in a little extra sway of her hips. The *what* and the *why* didn't matter; all Aelissm needed to know was that she hated the woman.

"Should I be flattered that you hate me so much you'd come all the way out here?" Pat asked coolly. "Northstar's not exactly your style."

"You have no idea how much I hate you, Patrick," she replied sweetly. She turned to Adam and said, "If you've finished your chat, you may go find your little darling, Adam."

"I hadn't, actually, so—"

"I wasn't giving you a choice, my pet," Sara said in the same tone of sugared poison. "You've done your part, and you've had your say. I'll deal with you later. Now, be gone."

Adam glanced at Pat and Aeli, obviously wanting to stay. Aeli found herself reacting to him like she once had, as a friend. It was as if the past year had never happened. That he felt horrible about bringing Sara into the mix was obvious from the expression on his face, but there was another emotion alongside it. He felt duty-bound to protect not just Aelissm but Pat as well.

"There's no point in you getting mixed up in *this* mess, too," Pat told him. "I'm sure Amber needs you right now. Aeli, why don't you join him, and you can help him explain things to her."

"I'm not leaving you alone with *her*," she replied.

She placed herself between him and Sara, gently but firmly wrapping his arms around her again. There was no way she was going to give that bitch any opportunity to undo all the work she'd done to teach Pat how to live again. Maybe if she and Adam were there, Sara wouldn't fall into old habits.

"Please, Aeli," Pat pleaded softly in her ear.

"No."

"Oh, let her stay, Patrick," Sara remarked. "I'd like to meet your new whore. I'm Sara Montgomery, by the way."

Aelissm lifted her brows and nearly laughed. "I'm Aelissm Davis, and the only whore around here is you, honey."

"Oh, Patrick, she has a wicked little tongue on her, doesn't she?"

"Aeli, my love, please go inside. I'll be all right." He leaned down to kiss her neck and whispered, "If I need you, you won't be far out of reach. Take Adam inside and find Amber."

"I think I'm going to be sick," Sara muttered. "I never knew you were such a woman, Patrick."

"I'm shocked you know what a woman is, Sara," he retorted without missing a beat. "Because you sure as hell aren't one."

The shadow of surprise on her face was priceless. Maybe Pat would be all right after all. Sara obviously hadn't expected him to snap back like that. Still, Aelissm didn't want to leave him alone with her. God only knew what she'd do. But he'd asked her to, so she had to assume he knew what he was doing.

"Touch him and the scar you gave him will look like

a pin prick compared to the one I'll give *you.*"

Aelissm followed Adam inside and settled down near the doors. She leaned against a table, refusing to be distracted by anything. Not even her grandparents' demands to know what was going on or Amber's desperate plea for information broke her concentration. She stared intently at her lover and his ex-fiancée, concentrating on every minute change in body language. Her heart began to race as Sara quickly descended from haughty disdain to graceless aggression. It wasn't long until Sara did something that made Aeli's stomach clench. When Pat jerked away, the petite socialite reached to strike him, and Aelissm ran to the kitchen to grab the old .38 pistol she kept there. It hadn't worked in years, but Sara didn't know that.

Twenty

PAT APPRECIATED AELISSM'S SUPPORT and missed it, but he was glad she'd gone inside. He'd rather have her safely out of Sara's path than trying to protect him. Besides, this was something he needed to face on his own, or he'd never be free of this manicured demon.

His time in Montana and the knowledge he might have to face her had given him the stability of mind to deal with her, but he couldn't have prepared himself for seeing her again. He felt the same aching nausea as if he'd been kicked in the groin. Whatever attraction she'd held for him had died a long time ago, and now, with Aelissm for comparison, he was revolted by the thick, concealing make-up she wore, the artificial highlights in her rich chestnut hair, the designer clothes, and the air of superiority. The last he recalled all too clearly and found it no more appealing than he had since he'd first realized the nastiness that came with it.

"Ooo, Patrick, your little kitty has teeth," Sara said laughingly. "Did you hear her threaten me?"

"Leave Aelissm out of this, Sara."

"Why should I? She currently has something I wasn't finished with."

It was just like her to think of him as a possession. He'd never been anything more to her, and he was wise enough now to know it. He understood enough about her that he wouldn't slink away from her in horror. What he still couldn't figure, though, was how he'd ever let her dominate him. He'd forgotten how tiny she was.

"What's the matter, Patrick, little miss kitty got your tongue?" Sara stuck out her own tongue and wiggled her eyebrows suggestively. "I bet she does. Tell me something because she seems like such a plain girl. I'll admit she has a pretty face, but there can't be much else about her to hold a man. Is she at least a good lay?"

"Better than you by a long shot because she isn't just a 'lay'."

"And that's all I am, is that right?"

"Ignoring the pain and humiliation you caused me…. All right, the sex was never good with you, and compared to Aelissm…. There is no comparison."

"You son of a bitch," she hissed.

"It doesn't feel good to be found lacking, does it, Sara?"

"You would know."

He sighed tiredly, wishing he was back inside with the people of Northstar and the woman he loved. He'd rather be anywhere but standing out here in the face of an approaching storm, confronting a woman he should have been through with years ago. "We've been here before, Sara, and it's never gotten us anywhere. What do you want from me? You certainly don't want *me*. You never did. So, you can't be jealous that I'm moving on."

"You're right about that, at least. But I do want you, Patrick."

The smile that curled her lips was predatory. She took a step toward him, her eyes glittering with malice. Still the old fear did not stir. She must have noticed because her brows momentarily furrowed in confusion. He stared down at her, tense and anxious, but angry rather than afraid. What could she do to him now that she hadn't already done? Not a damned thing because he wasn't going to let her, and if he didn't let her, she wasn't strong enough.

"So, you found your balls, huh?" she asked and reached for his groin.

He saw the intent in her eyes and backed out of her reach. "Those don't belong to you anymore, darling. *I* don't belong to you anymore."

"I'm sure you'd like to think so, Patrick, but you see, you owe me, and until that debt is paid, I *own* you."

"What are you talking about?"

"The six months of my life I'll never get back. The restraining order. And the shame of it all."

Restraining order? He'd never…. Bill. No wonder he hadn't personally seen her in a while. In fact, the last time he *had* seen her, she'd sheathed a paring knife in his chest. Remembered pain lanced through the three-year-old scar. He'd spent almost a week in the hospital from the infection and the surgeries to repair the damage. He was lucky he had full use of the muscles and tissue she'd torn through, but he'd have the scar for the rest of his life as a reminder. He should have let Bill charge her with attempted murder. Instead, she'd been charged with aggravated assault and spent a mere six months in prison for it.

"I paid for that ten times over long before Bill filed the charges. I don't expect you to understand that you were abusing me, but surely you haven't forgotten all your other indiscretions. It's a long list, Sara, and I'm not sure I can count them all. You debased me and controlled every aspect of my life. I lost touch with every friend I had but Bill, and I even pushed my family away because of you. Do you know I've barely spoken to them since before I left you? And let's not forget that night at the diner, when you accused me of cheating on you. That in itself was bad enough, but I was in the middle of an interview with an assault victim. It took me a long time to convince her to talk to me again. But I couldn't tell you who she was. I couldn't even tell you why I was there, and you didn't trust me enough to believe I'd never cheat on you. Maybe that's because a cheater thinks everyone cheats like they do. For the record, I was *never* unfaithful to you." Pat shook his head as understanding dawned. Nothing he said could make her see the truth because she lacked whatever component was required to feel empathy. "I don't know why I'm wasting my breath because you don't give a damn about *any* of that."

"Boo-hoo. Poor little Patrick."

"Bill wanted the judge to lock you away for the maximum, and the judge was going to, but I pleaded with them for the most lenient sentence. I just wanted it to be over."

"So, I should be grateful? Never. No one shames me, Patrick. *No one.*"

"You should've thought about that before you stabbed me."

His lack of submission was beginning to wear on her patience. He could see it in the deepening scowl on her face. It was incredible how such a physically beautiful woman could be so ugly. He should walk away right now and end it before things deteriorated further, but he couldn't swallow the need to retaliate. She felt she'd been wronged? He'd begged for leniency on her behalf after everything she'd done to him. More than wanting to be done with her and foolishly thinking she'd appreciate his generosity, he'd actually felt guilty for the bruises he'd left on her arms and on her cheek.

"Don't worry, I've thought about it."

"Just how were you planning to exact your delusional vengeance on me, Sara? From where I'm standing, I don't see a damned thing you can do to me."

Sara's attention shifted momentarily away, and he followed her gaze. Aelissm rested against a table, watching them with taut intensity. All at once, he felt as if ice water had been poured over him.

"That's the beauty of it," Sara purred. "I don't have to do anything to *you.*"

Before he could stop her, Sara grabbed a fistful of his hair, yanked his head down, and kissed him. She threaded her arms around his neck and pressed her body tightly against him, moaning as if she thought it might still arouse him. He jerked his head back, peeled her arms open, and pushed her roughly away. For a moment, he thought he was going to vomit. Memories of past encounters with her flooded his mind. In brilliant, painful clarity, he remembered rutting with her—there had been no love, so it had been nothing like the thrill of making love to Aelissm, just mindless, visceral oblivion driven by the hatred of how she made him feel and act. He remembered, too, the soul-destroying insults. It would *never* be like that with Aelissm.

All at once, he wanted her reassuring presence. At the same time, he knew Sara had nearly lost control of her temper, and he wanted Aelissm far away from his venomous ex.

"You must have lost your touch, Sara," he said. His voice trembled, but there was nothing he could do about it. "You never used to make me want to puke with only a kiss."

He saw her coil to strike and grabbed her wrist before her palm connected with his face. He caught her other hand in plenty of time, too, and pushed her back against the deck railing. Either she wasn't as quick as she used to be or his instincts and reflexes had sharpened. An emotion he was more accustomed seeing in a mirror widened her amber-colored eyes. For the second time in their tumultuous history, Sara was frightened of him. Realizing what he'd become—what she'd again made him—he released her and backed away. She lunged at him but stopped in her tracks before she reached him.

"I thought I told you not to touch him."

Relief flooded through him at the sound of Aelissm's voice, but it was short-lived. He turned to find a pistol in her hand aimed at Sara's head. The adrenaline ebbed, leaving him shaking in fear. Not for Sara's life, but for Aelissm's freedom. The look in her eyes terrified him like nothing ever had. He didn't doubt for a minute that, given the opportunity and further provocation, she'd kill Sara.

"Aelissm," he entreated. "She's not worth it."

Slowly, she lowered the gun. She slid a reassuring hand across his shoulders, letting him know she wouldn't do anything foolish. And that she was there for him. Still reeling from Sara's kiss, he couldn't find the words to thank her or the strength to tell her he was all right. Even if he'd been able to speak, it would have been a lie because he wasn't fine. He felt his grip slipping, and it took everything he had left to hold on to the courage to continue this ridiculous battle.

"I hope you understand that I'll happily go to prison to protect him," she said to Sara.

"I was merely defending myself from him."

"Oh, give me a break! You can't honestly think I'd believe you."

"You should. Go ahead. Ask him about the last time he hit me."

"Are you referring to the time he hit you *after* you stabbed him? Sorry, honey, but he had every right to knock you on your ass. In fact, he should've done it a lot sooner. An abusive little bitch like you never deserved him."

"Think you're tough stuff, honey?" Sara asked. "Go ahead. Unleash those claws, little kitty."

"No!" Pat bellowed too late to stop her.

Aelissm's head snapped around with the force of the slap. She landed a punch to Sara's jaw before the other woman could duck. Pat stepped between them before it could get any worse. As he did, something caught in the sleeve of his shirt, and Sara stumbled into him, thrown off balance by the unexpected snag. He turned on her and snatched her by her arms. Then he saw the small blade in her hand. He twisted her wrist until she dropped the weapon, spun her around, and pinned both hands behind her back. It shocked him how easily he overpowered her. The harder she struggled, the tighter he held her. She fought herself right into a wrenched shoulder, and she squirmed and whined in pain, but he didn't loosen his hold.

A quick inspection of Aelissm found her whole and impressively calm.

"What is it with you and knives?" he asked Sara without much vehemence. His relief that she'd failed to cut Aeli overwhelmed his anger.

"I think this has gone on long enough," Aeli said. Only the slight tremble of her lower lip revealed the lingering effects of the fight. "If she pulls another stupid stunt like that…. Why don't you bring her inside, Pat? Aaron can deal with her from here."

"*Who* can deal with me?" Sara snarled.

"Sheriff's Deputy Aaron Hammond," Pat replied.

"Oh, how quaint. You even have your own little Wyatt Earp. Good. I'm sure he'll enjoy an explanation of your treatment of me."

"Are you really that deluded?" Aelissm asked. "He's my neighbor and friend. What makes you think he'd be on your side?"

"He's a cop," she replied.

"So's Pat. What's your point?"

Unwilling to continue the conversation any longer, he said, "Why don't you bring Aaron out here? I don't want to ruin everyone else's night by dragging her in there."

Aelissm obeyed. For the few moments she was gone,

he stubbornly refused to be pulled back into an argument with Sara. Nothing had been accomplished, and nothing had been proven tonight except that she no longer had any hold over him. Before he had time to consider what needed to be done to ensure she'd never bother him again, Aelissm returned with Aaron and Adam on her heels.

"This must be Sara. Aeli tells me this little vixen is causing some problems," Aaron said.

"In a manner of speaking," Pat replied.

"She threatened me with a gun," Sara spat.

"A gun with a broken firing pin," Aaron remarked. "It hasn't worked in a long time."

Pat glanced at Aelissm, who was quite pleased with herself. She'd never told him the pistol her grandparents kept in the kitchen of the inn didn't fire. The urge to laugh struck him as being very inappropriate, but it was hard to swallow.

"How was I supposed to know that?" Sara asked.

"Doesn't matter. You pulled a perfectly good, functional knife on them. And you didn't just threaten; you tried to use it. I should arrest you for assault, but since I didn't actually see what happened, it's Pat's call."

"I told you the last time around. I'm finished. I want you out of my life," Pat said. "If you leave now and leave me the hell alone from this point on, I won't press charges."

"She won't leave on her own," Adam observed. "She's the wrong combination of selfish and stubborn. She won't leave without getting what she came for."

"Shut your face, Adam," Sara snapped. "Or I'll tell your lover you killed your own best friend."

"*I'll tell on you*," Aeli mocked. "How childish.

Technically, a burst aneurysm killed Brent. Give it up, honey. You've lost. Walk away or be dragged away. That choice is still yours, but you're never going to hurt Pat again."

Pat could have swept Aelissm up in a massive hug. God knew he wanted to, but that could wait. He carefully let loose of Sara, praying she was smart enough to know she was beaten. Before he'd fully released her, she spun on him and lashed out. When her nails raked across his neck, he hooked a foot around her ankles. She crashed to the deck and scrambled to recover from her sprawl. He pounced, straddling her waist and pinning her arms to her sides with his knees.

"You just don't get it do you? It's *over*. And every stupid move like that one takes you another step closer to more jail time."

"I guess I need to take it from here," Aaron said, his voice trembling.

"Looks like it. I'd recommend cuffing her."

Aaron wiggled his eyebrows suggestively. "I always keep a spare pair in my truck."

"And people say *I'm* shameless," Aeli muttered. "Now, this is going to be interesting to explain to everyone. My stalker is invited to enjoy dinner with us and some strange woman no one here has heard of has to be taken away by our local…. What did you call him? Ah, yes, that's right. Our own little Wyatt Earp."

Aaron chuckled and went to his truck to get the cuffs.

"He'll be back in just a few moments, Sara," Pat said. "Will he need those handcuffs? Or are you going to leave of your own free will? That is, if he decides to give you the choice after that last stunt."

"She isn't going to just leave, Pat," Adam repeated. "You of all people should know that."

"I do, but sometimes people change. I did. So did you." He turned his attention back to Sara. "It's amazing, isn't it, Adam, what a *good* woman can do for a man."

"It really is. Aelissm, you're an incredible woman, but Amber—"

"I know, Adam," Aelissm said laughingly. "And I'm sincerely happy for the both of you. I just hope we can help her see the truth."

"I think I'm going to puke," Sara snarled.

"You know, if you were as human as they are, you would never have spent a day in prison," Pat remarked lightly. Sara squirmed uselessly beneath him. "But you couldn't stand it that I would leave you. No one's ever insulted you like that. We both know it wasn't love. Personally, I don't think you're capable of it because love requires a heart, and you don't have one."

"Fuck you."

"No, thank you. Been there, done that, and it was horrific. Here's something else I figured out, Sara. Despite what you'd have me believe, I'm better than you. Adam's done some insane things, too, and he's better than you. By a long shot."

She screamed and fought, but there was nothing she could do to free herself. Gold-plated, Aelissm had called Brent. Sara was exactly the same as her best friend's brother. Shiny and expensive at first glance, but worthless underneath.

"Are we all ready to go, miss?" Aaron asked as he

mounted the stairs.

"Kiss my ass," she snapped.

"Guess it's gonna be the hard way," he said with a melodramatic sigh. "I hate the hard way."

As soon as Pat stood to haul her to her feet, she thrashed free. She jerked a tiny pistol out of her handbag and aimed it at Aelissm. Before he could blink, she released the safety and pulled the hammer back, the clicks pierced him with pure terror. He stepped between her and Aelissm fully aware that she was capable of shooting him. Reacting purely from instinct, he knocked her arm away as she squeezed the trigger. The shot raced wildly off into the sky, harmlessly above him and everyone nearby.

Within moments, she had the gun cocked again. She pointed it at Aaron, then Aelissm, then Adam, and lastly at Pat. "I said… kiss… my… ass."

"Don't do it, Sara," Pat said calmly. "Do you really hate me enough to spend the rest of your life in prison?"

She didn't respond, and for a moment, she didn't move. Time stretched in tense silence. Then, finally, she began inching her way back toward the stairs, but her aim didn't waver, held squarely on Pat's chest.

"I'll leave," she said quietly.

Pat jerked back as if he'd been slapped. It felt like he had. She looked nothing like the Sara Montgomery he knew. Her clothes were rumpled, and her hair was disheveled. More even than the broken nails, the runs in her nylons, and the darkening bruise on her chin, what shocked Pat the most was the defeat in her honey-brown eyes. It was difficult to make out with the fire of animosity still burning, but it was there. This was a woman who'd never been left before, who'd never been beaten. Until him. He wondered what would happen when she finally admitted that to herself.

She didn't lower the gun until she was at the driver's side door of her car, and no one else moved until she peeled out of the driveway, spraying gravel over the parked cars. Pat let out the breath he'd been holding and folded his arms around Aelissm. They both trembled as relief mingled with adrenaline. His heart pounded, and all he could do was hug Aeli tightly and thank God everyone was all right.

"I can't just let her leave," Aaron said. "Not after that."

"I know."

"I'm going to follow her in, so would you call it in, Pat?"

"Gladly," Aelissm replied first.

"Where's she staying in Devyn, Adam?"

"The Comfort Inn."

"Let's hope someone from the Devyn Police Department will be at the hotel waiting for her. Aeli, can you tell my folks I'll stop by the house if I'm not back in time to catch the end of the potluck?"

"Sure thing."

"Whatever happens, I'll call here when I get to Devyn."

"Thank you, Aaron," Aelissm said.

"Hey, just doing my job. Not very often that I actually get some action."

"I guess it's all over. Again," Pat murmured. He couldn't let go of Aelissm just yet, and she didn't seem anymore inclined to leave his arms. For a few moments, he rested his cheek against the top of her head and focused on every place where their bodies touched as his pulse at last began to slow. "I owe your dad a new flannel. She caught the sleeve with the knife."

Aelissm leaned back in his arms and grinned. "I'm sure he won't miss just one flannel. You're sure she didn't get you?"

He spread the hole in the shirt and inspected his own hide. There wasn't a mark on him. "All clear."

"I really hope that's the end of it. For both of us," she said, directing the last at Adam.

The man nodded solemnly, then glanced over his shoulder in the windows. "How am I going to explain this all to Amber?"

"Tell her the truth," Aeli replied. "Or, most of it, anyhow. I'll help. C'mon, boys, let's go inside."

"Now, *that's* a good idea," Pat replied.

Without letting go of his hand, Aelissm led him inside. All at once, they were bombarded with questions. Aelissm handled them all with her innate grace and charm, giving just enough details to satisfy them but not so many that either Pat or Adam felt uneasy. June helped where she could, and Pat had never been so grateful to two women in his life. Listening to the abridged tale of his relationship with Sara laid the foundation for putting distance between his past and future. He knew it might be a long time yet before he could fully comprehend that Sara's hold over him was well and truly broken, and she'd probably never give up on her irrational need for vengeance as long as she lived, but at least he wouldn't *let* her torment him. When he finally realized just what that meant, it wouldn't matter what she tried because he would truly be free of her.

At first, Amber had trouble coming to terms with her boyfriend's deceit, but eventually, she came around. Aelissm coaxed her into believing that what Adam had done—she left out the worst of his stalking—had not only been a terrible accident but a noble act. By the time Aeli finished, Amber had threaded herself around Adam, and both had the same, glittering, love-filled eyes. Pat remembered the terror in Aelissm's eyes those days when a letter from Adam had come or when he'd called her, and found a whole new level of respect for her. It took an incredible, selfless woman to have faced all that and still be able to say such things about the man who'd put her through that hell. She called herself sarcastic and cynical and frequently said she lacked June's compassion, but Pat knew without a doubt how wrong she was.

"That's all you're getting out of me," Aelissm said. "If you want to know more, ask Pat and Adam, but not tonight. Tonight, we're all going to have fun and forget what happened just a few minutes ago. Got it?"

After the crowd affirmed her declaration, Aeli turned the radio back on and gave everyone a free round of drinks from the bar or the fridge. Pat doubted anyone would soon forget the strange events that had taken place tonight, but bless their hearts, they knew how to enjoy themselves regardless. It wasn't long before it felt like nothing had happened, and Pat marveled at the ability of these people to move on. They had the right of it, though. Work hard and play hard and enjoy life as best you can.

"Aaron should have called by now," Aelissm told him. "It's been almost an hour and a half."

"Has it really been that long?"

"Yup."

"Wow."

As if she'd planned it, the phone rang. She raced back to the kitchen to grab it. "Bedspread Inn, this is Aelissm. Hi, Aaron. About time you called." Her face suddenly slid from amusement to surprise. "You're kidding, right? Hold on, let me give you over to Pat so you can tell him."

Pat took the cordless. "What's up?"

"The tires on your ex's Mercedes."

"What?"

"She was driving at least ninety. Crazy bitch. Anyhow, you know that creek at the bottom of Badger Pass? The one with all the willows where you always see about half a dozen deer?"

"Yeah."

"There was a moose crossing the road right there, and she swerved to miss it. She went through the guardrail on the bridge and ended up upside-down across the creek. The moose is fine. She's not."

"How bad is it?"

"The ambulance and my buddy Jimmy got here fast. We cut her out with the jaws, but she was already gone. Freakiest thing I've ever seen. She got a piece of rebar straight through the heart, so apparently she *did* have one. Must've been left behind from when they repaired the bridge last year. Anyhow, the EMTs pronounced her dead at the scene. We're all at the hospital right now. I've gotta get over to the courthouse, get the paperwork started, and all that. I'm sorry I have to miss the rest of the party."

"Me, too, Aaron."

"Hey, I'm sorry, man."

"For what? She brought it on herself. You did what you could."

"Yeah. I know it's wrong to speak ill of the dead, but at least she's really out of your life now."

"Guess she is. Take care of yourself, Aaron. And thanks for calling."

"You bet."

Pat ended the call and stared at the handset for a long time, unable to digest what he'd just heard. When he found his voice, he relayed to Aelissm, June, Luke, and Adam what Aaron had told him. Aelissm put her arms around him and held him for a long time. As it began to sink in that Sara was dead, he was able to lift his head and look around. June and Luke were nearby, ready to jump in if he needed them. No one else seemed to have noticed anything. It was Adam's expression that piqued his curiosity. There was a smile of gratification on his face.

"Karma," was all he said.

A blinding flash split the gloom outside. Moments later, the boom of thunder rolled through the valley, rattling the windows of the dining room. The dancing and chatter paused only briefly as the music and voices were drowned out. Pat and the small group gathered around him silently watched the windows as the wind picked up. He felt Aelissm take his hand.

"C'mon, old man," she said, pulling him toward the front doors. "June, you and Luke, too. Let's go play in the rain."

"You want to play out in the rain in the middle of a thunderstorm?" Pat remarked. "Isn't that tempting fate a bit too much?"

"Your sociopathic ex damn near shot you a couple hours ago. I think the angels are keeping a close eye on you today, and I doubt they will let anything else happen to you."

The air outside was heavy with humidity and the refreshing scent of rain. The wind was spiced with the fragrance of the lodgepole pines and sagebrush, and Pat inhaled deeply. The people of Northstar gathered with them under the shelter of the eaves. They watched as the leading edge of the thunderstorm moved through the valley, spearing the gloom with bolts of lavender and striking up a continuous roll of thunder. The first drops of rain fell as the storm paraded east over the mountains and out of the valley.

Behind it, the skies opened up, and Aelissm darted down to the driveway, turned, and dared anyone brave enough to join her. In the torrential downpour, the parking area quickly became a mess of mud puddles and rivulets. Laughing, Pat joined her. He was rewarded with a shower of water from a puddle. In retaliation, he kicked water back at her, and she screeched in delight. Luke and June took up the battle, and they were all soon joined by the younger generations of Northstar while the elders watched from the roof overhang. The water fight quickly descended into a mud bath as saturated, earthen balls were hurled across the parking lot. When Aelissm chucked a ball of soft mud at Pat and it splattered all over the front of his shirt, he captured her around the waist and was about to dump her in a puddle much like he'd dumped her in the snow bank, but the pure adoration and youthful amusement in her gaze stopped him.

He realized then just how old Sara had made him feel… and how old Aelissm made him forget he was. In that moment, he was Luke's age, and he was having a fantastic time playing in the rain and the mud.

There was still a long road ahead of them, especially concerning Sara's family, but he didn't care right then. Sara was gone forever. He was free to live the rest of his life in peace.

"I love you, Aelissm Davis!" he yelled over a weakening grumble of thunder.

She smiled up at him, looking so cute and beautiful with her soaked hair hanging limply and rain streaming down her face. "I love you, too, Patrick O'Neil."

Twenty-One

PAT HAD INTENDED to leave right after the car accident that had killed Sara. Instead, he'd lingered in Northstar with Aelissm for over two weeks to assist Aaron with the Montana-end of the case. Finally, yesterday morning, Bill had called to let Aelissm know the restraining order on Adam had been lifted, as per her request, and to ask Pat when he was planning on coming back to work. So, he'd spent all of yesterday packing. Now, it was just past eight in the morning, and he stood beneath a dismal sky as he tossed the last of his bags in the back of his truck. He didn't want to leave. Aelissm didn't want him to leave. But he needed to return to his job if only to see if he loved her enough to give up his dream. If he couldn't get through a couple of weeks back in Washington or if the memory of her fiery passion and insatiable wit faded once he was back in the routine of his life, he'd have his answer. Besides, he needed to go back to help Bill settle the remaining matters of Sara's death.

With a sigh, he turned around to face the cabin. Aelissm leaned against the door jamb with her arms and ankles crossed. They'd talked about this a lot over the last two weeks, and they both agreed it was for the best. If this was meant to be, they'd know quick enough when they couldn't stop calling or thinking about one another long enough to get through the day. If that was the case, Pat knew he'd be back in Northstar in twelve hours.

"All set?" she asked.

"Yeah, I think so. Guess this is it."

"Yup, guess it is. I'd come with you, you know."

"I know. But I couldn't let you. You belong here. This place is part of you."

Even from where he was standing, he saw the tears in her eyes. It broke his heart. She'd had enough pain in her life, and now he was causing her more.

"Aeli, sweetheart, don't cry."

"I'm not. Yet. I'll wait until you leave to do that." She sniffed. "I have my pride, you know."

"Yes, you do," he said, chuckling.

"Besides, I knew from the beginning you'd have to leave. I just didn't expect it to be quite like this."

"Goodbyes are never fun," he agreed. *Especially ones like this when so much is left unsaid and unfinished. What if I'm making a huge mistake?* He couldn't think like that or he'd never get back to Washington. "Whatever happens, Aeli, I do love you. So much more than you know."

She was too intelligent to ask it, but the thought was in her eyes. *Then why leave?*

"You'll tell everyone I'm glad to have met them and that I'll try to stay in touch, won't you?"

"I said I would, didn't I?"

"You did."

There wasn't anything left to say, so he closed the distance between them in ten long strides and kissed her one last time. It was everything they had become wrapped into one caress—lovers and friends and kindred spirits. Pulling away was the hardest thing he'd ever done, but daylight was burning, and he had a long drive ahead of him. He should have left hours ago but, like now, couldn't force himself to go. The rate he was going, he'd be lucky to make it home by midnight. Thought of what he was returning to made it even more difficult to walk away from Aelissm. That bare little house wasn't home anymore. Washington wasn't home.

"You planning on leaving before Christmas or not?" Aelissm asked.

He winced at the bitterness in her voice. It should have made it easier to get into his truck and drive off, but it didn't. It made him want to hug her until that resentment had been replaced with the fire he loved so much. He leaned down to kiss her again, just a simple peck on the lips to say goodbye.

"I have to go," he murmured.

"I know. Call me when you get there."

"I will."

At last, he turned away from her, walked to his truck, and got in.

"Hey, Pat!"

He leaned out the window.

"The wildflowers are blooming on the way to Devyn," she said. "I know I said you should go back through the Bitterroot Valley, so it's out of your way, but you should stop and see them. Now, go, if you're going to!"

Through sheer willpower, he turned the key in the ignition. The rumble of the engine made his chest ache. This was only the second time he regretted leaving a woman, but for an entirely different reason than the first. He should have ended things with Sara a lot differently. Maybe she never would have come out here to find him. He wondered at his own cruelty for not feeling the least bit guilty or remorseful that she was dead. He was sorry the people of Northstar had been exposed to her. Especially Aelissm.

"Quit thinking like that and just go," he muttered.

He glanced in the rearview mirror as he drove away. Just as he started down the hill and he lost sight of Aeli, he saw her sit down on the steps and drop her head in to her hands. It nearly broke him, but he had to leave, and going back to soothe her would only make things worse. He'd already done a fine job of breaking her heart; he didn't need to pour salt in it. So, he kept going even though his heart screamed at him to turn around.

He drove more slowly down the mountain than he had since he'd first come here, intent on memorizing every detail about this place. He had more than twenty rolls of film he'd need to have developed, but photos only told part of the story. He'd have to rely entirely on his memory to relive the scents and sounds and the feel of the soft, warm air on his skin as he drove with his forearm resting on the windowsill.

When he reached Northstar Road, he hesitated at the stop sign. He'd already said his goodbyes to June and Luke last night, and he knew dropping by the Ramshorn was a bad idea, but he couldn't stop himself from turning right instead of left. As he pulled up in front of the lodge, they both came out onto the porch.

"I thought you'd've been long gone by now," June called.

"So did I. I wanted to stop by and say goodbye one more time. And to thank you for everything you've done."

"Don't know that I've done all that much, but if it makes you feel better, you're welcome."

They came down the stairs, and he got out to hug them both.

"Are you sure you have to leave?" Luke asked. "Aunt Aeli's going to be really lonely without you."

"I'm sure. Listen, Luke, do me a favor, will you?"

"Sure," the boy replied.

"When you finally stop growing, give me a call. In the meantime, you two take care of each other. And take care of Aeli, too."

"We will," June said, wrapping an arm around her son and pulling him close. "Drive safe, Pat, and come back soon."

She might have meant for a visit, but he doubted it. When he met her eyes, her meaning was perfectly clear.

"I will," he replied without thinking. "I'll keep in touch."

"You'd better," she replied.

Twenty minutes and twenty miles later, he was still

pondering her unspoken request. She'd been right about him and Aelissm so far. She was probably right again, but he had to know for himself. He had to know that he loved Aelissm enough to sacrifice everything he'd once wanted.

Remembering the last thing Aelissm had said to him, and against his better judgment, he took another detour and headed toward Devyn. It only took him a few minutes out of the way to find the exact wildflowers she had mentioned. He pulled off the highway onto one of the ranch access roads to park and walked the rest of the way.

The guardrail had been repaired, and the new steel glinted even beneath the rare, overcast sky. The gravel around the new posts had been raked, leaving only the tire tracks on the highway to show where Sara's car had gone off. Someone had added a little white cross to the one that had been there for years, and he wondered if she would have appreciated the sentiment. Taking a deep breath, he walked farther and peered over the embankment to the creek below. The willows on the east bank of the creek bore broken branches, and there were a series of deep scars sprinkled with shattered glass in the soft earth just beyond that would take a long time to heal. He knew what had happened from Aaron's official report, but he could see it more clearly here. The front of her car had dug into the marshy ground beside the creek, and the velocity had pushed the rest over the top. She'd landed roof-side down and skidded into the hillside not far beyond, where her rear bumper had bitten into the stony dirt and uprooted several sagebrush. If she was going as fast as Aaron had claimed—he could see no reason to doubt it—there'd been no chance of survival. The one thing he couldn't quite imagine was how the rebar from last year's construction had embedded in her chest. And he'd seen the pictures, so he knew it had happened.

Adam had said it was karma. Maybe he was right.

He walked a little farther and plucked a few stems of periwinkle flax, a couple spears of lupine, and two wild sunflowers and placed all but one stem of flax beside the new cross. The voice that argued she didn't deserve it was so faint he barely registered it because it wasn't about whether or not she deserved it; it was about the significance to *him*. It was another step toward gaining closure, and Aelissm understood that. Otherwise, why would she have told him to stop and see the wildflowers?

"My sweet, beloved Aelissm," he murmured.

He stood there for a while, gazing at the landscape around him. He'd felt it almost since he'd first arrived. This was home. He looked down at the flax he still held and twisted the stem into a loop. He thought about what he was going back to and what he was leaving behind. As a uniformed officer and as a detective, he spent most of his time pondering the dark side of humanity. He'd seen just about every cruel, vicious, and devious thing a person could do, and at the end of many a day, he'd gone home wearied by it all. His time in Northstar had shown him a totally different side. The people of that valley lived and loved together, helped each other, and protected each other. As much as he loved his job, he'd lived through enough of his own nightmares. Seeing what he'd lived through repeated over and over was no way to spend his life. Not when he could spend the rest of it in peace and enjoyment.

Comprehension hit him so hard that he couldn't breathe for a moment.

"What the hell am I doing? I already know I love her."

He ran back to his truck, hopped in, and gunned the engine to life. His tires squealed as he spun around and headed back toward Northstar. He raced up the valley and up the mountain. Feeling light-headed and giddy and entirely childish, he parked his truck down at Aelissm's grandparents' cabin and, with the blue-purple flax ring in hand, snuck up the hill to surprise her. The sound of angry singing and the determined *thunk* of an ax led him toward the back of the cabin where he found her swinging away with her flannel tied around her waist. It was so classically Aelissm and so embodied what he loved about her that he couldn't speak for a moment.

* * *

Aelissm told herself she wouldn't cry. Pat hadn't even vanished from view before she realized she was a liar. She dropped her head into her hands and sobbed. She choked on the tears and cursed herself for giving in. She'd known all along that he wouldn't stay, and she'd gone plowing on ahead anyhow. It was her own fault. She hoped she'd get over him someday, but she doubted it because the mere thought of his name reminded her of all the wonderful memories they'd made. She'd never forget that night by the lake or the many times they'd made love since, and remembering would always make her yearn for him. The best she could hope for was being able to recall him without crying every time. She'd become so entangled, so deeply in love, that she couldn't think of what else his leaving meant.

She had longed for this day when the nightmare of the last year was finally over and she could breathe freely again. But it wasn't supposed to be like this. She wasn't supposed to be fighting back tears. She should be rejoicing that Adam wouldn't bother her anymore and that she was free to be herself and do whatever she wanted with her life. It was *supposed* to be a happy ending. Instead, she was sitting on the front steps of her parents' cabin, chewing on her bottom lip to keep from breaking down again, and nursing the worst pain she'd ever experienced. The memories that were at the moment her only company emphasized how alone she was. The gray sky above her seemed so mournful and empty.

It wasn't as if she'd never hear from him again. He promised he'd call. And he was Bill's detective, so if she had to, she could reach him through her uncle. Besides, he hadn't said he was leaving forever. But neither had he said he'd come back. He needed to find out if what they'd shared was the real thing and if he could give up his dream of being a detective for her. Bitterly, she hated herself for putting him in that position. No one should have to give up that much for love. Love was supposed to be some great thing that knew no bounds and healed all wounds. From what she knew of it, love was much more like an invasion force.

Swearing, she pushed to her feet and sought something—anything—to distract her. She yanked open the door of the shed her father had dug into the side of the hill and rummaged around for a while. It took her a disappointingly short time to straighten all the shovels and miscellaneous tools her family stored in there. Frustrated by the tears that still burned her eyes, she marched out back to her woodpile. Now, *there* was some honest work, and it would take her hours to chop it all. And, when she was done with that, it would take her hours more to stack it. Then she could ask Grandpa to come up and help her cut some more. She'd probably cut her winter's worth before she was able to think about Pat without crying. Next year's, too.

She snatched her ax from the shed beside the back door and went to work. She started to sing as she chopped, mostly Christmas carols, as was tradition. Each time the ax fell, she emphasized whatever word, not caring how angry she sounded. Better angry than sad and depressed. Besides, there was no one up here to hear her anymore. June and Luke were down at the Ramshorn, her grandparents were down at their house, and Pat was gone. Thoughts of him made her tear up again so she swung harder and faster and tried to think about anything but him. It was a useless endeavor.

Damn him for doing this to her, and damn her for so stupidly plunging in head first. June had warned her but in the same breath encouraged her. Damn her, too. And definitely damn Uncle Bill. This was all his fault. He'd sent Pat here on vacation and asked her to help Pat relax. Oh, she'd helped him relax all right, and ended up with a broken heart for her trouble.

Why was it that the greatest joys so often came hand in hand with the bleakest sorrows? She had found the most incredible love in Pat's arms, and yes, she was glad to have known it and knew she would never regret it, but now she understood what it was to be alone. She'd always had someone—her family, her friends, her colleagues. Right now, there was no one within five miles, and she desperately needed some company.

Thinking she heard a vehicle, she paused for a

moment. When nothing other than the soft sighing of the morning breeze reached her ears, she brushed it off as wishful thinking and went back to her chore.

The worst part was, knowing what she did, she'd do it all over again.

"Maybe I'm just stupid."

"I doubt it. If ever again *I'm* stupid enough to believe I have to leave you to realize how much I love you, promise me you'll knock some sense into me."

Aelissm nearly screamed. She dropped her ax and spun on her heel, certain she was dreaming. There he was, standing not twenty feet away. "Pat...?"

"I couldn't leave," he replied. "I love you too much."

Abandoning all pride and self-preservation, she ran to him and jumped into his open arms. She knew she was an idiot and behaving like a love-dumb teenager. She didn't care. He'd only been gone an hour, but it felt so good to be back in his arms.

"I couldn't even get forty miles away from you."

"I love you, Pat."

"Then marry me."

She jerked back and stared at him in shock. "But... what about your career?"

"My career can't make me as happy as you do. I've known that for longer than I realized, but I wasn't willing to admit it. So, I ask you again," he said as he dropped to one knee and presented her with the flower ring. "Will you marry me?"

"I'd be a fool not to," she replied.

"You can't give a straight answer, can you?"

"Nope. But would you have me any other way?"

"Not on your life. I'll take you just the way you are."

Tears welled in her eyes again, but this time, she didn't curse them or refuse to acknowledge them. "In answer to your question, you bet your sexy ass I'll marry you. I just hope you aren't going to change your mind when you realize what you're giving up."

He slipped the ring on her finger, then took her in his arms and kissed her long and deeply. "I'd be giving up a lot more if I left you. I'm never going to change my mind, Aelissm. I love you. I want to marry you. And I want to grow old with you. I know it's not too far away, but I thought it'd be nice to have a wedding under the aspen when they turn yellow."

"Last week of September, then. That only gives us about four months. Where do we start?"

"Well, I did promise Bill he'd be the first to know if there were wedding bells in our future."

She grinned and wiped her tears away. "You realize, don't you, that we'll have to invite most of Northstar?"

"I'd be disappointed if they didn't show up, invited or not."

They both laughed. Aelissm knew what she'd suspected for a long time now. Pat had found more than love. He'd found home. She understood now that she could have gone to Washington with him, but she also knew that something would always be wrong for them. They both belonged here, in Northstar, where their traumas had been faced and passed by. They could build the life that suited them here, surrounded by mountains, sapphire skies, emerald forests and hayfields, and air so pure every breath was happiness. This was right.

"Looks like your dream is going to come true, after all," Pat said, his voice soft. "You know, the one about you and June raising your kids together up here on the mountain."

"But yours has to be broken in order for mine to come true," she replied.

"That's not entirely true. I am—or was—a detective. I got to live my dream for a little while. Now I have a new one. And it involves a gorgeous blonde with dark green eyes, a cabin in the middle of the Montana backcountry, and a kid or three we can raise to love everything we do."

"Pat, quit making me cry," she muttered as she had to wipe her eyes again.

"But these are good tears, right? To wash away the past."

She nodded. It seemed so unreal and yet so natural to be standing in the driveway of her parents' cabin with Pat woven around her, discussing their future together. Recalling a conversation they'd had weeks ago, she couldn't help but smile. Then, both of them had expressed a belief that marriage and children seemed out of reach for them. Now they had taken the first step on the path that led them straight toward those fairytale, happily-ever-after joys. And she could picture them chasing their squealing children all over the mountainside with a stunning clarity. There would be no more shadows in Pat's eyes, only the glow of happiness.

"A kid or three, huh?"

"Sure."

"How 'bout we start with one and go from there?"

"Whatever you want, sweetheart."

"C'mon inside, my love. We need to break the devastating news to my uncle."

"Mmm. Yes, I'm sure he'll be absolutely crushed."

Aelissm snorted. Everything was happening quite quickly, but she wasn't about to slow down long enough to question it. She was afraid if she did, she'd wake up and find out his proposal and this whole wonderful experience was no more than the most incredible dream. Standing on her toes to kiss him, she grabbed his hand and dragged him inside.

Without hesitating, she grabbed her phone and dialed her uncle's office number.

"Aeli?" he asked, concerned. "Is everything all right?"

"Yes and no. I have some good news, and I have some bad news, and you don't get to choose which one to hear first." She winked at Pat. "I'm sorry to have to tell you this, Unk, but you can't have your detective back. I'm keeping him."

"Can you put him on speaker?" Pat asked. "I want to hear this."

Nodding, Aelissm led the way into the living room where the base sat and turned on the speakerphone. There was silence on the other end, and for a moment, she was worried she'd accidentally disconnected the call. But then she heard sounds in the background.

"Does that mean what I think it does?" her uncle finally asked.

"Depends on what you're thinking. But I can tell you, you'd better clear your schedule for the last week in September because if you're not at my wedding, I'll never forgive you, Unk."

Bill's laughter reverberated through her living room, as long, loud, and happy as she'd ever heard. She turned to Pat and threaded herself into his arms.

"I think we just made my uncle a very happy man," she purred.

"You're damn right you did."

"You *were* right, Bill," Pat said. "Your niece is very… *very* good for me."

Bill continued to chuckle. "I guess I win that bet. I'll miss you around here, Pat, but I'm glad you'll be part of the family. And soon, too. The end of September, huh?"

"Yep," Aeli chirped. "What can I say, Unk? I've never been much for society's traditions."

"That's for sure. But your own fit you well. I'd better get off here so I can tell your Aunt Mary."

"All right. Give her our love," Pat said.

"Will do."

When her uncle hung up, Aelissm looked up at Pat. "I know we just called my uncle, but I can't help but wonder… is this real? Did you really ask me to marry you?"

"I did. And this is real. Every bit of it."

He slipped one arm behind her back and the other behind her knees and swept her off her feet. She squealed and giggled and instinctively wrapped her arms around his neck.

"God, I love you," she said, still laughing.

Grinning like a fool, he gave her a quick peck on the lips. "I know."

"We need to tell June and Luke, but I want to do that in person, and there are a few other people we need to call first. Your family."

Pat nodded and reluctantly set her back on her feet. She thought she'd see sadness swimming in his eyes, but there was only a trickle. The rest was overpowered by his love for her. He held out his hand for the phone, and she handed it over. With pride and pleasure and a range of other wonderful emotions, she watched as joy overcame the last threads of anguish.

Three people answered the phone, and a quick argument ensued over who had the call.

"I'm happy to hear nothing's changed at the O'Neil residence," Pat remarked with amusement thick in his voice.

"Patrick?" the older of the two women asked.

"Hi, Mom."

"Oh, goodness, Darren, it's Patrick!"

"I know that, dear."

"Hi, Dad," Pat said. "And hi to you, too, Shannon."

"Oh, honey, it's so good to hear from you!" his mother cooed. "Bill's been keeping us updated, but it's better to hear from you."

"I know, Mom, and I'm sorry I haven't called. I'll work on that."

They asked him how he'd liked Montana, and Aelissm listened as he detailed his vacation. The way he described everything drove home the reality of their situation. He really was staying, and they really were getting married. When he told his family what had happened last week, there was no hesitation and no bitterness in his voice. He described the fight with Sara and her death matter-of-factly as if she hadn't nearly destroyed his life. Aelissm was surprised when he didn't leave out the bit about Sara trying to kill him.

When his father asked about Bill's niece, Pat started grinning like a fool again and listed out all her attributes, both the ones she liked about herself and a few she didn't. In his eyes, apparently, she was perfect even with her flaws. Now, that was love.

"Oh, honey, you sound so happy. I haven't heard that in your voice in so long."

"It hasn't been in my voice, Mom. You have your son back."

His mother started crying then, and Aeli thought Pat might join her, but he held it in check.

"You're coming home today, aren't you?" Darren O'Neil asked.

Pat looked at Aelissm and his smile softened. He beckoned her over and again tucked his arms around her. "Funny thing about that, Dad. I am home."

Epilogue

"I SWEAR TO GOD, I'd better not hear the birthday song again. I've already heard it five times today," Aelissm grumbled as she poked her nose over June's shoulder. They were standing in the kitchen of her grandparents' cabin, icing her birthday cake. She lifted her gaze to the window above the counter to see Luke and Pat trudging down the hill from her cabin and smiled. "I suppose I should be grateful. I did get the snow I asked for, although I don't recall wishing for two feet!"

"Be quiet and quit complaining, or I won't let you help finish icing your cake."

Obediently, she took a step back and smiled demurely at her best friend. The last thing she wanted to do right now was sit down while June and her grandparents got everything together for her birthday dinner. She had to do something, or the nerves would overtake her. It might have been *her* birthday, but she had a surprise for her husband. Thinking of him as her husband made her heart flutter, but it was a wonderful sensation reminding her that every beloved inch of him and every beat of his heart belonged to her and that she belonged to him just as completely. Her lips lifted higher when she again looked out the window. They'd been married for just over a month now, and her appreciation of him had only grown in that time. Loving him, unlike what she'd once feared, was not a mistake. Marrying him after so short a courtship hadn't been a mistake, either.

Oh, and what a beautiful ceremony it had been, too. As he'd wanted, they'd been married beneath a grove of shivering gold aspen. The grove they'd chosen had had some people wondering at their sanity and others shaking their head in amusement. Most of their guests had arrived on four-wheelers. She and Pat had, too. June had taken pictures of the turn around in the road leading to the Sheep Field, and the memory of it packed with dirt bikes and four-wheelers still made her giggle. Everyone had had to walk a quarter mile to get to the grove at the top of the last hill before the road dropped in to the Sheep Field, but not one of them had complained about *that*. By a miracle, her gorgeous, full-skirted, white wedding gown had made it there without a trace of dirt.

She glanced at the new photo on the wall behind her. Pat had been drop-dead gorgeous in his midnight blue tux. She hadn't looked too bad either. The strapless bodice had shown off her neck and shoulders marvelously. June had taken that photo, too, of the wedding kiss. The smile on their faces hadn't faded.

"It was a beautiful wedding, Aeli," June remarked. "And it suited you both."

"Not every little girl's fantasy, but I liked it."

She liked her ring, too, which Pat had designed himself. Being the crafter she was, she'd wanted to do it but was glad he hadn't let her. It was truly beautiful. He'd chosen to immortalize the flax ring he'd given her in diamond, tanzanite, emerald, and white gold. It was dainty and elegant and absolutely the most stunning ring she'd ever seen. Five round tanzanite petals surrounded a small diamond on the engagement ring and the wedding band interlocked with two teardrop emeralds for leaves, one on each side of the flower. The white-gold channel band they'd selected together for Pat's wedding ring had been set with matching tanzanite. Their wedding set, though far less flashy and expensive than the massive engagement ring Pat told her Sara had bought herself, was far more exquisite. The love they'd found glittered in every cherished stone and every curve of white gold. Sentimental value had no monetary equal, she thought, smiling again like she had in June's photo.

Just then, her grandparents came in. Both their coats were dusted with snowflakes. Her grandfather had an armload of logs for the fire and her grandmother had a sack of groceries and the mail.

"I thought I'd bring it up," Marge said. She handed a couple of envelopes to June and a larger stack to Aelissm. "I can finish up the cake if you girls wouldn't mind helping your grandfather with the wood."

"Sure thing, Grandma," June said.

She scooted out the front door just as Pat and Luke

arrived with the board games Aelissm had sent them up to fetch. She greeted them both with a smile, though the one she gave her husband was considerably hotter. Holding up the mail, she asked, "Want to help me go through this in a minute? Looks like it's mostly cards and congratulations."

"Sure, but didn't I just hear Grandma ask you and June to help with the wood?" he asked.

"That's why I said, 'in a minute.' You and Luke can help, too. Five people will make it quick and easy."

They each brought in a load and stacked it beside the stove in the corner of the living room. Aelissm had always loved the open layout of her grandparents' cabin. The living room and dining room made up the front half with the kitchen attached to the dining room. Only the bedroom in the back corner, the little pantry and the bathroom were closed off. Like her cabin, it was efficient to heat, even with the big front windows that looked out over the clearing all the way to the mountains south of the Northstar Valley. Aeli narrowed her eyes. The clearing wouldn't be clear much longer. It was already carpeted with sapling lodgepole pines.

"You know, I'm a little surprised that I'm not sick of being happy all the time," she remarked. "It's not like me at all."

"Hush up and help me open all this," Pat said.

She joined him at the dining room table. They made quick work of the pile. There were a couple of bills and numerous cards offering congratulations, gift cards, and money. The last envelope Pat handed to her to open. When she saw Adam's name and return address—he was still in Devyn and would be until Amber graduated in the spring—

she shook her head and smiled. Six months ago, seeing Adam's handwriting had made her cower. Now she looked forward to hearing from him. She took the letter opener from Pat and cut the envelope open.

"It's a wedding invitation," she said, opening the card. "Adam and Amber are getting married in the first week of June down in West Yellowstone."

Frowning, she counted on her fingers. November, December, January… June. Eight months. "I'm gonna be huge," she muttered.

"What did you say?" Pat asked.

She looked up, blanching. He watched her with a frown of confusion. "Oh, dear. This isn't how I was planning to tell you."

"Tell me what?"

"Well, you remember that night on our honeymoon… we, uh, got a little rambunctious and something broke?"

"You're pregnant," he said.

She nodded shyly, acutely aware of the five pairs of eyes on her. "According to the little stick I peed on this morning."

"But you just went off the pill before the wedding." Pat sat back in the chair, resting his hands on his thighs. "Wow. We'd talked about not waiting *too* long to have kids, what with me being so *old*, but…. Wow."

"Hey, twenty-nine, isn't old, Mr. O'Neil," Aeli remarked. "And I know we were thinking of starting our family in a year or two, but apparently, Mother Nature had other ideas."

"Well, seems to me that starting a family around here

doesn't follow tradition any more than anything else does," he replied, glancing at June and Luke.

Aelissm laughed. "I really had planned to tell you differently."

He leaned across the table, took her by the chin, and kissed her. "Grandma, can we have some juice for a toast, please?"

When the glasses had been distributed, Pat raised his, grinning. The only time she'd seen that exact smile had been on their wedding.

"June, get a picture of him, will you?" Aeli requested. "He's smiling like an idiot again, and I want proof."

Everyone chuckled. June obliged and Pat patiently waited for them to stop laughing.

"Here's to my beautiful wife," he began. "Mrs. Aelissm O'Neil, the woman who showed me life wasn't over. And the woman who's currently in the process of making me a father, something I thought, not too long ago, would never happen for me."

They all drank to that and Aelissm felt her face warm.

"Here's to my husband, who taught me what *real* love is." They drank to Pat, too, before she added, "And to making our own traditions. Because this family seems fond of it."

* * * * *

Summer Angel

When Ben Conner killed a man in the line of duty and orphaned a young boy, he pushed everyone away, including his friend June Montana—the one woman who might've been able to heal his heart.

With the guilt and nightmares getting worse, Ben is desperate for a change. He needs June's soothing compassion, so he heads home to Northstar… only to discover her adopted son Luke is the very same boy he orphaned.

When June adopted Luke, she promised to put his well-being before everything else, but she keeps a special place for Ben in her heart, and seeing him again sparks something she never expected—a love that could last a lifetime. But as Luke and Ben work to overcome their entwined traumas, a new threat arises. Someone from June's past doesn't want to see them get their happily ever after, and he's willing to kill to stop it.

AVAILABLE NOW
Visit www.suzieoconnell.com for more information.

About the Author

Suzie O'Connell is the *USA Today* bestselling author of the Northstar romances. The series is the product of a love affair with Southwestern Montana that began with a two-week adventure at her stepsister's rustic cabin in her teens. That love affair shows no sign of abating.

She has been writing stories for as long as she can remember, and her love of writing and of Montana pushed her to earn a Bachelor of Arts in Literature and Writing from the University of Montana-Western. What else would you expect from a self-professed mountain-loving nerd?

When she isn't writing, you'll probably find Suzie in the mountains with a camera in hand and enjoying the beauty of Montana with her husband Mark, their daughter Maddie, and their golden retrievers Reilly and Angus.

Find Suzie online at www.suzieoconnell.com